ELIZABETH LONSETH

Leave It With Him

A NOVEL

Deer Harbor Marina, Orcas Island

Leave It With Him

by Elizabeth Lonseth
Cover Photo and Illustrations by Stan Lonseth

This novel is a work of fiction. Names, characters, and incidents are the product of the author's imagination or are used fictitiously. Some events are loosely based on the author's life experiences.

Unless otherwise noted, all Scriptures are taken from the King James Version of the Bible.

ISBN 13: 978-1-4392-8041-6
ISBN 10: 1-4392-8041-x
Library of Congress Catalog Card Number: 2012923163
CreateSpace Independent Publishing Platform
North Charleston, SC

Dedications and Thanks

In memory of my grandmother,
Hazel Grace Cunningham Wheat—
An incredible storyteller and a grace lady of the Lord
who always looked to her Savior, Jesus Christ.

A special thanks to my husband, Stan Lonseth,
for his photography and wonderful support.

Thanks to my daughters, Meredith Ellis, Lindsey
Lonseth, and Witney Lonseth, for telling me often that
I "needed to write a book".

To my friend, Carol Lee Clayton, who used a red ink pen
and a computer to my advantage, thank you.

Table of Contents

BOOK 2: SUMMER AT ORCAS

BOOK 3: SENIOR YEAR

BOOK 1
Unwanted Changes

Boston Harbor Marina

CHAPTER 1

The Split

"What?" Luke put his fork down on his dinner plate. "We are getting a divorce." A tear slid down his mother's cheek as she spoke.

Luke's head swam; he could vaguely hear his father's voice. "I'm moving to Olympia, the state capital. I've got a new job there. I will be leaving in the morning."

Luke pushed his chair away from the table. "Excuse me," he mumbled as he stood up. With the screen door slamming behind him, he headed for the beach. A strange pain formed in his chest as he neared the shore.

"Why?" Luke yelled. He picked up a large pebble off the beach and threw it as far as he could out into the water. How could this be happening? Not *his* parents! This pain in his chest just kept building and building.

Olympia, Washington, was about three hours south after reaching the mainland at Anacortes. Luke had never been there. How could his dad move so far away? They all belonged here, on Orcas Island.

Fifteen-year-old Luke Johansen sat down on the beach in front of his parents' house. His elbow rested on his knee, his chin on the palm of his hand as he stared across Deer Harbor. Here he usually found solitude to think and pray, but not tonight. Anger, hurt, shame all ravaged his soul at the same time. He threw several rocks into the water not caring if they skipped or not.

Marriage was for life! That's what his parents, grandparents, pastor, and Sunday school teachers had taught him. He had known there were problems between his parents the past four years. Just last week he had discussed it with his younger brother, Adam, when they were fishing off Matia Island. Had it all started when his dad had stopped going to church? Perhaps, but most likely the end of his father's church attendance was just the first visible sign.

Luke shivered in the cool evening air. The sun had set, but he did not want to return to the house. What would school be like in the fall? How would he face the other kids? Worse yet, on Monday morning how would he face the crew on *The Claw,* the crab boat where he worked? It might be better if he told them. News traveled so fast on the fifteen-mile-wide island—everyone would know by Tuesday morning. At least he had the weekend to adjust to it.

Failure swept over him—failure as a son and as a Christian. What would other people think? He had grabbed every opportunity at school to talk about his Lord and Savior, Jesus Christ: in science class, when the subject was evolution; going to the school board requesting that prayer be allowed back in the classroom; and, in seventh grade, giving the gospel to the whole class. (They had been studying various religions—the first one, Christianity.)

"Christianity is not a religion; it's a relationship," he had mumbled under his breath.

He recalled the teacher was defining Christianity as a person working at being good to get into heaven. Luke could no longer stay silent. Instinctively he jumped to his feet, asking if he could speak. Luke smiled, remembering his teacher's stunned look. Wide-eyed she had nodded. Maybe her shock explained why he got to recite John 3:16, explain how Jesus died for everyone's sins, and got through Ephesians 2:8 and 9, telling how it wasn't works or being good but faith that God wanted, before she put a stop to his explanation and asked him to sit down.

But now, as the last bit of daylight disappeared, Luke stood and headed up the grassy knoll to the house. There were sounds from the study; his father must be still packing. Luke noted the sleeping bag on the couch as he walked through the living room. Anger burned inside Luke as he headed up the stairs to his room. How could his father desert them?

Luke tossed and turned in bed, unable to sleep. Did he hear crying? He checked his parents' room, but his mother was asleep. Then he checked on Adam. He was sobbing into his pillow. Luke sat on the side of the bed and patted Adam on the back. "It's OK, it's OK, kid. God's gonna take care of us."

Saturday morning seemed to last forever as Luke watched his dad pack up the 1967 Chevy Caprice station wagon that they had bought new the year before. It was the first time the family had been able to afford two cars. Luke knew he should be helping, but resentment did not let him move from his bedroom window.

Luke stared at the six-foot-two blond who always had a smile for everyone. He still loved him, but did he even know him anymore? Dad had quit crabbing and fishing for a living and taken a job on the mainland. The long commute to Bellingham had kept him away from home.

Some nights in the winter when the weather was bad, he would call, "Just getting a room....Roads are too bad, and I won't make the last ferry. Plus, I need to be at work tomorrow."

Luke remembered the "guys only" camping trips with his father. They'd pack up the forty-two-foot crab boat on Friday afternoon and head for Spenser Spit with a tent and a few supplies. Mom always made sure that they had extra food in case they didn't catch any crab for their meals. They'd pitch a tent on the sandy beach, and Dad would tell them stories until he and Adam fell asleep. The camping trips stopped altogether when Dad took the job in Bellingham.

The pain in his chest grew as Luke revisited his childhood dream of working on the crab boat with his father. That day never came. Until he was older, his mother did not want him out fishing on the open water where his father liked to troll. And he wasn't strong enough to haul in the crab pots. His parents had agreed that he would have to be twelve before he could work with his dad. However, the summer he turned twelve, his dad sold the boat in search of more money on the mainland.

"OK, boys, it's time for me to catch the ferry. Come say good-bye," Mr. Johansen called up the stairs. Luke and Adam moved slowly down the stairs, trying to postpone the inevitable. There was no sign of their mother, Rosa. They each hugged their father, watched him back the car around and head out the driveway.

"Dad! Dad!" Adam yelled, running after the station wagon. Luke ran after Adam, quickly catching up with him. Luke grabbed him and held Adam tight as he sobbed on Luke's shoulder.

Sunday morning, silence hung heavy in the '57 Chevy on the way into the town of Eastsound, where the small Baptist church was located. Luke glanced at his mom. She had been very quiet all weekend, her eyes red and puffy. He looked again. She had on pancake makeup to cover up the red around her eyes! He had seen some of the girls at school wear stuff like that. He had not been thinking of her at all, only himself.

Just before they got to church she pulled off to the side of the road. "Boys," she said slowly, "I did not want this. I tried to keep it from happening….But there's a situation I cannot tell you about." She continued, her voice cracking. "Anyway, no one at church knows about anything yet. But I have an appointment this afternoon with Pastor Bob and Marie. Would you two join me?"

Adam and Luke nodded in agreement.

After church they ate lunch at the nearby café, then walked two short blocks to the pastor's house, past little summer cottages, some permanent homes, and a few small shops. One shop displayed Rosa's placemats, rugs, and wall hangings which she wove. Pastor Bob Larson and his wife, Marie, met with Rosa first as the two boys played with the Larsons' three young children in the small, cramped living room. Then Adam met with Pastor Bob. Luke was last.

Pastor Bob allowed Luke to settle into the large leather chair and look around the study for a moment. He cleared his throat. "Tell me what you think about your parents' divorce."

"This isn't how God designed the family to be." Luke knew the hurt he was feeling showed on his face. "There has to be a way to fix it!"

"There's no fixing this, Luke. This is not your decision. It's out of your control. It's a test for you. Are you going to turn to the Lord or let this ruin your life?" Pastor Bob looked Luke square in the eye.

Luke looked away, ignoring the question. "What will the kids at school think? They know I'm a Christian. They'll think I'm a phony."

Pastor Bob's voice was firm but compassionate. "Our lives aren't perfect, Luke. Timothy was from a fragmented family. God still used him. You need time to heal....Make sure you spend time with God and keep reading your Bible. I'm going to write down some verses for you to look up and read on your own." Pastor Bob paused as he wrote on a notepad. He carefully folded the paper in two. "Go to God with your hurt. When people see you draw closer to the Lord through this, it will make them realize that Christianity does work. It brings you through the hard times."

"Thanks," Luke said as he took the piece of paper Pastor Bob handed him.

"Now let's go into the living room. It might be good if we all prayed together before you leave."

On the way home Rosa seemed a bit more relaxed.

CHAPTER 2

Crabbing

"Hey, we caught a special one!" Steve exclaimed as he sorted out the crabs from the last crab pot.

Luke looked up just in time to see a dogfish flying through the air. He deflected the slimy fish, preventing it from hitting him in the face, then picked it up and raised it above his head to throw it back at Steve.

"Now you're asking for it!" Luke laughed and stepped toward Steve just as Captain Tom came out of the cabin.

"Am I paying you two to work or to play?" Captain Tom scowled.

"Sorry, sir," both Steve and Luke said in unison and returned to sorting the crabs in silence.

Had it been a year since the news of his parents' divorce? Luke looked up at the shimmering blue water. Yes, a year, a difficult one. He bent down and started sorting crabs again. *My anger and self-pity keeps getting in the way of fellowship with the Lord. But I am taking more problems to Him and leaving them there. And, Lord, You do answer each one. Even the tiny ones.*

Luke paused, looked out at the water again. *But, Lord, this grace thing. Do I have to treat my dad in grace?* Pastor Bob had explained that treating someone in grace did not mean that you agreed with what the person was doing.

Luke stood up and threw two small crabs back into the water. He enjoyed working on *The Claw,* a forty-eight-foot trawler, setting and hauling in the large crab pots, because he was out in God's creation. The wind and waves reminded him of God's great power. Only God was more powerful than an angry sea. A large wave could flatten a grown man onto the steel deck or throw him overboard in a second. On sunny and hot days, when there was only a slight breeze, the water would shimmer and look glorious, like heaven. Pastor Bob talked about heaven being better than anything on earth. It must be absolutely unbelievable, Luke thought, because crabbing in the islands was as good as it got. He enjoyed looking at the bug-eyed crabs and watching them squirm to try and get away. The orca whales, seals, and sea lions were fascinating to watch. Luke liked the hard work and the time he got to reflect on life, the Lord, and the way problems seemed to get solved at sea.

They had finished sorting the crabs. Luke grabbed a crab pot and baited it, then let it go over the side.

"Hey, do you have that pot set?" Captain Tom yelled.

"Yes, sir," Luke yelled back. The red and white buoy bobbed happily at the surface, letting them know the pot's location.

"That's the last one in this area. We'll go back around to the other side of Decatur and check the pots we left this morning." The captain yelled so the whole crew could hear.

"Here's your lunch." Steve handed Luke the first sack he took out of the cooler, and the two headed forward to sit on the bow. Steve and Luke had been friends since first grade, but this was Steve's first summer working on *The Claw*.

"We need to eat fast. Won't take Captain long to get to the pots," Luke said just before taking a bite of his sandwich.

"Did you get your grades?" Steve asked.

"Yeah, how did you do?"

"Pretty good. Let me guess you got all A's again, right?"

Luke smiled. "Yeah."

"Have you told your dad?"

"No." Anger boiled up inside Luke again. "He's pretty busy. Haven't even seen him since Christmas, when he visited for *three whole days*. At least he sends Mom the support checks on time. And he calls once a week. He doesn't like to talk about the Lord anymore. Every time I mention Christ, he changes the subject."

"Sorry to hear that. Say, there are the pots we set this morning. We'd better get back to work." Steve stood up and stuffed his remaining lunch back into his sack.

Steve had been a Christian for three months. Though his family were long-time members of the same church that Luke's family attended, Steve had never understood what it was all about.

"I've been watching you these past eight months, Luke," Steve had told him in the early spring. "You've had it bad this past year, and you always seem to surface and do just fine. What is it that keeps you going?"

Luke took his time answering; they had discussed the Christian life before. "It's Christ that has given me the strength to keep going. At times it's been hard. I know you believe in God, and we've talked many times about Christ dying for your sins. When are you going to believe?"

"I need to think about it some more," Steve had answered. Less than a week later at school, Steve broke the news to Luke that he was a believer. It helped to have a Christian friend at school. The class of 1970 only numbered fourteen students, and nine were girls. The remaining guys were taking a path that Luke wanted nothing to do with.

As he hauled in a crab pot, Luke reflected on the fact it had not been a good year for his mom. Rosa's small frame had become even smaller, and lately her skin was starting to have a yellow cast. Thankfully she had finally agreed to go to Seattle for a doctor's appointment at the University of Washington hospital. She had caught the 6:30 A.M. ferry. After the appointment, she planned to meet up with her sister, Sophie, who lived in Seattle. *Lord, please take care of Mom,* Luke prayed as the full crab pot landed on the deck.

It had been a good day; they had a large haul. Just as Luke and Steve were finishing sorting out the males from the female crabs, and returning the females and any males under six inches to the bay, Captain Tom came out of the cabin. He had a concerned look on his face.

"Just got a message from Pastor Bob on the radio, Luke," explained Captain Tom. "Seems the doctors want to keep your mother overnight for more tests. She would like you and Adam to come down and be with her for a few days, so Pastor Bob's meeting us at dock. He and Adam are packing a bag for you, and you're to catch the next ferry. Pastor Bob will take you two into the city."

Luke sat down hard on the steel deck. His face turned white. *This can't be good,* he thought.

For five days Luke spent most of his time at the UW hospital by his mother's side, watching the doctors run test after test.

"Luke, we have all prayed so much about this....Come sit down." Rosa patted the hospital bed and scooted over to give him room. She took his hand. She looked yellow, and the IV in her lower arm made the blood vessels in her hand bulge. "This is the answer God has given us. We have to make the best of it."

"The doctors seem to think she stands a good chance, and we know she's a fighter." Aunt Sophie smiled, giving her sister a pat on the arm. Liver cancer had been the diagnosis.

"But I won't let you stay here in Seattle and watch me struggle through all the treatments. Sophie is going to take good care of me." Rosa said. Aunt Sophie and Uncle Hank had a huge house on the west side of Queen Anne Hill. They had no children.

"And I don't want to live with Dad," Luke insisted.

"OK, then you and Adam will have to take Pastor Bob and Marie's offer. The loft above their garage is good-sized. This way you can both keep your jobs. Several people from the church have offered to help. You'll have their support if you need anything. Do you think you can handle it and keep an eye on Adam for me?"

"Yes, I can handle it. Don't worry about Adam; I'll keep him in line. I love you, Mom." Luke stood up, bent over, and gave his mother a kiss on the check before leaving the room.

The summer passed quickly. Luke not only worked days on *The Claw,* but worked nights taking over the bookkeeping for Captain Tom. With his mom not weaving, and the medical expenses, they could use the extra money.

Luke and Adam were able to visit their mom every Saturday and talk to her every other day. Aunt Sophie was footing the bill for the calls. The church members were very supportive. Adam worked hard at his job at the Eastsound Grocery Store during the day and still played baseball in the evening.

As the days grew shorter and the foggy August mornings made their work more difficult on *The Claw,* it became evident that Rosa would not be home for the beginning of school in the fall. Although the surgery had gone well and the doctors were fairly sure the cancer was gone, she was very weak from the treatments and not able to care for herself. She definitely couldn't handle the cold island winter ahead.

Though Pastor Bob and his wife had been very hospitable, Adam and Luke could not stay with them during the school year. Pastor Bob and Marie's small house was very full with their own three children, and the loft above the garage where Luke and Adam had been staying didn't have heat.

It is totally unbelievable, Luke thought, that he and Adam were going to have to live with their dad in Olympia! Why on earth would God want them there?

CHAPTER 3

"Oly" Bears

With the car windows rolled down and the warm autumn breeze ruffling his hair, Luke sang along with the radio, enjoying the view of the south tip of Puget Sound meeting up with the north end of Capitol Lake. The narrow isthmus that divided the two bodies of water connected the west side of town to the east. As he drove his mother's '57 Chevy across the isthmus, he gazed up at the state capitol building with its large light gray dome looming between tall evergreen trees. High on a hill, it could be seen for miles in almost any direction. At night with the lights shining on it, the capitol took on a white glow.

Once downtown Luke took a right on Capitol Way and drove up the hill past the capitol and on to his new high school, William Winlock Miller High School. His father had warned him that everyone in town called it Olympia High School and the students called it "Oly."

Wow! Luke pulled the car off to the side of the road. He wanted to take this all in. There it was—Oly. *It looks like a college campus—eight buildings with covered sidewalks in between. It's huge!* But it would have to be to house over 1,600 students. The school packet his father had given him said the junior class had 565 students. Luke's eyes darted from one building to the next as he wondered how he'd ever find his classes without looking like a total idiot.

He glanced down at the map of the campus on the seat next to him. A picture of the school's mascot, a funny cartoon bear with a very lopsided smile, occupied the corner of the map. That…that must be the student parking lot. Yes, straight ahead. It was quickly filling with cars. Well, he'd better get a spot before they were all taken.

"Welcome to chemistry. I'm Joe, the TA." A short, well-groomed young man held out his hand to Luke.

"Luke Johansen, from Orcas Island." Luke shook Joe's hand.

"Oh, a newcomer. Well, then, welcome to Oly. Here's an outline of the course. Take a seat, and be careful who you sit with, as that person will also be your lab partner." Joe smiled, pointing to the tables that sat two students each.

"Well, the TA seems friendly enough. Mind if I sit here? I'm Luke."

"Don't mind if you do. I'm Zach. Yeah, Joe's pretty popular. He's student body vice president and captain of our wrestling team. We win state almost every year. Guess we better pay attention. Mr. Casey is here." Zach nodded to the front of the room. For fifty minutes Mr. Casey took the stage, acting out stories and anecdotes, while introducing the basics of chemistry to them.

"Mr. Casey's quite the actor," Luke mentioned to Zach when class was over.

"Oh, this is nothing. At the end of each semester he does a complete rendition of 'Casey at Bat.'"

Joe came over to their desk. "Do you know where your next class is?"

Luke nodded.

Joe glanced at Luke's class schedule. "Say, you have mixed chorus with me. What part do you sing?"

"Bass. How about you?" Luke stood up. He didn't want to talk too long; he only had ten minutes to get to his locker and to his next class on the opposite side of campus.

"Tenor. See you third period." Joe waved and headed off in the other direction.

Luke stopped at his locker one more time before mixed chorus to get his coat. The walkways between the buildings had metal roofs but no sides, poor protection from the wind and rain, which started partway through second period. As he picked his way through the mass of students in the hallway of Building One, he wondered what mixed chorus would be like. He liked to sing and he hoped the class wasn't filled with people looking for an easy A. Luke was assigned to stand next to the tenor section, and as he found his place on the bleachers, he was surprised to find himself standing next to Joe. They nodded to each other. Mrs. Miller had just played a note on the piano for warm-up exercises, and the whole chorus started in.

"Say, you have a decent voice. Our madrigal group needs a bass," Joe whispered to Luke between songs. Luke nodded. Mrs. Miller was still talking. She had called out someone else for talking earlier, and Luke did not want to be singled out in front of the seventy-five-member chorus. Everything here at Oly was so much bigger than his old school. It was almost too much to take in.

"OK, what about it? How about singing with the madrigal group?" Joe asked after class. "All the madrigals were selected last spring, but one of the bass singers unexpectedly moved away this summer. Auditions are this afternoon after school to fill the spot. Think about it." Joe slapped Luke on the shoulder and headed off to his next class.

Madrigals could be a great way to meet people, Luke thought as he walked through the door of his last class. He was early. He had finally figured out why everyone carried several books around. There was not enough time to go to your locker between each class. Luke put his books down on a desk near the window and gazed at the garden between the buildings. He heard someone walking through the door. He turned, and for a moment he could not breathe or speak.

"Hello, I'm Bobbi. This is level six English, right?" the small dark-haired girl spoke first.

Luke cleared his throat nervously, "I—I hope so. I'm Luke Johansen, from Orcas Island."

"Oh, so you are new here."

"Yeah…" as Luke fumbled for words, several other students and the teacher came through the door. Bobbi turned to talk to one of them. All during class his eyes kept wandering over to her, and afterward he realized he had little idea what the teacher had been talking about.

Wednesday morning was Luke's first madrigal practice. As he walked through the door he spotted Joe talking to several guys. Joe immediately introduced Luke to them.

"Luke, there is someone else I want you to meet." Joe turned and put his hand on the shoulder of a girl sitting on a chair. She turned to Luke. "Luke, I would like you to meet my girlfriend, Bobbi West."

Luke's heart sank. "Yes, we met in English class, yesterday," Luke explained to Joe, smiling at Bobbi as he spoke.

Mrs. Miller walked into the room. "OK, enough socializing. Let's warm up." "Luke, I want you to stand behind Holly here." She sat down at the piano, and practice began.

Hemingway! A whole semester on Hemingway? Luke slumped down in his chair in English class. It was Friday afternoon and he let his thoughts wander. *I like it here. The campus is huge, but I know where all my classes are. The kids are friendly and easy to talk to. It's comfortable.* If he could just get used to the smell of hops. The last two mornings had been foggy, and the still air held the odor of beer brewing at the nearby Tumwater Brewery. The strong, stale stench turned his stomach.

"Well, since you can't answer the question, Mr. Johansen, can anyone else help us out?" asked Mr. Henderson.

Luke suddenly realized that he had been deep in his own thoughts for the first ten minutes of class! His face turned red.

Mr. Henderson was talking again; Luke focused on the words. "Yes, Miss West."

"Hemingway is considered a great author because of the way he pioneered..."

Luke had spent two days trying to ignore Bobbi and his attraction to her. Now she was upstaging him, and it was embarrassing. She must be one of those snooty "Westside girls" who spent every spare minute at the mall shopping and getting their hair done. Her stylish clothes and painted nails seemed to fit with that crowd. He had to forget about her. She was Joe's girl. Besides she wouldn't even have a clue on how to get into a boat, much less row one, fish, or set a crab pot.

As soon as the 2:45 bell rang, the school week would be over. On Saturday morning he and Adam would drive up to Seattle to visit their mother at Aunt Sophie's. Rosa had improved this week, and the doctors were more hopeful that she might be able to return to the Island by Christmas. It was a day-by-day thing.

Sunday would bring the big question: Where would he and Adam go to church? His father had made it clear that he would not be joining them. In fact Dad had a date starting late on Sunday morning. Luke wondered where Dad had met her. Yesterday, after school he had taken a look at the list of churches in the phone book. *How does one pick a church?* he'd wondered. Where should he start? They would start with the first one on the list.

CHAPTER 4

Bobbi

"Oops!" Bobbi steered her car back onto her side of the road. Ending up in the ditch would not help. She kept driving as fast as she dared on the winding country roads, trying to make the early morning madrigal practice on time. Finally…today's Friday! It had been a busy first week of school.

She could not be late to practice. As the youngest, the only junior girl who had made the sixteen-member group of eight boys and eight girls, she had to be on time. She loved singing the classical music in such close harmony. She could hardly wait to wear the long dress her mother had been working on for the past week, with heels dyed to match, and long white gloves. That was the girls' outfit for each performance. And the best part of all, her new boyfriend, Joe Thorton Jr., was her partner. How perfect! They would walk in to each performance, her arm through his, and he would seat her and stand behind her. How romantic!

Dating Joe was an answer to prayer, she thought. Her parents had not liked the young man she had dated the year before. He wasn't a Christian, and that had caused a lot of family friction. Joe was attractive, very pleasant to talk to, and from a wealthy, respected family. In fact, her family had known his family back in the Midwest. His family had homesteaded in Iowa, becoming one of the most prominent families in the state. Her mother had sisters back in Iowa, and she enjoyed writing to them about whom her daughter was dating.

She had officially met Joe at the first madrigal practice in late July. She had known who he was for an entire year before he had noticed her. After that first practice, during her devotional time that night she prayed and asked God to work out the details so that she could date Joe. By the next madrigal practice they were dating. She had not expected an answer that fast!

Joe was also a gentleman. They had been dating for over a month now, and he had only held her hand once. She liked not having the pressure to become physically involved. She had gotten tired of telling her boyfriend "no" last year. He had always wanted to take things a step further. So many of the girls she knew were getting involved physically with their boyfriends. She had decided that she wanted to do it God's way and keep sex for marriage.

Joe was only three inches taller than her petite five foot two inches, but he had a good physique, as he'd been wrestling for years. Bobbi loved his blue eyes. She was so attracted to blue eyes.

The only drawback that she could see in their relationship was that Joe had just become a Christian. He liked going to church with her, but she felt she had to explain everything. It would be nice to have some spiritual leadership in a relationship, especially since she had only been a Christian for a year. Even though she had been raised in a Christian family and always gone to church, it had taken her a long time to understand what the issue was. She had loved learning about God and believed there was a God, but not until the summer before her sophomore year had she realized why Christ died on the cross. He died for her sins.

As she continued to drive into town, Bobbi thought about how perfect this year would be. Madrigals, art class, plus in the winter months, ski team and watching Joe wrestle. It was going to be a great year.

But the new guy in madrigals—Luke. Why had her heart skipped a beat when he showed up for madrigals on Wednesday morning? She had met him the day before in English class, and nothing happened then. Joe had told her on the phone that night that Luke had joined the group, and she had not thought a thing about it.

Luke was tall, six feet, with blond hair and blue eyes. He was in good physical shape, with broad shoulders and sharply defined arm muscles. She had noticed *that* under his short-sleeved knit shirt. Joe had mentioned that Luke had worked on a crab boat and was from Orcas Island.

Ever since she was a child, Bobbi had wanted to live on Orcas Island. Her grandparents had taken her family on a ferry ride through the San Juan Islands one summer. The islands were so beautiful. She would have to ask him what it was like to live there.

But why was she thinking about Luke? She was dating Joe. Even if she wasn't dating Joe, Luke was out of her league. He was too good-looking to be interested in her. She did not have Maggie's big green eyes, Carol's beautiful red hair, Becky's great figure, or Vicky's height and long legs. Her nose was straight, thin, and boring. Luke Johansen would never be interested in her. Besides, she didn't know if he was a Christian or not. He was definitely the new cool guy at school. Bobbi had overheard several groups of girls discussing him. It would only be another week and one of those Westside girls would tag him as hers, and that would be the end.

Anyway, enough of the wandering thoughts. She was going to make madrigal practice in time after all. Tonight was the first school dance, and she was looking forward to Sunday night and the first big meeting of the youth group at church. Yes, it was going to be a great year.

CHAPTER 5

Church Hunting

*H*ow could they spend a whole hour talking about nothing but social issues and never talk about the Lord? Not once was the gospel given or Jesus Christ mentioned. People ignored us, and I felt like an intruder. Didn't you?" Adam looked at Luke intently as Luke drove them home from church. "Someone needs to tell them what church is all about!"

Luke agreed. "Yeah, you're right. It was strange. That one will be crossed off the list. Hopefully the next church will be better."

Once at home, Luke was surprised to find his father and a very attractive young woman, Deanne, just finishing lunch. He thought they would be out somewhere on their date. It quickly became apparent that this wasn't the first date that these two had been on. She had known his father for quite some time.

"Luke, I forgot, someone called for you just five minutes before you got home," his father said, walking into the kitchen as Adam and Luke were finishing lunch. "His name was Joe…Joe Thorton, I think. He left his number; I have it right here."

"Hey, Joe. My dad said you called."

"Yeah. I was wondering if you'd like to go to youth group at church tonight?" Joe asked.

Was Joe a Christian? "Which church?"

"Westside Baptist. We do some singing, and we'll be studying in Ephesians the next few months."

"Let me check with my dad. I'll give you a call back." Luke hung up the phone and walked into the kitchen.

"No," his father answered quickly. Luke started to turn red. How dare this spiritually defunct man tell him he could not go to church! His anger rose, he started to object, then realized he needed to be respectful and obey his father. This was going to be a difficult year.

"Deanne and I are taking you and Adam out for dinner at the Falls Terrace Restaurant tonight, and we're going to show you some of the sights around town before and after that. We have a busy evening planned. It will be a good chance for you to get to know Deanne better," Luke's dad explained.

"Well then, how about next Sunday?" Luke thought he better get his reservation in quickly before Dad got some other thing going to interfere with church.

"I suppose so," his dad answered. "You're going to be just like your mom—church, church, church."

Luke called Joe back. "Sorry, not tonight," he said reluctantly, "but I'd like to come next week. Adam and I tried a church this morning, but we didn't care for it. What's your church like?"

"Well, it's really Bobbi's church," Joe explained. "I started going with her to church when we started dating. Then I realized I had never understood that I needed a

Savior, Jesus Christ. I became a Christian just recently and have a lot to learn."

Luke was excited. "That's great! I'm a Christian too."

After the conversation, Luke realized that God had really been working out the details for him. The first guy he met at school was a Christian! He also realized that he had been thinking a lot of negative thoughts about moving to Olympia and not trusting the Lord. With everything going wrong with his family and with his mother's illness, he had gotten his eyes on the problems and not on the Lord. He went to his room, prayed and got right with the Lord, finished a bit of homework, and then dove into a Bible study that he had brought from home. His father could keep him from church tonight, but he was not going to keep him from learning God's Word.

The city sightseeing and dinner with Dad seemed very shallow to Luke. Deanne, who could have not have been more than twenty-five, seemed to "ooh" and "ah" at every word that Dad said, and she was overly nice to him and Adam. What on earth did Dad see in her?

"Order anything you want. It's a time to celebrate all of us being together," Dad offered as they sat down at the Falls Terrace Restaurant. "Now, that's the Deschutes River out there." The river took a gentle turn in front of the restaurant, widened, and descended into a fifteen-foot fall.

When the waiter brought the food, both Adam and Luke looked at their father and waited for him to pray, but he did not bother. Instead, he and Deanne just began eating. Luke looked at Adam; they each bowed their heads and prayed silently.

It was obvious that Dad and Deanne were holding hands under the table so he and Adam could not see. Something about them seemed to really ruin his appetite, and Luke could not finish his dinner. Was it Deanne, or seeing his dad with anyone else besides Mom?

"We had an interesting time at church this morning," Luke said as he tried to make conversation.

"Deanne doesn't want to hear about all your religious stuff," his father exclaimed, loudly enough that people at the other tables turned to look.

Luke turned red. He remembered sitting on his father's lap when he was small. His father had read to him about David and the lion and the bear from his Bible. He told Luke all about how God needed to be first in his life, that no problem was too big for God. He remembered being on a camping trip and his dad talking about Christ dying for his sins. How did a man go from loving the Lord to not even wanting to talk about the Lord? Luke didn't understand but hoped that would never happen to him.

After dinner they all took a stroll on a rustic path around the Tumwater Falls. There were lots of trees, rhododendrons, and little springs of water cutting across the trail that hugged the Deschutes River. The last narrow fall plummeted thirty feet into the south end of Capitol Lake just south of the I-5 freeway. They crossed the wooden footbridge that spanned the top of the last fall and took stairs down to the concrete platform that jutted out close to the cascading water.

The next morning Joe waited for Luke before madrigal practice, outside the Music Building door.

"I brought some things for you. Here's a study guide for Ephesians, and this is a church doctrinal statement that explains what Westside Baptist believes."

"Thanks, I'm looking forward to next Sunday." Luke had never heard of a doctrinal statement. At lunch he found a quiet bench outside behind the science building and read the material. It was great. He could hardly wait to tell Adam that, most likely, they had found their church.

CHAPTER 6

Rosa's Setback

*T*wo weeks of school down and many more to go." Luke turned to Adam in the front seat next to him. "Aunt Sophie said that Mom's had a rough week. She's had a lot of pain, and the doctors want to do more tests next week just to make sure the cancer has not returned."

"Yeah, it's scary. Every night when we talked to her this week she mentioned the pain. I don't like it when she gets confused and doesn't make any sense." Adam grimaced as he spoke.

"It's the pain medication. But when she gets better, she'll be off of it and clearheaded again. She's the mainstay, the true glue that has held our family together through the years. How could Dad have ever gotten so mixed up and left her?"

"He's crazy," Adam replied.

"You shouldn't say that!"

"But it's true," Adam insisted.

Luke drove in silence for a while, trying to figure out how to reply to his younger brother. "I know it's hard without Mom. She always listens and has great advice, but I find it helps to find a quiet place at lunchtime to read my Bible and pray." If he ever got married, it would be to a woman like his mother, a strong Christian with a giving and forgiving spirit.

Once in Seattle they drove up steep Queen Anne Avenue, west on Galer Street, then took a right onto Eighth Avenue West and looked up at the three-story house. "There's Mom, sitting on the patio. Look! She's waving! I thought she'd be sleeping," Adam exclaimed. As soon as Luke brought the car to a stop, Adam darted out.

Luke was glad that his mother was awake and able to talk to them. He wanted to have a long talk with her alone.

Aunt Sophie met Luke at the top of the steep stairs. Adam was already sitting on the patio next to his mother.

"She slept all night and woke to much less pain," Aunt Sophie explained to Luke. "But we're still going in for the tests on Tuesday and Wednesday. Hopefully we'll have answers back by Friday."

Uncle Hank showed up about a half hour after they arrived. "How about throwing the ball around with me for a while, Adam? On the way home I noticed that the baseball diamond was free at the school."

"Sure. That pitching mound is cool. Do you have an extra mitt I could borrow?" Adam and Uncle Hank quickly disappeared.

"How about if I wheel you over to Parson's Gardens, Mom?" Luke stood up and picked up an extra shawl from the bench and spread it over her legs.

"That would be great. It seems to always have flowers blooming." Rosa smiled.

Luke wheeled her out back to the alley to avoid the stairs, then up the street, passing one old traditional house after another; most had been built in the early 1900s. They took a slow turn through the public garden then headed across the street to a scenic lookout with a great view of the bay.

A historical marker explained that in 1792, George Vancouver had anchored his ship, the *Discovery,* off Restoration Point directly across on the other side of the bay. He and his men were looking for the Northwest Passage and spent a year exploring the bay they named Puget Sound.

Luke shared with his mother about school, the madrigal group, his friend Joe, and trying to find a church.

Rosa started to cry when he mentioned the latter. "I'm very proud of you for taking on the responsibility of finding a church. I pray for you and Adam many times each day. I try to spend a lot of time reading my Bible, too." Rosa wiped a tear from her eye. "But often the pain gets bad, and I can't focus my eyes. Sophie's good and reads a portion of the Bible to me every day. But praying? *That* I can do even if I can't do anything else."

Though he ached to talk about it, Luke left out information about Deanne, as he did not want to cause his mother more pain. He suspected that his mom would remain in love with his dad all her life.

Before Luke and Adam left, they all prayed and read a few psalms together. How he missed the family devotional time.

"Have you been praying for Mom?" Adam asked as Luke merged on to I-5.

"Sure, I keep asking that the doctors will find a cure, that she will get stronger and will be able to return home again soon."

"So do I. I miss being home on the island."

"I miss being out on the water and not having a beach to sit on. It's great that Dad's house has a view of the water, but it's not the same." Their father's house was on the west side of Olympia, the "rich" side, where the homes were fancier. The country club, golf course, and yacht club were on that side of the bay. The house sat close to the yacht club, just up the hill a few blocks. It was a nice house, but it didn't feel like home. Home would always be the large craftsman-style house that he had grown up in on Orcas. It had been in Mom's family for sixty years. The solid structure made Luke feel secure.

"I've been thinking about finding a part-time job after school, something to do with the water, if possible," Luke said. "There's a marina at the end of the bay. They might need part-time help to pump fuel, be a cashier, do dock maintenance, or even to sweep the docks and floors. Just being out on the docks would help." He would look into it after school on Monday.

"How's that singing group you're in going?" Adam asked.

"Madrigals? It's fun. Two of the other bass singers are football players and like to joke around a lot. We haven't performed yet. I'm assigned to walk in with Holly; she's OK."

"Someone you might want to date?"

"No, she's dating another guy who's not in the group. One thing I don't like is that for performances we have to wear a suit and tie. If I'd known that, I might not have tried out." Luke hated putting on a suit and tie.

Adam changed the subject. "So, we're going to try Joe's church tomorrow. I hope we like it."

"Yeah, I hope so."

Then it dawned on him. Hadn't Joe said last weekend that Bobbi attended that church? She would probably be there. In all the turmoil about his mother during the past week, he had been able to keep his mind off Bobbi. Maybe she was a Christian! Maybe she wasn't a snooty, rich Westside girl after all, just a Westside city girl. He still couldn't imagine her out on a boat.

Luke looked over at Adam. His younger brother had conked out and started to snore.

CHAPTER 7

Back to the Water

As Luke sat in Westside Baptist Church Sunday school class, he saw several teens he recognized from school and some he didn't. He kept looking for Bobbi.

"Too bad Bobbi's not here today." Joe interrupted Luke's search. "She went with her family out to the coast for the weekend."

Well, at least I can settle in and get to know my way around without that distraction, Luke thought.

During the morning church service he and Adam sat with Joe. The service was excellent. The pastor really knew his Bible. He had studied Greek and Hebrew in seminary and explained what each verse meant. Luke could tell that Pastor Ralph really lived what he was preaching and wanted others to do the same. He wasn't just teaching some abstract theory.

That evening, Joe picked Luke up for the high school youth group. Luke liked the assistant pastor who led the youth group Bible study. He found out that there was a junior high youth group at the same time as the high school group and an evening church service after the youth groups. Next week he would make sure that Adam got to come.

Monday after school, Luke drove to the Olympia Marina.

"Is the marina owner in?" Luke asked the middle-aged man behind the counter.

"I'm the owner. My name's John." He held out his hand and Luke shook it.

"I'm Luke. I'm looking for part-time work, after school."

"Sorry, we have full-time help. Don't need anyone else. However, there's a small marina out north, on the east side, that could use some help. It's called Boston Harbor Marina, in the cove right after the Dofflemyer Point Lighthouse."

"OK, I'm new here. Where is that?"

"Just head out East Bay Drive and keep going north through Priest Point Park. Then stay on the main road, Boston Harbor Road. You'll pass Gull Harbor Mercantile and a fire station. Don't take any of the Y's that go to the right. When you hit Main Street, take a left. It's about eight miles north of town," John explained.

Luke left, disappointed. That seemed a long way to go for a part-time job.

That evening Dad put a small package in the center of the table before they sat down to eat dinner.

"It's not anyone's birthday," Adam commented as he sat down. "What's this about?"

"You will both open it after dinner. It's something that I think you'll find helpful in making your transition to Olympia."

Adam started to wolf down his food. Luke laughed.

"You have to wait until I finish, so you might as well slow down." Their father smiled.

Finally they got to tear into it. Inside the box sat a card that had "B-18" written on it. Was this a joke?

"Well, that's a clue to something at the yacht club. I think we need to take a walk down there and have a look," his father explained.

Not a scavenger hunt. Luke had homework to do and didn't have time to play games.

"Take a look at the marina. See if there are numbers that match," Dad instructed them once they got to the yacht club. Quickly they realized that the slips were numbered the same way. Slip B-18 enclosed a brand-new, sixteen-foot runabout with a powerful outboard engine. Adam and Luke stood on the dock, staring at it for a minute.

"A new boat!" Adam yelled.

"Both of you can use it," Dad said. "It's now our family boat. Hopefully you can feel more at home here being out on the water. How about if we take it for a quick spin?"

Homework forgotten, both boys quickly climbed in. Dad started the engine, and they untied the lines and shoved off. The waters at the end of the bay were calmer than the water around the San Juan Islands, most likely because these were smaller bodies of water. They headed out north past Priest Point Park, which Dad pointed out.

"Do you think we could make it out to Boston Harbor Marina?" Luke asked his dad. He wanted to see what the place looked like.

"Sure." The small boat skimmed across the smooth water at thirty knots. "With this engine, it won't take long to get there."

The lighthouse came into view first. It stood like a lonely statue on the point. Then they came around the sandy point to the most run-down marina Luke had ever seen. Groups of houses were nestled among the evergreen trees on the hills surrounding the pretty cove. Luke looked back at the marina. He feared some of the docks might sink into the water. The gas dock floated precariously, looking like it, too, might sink at any moment.

"Wow!" Adam exclaimed. "What a dive!"

"Careful," Dad reprimanded. "Remember voices carry across the water."

Luke did not tell either of them that he had considered applying for work there. He would have to think it over. He had the means to spend time on the water now with this new toy. Maybe he wouldn't have to find a job.

Dad pointed out Harstine, Hope, and Squaxin islands and then turned the boat back toward Olympia as the sun started to sink behind the Olympic Mountains. It was best to be at dock before dark in unfamiliar territory.

Luke had a hard time falling to sleep that night. He kept thinking about the new boat. Tomorrow after school he would head out to the islands northwest of Boston Harbor that his dad had pointed out. They would be fun to explore. He needed to pick up a chart and a tide book at the Olympia Marina before heading out. He doubted that the Boston Harbor Marina carried anything like that.

Tuesday after school, Adam and Luke took off to explore the islands. They found out that the northeast side of Squaxin Island had a state park with a dock in a small cove and several acres of land and beach to the south of it. The rest of the island belonged to the Squaxin Indian tribe. Luke slowed the engine and came in quietly. No one was there, except eight seals playing on a rough raft of logs and snags several hundred feet off the dock. Luke quickly cut the engine so as not to scare them off. They floated for a while just watching the seals play "king of the log pile."

Just north of Squaxin the south end of Harstine Island ended with a long narrow point. The point and the mainland came very close to touching, creating a very narrow channel.

"That's Dana Passage, Adam." Luke pointed to the narrow channel. "The dockhand at the Olympia Marina told me it's a place with dangerous currents during tide changes. He said we needed to be careful and watch out for ships coming through. They won't stop for you. At low tide, there is not that much room. The passage is plenty deep, just fairly narrow, and it's the main connection from the middle of Puget Sound to the south sound."

"Well, the tide must be changing now. The center looks pretty choppy. Look at that old wood lighthouse on that steep cliff. The chart says that point is called Bristol Point." Adam pointed to the end of Harstine and then looked down at the chart again.

"I like that sandy beach. What a place to read."

Adam looked up from the chart and pointed to the east side of Dana Passage. "There's a lagoon over there called Little Fish Trap. But it's only a half-fathom at low tide."

Luke turned the boat toward Little Fish Trap. Several modest homes lined the cliff above the lagoon. They passed it and headed into Zangle Cove, north of Boston Harbor.

"Luke!" Adam pointed to the instrument panel. "Look at the fuel gauge!"

It read empty. That couldn't be right! They were careful to fill just before they left Olympia. Something must be wrong with the gauge.

"We're close to Boston Harbor Marina; it's just around that point." Luke calmly answered his brother. "Besides we do have oars if we need to row."

"That dump!" Adam exclaimed. "The dock might sink and take our boat with it if we tie up there!"

"I don't think we have a choice, Adam. We aren't going to make it back to Olympia without getting fuel."

Luke slowed the boat down and limped into the run-down marina beside the tilting fuel dock. Luke figured he would pass the fuel dock and swing back around so the dock would be on the port side of the boat. As he made the loop and headed for the dock, a strong south current swung him away from the dock, and even though he gave the engine a bit of gas, he missed the dock completely.

"What's wrong?" Adam asked. "The dock is over there."

"Sorry, just misjudged the current here. We'll try it on the starboard side." That worked well.

"You're beginning to steer like a girl," Adam mumbled under his breath as he helped tie the boat up.

"Do you want gas or diesel?" A loud voice came out of nowhere and caused Luke to jump. Then he saw the loudspeaker on the edge of the gas shack and a microphone below labeled "ORDER FUEL HERE."

"We need gas." Luke spoke into the microphone.

"Do you have cash?"

"Yes, I have a twenty, and we won't be needing more than that."

"I'm turning on the switch. When you're done come up to the store and pay me, OK?"

"Yes, sir." Someone was sure lazy not to come down to help his customers dock and collect the money from them. Especially with such a nasty current here, Luke would have appreciated some help docking.

The fuel tank topped off after only two gallons of fuel.

"Something must be wrong with the fuel gauge," Luke surmised. "At least we're not leaking fuel and messing up the bay. I'll go up and pay, and you stay with the boat."

Luke prepared his apology to the person in the store as he climbed up the ramp from the dock. Astonishment took away his words when he walked into the small, run-down store and saw an elderly man in a wheelchair behind the counter. He had only one leg and did not look to be in the best of health. Someone wasn't lazy; someone needed help. No wonder the place looked like it did.

"I—I'm sorry we didn't buy more gas," Luke stammered, still stunned. "Something must be wrong with our fuel gauge. It read empty. Might be the wiring."

"That's OK, son. Just glad you came up to pay me. Some of the teenagers around here like to try to get away without paying. That is why I don't flip the switch until I know you have cash. I check each one out." The man pointed to his binoculars sitting next to the microphone on the window ledge.

As the man rolled over to the cash register to get Luke change, Luke looked around the store. To the right of the L-shaped cashier's counter were two short rows of free-standing shelving in the center of the room with nonperishable food items. The south side of the room had refrigerated and frozen items. The west wall was a mix of hats, hardware, fishing tackle, oars, flashlights—one or two of everything you might need in a pinch. To the north, the room jutted out toward the water, and with sofa and coffee table against the east wall. A small kitchen with an old propane stove filled the northwest wall. In the center, a dining table stood all alone. There were two doors on the west wall, and Luke wondered where they went. His eyes returned to the magnificent view out the north windows. You could see the entire marina and the harbor, and off in the distance Hope and Squaxin islands, with the Olympic Mountains standing tall behind.

Luke looked out the east window and noticed a pile of cedar boards, perfect for fixing docks, sitting by the path up to the road. They had been there awhile.

"Do you ever need any help around here?" Luke asked quietly.

"Help? Sure, I could use help! Can't pay much. Minimum wage. Do you know anything about boats, fueling, or docks?"

"Yes sir, I do, although you couldn't tell it by the way I docked my boat just now. Up until recently I lived on Orcas Island, and my whole life has revolved around the water."

"Oh, don't worry about the docking; everyone has problems with that current. It constantly changes direction, depending on the tide. Even the locals have trouble with it." The man put Luke at ease. "By the way, my name is Charlie, Charlie Swain. You have a job, young man, if you want it. You're in school yet?"

Luke nodded.

"I'd like you to work as many hours as you can." Charlie put out his hand and Luke shook it.

"Work at that old dump?" Adam exclaimed loudly. Luke had made sure that they were a long way away before breaking the news to his brother.

"The man needs help." Luke explained, "He's in a wheelchair. I'm not doing it for the money. I just want to help the guy out. I know how to rebuild a dock. You could help too."

Adam shook his head. "I have better things to do."

CHAPTER 8

The Marina

*I*t was so foggy out no one would be coming in for fuel, Luke figured. He might be able to get all the old rotten boards on the fuel dock replaced this afternoon. The thick fog cut the visibility to less than one city block at times. Luke could barely see Charlie up at the marina store. It had been like that all day.

As he hammered his last cedar plank in place, Luke reflected on the past week. He couldn't believe it had only been a week since he and Adam had come into Boston Harbor Marina. A lot had happened since then.

Madrigals had their first performance for the Olympia Rotary Club monthly luncheon, which went well. Most of the kids loved having an excuse to miss class, but Luke hated missing his physics class. This was the first time he had been exposed to science labs, and both physics and chemistry were quickly becoming his favorite classes.

It had been a week of lots of telephone calls between Olympia and Seattle. His mother's tests had come back early Thursday afternoon. The news was not good. The cancer had returned to her liver. But the tumor was not very big, and the doctors were sure if they did surgery soon they would have a good chance of getting it all. The second surgery was scheduled for the next week.

Adam and Luke had driven to Seattle several times to spend an evening with Rosa. Each time she had been in good spirits, and they left, praying for the best. Luke refused to let himself think of anything but a good outcome for his mother.

As Luke walked up the main dock past the store to get more cedar planks, he gazed in wonder at the beautifully floating docks and finger piers peeking through the fog. Last Saturday had been the most amazing day. Luke had told Joe all about the Boston Harbor Marina at lunch on Wednesday. By Friday night, Joe had arranged a work crew of thirty men from Westside Baptist to help fix the marina docks the next day.

Charlie had given Luke the money to buy the badly needed Styrofoam pontoons that would keep the docks afloat. After school on Thursday, Luke had bought them at a marine supply place in Olympia and scheduled the delivery to the marina.

Luke was disappointed that Joe was not able to help on Saturday due to a family outing. But with all the experienced carpenters and handymen who showed up, Joe was not needed.

Luke had taken several men at a time to the finger piers and showed them what needed to be done. He took off a sideboard, removed an old worn-out pontoon, slipped in a new one, and secured it in place. Soon he had ten fully trained crews working away. Several women from the church brought out a fabulous lunch and served it on the marina deck to all the workers. Before nightfall they had all the main docks and most of the finger piers fitted with new pontoons and floating proudly in the water. Boston Harbor Marina was not going to sink to the bottom of the bay after all! With almost everything floating, Luke figured he could take his time replacing the rest of the pontoons and the rotten cedar planks. Best of all, Charlie was beside himself with thankfulness.

Luke loaded up with cedar planks and smiled at Charlie as he walked by. As he made his way down the main dock, he heard a small engine through the fog. Who would be coming in for fuel today? Luke hoped they knew what they were doing. He tried to hurry so he could make it to the dock to help them. The tide had just changed, and that nasty south current was in action again.

As he got closer to the fuel dock he could see a twelve-foot pram, with a small figure in a yellow slicker huddled next to the outboard motor, cutting through the fog. He wasn't going to make it in time to help. Luke dropped the cedar planks on the side of the main dock and ran for the fuel dock. About five feet before the fuel dock, he tripped over the hammer he had left there and did a perfect belly flop onto the dock. The hammer did a nosedive into the water. With the wind totally knocked out of him, Luke looked up to watch as the boat came gliding in, and the small figure jumped out onto the dock in perfect rhythm to tie up the pram. This person knew how to handle a boat!

Luke gathered up his tall frame and walked over to the little yellow figure. "Would you like some gas?' he asked.

The figure turned. "Yes, please." It was a female voice. She lifted her head and pulled back her hood. It was Bobbi!

Bobbi took a few steps back and almost went into the water. "Luke! What are you doing here?" she said, gasping.

"I started working here a week ago." Luke wondered why she didn't make some comment about his belly flop on the dock. Either she hadn't seen it or she was being very kind.

"That's wonderful!" she said. "Poor old Charlie could really use the help."

"Poor old Charlie is going to be very upset if his favorite customer does not come up and visit him," the loudspeaker squawked. "Luke, would you please fill up her fuel tank and let us know the total when you're done?"

"Yes, sir," Luke answered and watched with pleasure as Bobbi stopped and looked around at the dock.

"What happened here? The dock's not sinking at this end. It's floating, and there are new boards!"

Luke gave her a shortened version of Saturday's work party.

"I knew Joe was organizing something for the church, but I didn't know what for. This is great!" she exclaimed.

Bobbi visited with Charlie awhile, and Luke filled up her fuel tank. After she left, Luke went up to see Charlie. "I owe you for a hammer. You can take it out of my pay, or I can bring you the cash tomorrow."

"Nothin' doin'," laughed Charlie. "I haven't had that much entertainment in a long time. It was well worth the price of the hammer. Didn't your parents teach you to pick up your feet? At least you finally got to meet Bobbi."

"Bobbi and I have already met at school," Luke informed Charlie. "We have English, mixed chorus, and madrigals together. Plus, her boyfriend is one of my friends."

"Yeah, another city slicker who doesn't know anything about the water." Charlie snorted. "That girl needs someone who can help get her out of the predicaments she gets into sometimes. There's a whole group of girls her age who are very adventuresome and are always up to something."

"Joe is a really nice guy." Luke defended his friend. "In fact, Joe is the one who did all the calling and organizing for the work party last Saturday. By the way, what was Bobbi doing out in soup like this?"

"Oh, nothing stops that girl! If she wants to be on the water, that's where she'll be. Drives her mother nuts with worry sometimes. It doesn't matter what time of year either; she loves to be on the water. She and her friend Mary almost got stranded on Bristol Point after school with their boy-friends last February—in eight-foot rowboats. Mary's guy had lost one oar and broken the other. So Bobbi's boyfriend had to row, towing the other boat across Dana Passage in the dark, during a small winter storm, and with no lights! Fortunately, they didn't meet up with a ship comin' in. Her mother called here four times wondering where she was. Storms come in here real quick sometimes and can catch everyone by surprise."

Luke walked back down to the fuel dock, mulling over the events of the last half hour. Bobbi—a country girl and she loved to be on the water.

The next morning as Luke walked toward the music building, Bobbi came running up beside him. "I'm so excited that you're working for Charlie. Have you had a chance to talk to him about the Lord?"

"No," Luke said, "but I've been praying about it."

"So will I. I've tried to talk to him, but he always shuts me down. He says all church people are a bunch of hypo-crites," Bobbi explained. "Maybe that work party will change his mind."

"I hope so. Thanks for the info on his past. Something must have happened to make him feel that way." Luke and

Bobbi walked into madrigals together. Luke felt comfortable talking to her. It was like talking to someone he had known all his life.

CHAPTER 9

The Storm

Octor 10! *Wow, time sure has flown by*, thought Luke. With his mother's second surgery, madrigals, church, schoolwork, and the marina, he had been falling into bed late at night, exhausted.

Charlie and the school officials had been very understanding the day of his mother's surgery. He and Adam had been able to take that Friday off from school and sit with Aunt Sophie in the waiting room. The minutes seemed to tick by very slowly, but finally the doctor came out with the good news that his mother was resting and the surgery had gone well. They each got a few minutes with her, but she was sleeping fairly soundly from the medication. Aunt Sophie put the boys up for the night so that they could be back to the hospital early Saturday morning.

The next week they made two trips up to Seattle instead of the usual one. Rosa was doing well and had just made it out of the hospital and back to Aunt Sophie's house. Her spirits had seemed to pick up when she got there.

Luke had finished almost all of the dock work at the marina. He had also found two other guys who lived in Boston Harbor that were willing to work at the marina so that he didn't have to work every day after school. The other boys took turns working the weekends, and Luke worked two weekday afternoons. Luke was glad to have a little free time for himself. Plus, schoolwork was getting more demanding, and he needed more time for that.

There were actually more people coming in for fuel, and some were even mooring their boats at the marina, now that the place didn't look like it was going to sink. Charlie was very excited about the expanding business.

What a wonderful warm day for October. Luke sat on the sandy beach south of the cove at Squaxin Island State Park trying to finish *A Farewell to Arms* for the English exam tomorrow. He had brought the anchor up onto shore so his boat would not float away. He only had a few more chapters.

Splat! Splat! Luke jerked awake. He had fallen asleep on the beach. He brushed a few raindrops off his face. What time was it? Five-thirty! Oh no! Time had gotten away from him. He sat up and realized the weather had made a drastic change for the worse. The park was around the point from the main channel of Puget Sound, and even in this sheltered body of water some of the waves were a good two feet tall. The sky loomed dark and menacing. He better get moving before things got worse and it got dark.

Luke gathered up his anchor and pushed the boat off from shore. He found his sweatshirt in the bow of the boat and a life jacket and put them both on. He pointed the boat toward the main channel but took a look back at the park. He saw a small red rowboat coming out from the dock area, struggling against the waves. Apparently this person did not have a motor. He would never make it, rowing back to the mainland in this weather.

Luke turned his boat around and headed back for him. He couldn't leave the guy out there. As he came up on the rowboat's port side, Luke realized it was Bobbi.

"Do you want a lift?" shouted Luke over the wind.

"That might be a good idea," Bobbi shouted back.

"I fell asleep trying to finish the English reading. I didn't see the weather change. I had tied up at the dock. Sorry to inconvenience you, but thanks for the lift," Bobbi explained after she was safely in Luke's boat. The pram bobbed behind, being towed with a ski rope.

"I fell asleep too. Guess that says a lot for Hemingway," Luke joked.

Bobbi laughed, then pointed at the waves. "This could be a bad one. The main channel will be nasty if the waves are this big in here. Remember, the tide is changing right now, too, so the center of the channel will be full of riptides and whirlpools. I suggest we head south to the marina and cross the middle down there."

As they rounded the southeast point of Squaxin Island, they saw what was ahead and both started silently praying. The turbulent sky had turned black, and the wind hit them hard from the south. The whitecaps on the two- to three-foot waves were a stark contrast to the dark, midnight-blue water. Luke could see the center of Dana Passage to the northeast of them churning like a boiling caldron. It was a raging river separate from the rest of the sound. The waves were going in every direction and had swelled to three to four feet tall. The separate river extended down past Zangle

Cove and seemed to stop just north of the marina. Bobbi was right—instead of going across to the mainland at this point, it would be better to head south and cross near the marina where the sound was wider and the center current was dissipated. That current would take a boat and push it wherever it wanted.

"Find a lifejacket under the bow and put it on," Luke commanded.

Bobbi did not hesitate, quickly and calmly donning the first one she found. Luke was doing a good job steering the boat across these waves. She was not too concerned, but took a few minutes to pray again and ask the Lord for His help.

Bobbi turned to look back at the rowboat and gasped. "Look! There are people out there in the middle. Luke! Their boat is going down!"

Luke turned to look just in time to see the small boat capsize and two men in lifejackets thrown in at the edge of the boiling caldron.

"We can't leave them there." Luke looked at Bobbi, not wishing to put her life in danger, but not wanting to watch two men die without at least trying to save them.

"Can you take the helm and keep it steady? You will have to stay close to the center current without letting the boat get into it. Can you do that in these waves?" Luke questioned Bobbi.

"Yes, I can handle it," she replied.

"Then take the helm and go back. Get the boat as close as you can to them without getting into the center current. Face the boat south when you get there. I'm going to get things ready."

Turning the boat around in these waves was not going to be easy. But Bobbi recalled everything Charlie had ever taught her and carefully brought the boat around at the right time between the bigger waves. She was not too sure she could do this, but she was going to give it her best shot. She kept asking for the Lord's help as she headed the boat back towards the men.

Luke found two fifty-foot lines and put one eye end through the other line's eye end as if it were a cleat. *That ought to hold against anything,* he thought. He found a flotation cushion and tied it on to the other end of the line then tied the bitter end to a cleat on the side of the boat. That would give him one hundred feet to work with. He hoped he could just throw it to the men and then pull them in.

As they came closer to the men, Luke realized that the one man was struggling to hold on to the other man and swim. His plan of throwing the cushion was not going to work. Luke stripped off his life jacket and sweatshirt and put the life jacket back on. He did not want extra wet clothing weighing him down. Then he took off the cushion and tied the end of the line to the rings on his life jacket.

"Get me as close as you can," yelled Luke over the wind and waves. "We'll use water-skiing signals, OK?"

Bobbi agreed but was dismayed that she would be left alone in the boat to keep it out of the current. Waves were constantly breaking over the bow as it was. Her heart sank as she watched Luke jump into the black, churning water. She did not want to watch but knew she had to keep a close eye on the men, Luke, and the current. It seemed to her that the winds were even stronger and the waves higher. Maybe she was imagining things.

Luke fought to keep his sense of direction as he swam toward the men. At the crest of a wave he would look to make sure he was going the right way. Between the wave crests all he could see was angry water and black, noisy sky. With the wind coming from the south, the waves were helping push him toward the men, but they were being carried farther away. It took all his strength to make progress over the turbulent water.

"He's unconscious," yelled the struggling swimmer.

"I'll take him. Grab on to the rope and pull us in," yelled Luke.

As soon as Bobbi saw Luke had gotten to the men and had the injured man securely held, she started to slowly move the boat out away from the current. When she got the men a safe distance from the current, she gave up the helm for a minute and tried to pull the line in. She was not sure she was helping much; upper body strength was not her forte.

"Go back to the helm. Straighten us out," yelled Luke as he neared the boat with the men.

Once all three were on board, Bobbi gave the engine more gas and headed for the marina. The waves were definitely bigger and the wind stronger, she decided. The roar of the wind had increased. She looked back at Luke working over the unconscious man. All three men were soaking wet and must be chilled to the bone. She started praying again. It was getting more and more difficult to hold on to the wheel and keep control.

Luke started pumping the man's chest as soon as all three were in the boat. *I need to get this man breathing now,* he thought, as he kept pumping. He also needed to relieve Bobbi at the helm. She had done a good job, but the waves were bigger, and she wasn't strong enough to keep this battle up much longer.

"Lord, please! Let him breathe. And soon!" Luke prayed, not realizing he was praying out loud.

"Here it comes!" Luke hollered as the man belched up a pint of water and then began to breathe. He turned to the other man and shouted, "Come take care of your friend. I need to take over the helm!"

Luke turned to the helm. He tapped Bobbi on shoulder. "I'm taking over." She seemed relieved and sank into the seat directly across from him and closed her eyes. Was she praying?

Please, Lord, guide Luke and keep us safe. This reminded Bobbi of past storms. The last big one she remembered had happened several winters before.

From their living room over the roar of the wind and the waves, they had heard men yelling and screaming for help. Her dad had called Mr. Connor, the only neighbor who had a boathouse with an automatic launch. Everyone else had their boats in for the winter season, and the Coast Guard was at least an hour away. Her dad had gone out in her eight-foot pram with a lantern. Mr. Connor had come out in his twenty-six footer, and they searched for the men. They found two, one already dead. The third man they never did find. Their boat had gone down. A person could not last too long in the frigid water. Bobbi would never forget the screams of those dying men.

Charlie had been listening to the radio and the warnings about the storm. It had come up so suddenly. There might be people caught out there! This could be a bad one. If one was a praying man, this would be the night to be praying hard.

Just as the radio station in Olympia said the winds were at fifty miles per hour, Charlie saw Luke's boat coming into the marina. Luke had an emergency megaphone to his mouth. What was he shouting? Charlie rolled himself to the door and opened it.

"Medic! Call a medic now!"

Charlie could barely hear Luke over the roar of the storm. Were the phones still working? Oh no! That was Bobbi's little red rowboat behind Luke's. Was she hurt? Charlie rolled back to the phone in a panic.

Thankfully the phone lines weren't down yet. He made it through to the operator, and she said she would get someone there right away. As he rolled back to the window, Charlie noticed Bobbi out on the dock helping Luke tie down the lines. There were two other people in the boat, and one wasn't moving.

Charlie went back to the phone and called Bobbi's mother. "She's here and OK."

"Please get her under cover and keep her there," pleaded Mrs. West. "Don't let her walk home. Trees are coming down everywhere. And they're predicting sixty to seventy mile per hour winds before it's over."

Charlie stayed on the party line and asked the operator to call Luke's dad.

"Mr. Johansen, this is Charlie at Boston Harbor Marina. Luke's here and he's OK. I suggest—" A huge crash shook the store, interrupting Charlie. Then phone line went dead. At least Mr. Johansen knew that Luke was safe. *Luke and Bobbi are staying here till this storm is over.* The radio updated the wind speed. It had strengthened to sixty miles an hour.

Charlie began to wonder if the medics would be able to get through, when Dr. Peterson, a volunteer fireman, showed up. He lived just a block away. "Heard there was a medical emergency here over my ham radio, and the medics from Olympia don't think they'll be able to get through." Dr. Peterson had his black medical bag.

"Charlie! Charlie!" It was Bobbi bursting through the door before Charlie could answer Dr. Peterson. "Do you have a stretcher? Luke can't carry the injured man up here alone."

"Yes, I have one in the shed on the side of the deck. But you're not going out there in this wind again! The winds are at sixty miles per hour, and you might get blown away. Dr. Peterson can take it down to the boat."

Dr. Peterson agreed that was the best plan and headed out for the dock.

"Now, young lady, your mom knows you're safe, and you and the rest of the men out on the dock will be spending the night here. So, we have some work to do to get ready for our guests. Get me a new tarp off the shelf. We need to put that over my bed for the wet patient, and find extra blankets."

Bobbi filled pails, one-gallon containers, and the bathtub with water. She put water on the old propane stove to boil and brought out as many extra blankets and sleeping bags as Charlie and she could find. They got out all of Charlie's gas lanterns and candles. Bobbi finally sank down next to the old propane stove, cold, wet, and tired.

"It's just a matter of time before the lights go out. The phone lines are already gone," Charlie informed her. "Now you need to get out of those wet clothes. I have some old jeans and a flannel shirt that belonged to one of my nephews when he was a boy. After you change we need to find things that might fit Luke and the two men on the dock."

CHAPTER 10

A Glorious Morning

Luke woke to the smell of frying eggs and hash browns. He saw Charlie working over the propane stove, and the sun shone into the little store. He sat up and remembered that Bobbi was just one aisle over on the store floor in a sleeping bag, snoring away. Even though her hair was a mess and she was drooling, Luke couldn't help think how pretty she looked.

Luke smiled at Charlie, whispered, "Good morning," and went to the window to look out on the bay. It was shimmering in the early morning sunlight and perfectly smooth like glass. How beautiful.

Thank You, Lord, for keeping us safe all night, Luke prayed. This old store must be much sturdier than it looks. The winds had persisted late into the night. Luke had stayed up until midnight, trying to finish *A Farewell to Arms* and making sure everyone was OK. Even as he went to sleep, the wind still howled, and the old store shook.

"Have you heard any news on the radio, yet?" Luke asked Charlie.

"Yes. Everything's canceled, and even people in town are without power. Trees are down everywhere, and lots of roads are closed. One couple was killed by a tree that fell on their car. The utility company is just starting to find out the extent of the damage. Guess the gusts were hitting seventy miles an hour for a long time."

"How's the patient doing?" asked Luke.

Just then, Dr. Peterson came through the entry door, waking up Bobbi in the process. Dr. Peterson had bandaged up the man's head wound the night before and said the man would make it.

"He's awake and hungry." Charlie answered Luke while nodding hello to the doc. "This is for him and his friend. I'll make some for you and Bobbi in a minute." Charlie loaded up two plates; Luke intercepted them and took the plates into Charlie's bedroom for the rescued pair.

"My, those are interesting pants you have on. Setting a new trend?" Bobbi giggled at Luke's high-water pants as he walked back into the main room. She sat up in her sleeping bag and ran her fingers through her hair.

"Well, I was informed that you were the one who picked them out for me." Luke smiled. "They are definitely a better choice than the wet swim trunks I had on last night. Besides, that flannel shirt would be a big hit at school, and you'd get expelled if the principal caught you in jeans."

After breakfast, Luke and Bobbi went down to the dock to survey the damage. Charlie had thanked Luke again for fixing the docks, as the marina would not have survived the storm in its previous condition. They noticed some damage to several of the finger piers and a few of the boats, and Bobbi's pram was upside-down, half-sunk in the water, minus the oars. They turned it over, got all the water out of it, and it floated just fine.

The two men decided to try to drive into town once Dr. Peterson declared the patient well enough to travel. They thanked Luke and Bobbi profusely for rescuing them and kept calling Luke a hero.

"How about if I take you home, Bobbi? You live in Zangle Cove, right?" Luke asked.

"Well, you might need to help her up the trail. There could be brush over the path. Why don't you take my machete out in the shed?" Charlie wanted to add "and spend the day with her," but that might be pushing things.

"That would be great. Otherwise I'd have to borrow oars from Charlie."

Bobbi sat out on the bow of Luke's boat as they headed north around the point to Zangle Cove, dangling her legs off the side and watching for sunken debris, called "deadheads." She also kept an eye on her red pram in tow. Luke took it very slowly, knowing full well the dangers after a storm. Higher waves could wash old logs and debris into the water, boats that had been set adrift by the winds could be half sunk, and tree branches could be blown into the water. The water was shimmering in the sun. It was as if the storm had never existed, and the Lord had swept the earth clean. Now, everything was fresh and new again.

"This is so beautiful!" exclaimed Bobbi as they carefully crossed the cove to Bobbi's beach. "A bit different than last night!"

"Yes," Luke agreed. "Our pastor on Orcas often reminds us of how perfect heaven will be. It must be fabulous, because there is nothing more perfect than smooth water glimmering in the sun."

"Hadn't thought about that, but you're right," Bobbi agreed. "There, see the eighty-foot bank with the concrete bulkhead below and the two boats tied to the raft? That's our place. Since it's high tide and the beach has fairly small rocks, you could bring your boat up on the shore. At low or mid-tide you don't want to try it because the beach is full of big rocks and barnacles."

Luke looked up at the high bank covered with trees. Thinking that it might take a while to work their way through the storm debris on the trail, he opted to tie his boat to the raft with the others and row Bobbi's pram to shore with the extra oars he kept in his boat.

Luke and Bobbi were pleasantly surprised. Except for a few branches that were easily removed at the bottom of the trail, they did not find much debris on the trail. On the second switchback they found out why. There was a freshly cut log off to the side.

"My brother must have been here this morning," Bobbi said when she saw it. "He loves working with the chainsaw, and Dad is out of town on business."

Mrs. West came out of the house as they reached the top of the trail and she walked across the patio to the yard. "I'm so glad you are home! Thank heavens Charlie called last night or I would have been frantic," she exclaimed, leaning over to give Bobbi a big hug. "Who's your friend? You look familiar."

"This is Luke Johansen, Adam's big brother, Mom," explained Brad as he strolled up to the group, chainsaw in hand. "Saw you coming across the cove. Thanks for bringing this little troublemaker home." He grinned down at Bobbi and put an arm around her.

Luke had to smile. They looked so much alike but totally different at the same time. Though Brad was three years younger than Bobbi, he stood almost ten inches taller and acted and looked much more mature than she did. He looked liked the older sibling. Luke had noticed one Sunday morning during church that Bobbi was the runt of her family.

"Well, it's almost lunch time. Let's go inside and start working on some of the food in the refrigerator. Things are not going to last too long without power." Mrs. West pointed toward the house.

Luke tried to decline, stating that he needed to head home. Mrs. West insisted that he would need food before heading back into town, so he gave in and agreed to stay.

Mrs. West served lunch on paper plates, in a modest pine-paneled dining room. "I just don't want to start piling up dirty dishes when the power may not be back on for a while, and we need to conserve the water that we do have. So please excuse the paper plates."

The Wests were on a well just like everyone else in that neck of the woods. It took electricity to pump it, and so now they were left with the water they had saved in the bathtubs and containers to get them through the comings days.

"The last big storm we were without power for a week," Brad said.

"It happens to us up on Orcas, too," Luke replied. "My dad finally got a generator four years ago, and that helps."

"I just wish my husband would be home for one of these storms for a change, and I really wish I could call him and tell him that we are safe. He's at the University of California, Berkley, giving several lectures in the forestry department there," Mrs. West explained to Luke.

The foursome compared storm stories throughout the lunch. After lunch, Brad gave Luke a tour of the place. Bobbi disappeared into her bedroom. Luke and Brad walked around the yard and stopped at the basketball court on a lot north of the house.

"How many acres do you have here?" Luke asked.

"Almost three on this side of Zangle Road. Twenty-nine of pasture land on the other side and one hundred fifty acres of woods beyond that." Brad took Luke up the steep driveway and across the road and showed him the barns, machine shed, pastures, a small herd of Black Angus cattle, and a horse. At the barns the land was flat but then dropped away down another steep hill to the lower pastures and the woods. To the southeast, Mount Rainier stood tall above the trees in the distance. What a place to grow up!

"We grow our own hay every year on the lower pastures and store it up for the winter. Bobbi and I take turns feeding the animals. She bottle-fed one orphaned calf from two days old on. She named him Glenn, after the astronaut John Glenn. Until the day he was butchered, he thought she was his mother. He was a large Guernsey, about fifteen hands. He would charge across the pasture at a full gallop to get to Bobbi. It was quite the sight." Brad smiled.

Luke chuckled at the picture he was forming in his mind.

Back at the house Luke thanked Mrs. West for the lunch and said good-bye to her. Brad hiked with Luke down the trail to the beach.

"Do you enjoy riding the horse?" Luke asked.

"No. Her registered name is Miss Shorty Fore, we call her Missy. She belongs to all of us, but Bobbi is the only one who rides on a regular basis. Mom and Dad have never been into horses. The mare is expecting her first foal this spring, around Easter-time."

"What about the basketball court? Who do you play with?" Luke asked while they rowed out to the raft. Luke was glad he had not brought his boat to the beach. The tide was down midway, and the boat would have been stranded on the barnacles if he had.

"I play with Bobbi and several of the neighbor boys. Do you like to play?" asked Brad.

"Not really. We always played more baseball on the island. But Adam is fairly good at basketball; he's good at all sports. He'd enjoy playing with you. By the way, thanks for being a friend to Adam. It's always hard being the new kid in town."

Brad and Luke said their good-byes, and Luke headed back into town slowly, still watching for deadheads and debris along the way.

CHAPTER 11

Christmas in Seattle

What a wonderful Christmas with so many answers to prayer! Luke thought as he leaned back against a Windsor chair leg in front of the fire at Aunt Sophie's place. Wonderful, but unusual. They had never had Christmas at Aunt Sophie's before. It was always at the family homestead on Orcas. But his mother was feeling better. In fact, tonight she had been the life of the party again. Luke had not seen her so spirited in a long time. The last time he had seen her this happy was about a month before his father had left for Olympia. But tonight she tired easily and had to go to bed early before the rest of them.

The second surgery and round of treatments had been successful, and she kept getting stronger at a slow, steady rate. She was on the road to a full recovery.

He and Adam had two weeks off from school. They were going to spend most of the time at Aunt Sophie's. Aunt Sophie and Uncle Hank were going to go on vacation for four days toward the end of the two weeks, and Adam and Luke would look after their mother. But first, the boys were going to take a few days and drive up to Orcas and check on the house. They had closed it up for the winter, and Pastor Bob and Steve were checking on things, but Mom was getting restless and wanted a firsthand report on her old family home. Luke couldn't wait to see Steve again.

Thank You, Lord, for making this Christmas happy and full of great memories. They had read the Christmas story from the Bible, sung Christmas hymns and carols, played board games, and laughed themselves silly. Aunt Sophie had baked all the wonderful old cookies that Grandma and his mother always made.

Luke thought about all the happy childhood memories in their home on Orcas. The Christmases his grandpa and grandma Miers had celebrated had been fantastic, full of surprises and goodies. His grandparents died when he was in fifth grade. His parents took a few months to fix up the old home before they all moved in. His grandfather had died first, from a heart attack while he was out fishing. He had dropped anchor off Fawn Island, and the boat was sitting out there all day. At dinnertime his grandmother had called the marina and asked for help. She could see the boat with the binoculars.

His grandmother had lasted a few months after that. She had lost her will to live. They had been married over forty years and were a very close and happy couple. She caught the flu late that fall and never recovered.

Luke missed them terribly. They always made time for the boys and had great stories of the island and sea. But the best thing was their knowledge of the Bible. Grandma had a way of making David and Goliath so real. She could walk you through the Bible and make you feel like you were there, watching each life unfold.

They would be so happy if they knew about the great Bible teaching that he and Adam were getting at Westside

Baptist. Luke could hardly wait for each sermon and Bible class. Every time, it was just what he needed to meet the next challenge. Pastor Ralph seemed to be reading his mind. Luke knew from Pastor's teaching about the Trinity and God's essence that it was the Holy Spirit using Pastor Ralph to take care of each member of the flock, giving each one what they needed every Sunday. Luke appreciated Pastor Ralph taking time with him and answering his questions. Maybe Pastor Ralph was the reason he had been brought to Olympia.

Aunt Sophie brought Luke a cup of hot chocolate. "Uncle Hank and I are going up to bed, and Adam has turned in, too. You're welcome to stay up. Just make sure the fire has died down, and close the screen and glass fire doors when you go to bed."

Luke nodded. He was way too keyed-up to go to bed, too many thoughts. He hadn't had much time to reflect during the past two months. School, madrigal performances, church, work, and driving to Seattle to see his mother—it was almost a blur.

The madrigal schedule had gotten really hectic in December with four or five performances a week. Singing all the old Christmas carols really put a person in the mood for the season. They were sounding pretty good as a group. However they were missing classes left and right, which he did not like. The science labs were hard to make up. Joe had been helping him with chemistry, which Luke appreciated.

Bobbi had thrown a surprise birthday party for Joe just before Thanksgiving. She had called Luke at home a few weeks before and asked him to help. She assigned him the job of decoy. Luke drove Joe to the home of a madrigal friend the night of the party. They were just going to have a fun time, the three of them playing pool in the rec room.

When they went downstairs, everyone jumped out and surprised Joe! Bobbi's energy and excitement about the party made it hard not to get involved. Bobbi loved doing things for other people, and it was contagious. Luke had been trying hard to keep his distance from her ever since the storm. He still found it hard not to think about her. He had asked the Lord many times to take this attraction away from him, but that prayer was not being answered yet.

He had learned a lot about her during that October storm. She wasn't what he had thought she would be like at all. Who would have thought that they would have so much in common? The Lord, a love of the Scriptures, music, and the water. Luke just hoped that Joe realized what a special girlfriend he had. It bothered Luke sometimes that Joe didn't want to talk about Bobbi much. Joe would change the subject when Bobbi's name came up. It should be a subject Joe couldn't stop talking about if he cared about her.

But God had answered Luke's prayers about Charlie. Luke thought about his visit to Charlie after the storm. As soon as the roads were cleared enough to drive out to the harbor, Luke headed out with ice and water for the West family and Charlie. They were very grateful. The phone lines were back on, and Mr. West was on his way home from California.

Luke spent the first few hours at Charlie's cutting up a three foot diameter old tree that had gone down over the wheelchair ramp that ran from the store to the road. It must have been the cause of the crashing sound Charlie had heard when the phones went out. Luke was glad that it had not hit the store.

Once he cleared the ramp Luke took a break and came into the store. Charlie was not looking too good. "Are you OK?" Luke asked.

"Just off my schedule a bit," Charlie had answered. "You see, I'm a diabetic. I'm almost out of my insulin. So I've not been eating as much as I should. If I eat more, I'll need more insulin."

"Charlie, you tell me what you need right now, and I will go into town and get it! You should have told me you needed help!" Luke was upset. Why was this man so proud?

Charlie started to roll over to his desk to get Luke the prescription, and Luke noticed that he was shaking.

"That's it, Charlie. I'll get your coat. You need to see a doctor, and you are going now!" Luke turned the "open" sign to "closed" and locked the back door. He grabbed Charlie's coat and gloves and made him put them on before wheeling him out the front door and up to his car.

Luke called his father from the medical clinic in town. "I think I should stay with him tonight."

"Well, school is still cancelled for one more day. It's fine with me," his dad had answered.

Finally, the doctor wheeled Charlie out and said he would be fine once he started eating right. After picking up Charlie's insulin, Luke decided he would treat Charlie to dinner. Some good steak would do Charlie a lot of good.

"Why do you care about an old coot like me?" Charlie asked Luke as they were finishing dinner.

"Oh, I don't know." Luke smiled. "There's just something about you," he teased. "In some ways you remind me of my grandpa Johansen. He was gruff and independent like you, but underneath he had a heart of gold."

"Did he live on Orcas too?" Charlie asked.

"Yes, most of his life. He came to the States from Norway when he was in his twenties. Fell in love with the Northwest, and after several years of fishing on commercial boats, in several different areas, he settled on Orcas. The sad thing with him was that I could never talk about the Lord with him."

Charlie started to make a face and act like he was going to brush Luke off. Then he looked Luke straight in the eyes and said, "That is what I can't figure out about you and Bobbi. You're both so different from other young people that I've known. You care about other people, not just yourselves. And you take time for old folks like me."

"It's not us that you're seeing," Luke said. "It's the Lord. Have you ever heard about what Jesus Christ did for you?"

Charlie was quiet all the way home. Luke had brought out his pocket Bible and showed Charlie salvation verses in the Bible. When Luke had brought the question home to Charlie and asked him if he had believed, Charlie did not answer, and after a pause stated that it was time to get back to the marina.

Luke had been praying for two months now that Charlie would realize his need to be saved. At least the seed was planted.

CHAPTER 12

Snowed In

*I*t's snowing! It's snowing!" Luke awoke to Adam dancing around his bed.

"What day is it?" Luke sat up. His alarm clock said eight o'clock! He jumped up and yelled, "I'm late, so are you! We need to get to school. Now go and get dressed, Adam."

"No, no. Look outside!" Adam insisted.

Luke went to the window and stared. It was February in Olympia, Washington, and there was at least four inches of snow on the ground, and it was continuing to come down thick and hard. Adam was right. There would be no school today. He could barely see the bay through the falling snow. The water looked dark and gray like a painting with the snow all the way down to the water's edge.

Western Washington was usually green and wet all winter long with rain and fog, and all the snow stayed up in the Cascade and Olympic mountain ranges. Every once in a while they would have a winter with snow. Sometimes just for a morning, but sometimes for several days. Every time that happened, life came to a screeching halt. It was wonderful, really. All of a sudden, everyone had to take things slow, and life became simple again.

Dad poked his head in the door to Luke's room and said, "Who wants to have a snowball fight? Everything is closed down for the day. They say it's going to snow all day and night. We might be here for awhile."

They chased each other up and down the streets, throwing snowballs and watching out for the occasional car that chanced driving around the unplowed roads. Then, the three of them took a walk down to the marina and brushed the snow off the canvas of the boat. On the way home they took the long way and stopped by the store to stock up on supplies. The snow kept coming, and there was about eight inches on the ground.

They watched an old movie in the afternoon on TV and played gin rummy. At dinner time, the evening news showed all of western Washington covered in snow. The weather forecaster said that it might go on for several days!

"It's Joe on the phone for you," Dad called upstairs to Luke.

"So, there's no madrigal performance tomorrow night," Joe informed him. "I am supposed to call several other members, so I can't talk long now. How about if I call back in an hour or so?"

"That's fine. If this keeps up, things could get kind of boring around here." Luke hoped that Joe would want to get together and do something tomorrow. Luke enjoyed Joe's happy outlook on life.

He called his mother and Aunt Sophie. They were doing well. Uncle Hank had been to the store with his backpack and had stocked up on food. They were enjoying the view of the water and the snow-covered hills of Magnolia.

Then Joe called back. "We have to figure a way to get out to Bobbi's house tomorrow. They're skiing out in the Garbianni pastures, just north of the Wests' barns." Joe explained. "One of her neighbors has an old rope tow, and he set it up in the hill pasture. They have built a huge bonfire and set up floodlights. Bobbi said that there are about twenty people night-skiing up there, and more are planning to come tomorrow afternoon."

"I don't know how to ski. Plus, it's too dangerous to be out on the roads." Luke didn't want to go. He wanted to spend time with Joe, but not skiing.

"We just have to think of someone with four-wheel drive." Joe persisted. "It'll be fun. They're saying we have twelve inches now, and they expect at least eighteen by morning. We may not have school all week! Do you know anyone with four-wheel drive?"

Luke did, but he didn't want to let Joe know. "Let me think about it," he mumbled back. "I gotta get off the phone; Adam wants to use it." Luke felt guilty as he hung up the phone.

"Luke, we have to go out to Brad's tomorrow!" Adam burst into the living room. "They're skiing out there, and Brad has an extra pair of skis he'll let me use. Dad says it's OK if you go with me."

"How are we going to get there?" Luke asked.

"You know Jake down the street has four-wheel drive. Dad says that he cross-country skis and might want to go out and try some trails in the woods."

Luke wanted to yell no. A trapped feeling came over him. He didn't want to go out to Bobbi's and in front of her and everyone else make a fool of himself on skis. It had been hard enough all winter listening to everyone's stories about what runs they had taken at White Pass over the weekend.

"I thought the idea was for everyone to keep off the roads. Aren't we supposed to stay at home and be safe?" Luke declared to his father.

"Who elected you party pooper?" his dad asked, and Adam laughed. "You will be perfectly safe. I have gone up to the mountains with Jake before and he knows how to drive in the snow. That Jeep of his can go anywhere."

Luke walked over to the top of the rope tow and watched several people take off down the steep hill, cutting a perfect path of beautiful curves through the untouched snow to the bottom. They knew how to ski. Luke had seen skiers like that at Mount Baker the few times he had been there to try skiing. His dad had taken him and Adam up twice and rented skis for them and placed them in lessons while he did paperwork in the ski lodge. Both times had been a disaster for Luke. He could barely make it down the bunny slope in rough snowplow form at the end of the second lesson. Adam had caught on quickly and was far ahead of him.

They were some of the first ones at the Garbianni pastures. Joe had been so excited when Luke had told him they had a ride out to the harbor. Jake had been more than willing to take them out. He had heard about the skiing from some teacher friends and had been thinking about going anyway. He taught sixth grade, so he had the time off. Dad had gone in to work. Luke watched from the kitchen window as his dad put chains on the station wagon and took off early in the morning.

The snow showers were light, gradually adding to the twenty-one inches already on the ground. Several more families arrived at the top of the steep ski hill. Two women arrived pulling a barbeque on a sled. Other ladies, including Mrs. West, brought hot dogs and hamburgers, chocolate chip cookies, hot chocolate, and cider. The festivities started in.

Luke walked over to help stoke up the fire in the fire pit when the first skiers came back up the rope tow.

"That was as good as Cascade!" Luke heard Bobbi exclaim. He knew that she was referring to a run at White Pass. She looked cute in her ski outfit, and he realized she had been one of those cutting the perfect curves down the hill. He could feel his face turning red. This wasn't going to be a good day.

"So are you going to spend the whole day standing around feeling sorry for yourself, or are you going to try skiing?" Jake asked Luke.

Luke suddenly realized that was exactly what he had been doing, wallowing in self-pity. He smiled at Jake and quickly named his sin to the Lord before answering. "I suppose I should give it a try. But the other times I have attempted this haven't been very successful." Luke glanced at Jake's downhill skis. "I thought that you cross-country skied, not downhill."

"I do both. I teach skiing at White Pass on Saturdays. Give me one Saturday this spring of yard work, and I will teach you to master this hill," Jake replied.

"It's a deal." Luke grinned and thought maybe this day wouldn't be so bad after all.

"Luke, come have something to eat. You have not had anything all day," Mrs. West called to Luke as he took off the skis he had borrowed from Jake.

"I appreciate it, but we did bring our own lunches," Luke replied.

"Well, the food is for everyone. At least have something hot to drink and one of Bobbi's cookies."

Luke noticed that Adam had brought out their cooler, and Bobbi, Joe, Brad, and Adam were all sitting together near the fire.

"You're looking pretty good. Especially this being only your third time on skis." Bobbi gestured at Adam. "Adam told us. Luke, keep going at this rate, and you will pass us all by."

"Well, you must not have been watching that much, as I sure have had my share of spills," Luke replied.

"That's part of the game when you're learning. Then when you have skied for a while, you begin to think you can really ski. You get a bit proud of what you're doing, and the hill slams you down again. A bit like life. Pride makes you fall," Bobbi confided.

"That's an interesting perspective on skiing. I've never thought about it much. Just go kill the hill!" Joe laughed.

"No, like any sport, once you get the basics down, it's all mental," Bobbi contested. "I'm always having a battle in my head over it."

"I thought it was just supposed to be fun," Brad said. "I'm not skiing with you anymore. You take this way too seriously, sis."

"No, I get what she means." Luke came to Bobbi's defense. "Whenever you get too cocky, God humbles you.

Just like anything in life, you have to stay in fellowship or it gets all messed up."

"Exactly! If you are trying to do well, you have to watch your motivation, or pride will get in the way." Bobbi looked relieved that someone agreed.

"Well, I am going to leave you two philosophers to mull over the meaning of life. I have a hill to kill." Joe jumped up and went to get his skis on.

Luke couldn't help but notice that Joe arrived at the ski storage area in time to catch Karen and take off skiing with her. She lived in the Big Fish Trap area and had walked over with her family. In fact, come to think of it, he had seen Joe walking with her at school a few times. He hoped that Bobbi didn't mind.

Luke lay back in the snow and closed his eyes for a minute. It hadn't been bad, but he could feel a few sore muscles. He had fallen a lot. Jake had taken him over to a little knoll at the top of the pasture and gone over the basics and taught him a few new things. Then, after an hour of that, Jake promoted him to the big hill and coached him all the way down. Jake had showed him how to do stem turns and that helped.

"Ready to work on your stem christies?" Jake asked. "Or are you going to sleep the rest of the afternoon?"

"No, I'm ready for the torture chamber." Luke laughed and sat up. Everyone had left.

"I think you have graduated." You'll do fine on your own," Jake said late in the afternoon. They had just gotten off the rope tow at the top of the hill. "I'm going to change skis and try a few trails in the woods."

Luke knew apprehension showed on his face. "You think it's safe? Me alone on the hill?"

Jake laughed. "Yeah, you've got it." And he slapped Luke on the shoulder.

Luke skied over to the edge and looked down. It looked steeper now that he was on his own. He tried a few turns—that worked—then a few more. Soon he was halfway down the hill.

"Hey, you're doing better." Bobbi skied up next to him.

"Thanks." Luke still felt out of place.

"Try relaxing your knees a bit. Like this." Bobbi bounced up and down with her knees moving and her upper body staying straight. "Your knees are your shock absorbers."

"OK." Luke laughed. "Relaxing and skiing in the same sentence?"

"Follow me down. We'll take it slow."

Luke followed her down. It helped to see what she was doing and then try to mimic her moves. They took two more runs. On the way back up the rope tow Luke looked around. He didn't see Joe anywhere. Karen and her parents had left a short while ago.

At the top of the hill he looked around for Adam. He was with Brad at the fire pit, munching on cookies. Luke waved at him and then took off after Bobbi. She was taking this run a little faster, and Luke struggled to keep up. As they neared the bottom he caught an edge. He fought to regain his balance. His skis were gaining speed as he headed straight for Bobbi. Swish. He could feel the edge of her coat as he zipped past her. The barbwire fence between the Garbianni pasture and the Wests' loomed ahead. Then his left ski hit something under the snow. It threw him forward, and he fell facedown in the snow. His skis came off and finished the run by themselves.

"Ski! Runaway ski!" Bobbi yelled. She came up next to him, laughing. "Well, that was graceful. Are you OK?"

Luke rolled over. Everything hurt but nothing major. "Yeah." He lay there for a moment.

Bobbi sat down in the snow. "I'm sorry I laughed."

"No, that's OK. Once I catch my breath, I'll be laughing too." He sat up and smiled at her. She looked gorgeous, her cheeks red from the exercise.

"It's so beautiful out here. I love it," she said, staring up at the snowflakes. It was snowing heavily again, and the temperature had dropped. Bobbi picked up some snow, formed a snowball, and lobbed it half-heartedly at Luke, not caring if it hit him or not.

Luke threw one back, hitting her on the arm.

Bobbi laughed. "I will tell you something I have never told anyone else. You seem to understand….but you have to promise that you will not tell anyone."

"I promise." Luke smiled and wondered what it could be.

"I have a love-fear relationship with snow and water. I love being out here in the snow and love being out on the water, but I always fight fear of both, too. I'm too aware of the dangers. It's a battle for me. Just when I start skiing really well, I get prideful and forget that the Lord gave me the two legs and the ability to ski, and I crash and burn. The same way with the water. Just when everything is tranquil and perfect, then some big storm comes along, and, well…you know the rest of *that* story." Bobbi's voice trailed off as she finished.

"I do understand. The waters around the San Juans are more dangerous than here in the south sound. You can't worry about what if. How about leaving it with the Lord? God will take care of you. He has so far, right?"

Bobbi nodded. "You're right. Thanks."

CHAPTER 13

Slumber Party

*L*uke awoke to the smell of bacon and pancakes. He rolled over and looked at Joe sleeping next to him. What a night! He had fought for every inch of space all night long!

Luke sat up in bed. *Ouch!* Man, he had some sore muscles. He looked around the Wests' guestroom. At least the guest bedroom was on a separate level from the rest of the house and had its own bathroom.

OK, Lord. Why am I here? I keep asking You to keep me away from Bobbi! Well, I was outvoted. Jake, Adam, and Joe had wanted to stay. As they discussed their options, the roads were icing up. Mr. West insisted that they stay for safety reasons.

So they stayed, had a late dinner of chili around the campfire, and skied until ten. A lot more people came that night, including two of Bobbi's girlfriends, Mary and Jill. People were singing and yodeling as they skied down the hill. It had been fun.

Jake had hiked down the road a half-mile to stay with his teacher friend. Adam slept on a cot in Brad's room.

"It snowed another six inches last night, and everything is still cancelled," Mr. West told Joe and Luke as they came up the stairs to the main part of the house. "Hope you boys had a good night's sleep."

"Oh, it was great! I slept like a log," Joe replied.

"I beg to differ. You sleep like a cheerleader at a pep rally," Luke said, rubbing his eyes. "I'm going to need a nap."

"Well, that's interesting information." Bobbi gave Joe a slight peck on the cheek. "Good morning." She nodded to both of them and motioned them into the dining room while holding a huge plate of pancakes.

There was hot maple syrup and strawberry jam besides the bacon. Mr. West said grace, and they all dug in.

"So, Bobbi, you must have been up early to get all of this made," Adam said.

Brad gave a snort of disgust. "She can't cook!" he said. "We all try to miss dinner when she's the chef."

"Now, Bradley, that is not nice. You owe your sister an apology. She makes beautiful cookies and cakes, even pies sometimes. You know you enjoy eating all of it." Mrs. West defended her daughter.

"I don't know why I have to apologize for stating the truth...." Brad began, but his father gave him a stern look, and he stopped. "I'm sorry, Bobbi."

Luke noticed that Bobbi was turning red through all of this, so he decided to change the subject. "I hear that you are a research forester, Mr. West. What got you into that line of work?"

"My sister. She knew I liked to collect plants and trees as a child. She suggested I try forestry." He went on to explain about getting his master's in genetics and starting his doctorate, but never finishing. It was interesting, and Luke was pleased he had been able to get the subject off of Bobbi.

As everyone finished eating, Mr. West grabbed his Bible off the sideboard. "We have been reading in Galatians. We are in chapter six."

Everyone listened quietly, and Luke could not help but think this was the way he wanted to lead his family. So different from his father, who had destroyed his family and now spent every spare moment at Deanne's place. With his father gone so much, Luke had to answer questions for Adam, help him with his homework, make Adam's lunch, and get him to school.

Mr. West finished up the reading. He looked up from his Bible and said, "So, Brad, you have the livestock to feed and wood to split. Bobbi, I think your mother has some housework for you. Once you finish your chores, enjoy the day skiing. You're all excused." He stood up and left the table.

"Mrs. West, may I use your phone to call Charlie and make sure he's OK?" asked Luke.

"Sure, if you can get on the line. This time of day, several of the neighbor women like to get on and talk for hours. Remember, this is a ten-party line, and there are people who like to listen in. So don't talk about anything you don't want this part of the world to know." Mrs. West smiled as she replied. "And I did call Charlie yesterday, and he's just fine. Rick's been there and has swept the snow off the docks and the canvases of the boats."

Luke picked up the phone. Good, he had a dial tone. The neighbor ladies must be taking a break. "Hi, Charlie. How are you doing?"

"Just fine. Nice of you to call. Are you enjoying the snow?"

"Yes, I'm here skiing at the Wests'. Do you need me to come over and work?"

"No. The two neighbor boys are handling everything. There aren't many boats coming in for fuel. You enjoy the time off."

Luke caught up with Joe, Brad, and Adam at the barns. The three were making quick work of feeding the livestock. So Luke helped Mr. West knock the snow off various trees, rhododendrons, and plants in the gardens around the house to prevent their branches from breaking.

Luke brushed the snow off his coat and stomped his boots outside the Wests' front door. He stepped inside the entry and took off his boots. The smell of sugar cookies drifted down the stairs.

He bounded up the stairs. "Mm, that smells good!" he said as he walked into the kitchen.

Bobbi stood there smiling. "You can have some." She pointed to a pile of cookies on the cooling racks, then opened the oven door and took out the last batch.

He walked over to the pile and grabbed one. "I wonder if they're showing pictures of the snow on the TV," Luke said, hoping they could see a bit of the noon news.

"We don't have a TV," Bobbi replied. "Dad believes it will stunt our creativity."

Brad walked into the kitchen. "Yes, and we already have enough stunted things around here." He laughed, patting Bobbi on the head. She made a funny half-smile back at him and marched off to her room to put on her ski outfit.

Jake showed up, and they all helped pack up food to take up the hill. Jake and Luke decided it would be a good idea to leave midafternoon to get back into town. They did not want to impose on their hosts for another night. It would be getting icy again once the sun went down.

Joe and Adam were disappointed but agreed. Luke skied with Brad and Adam for several hours, and then Jake drove them back into town.

The snow finally stopped on Wednesday afternoon. That night everything froze, and then Thursday afternoon the temperature started to rise, and the melting process began. They had missed a week of school.

CHAPTER 14

Birthday Surprise

On Monday everyone had snow stories, and the school was abuzz. Mixed chorus was no exception. Rumors were flying that Mrs. Miller had some big news. It had to do with some special opportunity to sing. Luke wondered if it had anything to do with the special tape she helped him record back in October. He knew Joe and Bobbi had been asked to make tapes along with most of the madrigal and Good Day Singers.

"We have the official invitation to All Northwest Choir," Mrs. Miller announced at the beginning of class, waving a sheet of paper in the air. "As you know, this is a choir made up of students from Alaska, Oregon, Washington, Idaho, and Montana. It is a two-hundred-voice choir. There are fifty students for each vocal section. Students will be gone for three days of school and will practice in Eugene, Oregon, with a performance that Saturday in the University of Oregon auditorium. I am very pleased to announce that we have six finalists who will be representing our fine school."

The room got deathly quiet. Not a single bleacher that the seventy-five-voice chorus was standing on squeaked. Mrs. Miller continued. "They are Joe Thorton...." She had to pause as everyone cheered, "Steve Dally, Scott Thompson, Brian Wells, Luke Johansen, and Bobbi West."

The room broke into pandemonium. People were cheering, crying, and clapping. Luke got slapped on the back several times. He glanced at Bobbi and saw her looking at Joe in disbelief. *She's the only girl,* Luke thought. He noticed that several of the senior girls were crying, and three of them, including the madrigal leader, left the room. This could cause problems for the group. Hopefully it would not destroy their teamwork.

"Now, quiet down. I have packets for those six students to take home to their parents, so please see me after class. We will also be having lots of extra practices for mixed chorus, Good Day Singers, and madrigals. We have two concerts this spring, plus the performance at the sunrise service on Easter morning at the state capitol, and in April, the Southwest Washington Music Competition. I will be handing out a schedule at the end of class. Make sure you get one. Now please take out "A Time For Us," and let's take it from the top. I will not be holding open auditions for the solo parts. I will assign them, based on how your voices work together, not if you're dating." Mrs. Miller smiled. There were three "couples" in the madrigal group—all of whom could easily sing the parts of Romeo or Juliet.

"Oh yes." Mrs. Miller continued. "This Thursday night, we have an extra mixed-chorus practice at seven. I will be deciding who has the solo parts. We will practice as long as it takes to select the soloists."

Thursday night Joe came in to practice during warm-ups. Mrs. Miller asked him in front of the whole group why he was late.

"I got caught speeding!" Joe explained, red-faced. "It's my third ticket this year. I'll probably lose my license."

"Well, then, if some of you who live on the west side could please make sure Mr. Thorton gets to practices on time, we won't be interrupted again." Mrs. Miller was usually cheery, but lately she had been uptight. They did have a lot of work to do.

"You can always catch a ride with me," Luke whispered to Joe when he took his place next to Luke on the bleachers.

"Thanks, I might be taking you up on that," Joe whispered back.

Mrs. Miller asked three girls to try the part with Luke. Then she had several baritones try the part with Bobbi. Luke noticed that Joe was not asked to sing, but the sheet music did suggest a baritone or bass sing the part, not a tenor.

"Luke, come down and try the part with Bobbi and the whole group. I want to start from the top," Mrs. Miller commanded.

He and Bobbi—Romeo and Juliet! *Great!* he thought sarcastically. Why wasn't the Lord answering his prayers?

"That sounds good! Practice is done. Luke and Bobbi have the solo-duet part. Now tomorrow we can move ahead with other pieces." Mrs. Miller ended the practice.

"March fourteenth," Luke wrote on his English notes. He stacked his books on his notebook and headed for the music building. They had an extra madrigal practice after school. Practice was being held in one of the smaller upstairs rooms. Everyone was there except Bobbi and Theresa, the madrigal leader.

"I'm going to ask Bobbi to be the nodder," whispered Mrs. Miller. "Theresa is keeping her in the bathroom for a few moments. It's Bobbi's birthday, so when she gives you the note, we'll all start singing 'Happy Birthday' instead of 'Sing We and Chant It.' Her mother is hiding in my office, and she'll be bringing in a cake." Mrs. Miller eyes were dancing, and Luke could tell she was really enjoying this.

"Oh no! Her birthday!" Joe blurted out, turning to Luke. "I totally forgot." He looked upset with himself.

This is intriguing, Luke thought. After the surprise party that Bobbi threw for Joe, how could Joe forget her birthday? For such a great guy, so friendly and personable, Joe could do a better job being a boyfriend. If Bobbi was *his* girlfriend, that would be one day he would not forget. But, she was not his girlfriend.

Theresa and Bobbi walked into the room and sat in their places.

"Bobbi, would you please take Theresa's place for the next song?" Mrs. Miller asked. "I would like you to have a chance to practice being the nodder."

Bobbi and Theresa switched places. Bobbi felt butterflies in her stomach. Mrs. Miller handed her a new pitch pipe. What did this mean? Was she going to be the leader next year?

"Let's begin with, 'Sing We and Chant It.' You start when you are ready, Bobbi." Mrs. Miller smiled encouragingly.

Bobbi glanced at the sheet music and found the note on the pitch pipe. She had to get the rhythm right. She nodded and they started in. But the music didn't sound right. At first she heard conflicting notes, and then it made sense. Everyone was singing "Happy Birthday" to her, and smiling. They turned to look at the door.

Bobbi turned and put her hands up to her face. "Oh, my!" she gasped. Her mother walked through the door, holding a large sheet cake with seventeen lit candles on top.

Bobbi walked over and helped her mother put it down on the table. Then she stood there enjoying the final chorus of "Happy Birthday" being sung to her. This was special. Why was Joe looking at her so funny? He hadn't mentioned her birthday all day. He must have something special planned for that evening.

"We will have a twenty-minute break," Mrs. Miller announced.

Bobbi cut and served the cake to everyone.

"Happy Birthday, Bobbi," Luke said as he got his cake.

"Thanks. When's your birthday?" she asked.

"Actually, it's in two days."

"Really?" her eyes got big.

"Yes, really. I was surprised to find out yours was today."

"Hey, everyone! It's Luke's birthday in two days! We need to sing to him, too." Bobbi started in and everyone joined her.

After practice, as Luke sat in his car waiting for Joe to say his good-byes to Bobbi, he marveled at the fact that all the girls in madrigals seemed to be genuinely happy for Bobbi that she had made the All Northwest Choir. There didn't seem to be any jealousy.

Since Joe had been to traffic court and the judge had suspended his license for three months, Luke was now Joe's chauffeur.

"Can we stop downtown at Ralph's Jewelry Store on the way home? I need to get something for Bobbi," Joe asked as he got into the car.

"Sure, I have some English reading to do, so take your time," Luke answered. "When are you going to give it to her?"

"Oh, I will most likely talk my sister or brother into giving me a ride out there tonight. My sister's home from college on spring break."

Joe came out of the store about ten minutes later and settled into the passenger seat.

"That was fast," Luke said.

"Yeah, I found this little duck pin and it looks cute." Joe opened up the box and showed it to Luke.

Luke nodded. "Nice." But he couldn't help but wonder what Joe was thinking. That was not Bobbi at all. It was very gaudy and little girlish. Something Joe's youngest sister would go for, and it was gold. Bobbi always wore silver. Luke had noticed that.

"I'm not going to be able to drive to the May dance. I was wondering if you could help me out and double date with Bobbi and me?" Joe asked Luke on the way home.

The May dance was Oly's equivalent to prom. Unlike other high schools, Oly allowed all of the students to attend, not just the seniors; the surrounding high schools kept prom exclusive for seniors and their dates.

"Well, I would like to help, but who would I take?" Luke asked. He wanted to help but not when it meant he would be spending more time with Bobbi.

"Come on now, Luke. There are lots of girls at school and church dying to go out with you. You don't have to marry them. Just ask one of them out! It's only for one night. I'll pay for your gas, your tux, your date's corsage, dinner, and the prom tickets."

"No. You don't have to do all that. That would cost you a fortune. Just pay for the gas, and I can take care of the rest. But I'll have to think about it. Are you sure there isn't someone else you two would rather double with?"

"No. It would be the most fun with you. You and Bobbi get along well. I'm sure we'll have a great time."

CHAPTER 15

New Life

So this is what three-thirty in the morning feels like," mumbled Amy as Bobbi rolled over and turned off the alarm. Bobbi stumbled out of bed, grabbing the first dress she found on the chair. She slid it over her head, and it almost went down to her ankles.

"That's mine!" Amy started to laugh, but put her hand over her mouth, trying to be quiet so she wouldn't wake anyone. The rest of the West family had planned to sleep for another half hour. "You haven't grown eight inches overnight!"

"You don't like it?" Bobbi turned on the light and did a little dance around the room.

"On me, not you."

Amy, Bobbi's closest friend from church was a year older than Bobbi and went to Tumwater High.

"So what's it like?" Amy asked as she drove Bobbi into town.

Bobbi looked at her straight-faced. "Well, it has marble columns and floors and a one-hundred-sixty-eight-foot-high domed ceiling. The twenty-five-foot-long Tiffany chandelier is suspended fifty feet above the floor—"

"No, silly." Amy cut into Bobbi's history recitation. "The Easter sunrise service. I've been in the capitol building. Though that was several years ago."

Bobbi smiled and fumbled in her purse for some lipstick. "Everyone sits on the marble stairs; mixed chorus is up on the south balcony. When we sing, it resonates throughout the whole dome. It's incredible. I love singing there, especially about the Lord's resurrection."

"I can't wait. You better sing your best. Dragging me out of bed at this hour, it's the least you can do." Amy laughed.

"I'll try. It's too bad we can't be more awake when we sing. Mrs. Miller brings hot tea for us to drink beforehand. I think she hopes it will wake up our vocal cords." Bobbi flipped the passenger-side visor down and put her lipstick on in the mirror.

The mixed chorus started the service with two pieces. Pastor Ralph gave a short sermon, and several other pastors from other churches gave prayers and read Scripture. The sun shone in through the windows. *What a beautiful sunny morning to remember that the Lord has risen*, Bobbi thought. After the service, Bobbi and Amy talked for a while with students from their schools and then left for church and the pancake breakfast.

"That was a good sermon this morning," Mr. West commented as they sat down at a table at the Tyee Inn.

"Yes, it was," Mrs. West agreed. "Amy and Joe, would you like to go with us to the stables after dinner to check on Missy?"

"That would be fun," Amy replied. "Why did you take her to the stables to have her baby?"

"If something should go wrong we want her where we can get help quickly," Brad explained. "She's due in two weeks, but next week she will be moved into a large birthing stall and she will have an equestrian midwife staying with her at nights."

"We lost a Black Angus bull a year ago during delivery because we couldn't get a vet to come out to the harbor in time," Bobbi said, thinking of her dad pumping and pumping on the chest of the newly born bull calf. He had tried for over twenty minutes. Finally, she had tapped him on the shoulder and quietly told him it was not going to breathe. He'd burst into tears. She'd felt so bad; she'd never seen her dad cry like that.

"Bobbi, you can't forget we are supposed to spend the afternoon with my parents at the house," Joe whispered to Bobbi behind his menu.

"We should have time for both," she whispered back.

Missy stood only fourteen hands tall, a small, compact, dark brown, registered quarter horse, full of spirit. They had bred her to a tall, light chestnut quarter horse that was very gentle, a retired "triple A" racer. The rest of the meal the conversation revolved around what kind of offspring these two beautiful animals would produce.

As they finished their main course Mr. West stood up. "You all order dessert. I'm going to call out to the stables and let them know we're coming to visit."

Joe had finally caught the eye of the waitress, and they were in the middle of ordering the desserts when Mr. West came back to the table looking very grim. "If you don't mind, we are going to have to skip dessert. I need the check as soon as possible," he told the waitress.

"Dad, what is it?" Brad asked.

"The foal came early. Most likely, early this morning. Missy was not in the birthing stall. She was all by herself. Something went wrong, but they don't know what. They still have two vets working with her. She has lost a lot of blood, and the little filly is very weak and can't stand up. I think we better get out there right away."

Bobbi wanted to burst into tears, but she didn't want to make a scene. She thought of Matthew 6:26 where God tells about caring for the sparrow. *Missy is God's creature too*, she kept thinking, trying to maintain her composure as they left the restaurant.

Amy drove out to the stables, watching Joe and Bobbi in her rearview mirror. She couldn't help but notice that Joe did not seem very sympathetic about the situation.

Bobbi jumped out of the car as soon as they arrived. When Amy, Joe, and the rest of the Wests arrived at the stall, they found Bobbi sitting in the hay—Easter dress, heels, nylons, and all—with the mare's head cradled in her lap. Bobbi kept stroking Missy's neck and talking to her very slowly and quietly. Over in the corner was a light brown bundle with a blonde mane and big brown eyes.

"We just stopped the bleeding," the vet explained to Mr. West. "We think Missy will be fine, but she's very weak and needs lots of rest. We are very concerned since the filly doesn't want to *try* to stand. We have given her some booster shots and a bottle, and we are hoping that some good feedings will give her the energy to stand. We took her out of here for a while and just brought her back in with her mother. She seems normal in every way but just not very strong."

"You still don't know what happened?" Mr. West asked.

"We don't know. Not having been here, it is hard to say. We think the foal might have been positioned wrong, making it a difficult delivery. Your mare was badly torn, and we had to sew her up in several places."

"Bobbi, we need to be leaving fairly soon if we're going to have any time with my parents this afternoon," Joe said. He wasn't pleased with the fact that Bobbi looked quite a mess, sitting in the hay and silently crying.

Each member of the West family had gone into the stall and petted their mare for a while, but Bobbi had not moved from her post.

"I'm not leaving. You will have to apologize to your parents for me," she replied. "Missy needs someone with her that she knows. I can stay, right, Dad?"

"Yes, it's probably best for her if you do. You've always been the one that has understood her." Mr. West thought about all the pranks that the small mare had pulled in the past few years. They had bought her at two years of age. She had just been saddle-broke two weeks before, so they boarded her at the stables for several months so she could get the best training. He had to laugh every time he thought of her pushing the dirt back into the holes he had dug for fence posts and stomping the dirt back in with her front hoofs. Or the time she tore up his tractor seat cushion when he left the tractor in her pasture during lunch. She was always getting into something.

"I will get some jeans and a sweatshirt for you and bring them in when we come in for evening church service," Mrs. West offered.

"Come on, Bobbi. You promised that you'd spend time with my parents," Joe persisted.

"Sorry, Joe, but I didn't know this was going to happen. Please tell them I'm sorry, but I can't come." Bobbi would not budge.

"I can take you home, Joe," Amy offered. "And I will be praying for you and Missy, Bobbi. By the way, what is the new one's name?"

"Olympic Lady," the Wests all answered in unison. They had picked out a colt and filly's name a month ago.

"OK, little Lady. You get well, and welcome to the world." Amy turned, grabbed Joe's arm, and walked him out of the stable.

"All that fuss over a simple animal!" Joe looked disgusted.

"It's an animal that they all love. You need to be a bit more understanding," Amy exhorted him.

It had been a great Easter, Luke thought as he picked up Joe for madrigal practice Monday morning. He'd really enjoyed the sunrise service at the capitol. Both of Pastor's sermons had been good.

"How did the day go with Bobbi yesterday?" he asked as Joe settled in the car.

"Not good. Bobbi won't be at madrigal practice this morning, and she may not come to school. I can't believe her parents let her spend the night at the stables with her mare! She didn't spend the afternoon with my parents like we planned." Joe was still upset with Bobbi.

"What happened?"

"Her mare delivered early and had problems. I can't believe all the fuss they made over a stupid animal."

"She seemed like a very smart mare to me. I played tag with her when we were out there skiing. She would run and stop suddenly, spraying people with snow. She hung over the fence and watched all the skiers. She really enjoyed the action. Is the mare OK? What did she have?"

"I don't know and I don't care. Just seems to me Bobbi has her priorities mixed up," Joe replied.

Bobbi and Trina, the vet's assistant, had gotten a few naps during the night. Each had taken turns feeding Lady a bottle every two hours. They kept force-feeding water and a small amount of oats to a very sleepy Missy.

"Look who's nursing!" Trina whispered, gently shaking Bobbi awake. It was 7:30 in the morning. Light shone from the high window above, gently streaming down on the hay.

Bobbi sat up and looked. Both Missy and Lady were standing in the corner! The filly kept nursing! Trina and Bobbi sat still in silence. It was beautiful, almost magical, with the beams of light playing on them and the dust from the hay glistening in the air. Tears of joy streamed down Bobbi's face. *Missy's going to be all right.*

"Hey, looks like things are headed in the right direction," Mr. West exclaimed softly as he joined them. "My wife packed breakfast for both of you. Hope everything's still hot." He passed a brown bag over the stall door to Trina.

Bobbi stood up and went to her father and gave him big hug. All of a sudden she started to bawl. All of the pent-up emotion came out at once. Mr. West held her tight. "Everything is going to be fine," he whispered.

CHAPTER 16

May Dance

M y, it's warm!" Adam said joining Luke on the deck. "Yeah, the radio said it's ninety-one. New record for May seventeenth." Luke yawned and stretched. He sat rocking on the chair's back legs with his feet on the deck railing, enjoying the warm breeze off the bay.

"Aren't you getting ready for the dance?" asked Adam.

"Not yet. I'm not picking Joe up till six o'clock, and our dinner reservation isn't until seven thirty. How did I get roped into this, Adam?" Luke stretched again, the chair started to fall backward, but Luke regained his balance.

"You were just trying to be a good friend. Now you're paying your dues. Besides, Amy isn't that bad looking and she's a Christian. Too bad she's a senior and won't be here next year for you to date."

"We're going as friends and she knows that. Who says I'll be back next year?" Luke answered crossly. "I may go back to school on Orcas."

"That I doubt. You have too much going for you here. You should stay. Mom and I'll be fine at home."

Adam ran to answer the phone. *It's probably Brad,* Luke thought. Those two were inseparable. Luke knew that they would miss each other, but Adam needed to be back at Orcas under the careful watch of Mom. Dad wasn't doing his job.

Luke glanced at his watch, then his thought turned to his mom. *Thank You, again, Lord for her complete recovery. I'm glad she's home and strong enough to weave again. Thanks for Aunt Sophie's willingness to stay with her until Adam and I return home. Amen.*

The two sisters had gone off to Hawaii for three weeks at the end of March. It had been Aunt Sophie and Uncle Hank's birthday present to Rosa. Rosa had returned tanned and well rested, and she had gained a few pounds. She looked terrific. She said she could take on the world.

Luke reminisced about when Mom, Aunt Sophie, and Uncle Hank came to Olympia for the mid-March concert. The concert had gone well. Luke filed in with the chorus and looked at the audience. He spotted his mother—she waved and he smiled back. Uncle Hank and Aunt Sophie were there....Adam? Oh. Sitting in the row behind them with Brad and Mr. and Mrs. West. Apparently, Brad and Adam had introduced everyone, as his mother kept turning to talk to Mrs. West. He started to sweat as he thought about his solo-duet with Bobbi. He shouldn't have looked at the audience.

Luke reminded himself of Philippians 4:13: "I can do all things through Him who strengthens me."

Mrs. Miller came in and bowed, and they started the first of three pieces. Though the orchestra and band had already played, the orchestra stayed on stage next to the mixed chorus bleachers. They were accompanying them on the last piece, "A Time for Us."

With the orchestra accompaniment and the chorus backing them up, it sounded wonderful. It seemed like he and Bobbi had one voice as they sang in perfect harmony on the duet parts. It did not even seem like he was doing the singing, just enjoying the sound.

Luke looked at his watch. Now he'd better get ready for prom.

"Wow," Luke said softly, then put his hand over his mouth. He hoped no one else had heard him. But all eyes were on Bobbi, who had just walked out into the Wests' living room all ready for the May Dance. She looked fantastic. Joe hadn't said a word. Luke watched Joe give Bobbi a look of disgust, walk to the coffee table, and grab Bobbi's corsage out of the box. Luke had not planned to come inside, but Mr. West had come out to the car and said it would be awhile and that he should come inside and keep Joe and him company.

"We have to get going." Joe frowned at Bobbi as he quickly pinned on her corsage. "You've really put us behind schedule."

"I'm sorry, Joe. There were some logistical problems that Mom had to fix. I'm sure that we'll be fine." Bobbi smiled and tried to make the best of it, though she looked like she might cry.

Luke drove as fast as he dared toward town, glancing in the rearview mirror at Joe and Bobbi. Bobbi sat near the middle of the seat, but Joe sat next to the door. Bobbi kept looking out the window looking like she might cry.

"Why did you pick pink for your dress?" Joe broke the silence. "It makes you look big."

Luke hit the brakes! He wanted to stop the car and let Joe have it.

Bobbi slid forward and almost hit her chin on the front seat. Through tears she asked, "What's wrong?"

"Nothing. My mistake." Luke gave her a smile. "Sorry," he said, and put his foot on the gas. It was none of his business.

When Luke walked into Amy's house, she was standing by the living room sofa all ready to go. Luke complimented her. "You look great."

"So do you," Amy replied. Luke pinned on her corsage and she pinned a boutonnière on his lapel. She looked him straight in the eye; with heels on she was as tall as he was. "OK, we're ready to go, Mom and Dad."

She grabbed Luke's arm, and they said their good-byes to her parents and walked to the entry. Amy stopped at the full-length mirror. "We look like sister and brother." She was right. The matching blond hair and blue eyes did make them look like siblings.

"OK, sis, let's go dance," Luke joked. Amy laughed, and they headed out to the car.

"Amy, order anything you'd like. We're here to celebrate." Luke smiled at his date. They all had been staring at their menus for several minutes.

"Oh, I'm not sure...the crab or the lobster." Amy debated.

The waiter came up to the table. "Are you ready to order?"

"Yes." Joe started in. "My date and I will have the New York steak, rare." He tilted his menu toward Bobbi as he spoke.

"But, Joe you know—"

"Bobbi, you're too picky. You need to try something new." Joe grabbed her menu and handed their menus to the waiter.

Luke noticed during dinner that Bobbi didn't say a word. She didn't touch the steak and took off for the ladies' room twice looking ill.

At the dance Amy and Luke found a table off to the side of the dance floor. "Poor Bobbi," Amy said. "I thought she and Joe had a great relationship."

"I don't know what's wrong with Joe," Luke said, "but there were problems when we were at All Northwest Choir in Oregon. It almost ruined it for the rest of us."

"I'm sorry to hear that. But you know, I've noticed that Joe hasn't been coming to church lately. When you stop taking in God's Word, things can fall apart."

Luke had not thought about that, but Amy was right. Joe had only been to church once or twice since he lost his license. Every time Luke offered him a ride he'd have some excuse. Luke hoped he'd have a chance to talk to Joe about it.

"What was All Northwest like, anyway?" Amy asked.

"Fabulous, amazing. We sounded like a professional choir from the beginning. Everyone came with the pieces memorized, and we were able to follow every move the director made. Even on the first notes we sounded like one unit. We had one funny time after the performance on Saturday night. Bobbi was driving Mrs. Miller's VW Bug with some of us guys in the car. Bobbi went the wrong way down a one-way street and stopped at a traffic light. All of a sudden we realized that there was a police car on the other side of the intersection facing us head on. Bobbi did a U-turn and took off. The amazing thing was, she didn't even get a ticket."

Amy laughed so hard tears ran down her face. " Oh, another addition to the 'Bobbi driving' saga. Bobbi's known for her wild driving. She only had her license two weeks and she had it taken away. She doesn't mean to do the things she does. She just isn't very good behind the wheel."

"Well, she sure doesn't have any problem steering a boat."

"OK, you two, let me in on the joke. I need something to laugh at." Bobbi joined them at the table. "Joe has this idea that it would be more fun if we dance with other people tonight."

Luke looked out on the dance floor and saw Joe dancing with Karen. *Poor Bobbi*, he thought, anger starting to well up inside of him.

"Luke just told me about All Northwest Choir and about the U-turn you pulled after the concert," explained Amy.

"Oh yes." Bobbi laughed. "I had hoped that people had forgotten about that by now. Amy, would you like to join me in the little girls' room?"

The song wound down, and Luke went over and tapped Joe on the shoulder. "I'm not asking you to dance," he joked. "Just wanted to know if you want to take a break and walk outside. The girls are off powdering their noses."

"Sure," Joe agreed.

As they headed to the door Luke wondered how to address the issues he had on his mind. *Lord, please give me the right words.*

"Just two more weeks and you are a free man." Luke started in as they walked along the inner courtyard of the Tyee Inn. The Tyee Inn had a big ballroom, the only place big enough besides the high school gym to hold such an event. It was often used by the state legislative branches for special functions.

"Yeah, and am I looking forward to it. Not so sure about college in the fall, though."

"I'm hoping that you'll write to me," Luke replied.

"Sure. No problem. Where are you going to be? Here or on Orcas? You should stay here. You love the science classes so much, and you know you'll be better prepared for college if you stay here."

"That's all true, but the best thing here is the Bible teaching. I really like my pastor on Orcas, but Pastor Ralph has taught me so much. That is something you'll be facing, finding a good pastor who teaches God's Word when you're in college." Luke knew that Joe had been accepted to a university in Iowa that his great-grandfather had founded. "We can't stray too far from getting fed God's Word, or our lives will just fall apart, you know."

Joe didn't answer, and Luke did not know where to take it from there. He just hoped his point had been taken to heart.

"Say, let's head back inside and give those two ladies a good time on the dance floor." Luke gave Joe a light punch on the shoulder. He had wanted to tell Joe to stop treating Bobbi so badly, but he knew the real issue was getting Joe back to God. Once Joe got right with God, everything else would fall into place.

BOOK 2
Summer at Orcas

Fossil Bay Inlet, Sucia Island

CHAPTER 17

Back to Orcas

*T*hank You, Lord!" Luke said as he looked around at the forested shores of Orcas, Decatur, Blakely, and Lopez islands. He stood on the aft deck of *The Claw*, the wonderful, magnificent, rusty old *Claw*. She still had a bit of blue paint left in places. Oh, how he loved being out here on the water. They were rocking slightly from the swells from the 10:00 A.M. ferry that had just passed. Boy, would Bobbi love being here, he thought, and then mentally slapped himself. Why couldn't he get that girl off his mind?

"Well, are we going to sight-see all day or set crab pots?" asked Captain Tom.

"Oh, sorry, sir." Luke bent over and got to work.

It was just Luke and Captain Tom this summer; the full-time hands had been hired by a larger company. Luke had been disappointed when he heard that Steve had taken a job on the mainland. But Steve would be home on the weekends, and they could get together then. Captain Tom hadn't bothered to find a replacement for Steve.

The first night back at home Captain Tom had called. "Work will be slower this summer. They are starting to cut back on the amount of time we can crab. I can't afford to keep a full crew anymore. Others are beating the system by buying more boats and adding more crews. I am just too old to try that; this will most likely be my last year. Besides, the missus is on my case to retire."

Knowing that he would have less crabbing money, Luke had picked up a few evening hours at the Deer Harbor Marina. But he did not want to get too busy; Mom needed him to make some repairs on the house, the guesthouse, the barn, and the fences. She had talked about renting out the back pastures and barn. They hadn't had any livestock on the land since Dad started working on the mainland. The old black mare had died of old age, and they had butchered the last steer the first fall his father had worked in Bellingham.

Sweat poured off Luke as he pulled up a crab pot. My, it's hot. Maybe all the talk about a warm summer is right. So far June's been like a typical August, warm and calm.

"Watch when you pull up the pots," Captain Tom yelled. "We have a pod coming through."

Luke looked up; he started to count: one, two, three, four, and five white and black shiny backs going up and down in the water. The orca whales were visiting for the day. Hopefully they wouldn't stop here to play, or it would really slow their work down. Evidently the orcas had some other destination in mind and kept on going right past *The Claw*.

By midafternoon they had a huge haul. Captain Tom set the course to the Orcas ferry dock, where they sent off their catch packed in ice to the mainland on the late-afternoon ferry.

It's great to be home, Luke thought as he walked in the door of the old homestead.

"Spaghetti, right?" Luke yelled to his mother. He had smelled it as he came up the walk. No one could cook like Rosa.

"Yes, and garlic bread. Your grades came from William Winlock Miller High School," she said.

"It's Olympia High, Mom. How many times—" Luke stopped and smiled when he saw her laughing as he walked into the kitchen. *Mom's well; she's teasing again.*

They ate out on the patio overlooking Deer Harbor and watched the boat traffic coming in and out of the marina.

"I got a letter today from Brad," Adam said. "Mr. West wants to trailer their boat up here, and they're planning to spend a few days boating between the islands. They're thinking of coming up right after the Fourth of July. Can we invite them for dinner one night, Mom?"

"Better than that. If you and I work on cleaning it up, they can stay in our guesthouse. Where were they thinking of staying?" she asked.

"At Morrison's Cabins," Adam replied, referring to a group of very rundown cabins right across from the Deer Harbor Marina.

"Oh no, they can't stay there! Our guesthouse looks like the Ritz compared to those shacks. After all, the Wests were very good to you while you were in Olympia. I know for a fact that you ate there once a week on average. We owe them more than a meal," Mom insisted. "You call them tonight, but remember to wait until after seven so we can get the best rate."

Adam nodded in agreement.

"So, we have two letters from Olympia to open," Mom teased, holding the envelopes high above her head. "Anyone want to guess the outcome? Who shall we start with?"

"Why don't you get mine over with first? We know they'll not be as good as 'Mr. Perfect' here." Remorse showed in Adam's voice.

"Come on, Adam. You know that you were really doing well, especially the second semester. Open it up, Mom! You might be surprised. He was really catching on to math." Luke knew that Adam had done better than his usual 3.0.

"Wow!" Mom's eyes got wide. "You did do better. A 3.4! Very good. Great effort, Adam. I am proud of you."

Adam smiled big, enjoying his mother's praise. "I owe a lot of it to Luke. He's a good teacher, you know."

"OK, let's see if Mr. Luke broke his perfect straight-A streak." Mom smiled and opened Luke's grades. A frown started to form on her pretty face, and Luke sat up straight and tried to take the paper away from her. Then she laughed. "I got you. Very good job. You keep this up, you'll set a record for this family. Straight A's from first grade on. You and I have some serious discussions coming up about your future, young man."

"Gotta go call the Wests and go over to Bill's. That's OK, isn't it, Mom?" Adam asked.

Rosa looked at her watch and nodded. Adam spent every spare minute at Bill's pasture. Bill's dad had built a baseball diamond. In the evenings there were always boys there. Adam had developed quite an arm and held the distinction of being the best pitcher on the island.

"But this weekend I thought you could work with me on the fences. You're going to have to know how to work with a hammer if I'm not here this next winter." Luke tried not to sound too much like Adam's father. For a second Luke started to get angry about his father's indifference to parenting.

Luke looked at the grade slip when Rosa handed it to him. Straight A's. These A's meant a lot to him; he'd worked hard to get them. "I don't know if I should stay here next year or go back to Olympia. It's a hard decision to make."

"I know. You have another month to think it over. I think you should go back. I know you wanted to have your last year here, but the island can't give you what Oly can. But we also need to start looking into colleges. You might be able to get some scholarships with those grades. Have you thought about where you might like to go and what you might like to major in?"

"No. Some kind of science, but where I don't know," Luke replied.

"Have you ever thought of being a pastor?" Rosa asked.

Luke shot her a look of surprise. "A pastor? Whatever gave you that idea?"

"Your love for God's Word, your ability to teach and explain, and your reflective personality. You're always praying, too. You would make a good pastor." Rosa smiled.

Luke gave Rosa a determined look. "That won't be happening, Mom. That is not the life for me."

"But if God calls you?" Rosa would not let the subject go.

"Then I'll have something to think about," Luke answered, standing up. "I want to finish the repairs to the west side of the barn tonight. Then move on to the fences next. If you can rent the pastures by July it would be good. The grass needs to be eaten down or we're going to have to make hay." Luke thanked his mom for the dinner and helped her clear the dishes before heading off to the barn.

A pastor, he mused as he put on his tool belt, then chuckled. Maybe Mom wasn't as well as he thought she was.

CHAPTER 18

Visitors

*D*o you think it looks presentable?" Rosa asked Luke. She put a bouquet of flowers in the center of the little dining table of the guesthouse. Luke stood in the door, afraid to come in. Adam had worked hard fixing up the guesthouse and getting it ready.

"I haven't seen it look this good in years," Luke said. The painted white wood floors were spotless. The white kitchen tiles had been washed till they shone. Rosa had washed all the rag rugs and added a new one in the living room side of the room.

"Come on in and take a look at the bedroom."

Luke took off his shoes and crossed the threshold. Looking out the window, he noticed Adam stacking firewood near the kitchen side door. The bedroom was stunning. Adam had painted the walls dark blue. Rosa had put a white bedspread and new, dark blue throw pillows on the bed.

"Adam did all the hard cleaning. I only dusted this morning and brought in the spread, rugs, and pillows. He did a great job."

"That he did, Mom, that he did. There might be hope for him yet," Luke joked.

Brad and Mr. West pulled in the next day, in the late afternoon. Adam had taken the early shift at the grocery store so he could meet them at the ferry dock. He helped them launch their boat at the marina, and he and Brad brought it over to the Johansens' dock. For once, the old dock looked busy, with the Wests' twenty footer, Grandpa Miers' old twenty-six-foot twin inboard, and the ten-foot pram tied up. The Wests admired Grandpa's old inboard.

"So this is *Matilda!* Wow! I bet she can really move!" Brad exclaimed.

"Yeah, she can do up to forty knots on smooth water. It helps to have that kind of power out here, especially if you get caught in a storm," Adam told Brad.

"Where did the name come from?" Mr. West asked.

"My grandfather named it after my grandmother. He had this boat custom built. Grandma would go out in it occasionally, but she liked being on land better."

"What a terrific dinner, Rosa, and this is a fantastic place. A great view of the harbor, your own dock, and a nice house and barn." Mr. West complimented Mrs. Johansen on the fresh crab dinner.

"We get the crabs for free when Luke is out crabbing. Nothing tastes better than fresh Dungeness crab," she replied.

"How did you ever find this place? When did you buy it?" he asked.

"We didn't buy it. My grandfather on my dad's side was one of the first settlers on Orcas, and he originally built a log cabin here. Then just before my parents were married, my father and grandfather built this house. My hope is that it will always stay in the family." Rosa watched a boat slide into the marina fuel dock.

"Once we clear the table, can Brad and I go over to Bill's?" Adam asked.

"Yes, if that's OK with Mr. West," Rosa said.

"What's over at Bill's?" he asked.

"Baseball," Luke replied. "Adam is king of the pitcher's mound. He lives each day just to get out there and pitch."

Rosa went into the kitchen to take care of the dishes, and Mr. West and Luke enjoyed the view and the warm breezes. Mr. West brought up the subject of the warm weather and the numerous forest fires that had broken out in the Olympic and Cascade mountain ranges. "It seems like the whole state is on fire when we listen to the news. It's been such a dry spring and summer."

"I know. Almost every night there's a new fire added to the list." Luke paused, took a deep breath, and then ventured to ask, "How's Bobbi doing?"

"Just fine" was Mr. West's reply. "She is taking care of her horses. She's been picking strawberries, but soon it will be blueberries. There is a women's Bible study she attends at church, and she's doing some babysitting. But mainly she plays out in her boat with her friends on the bay. She'd love it up here."

As Rosa returned to the table with fresh coffee, Mr. West asked, "Have you ever thought of renting out your guesthouse?"

"Not really," she answered.

"It could bring in some additional money during the summer, if you did not mind the intrusion. In fact, I will pay for one week's rent, you name the price, for a family that would be coming in two weeks," he offered.

"Who would want to stay here?" Luke asked.

"It would be perfect for Pastor Ralph and his family. Just yesterday he told me that he'd been too busy to find a place for their vacation. He didn't think they would find a place they could afford at this short notice. I've wanted to find something extra I could do for Pastor, and this would be perfect. What do you think?"

"Well, let me talk it over with the boys, as they would be doing the heavy work. That might be fun. I will check prices on the island and let you know tomorrow." Rosa smiled. She could use the extra money. Her weaving did not bring in a steady income. "By the way, Luke, the Olsens will be bringing their two horses over tomorrow afternoon. They already paid July's boarding fee."

Luke sat on the deck of *The Claw* eating his sandwich. They had just left the group of crab pots on the west of Blakely and were heading southeast through Thatcher Pass to the east side of Decatur Island. Pastor Ralph and his family had arrived last night and would be staying on the island for a whole week! *What an opportunity to get some more teaching on the Greek language. But I can't intrude on his*

family time. In the spring Pastor Ralph had introduced him to "Koine" Greek. The four private lessons had been just enough to pique Luke's interest in the common dialect of the New Testament. Thursday night they would be having a big dinner at the house. Mom had invited Pastor Bob's and Pastor Ralph's families and others from the church.

Luke smiled as he thought about how enthusiastic Adam had been about renting out the guesthouse. Again, Luke didn't have to lift a finger. Adam took over. He made sure it was clean, the bathroom and kitchen stocked, and the yard mowed. He planted fresh flowers by the front porch and added new mattresses to the old twin beds in the loft.

Luke wondered how much Adam remembered of that place and how they used to play in the loft as kids when they woke up in the morning. Sometimes, the pillow fights got so wild their pillows would fall over the edge into the kitchen and living room area. His parents had lived there ever since they were married. It had been cramped quarters for the four of them. After Grandma died, they moved into the big house, and the boys each had their own bedrooms. The pillows fights did not happen very often after that.

"So you're taking tomorrow off. That leaves me by myself. Good thing we got a good catch today," Captain Tom said, bringing Luke back to reality.

"Yeah, I'm taking our guests out on *Matilda* to give them a tour around the islands. We will most likely have lunch over here at Spenser Spit. I had thought of taking them up to Sucia and Matia islands, but the south wind is supposed to be kicking up tomorrow. So it's best to stay in the more sheltered waters with that many people in Grandpa's old twenty-six footer."

"That boat can withstand anything. I knew the man who built it, a good boat builder. His boats were built for storms.

You'd be fine going up there. But I suppose it doesn't hurt to be careful," Captain Tom agreed.

"Is this all the food?" Luke asked. He had a large casserole dish balanced on each hand. Earlier he had put out extra tables made of sawhorses and plywood. Mom had laid tablecloths over them.

"No, the desserts are on the dining room table. And there are extra casseroles in the oven in case we run out," Rosa answered. "Maybe we should leave the desserts in the dining room and let everyone come inside for that." She had been cooking all day and baking the day before.

Luke placed the casserole dishes in the last open space on the serving table. "Good idea, Mom." He looked around at a patio full of adults, and the children playing on the yard that sloped down to the beach. Adam sat near the dock. They didn't want any children going out there and falling into the water. Even with the chain across, a little one could easily wander out there and not be noticed in the commotion.

Mom rang the old silver dinner bell and everyone quieted down. She asked Pastor Ralph to say grace. Pastor Ralph and Pastor Bob seemed to really hit it off.

"So here's our young Greek scholar," Pastor Ralph said as Luke walked up to the two pastors.

"Greek?" Pastor Bob looked at Luke. "You're learning Greek?"

"Yeah, thanks to Pastor Ralph. He's given me two lessons while he's been here. It's an interesting language." Luke looked up to see his mother signal him. "Please excuse me.

Looks like Mom needs my help." He headed into the house to help her carry out more food.

"We have two more families coming up from Westside Baptist this summer," Rosa informed the boys as they helped her clean up after the dinner. "That Mr. West has become our marketing department. We won't need to advertise."

They both laughed at Rosa's joke.

"Are you sure you want to do this?" Luke asked. "It's a lot of work."

"It's fun having people around. We won't do it all year, and if we just book people when we want them it should be fine. Plus, the extra money is helpful, and Adam does most of the work."

Luke knew his mother needed to find a steady income to support herself. In three years, the child-support checks would stop, and she'd be on her own.

"Yes, she's paying me more than I get at the grocery store. I like the work and seeing the old house looking good again. Remember the pillow fights, Luke?" Adam asked.

So he does remember. Adam shares those happy memories too! Like dropping in at Grandpa and Grandma's uninvited for some of Grandma's famous cookies. Life was simple then—even though we were poor.

Luke put down his tray of dishes. "Like this?" He grabbed a throw pillow off the wicker settee, hitting Adam square on the chest. Adam laughed, threw it back, and tackled Luke. They tumbled down the grassy slope to the beach, play-fighting all the way.

"Come on, you two. It's getting dark and we need to get everything inside," Rosa yelled.

CHAPTER 19

The Letter

*T*his letter came for you in the mail." Rosa carried out the crab casserole for dinner and placed it on the table. It was just the two of them tonight, as Adam's baseball team had a game on San Juan Island. They were playing for the Island County championship.

Rosa had a curious smile on her face as she pulled a letter out of her apron pocket and handed it to Luke.

Luke couldn't believe the return address. Bobbi West! He carefully laid the letter next to his placemat as he sat down to the table. Then he proceeded to give thanks for the food.

Rosa looked up, gazed at the letter, then asked, "How did crabbing go today?"

"Good. We had the biggest haul of the summer. It was hot though. Ninety-two the weather radio said."

"Yes, it's warm."

"Dead calm all day—no wind to help cool us down. We had two seals that tagged alongside all day."

"Do you still have the next two days off?" Rosa asked, looking at the letter again.

"Yeah, Susan's going back for another doctor's appointment. Guess she was ill all winter." Susan was Captain Tom's wife. "I might be able to finish the repairs on the roof of the house. Then you will be all shipshape for winter."

When Luke finished eating he picked up the letter and opened it. Rosa watched Luke's facial expressions change as he read.

"Well, I take it the letter is good news?" she asked.

"Lots of surprises, that's for sure." Luke stared at the letter as he talked. "Bobbi's coming to Orcas in two weeks with her aunt Jane and her cousin Polly. They have reservations at Rosario Resort for seven days." Rosario was a deluxe resort on the eastern bay of Orcas, called East Sound. The town of Eastsound sat at the north tip of the bay. Rosario provided all the amenities for its guests: a pool, restaurants, a spa, and a marina. "But the biggest news of all is that Joe broke up with her three weeks ago!" Luke sat dumbfounded, looking out at Deer Harbor for over five minutes.

He reread the last two paragraphs again:

> By now you know that Joe broke up with me three weeks ago.
>
> I am really looking forward to my time on Orcas. It's a place I've always wanted to visit. Dad has told me so much about it.
> Sincerely,
> Bobbi

She's free to date! But more important—how is she doing? She didn't even allude to how she's feeling, Luke thought. He continued to stare at Deer Harbor for a while.

"Mom, I'm sorry, the repairs will have to wait. I've got to leave tonight. If I leave in an hour I could be in Port Townsend by nine, spend the night. Then, if I got up at six I could be to Boston Harbor by ten or eleven. Spend the rest of the day with Bobbi and make sure she's OK, stay at Boston Harbor Marina, and head back up the next day." Luke stood up and started to hurry off.

Rosa grabbed his arm. "Now, you just sit back down for a moment. That is crazy. Are you thinking of going by boat?"

"Yes, you two will need the car. Captain Tom checked the weather radio this afternoon. The weather forecasters aren't expecting any changes until Monday at the earliest. We were at the south end of Lopez this morning, and I've never seen the Strait so calm. I just filled Grandpa's boat with fuel yesterday. I'll pack lots of food. I promise I'll come back up the Inland Passage if things change. I've studied the charts several times this summer, because I was curious about the best way to get there by boat, and ran a course I can show you."

"Well, I can see that you are determined. But this is crazy. You'd better call her first and make sure she will be there tomorrow." Rosa gave in, seeing the look on Luke's face. "I will pack your food. The sooner you get started, the better I will feel. Remember there are several forest fires on the Olympic Peninsula. You might run into some smoke."

"Hello, Mrs. West, it's Luke. May I talk to Bobbi?" Luke did not want to talk long. It wasn't seven yet.

"Sorry, Luke, she's spending the night at a girlfriend's," Mrs. West replied.

"Oh, I thought I might come down tomorrow around eleven. I'd be coming in by boat. I'd hoped to see Bobbi."

"I think Bobbi would be delighted to see you. I'll call her and let her know that you are coming. So, we'll see you tomorrow then," Mrs. West said.

"Yes, tomorrow." Luke hung up the phone, hoping it would all work out.

Luke gave Charlie a quick call and asked if he could have the use of a slip for the night. Charlie seemed excited that he would be visiting.

"OK. Here is the plan." Luke put his backpack on the patio table and showed Rosa the chart. He had the course penciled in with all his headings marked out. "Cattle Point to Port Townsend, Port Townsend south through Port Townsend Bay through the Hadlock channel, past Port Ludlow, Point No Point, Kingston, Bainbridge Island, Blake Island, down Colvos Passage to Tacoma, under the Tacoma Narrows Bridge, between Anderson and McNeil Islands, around Johnson Point and into Dana Passage. I'll call you in a few hours."

Luke gave her a hug and headed for the dock. He glanced at his watch: six forty-five. Luke took it slow out of the harbor and then gradually worked up to full speed down San Juan Channel toward Cattle Point. Cattle Point was the southeast tip of San Juan Island and the gateway to the Strait of Juan de Fuca. Except for waves from boat traffic going into Friday Harbor, the water remained calm.

Rounding Cattle Point, Luke encountered gentle rolling swells from the strait. He could vaguely see the smoky Olympic Peninsula in the distance. *Matilda*'s instruments held a perfect course off Smith Island, Partridge Point on Whidbey Island, and on into Port Townsend. He referred to the tide book and chart—both important items for navigating the waters around Port Townsend. The extensive shoaling in that area had caught many vessels off guard over the years. He pulled into Port Townsend just after nine o'clock, as the sun went down in the west. The Olympic Mountains stood tall behind the city lights.

Several sea otters played a game of tag on and off *Matilda*'s swim platform as Luke tied up the boat. "Go on now. Time for bed." Luke scolded them as he headed up the dock to the pay phone.

After letting Rosa know that he had arrived, he took a short walk on the beach. Memories of the last time he had spent the night here flooded over him. Grandfather Miers and he had spent the night on *Matilda* and met Grandma the next day in town for lunch. She had spent several days here in her hometown with a longtime girlfriend, and they were picking her up by boat. The crossing back to the San Juans had been rough, and Grandma hadn't liked it at all. She spent the entire time down in the cabin. *Matilda*'s cabin had a bunk in the bow, a sink, a one-burner cooktop, a small icebox, and the head. Poor Grandma. She spent two and a half hours in the cramped cabin being tossed back and forth. Luke thought it was sad that his grandma didn't share her husband's love for the water. They were so close otherwise.

Grandpa had been sent to Port Townsend to attend high school. His mother did not want him "growing up ignorant." Back then the islands did not have schooling past the eighth grade. Grandpa told him the moment he met Matilda he knew she was the one. He did not have a fancy horse and buggy like the lumber mill owner's son had, but he decided to be her friend first. After three years, she chose him over the lumber mill owner's son. They married and moved to Orcas.

Grandma had always talked about Grandpa in a respectful, loving way. Once while baking Christmas cookies, she gave Luke her side of the story. "Your grandfather had a love for the Lord. He knew the Bible well and used it in his life. I knew with that kind of husband I would always be all right. Besides, he was the best-looking guy I knew." She blushed as she continued. "And he still is." Luke remembered laughing when she said that. He never thought of little Grandpa Miers as good-looking!

He wanted that, a close walk with the Lord and his partner. Could Bobbi be the one? But they needed to cement the friendship part first.

Luke woke up at five to splashing sounds off the swim platform. The sea otters were working on their diving form. He tried shooing them off to no avail. One of them even ventured to the cabin door as he fried his eggs and toast. As he ate his breakfast on the aft deck, seven of the sea otters sat on the dock, lined up in a row, hoping that he would share. They were like a pack of friendly puppies. When Luke finished his food and pulled out his Bible, they headed off toward the smell of bacon and pancakes coming from a larger boat nearby.

Matilda glided by Point No Point, famous for its rough seas and bad weather, heading south down Puget Sound. But today there wasn't a ripple on the water. After passing the point, Luke gave the engines a rest and just floated for five minutes in the calm bay. *What on earth am I doing? Why is this such a mission? Should I just wait till Bobbi comes to Orcas? No, I need to make sure she's OK.* He wanted to be there for her as a friend and let her know that. Oh yes, it would be nice if the relationship became more than that someday, but he didn't want to rush it.

Matilda needed fuel at Kingston, so Luke got out and stretched a bit.

Finally, after passing Fox Island and heading between McNeil and Anderson islands, Luke put the chart away. He knew the rest of the way by heart. Johnson Point was just ahead. He docked at Boston Harbor Marina at ten thirty and ran up the ramp to the store.

"Glad to see you made it. You're early." Charlie smiled and kept looking through the binocs at the dock. "That is quite a boat! *Matilda.* Your grandfather's boat you told me about, right?"

"Yes, that is the lady. Can I use your phone? I need to call someone."

"You mean Bobbi? You don't need to do that." Charlie nodded at the window.

There was Bobbi, docking a boat with two of her Boston Harbor girlfriends.

"So, you're here to claim your girl?" Charlie continued.

"No, nothing like that. I just want to make sure she's OK and let her know that I'm her friend," Luke replied.

"Oh, and then let another city slicker cut in and take her away? Make your move now!"

Luke didn't want to discuss it any further. He gave Charlie a smile and went out onto the deck. Leaning on the railing, he watched as Bobbi and her two friends walked up the ramp. She looked great! Her dark tanned skin gleamed in the sun, and she wore her long dark hair pulled back into a ponytail. She had on her swimsuit with a pair of light blue cutoffs over it and an unbuttoned long-sleeved cotton shirt. She waved, skipping up the ramp to him.

"I'm so glad you came." Bobbi clapped her hands together, and bouncing on her toes, she continued. "I couldn't believe it when Mom told me. She's expecting us for lunch.

Then I was hoping you could help me with the horses—unless you had other plans. How was your trip? Is that your boat?" Her excitement reminded Luke of a little kid.

"Calm down. I can only answer one question at a time." Luke laughed and put his hand on her shoulder, trying to keep her still. "Yes. That's my grandpa's boat, *Matilda*, named after my grandma. The trip was great, and lunch at your house and helping with the horses is fine." He turned to the other girls. "By the way, it's nice to see you, Mary. You too, Jill."

"We all spent the night at my house," Mary explained. "Bobbi couldn't wait to see you, so we brought her here."

"Bobbi wants to go in and talk to Charlie for awhile. Why don't you help me carry her bag from Mary's boat to your boat, Luke? I would love to see your boat." Jill grabbed Luke's arm and tried to lead him toward the ramp, smiling up at him and looking very helpless. Luke didn't budge. He smiled and gently took her hand off his arm.

"I need to talk to Charlie for a minute too. I'm sure you two can wait a minute. If not, just put the bag on the dock and we'll pick it up." She wasn't his type, and Bobbi's overnight bag couldn't be that heavy.

Luke held the door to the store open for Bobbi and followed her in.

"Look who's here! Look who's here!" Bobbi sang, sliding into the store in small little jumps, smiling, and waving her arms toward Luke.

"Well, it is good to see that you can smile again. It's been kinda gloomy around here the past few weeks. Never thought the sun rose on this big thug, but I guess it does." Charlie grinned from ear to ear. "Now, I hear that his time is limited and your mom is expecting you two for lunch, so you better be pushing off and stop wasting your time here. Luke, how about having breakfast with me in the morning before you leave? I'm sure I'll be in bed by the time you get back to your boat tonight."

Luke agreed and Bobbi gave Charlie a big hug.

"Now, it's your turn to ride. Let me adjust the stirrups for you." Bobbi finished up her ride on Missy and dismounted.

Luke stopped playing with Lady. "She's adorable. So spirited. And her blonde mane and tail have really bleached out in the sun. Against her light chestnut body, it's quite striking. She looks one of those blondes in a hair-coloring commercial, with a dark tan."

Bobbi laughed. "Yes, she does. I'm going to give her special vitamins while you ride. The vet has her on them to build up her strength and help her grow. She's small for a four-month-old filly."

Luke walked over to Missy and grabbed the reins.

Bobbi finished adjusting the stirrups. "Now when you want to trot or gallop, don't kick her. She will send you flying, and you'll be on your back. You just press your thighs and calves in and start to move your heels toward her side but *do not* touch her with your heels. She will move out. Her mouth is very sensitive, so just change the rein location to the side you want to turn and she will turn. It's called neck reining. Don't ruin her for me." Bobbi smiled up at Luke. They had talked at lunch about how well Missy had been trained. She knew he would be careful.

Luke rode Missy around the horse pasture. She was the most responsive horse he had ever ridden. No wonder Bobbi liked riding so much.

"OK. So now we have a few hours before dinner. How about taking a spin around Squaxin Island?" Luke asked Bobbi as they walked down the driveway to the house. "We could even do some waterskiing."

The waterskiing didn't happen. Instead, they ended up floating off Squaxin Island, sitting on *Matilda's* swim platform and talking.

"I got your letter at dinner yesterday. My mom's very excited about your visit and wants to have your aunt, cousin, and you over for dinner while you're there."

"That would be great! Aunt Jane has a number of friends on the island, so I know we will be very busy. I'm really looking forward to this trip...." Bobbi's voice trailed off, and she stared into the water for a minute. "Ever since I turned nine and first saw Orcas Island from the ferry, I've wanted to live there."

"Really? Cool."

"Yes, but I do love it here too."

They chatted a while about Orcas and Boston Harbor. Then Luke took the plunge.

"I came down here because I'm concerned about you. I was surprised that Joe broke up with you. Are you OK?"

"Joe didn't tell you? I thought he would." Bobbi looked amazed.

"No, I've written him twice and even called and left a message with his brother. Haven't heard from him since graduation. He's changed, Bobbi. He's not the same guy I met last fall. Seems like he's turned his back on the Lord, and that changes a person." Luke noticed pain on Bobbi's face. "I'm sorry he's hurt you."

"You know, the funny thing is our relationship kept getting worse and I wanted it to end. But it really hurt when he dumped me." Bobbi looked like she might cry.

"We both care about him. It bothers me to have him ignore me. I think he's afraid I'll tell him he needs to come back to the Lord, and he doesn't want to hear that."

"Well, it's been for the best. He never was the spiritual leader I want or need. You know what else? I've not been a good witness to Charlie. I didn't realize it until today when he said I've been so gloomy. I've had my eyes off the Lord and have been wallowing in my pain," Bobbi confessed.

"So now that you recognize your sin, move on. Confess the self-pity, give Him your pain, and spend more time in God's Word. God's giving you this test to make you stronger. Remember Job?"

"Oh, I don't think this is a test." Bobbi grimaced, "It's a correction. I don't think God ever wanted me dating Joe. I went down the wrong path, and God's showing me that."

Wow, what discernment, Luke thought. "It's hard to admit we are wrong, but it's a good start. I just want you to know that I'm here for you, if you need to talk."

Bobbi smiled at him. "Thanks." She stared into the water for a while, then looked at him with an impish smile on her face and pushed him off the swim platform into the water.

Bobbi pulled up to the intersection in her red VW Bug. She stopped.

Luke looked up at the light. "It's green!" he said softly.

Bobbi jumped. "Oh? Yes, it is. It looked red to me." She put her foot on the gas pedal and turned right into Bob's Big Burgers.

Red? Luke decided not to pursue it any further.

"I'd forgotten how good these cheeseburgers taste. It's been months since I've been here. Thanks again," Bobbi said as they finished up their burgers.

"My pleasure. Just wish that I could have driven," Luke said, embarrassed that Bobbi had picked him up at the marina. "How about we walk around the capitol grounds?"

They ended up on the capitol steps. Luke sat down and watched Bobbi walk up and down the stairs counting them. *She's cute.* Her tanned legs stood out against her pink skirt and white sandals. Her tanned arms shone in the evening light, and her long hair hung loose in soft curls.

Bobbi sat down next to Luke, and they talked about everything—his father, Orcas, her horses, Charlie, and Bobbi's driving record.

"Why did you stop at the green light?" Luke asked.

"I don't know why it happens, but sometimes I see the opposite of what things really are. It's like I see in reverse. I have had a hard time with traffic lights. In fact, that's how I had my first traffic accident." Bobbi made a face and then continued. "The light looked green to me, but it was red. I hit the side of a car with a nice, elderly couple inside. Fortunately they weren't hurt. We were both going under twenty miles per hour. I just felt awful. The judge took my license away for a month."

"But I heard that you got caught speeding."

"Yes, there's that, too. I got caught out on Libby Road. The sheriff just happened to be going home and caught me. But *the* worst was when I took out my dad's rhodies along the driveway."

"His prize rhododendrons?" Luke gasped. He knew how much those meant to Mr. West. He remembered Mr. West showing him how to shake the snow off the branches so they wouldn't break.

"I'm afraid so. The gas pedal got stuck at seventy miles an hour when I was on Esterly Road. I didn't know what to do. When I tried braking or slowing down, the engine sounded like it was going to explode. I even bent over and tried pulling the gas pedal up with both hands. I went down the big dip, and the steep hill on the other side slowed me down enough that I made the turn at the top of the hill onto Zangle and ran the intersection." Bobbi laughed. "Somehow, I made the turn into the driveway, but the car was going so fast I thought it would go right through the house and down the bank into the bay."

Luke started laughing. He was glad Bobbi did not seem to mind. In fact, she seemed to enjoy telling the story.

"So, I turned and went toward the plum tree. I missed it and circled the tree. Then, I went to the other side of the driveway and took out three of Dad's rhodies. That slowed the car down. My brother came running up and jumped on the running board, reached in, and turned the key. I hadn't even thought about turning the car off!" laughed Bobbi, and wiped a tear off her cheek.

"Dad was so mad. I went to the beach and hid out in the caves to the north of us for the rest of the day. It upset me too. I know how much he loves his rhodies," she ended the story on a more serious note.

"And I'm putting my life in your hands on the way home? Not so sure about this!" Luke teased her. "It is dark and we should be getting back. Would you like me to drive?"

"That would be nice," Bobbi said and handed him the keys to the VW.

CHAPTER 20

Dinner

Clank! As Luke pulled a crab pot from the water they were suddenly rocked by waves. The pot hit the side of *The Claw*. Luke had been so busy pulling up crab pots he didn't see the 10:00 A.M. ferry go by. All week Luke had been working extra hard, trying to please Captain Tom.

The news about Susan had not been good. She had some kind of very serious arthritis, and the doctor recommended they move to a warmer climate. Captain Tom had been cranky all week. Luke had hoped to ask Captain Tom for another day off while Bobbi visited, but he now knew it was out of the question.

"Do you know anyone coming on the ten o'clock ferry?" Captain Tom came out of the cabin with his binoculars in hand and a frown on his face.

"Yes, a girl from the Olympia area. Why?"

"Well, there were two girls out on the front, waving at us and looking through their binocs. I couldn't figure out what was going on. Sorry, I should've asked sooner."

Luke turned and watched the ferry disappear into the ferry dock on Lopez Island. It was too far away to see anyone on the deck even with the binoculars.

"That's OK. I hope to see her tonight."

It had only been five days since he had seen Bobbi, but he missed her. It seemed like a month had gone by. The trip back up to Orcas had been uneventful, the waters were fairly calm, and he didn't need to take the Inland Passage past La Connor.

The calm, hot day seemed to last an eternity. Luke wanted to drive over to Rosario in the evening to make sure that Bobbi and her aunt were all settled in and make final arrangements for tomorrow night's dinner at his house. Rosa had been baking and fixing up the flowerbeds and garden. She seemed to be looking forward to it as much as he was.

Finally, at three-thirty Captain Tom called it a good enough haul, and they headed into the Orcas dock to send their catch off on the afternoon ferry.

"Hey! Let's not brutalize the crabs before they get to market!" Captain Tom looked at Luke sternly.

Luke jerked and realized he had given the last crate too strong of a toss onto the dock. He had been lost in a fog and forgotten what he was doing. He wanted to get home soon and clean up before he saw Bobbi. The smell of his sweat and the crab might drive her away.

"Besides, you might want to put a smile on your face for your audience," the captain continued.

Luke looked up the hill to the road and saw Bobbi and a tall blonde girl standing there watching him unload the boat. Bobbi smiled and waved. Luke waved back. Then he finished up his work.

As he walked up the hill, she started to run toward him. Luke put up his hand to stop her. "I smell to high heaven. You might want to keep your distance." He smiled.

"Or we could just push you into the water!" She smiled back. "Luke, this is my cousin Polly. We talked Aunt Jane into letting us use the car for the afternoon, but we have to be getting back. We are having dinner tonight with Aunt Jane's friends over by Doe Bay."

"Nice to meet you, Polly. I would shake your hand, but mine smells like crab. May I call you tonight, Bobbi, when you get back to the resort?" Luke was disappointed that he was not going to have any time with Bobbi that evening.

"Sure. We are in cabin twelve."

"We should be back by nine," Polly added.

"That's some trawler. May we have a closer look?" Bobbi asked.

Bobbi seemed impressed with *The Claw*, even commenting on her classic fishing boat design.

"That was an incredible dinner! Dad told me that crab fixed by your mom is the best in the world, and he's right." Bobbi's eyes shone with appreciation as she walked to the beach with Luke.

Dinner had gone very well. Aunt Jane and Rosa seemed to hit it off immediately. Bobbi had helped Mom serve the dinner. They seemed to work well together. Polly turned out to be a big baseball fan and took off with Adam right after dinner to watch the guys play at Bill's. Luke was pleased. *Finally some time alone with Bobbi.*

"How about a little spin around Deer Harbor in *Matilda*?" Luke asked.

Bobbi loved the idea, and they took off, going very slowly around the harbor. Luke played tour guide, telling her about the marina, the people who lived in the different houses, and all about Fawn Island. They even floated for a while and watched the seals come up to the surface and play in the fading evening light. Bobbi looked beautiful in her blue and white summer pants outfit. Her dark hair lay loose over her shoulders. She seemed relaxed. From time to time she would dip her hand into the water and swirl it around for awhile. Luke could tell she really loved being out on the water. He felt like pinching himself. *Is this real? Bobbi West in my boat, on Orcas Island?* Four months ago he would have never thought it possible.

"She is a very special girl," Rosa remarked as Luke helped her put away the last of the dishes. She had been watching Luke as they cleaned up, and he kept smiling, almost glowing with happiness.

"Yes, she is. Does that mean you approve?" Luke asked, bending down to look into his mom's eyes.

"Definitely. But you are both young, too young, to get tied down yet."

"That's why my goal is to just stay friends as long as possible. But I'm not sure how to communicate that to her." Luke leaned back against the kitchen cabinet with a very serious look on his face. Aunt Jane had wanted to leave before it got totally dark. It was a ten-mile drive back to Rosario, and she wanted to be able to see on the narrow winding island roads.

"Have you asked the Lord?" Rosa always took everything back to the Lord.

"No, you're right. I need to be praying about this relationship. It's a big workday tomorrow. I'm going up and study my Bible for awhile, unless there is something else you need."

"No, I'm going to listen to the weather radio. I'll let you know if there is going to be any change. Boy, do you remember any summer like this one? I don't. They keep adding more and more forest fires to the list. It seems like the whole state is burning up."

"No, I don't remember any summer so warm and dry. Just look at me. Have you ever seen me so tan?" Luke jokingly showed off his arm muscle.

Rosa laughed as he headed upstairs. "Check on your brother. He is still brooding over his near loss tonight."

He and Adam had pulled mattresses out onto the upstairs porch facing the water. They had been sleeping out there since early July. It was too hot to sleep inside, and the occasional breeze off the water felt good. Luke read for a while in his room and then headed out to the porch.

He lay there for a long time watching the stars and listening to Adam's light snoring as he recounted every minute he had spent with Bobbi that day.

CHAPTER 21

Sucia

Luke jumped. The horn of the ferry coming into dock woke him up. He must have fallen asleep waiting for Steve. The ferry was at least ten minutes late.

"Hurry up! We're late," Luke yelled at Steve as he walked up the hill from the ferry.

"Yeah, yeah. Now you promised me if I don't like this Polly gal I don't have to go out with you guys tomorrow," Steve said as he sank into the seat of the '57 Chevy. He was referring to an outing Luke had planned for Saturday to Sucia Island.

"OK, I promised." Luke had done some tall talking to convince Steve he should give up a Saturday to be with some girl he didn't even know. Luke wanted the outing to be a foursome.

When they arrived at Rosario, Steve took one look at Polly, and from then on, you would have thought the trip to Sucia Island was his idea. They ate at the resort café and then walked along the docks and the beach. Luke didn't expect Polly and Steve to hit it off so well. He just wanted to see Bobbi, and this gave him another excuse.

As Luke drove Steve home, the talk was all about the girls.

"How Bobbi and Polly got to be first cousins is hard to figure out," mentioned Steve. "All that blonde hair and blue eyes. She's at least six inches taller than Bobbi."

"She must take after her father's side of the family, not the West side of the family," Luke surmised.

"Polly has the perfect face. She gorgeous! All the guys on the island are talking about her. I guess when she showed up at Bill's on Thursday night with Adam, they all fell in love with her on the spot. In fact they divided into teams, and she pitched for the other team. She almost out-pitched your brother!"

"Yeah, I heard about that. Poor Adam is still getting over almost being beaten by a girl. Guess she has quite the arm. Mom says Polly is what you'd call a classic beauty."

"Are you sure you don't want to be paired with Polly? She is definitely the prettier of the two," Steve said.

Luke shot Steve a look of disbelief. "Well, that goes to prove the Lord designed all of us with different tastes. I happen to think Bobbi's prettier."

"There it is. Just ahead at eleven o'clock, and that is Matia Island off to the right just a bit behind it. The whole island is a state park." Steve pointed out Sucia Island to Polly and Bobbi.

"So which side are you thinking of, Luke? Echo Bay or Fossil Bay? Steve asked.

"I thought Echo would be more fun, but we do have some time, so let's go into Fossil so the girls can see what it's like. Then head around the north side of the island to Echo."

Bobbi gazed in wonder. The narrow bay had no shore. Huge bare rock walls went straight down into the water with small holes in them like they were fossilized. She sat still, watching Luke navigate *Matilda* around Sucia Island. She couldn't help but be impressed as he moved the boat in and out of little coves, around reefs and dangerous rocky points. She had taken a close look at the chart posted on the wall of the lobby at Rosario Resort the night before. She had noticed all the dramatic changes in the sea floor around Sucia Island. Luke didn't look at a chart. She knew that he had it all memorized. Why was she so fascinated? Was it his control of *Matilda?* No, though his mastery of the vessel and the elements was an underlying reason. Then she understood. *He's completely at home on the sea.* Several times on the way up he had turned and smiled at her. They hadn't talked since they left Deer Harbor. A comfortable silence.

Besides, it would have been hard to say a word with Polly's and Steve's constant chatter. Bobbi sat in the stern on the port side. From her vantage point she could see everything that was going on in the boat and out. She had basically tuned out Polly and Steve and just sat back and enjoyed the trip. The salt water smelled so good!

Bobbi watched as Luke pulled into Echo Bay and tied up to a mooring buoy. They had brought a small inflatable dinghy along. Polly and Steve had quickly claimed it and headed into shore, leaving Luke and Bobbi alone on the boat.

"It's eleven in the morning and already ninety degrees!" Bobbi broke the silence. She was glad she already had her swimsuit on. She slipped off her shorts. Still wearing her favorite light peach-colored cotton long-sleeved shirt, she sat down on the swim platform, letting her feet dangle into the beautiful, clear, ten-foot deep water. She could see the sandy bottom scattered with shells. A few crabs quickly scurried away as Luke sat down on the other end of the swim platform.

"Uh-oh! You scared off the crabs!" she whispered, smiling at Luke. "Guess you didn't tell them that you have the day off."

Luke laughed. "I'm just glad to have some peace and quiet!"

"Amen to that!" Bobbi agreed. "I can handle Polly on her own, but around Steve she becomes another creature! I'm not so sure it's a good combination."

"Well, it is getting a bit warm, and if I remember right, I owe you one." Luke smiled and scooted closer to her.

Bobbi looked puzzled but quickly realized what he was talking about as he gently pushed her into the water. Luke laughed at the look on her face as she hit the water. He joined her. They swam around the boat several times and then into shore.

The hours went by quickly. The four of them ate lunch on the beach, hiked the island, swam in several different coves, and played the afternoon away. All of a sudden Luke looked at his watch.

"It's five o'clock! I promised your aunt we would be back at six! We need to wrap this up and get going." Luke looked frantic.

They came around the south point of Echo Bay and it was almost déjà vu. A stiff wind had kicked up from the southwest. But this time it was sunny and warm with light blue skies. Plus, the boat they were in was ten feet longer. The waves were just as big, though—at least two and a half to three feet high and breaking over the front of the boat.

Polly looked scared and immediately put on a life jacket.

"Polly, don't worry. Luke can handle this." Bobbi tried to reassure her.

"I'm going to the cabin," Polly declared. After a few minutes she came up, looking very green.

"Come over here." Steve guided her to the port side of the boat so she could "let go" over the side.

"Luke, should we all put on life jackets? Bobbi asked.

"Not a bad idea."

Bobbi found life jackets for the guys and herself and then got out a thermos of water and a clean rag for Polly to wipe her face with. She noticed a radio on the control panel. She sat down on the starboard side in the seat behind Luke. *Lord, please give us a safe trip. Please get us there in time for dinner, and help Aunt Jane to be understanding,* she prayed. They wouldn't be back to Deer Harbor by six. Fighting this headwind and the waves, it might be more like seven. Aunt Jane would not be happy if they were late, because they had a seven-thirty dinner to attend.

Finally, after an hour of pounding waves, they rounded Steep Point and headed into the calmer water of Deer Harbor. Polly had thrown up two more times. She still looked green. Bobbi felt sorry for her. Steve had been such a help to Polly.

"I'm sorry. I'll take the blame for being late," Luke said to Bobbi as he slowed the boat past the marina and headed into the Johansen's dock. He looked at his watch: six forty-five. "I should have kept better track of the time. The weather forecasters said it would be calm all day. No signs of any disturbances. I know better than to trust them completely, but this summer has been so warm and calm, I forgot they can be wrong."

"Well, the rest of us had watches, too. We share the blame. Besides, you did a fabulous job against that sea, getting us back this quickly and safely." Bobbi patted him on the shoulder and headed back to the starboard stern to put out the fenders and get ready to jump out on the dock and tie down the lines.

She had just finished tying off the bowline when Aunt Jane came charging down the dock, yelling all the way.

"Oh no! A full demonstration of the quick West temper," muttered Bobbi. "And in front of Luke, too."

Bobbi turned red and wheeled around to face her aunt.

"This is unforgivable! Forty-five minutes late! What were you kids thinking? Do you know how this is going to make us look to my friends?" Aunt Jane waved her arms in the air.

"Now you two young ladies head up to the house. I laid out your dresses on Mrs. Johansen's bed, and she said you may change there. We will not have time to go back to the resort. As for you two young men, I forbid you to see these two young ladies again! Totally irresponsible, you are! You need to return your dates on time!" Aunt Jane turned to march off the dock but suddenly noticed how sick Polly looked, as Bobbi and Steve helped her onto the dock. The green pallor was beginning to subside, but she was still very weak.

"What's wrong with you?" Aunt Jane stood there, both hands on her hips, glaring at Polly. Bobbi imagined steam rising off her.

"She's been seasick for an hour and a half, Aunt Jane, and she's not doing too well! We just came off of a nasty sea, and you should be thankful we were with good seamen and that we're safe!" Bobbi didn't want to talk any more.

She mouthed "sorry" to Luke and grabbed Polly's arm and headed for the house.

Rosa opened the door and helped Bobbi get Polly inside. "I'm so glad to see you safe. What's wrong? Is she seasick?"

Bobbi nodded and helped Polly up the stairs after Rosa.

"Boy, the weather radio sure missed the prediction for the afternoon. Here, let's lay her down on my bed. Why is your aunt going to the car? What happened down on the dock? It looked like she was yelling."

Bobbi glanced out of the window and noticed that Luke was still standing on the dock shaking his head and acting like he didn't know what hit him.

"I am sorry, Mrs. Johansen, but my aunt lost her temper. It is something we Wests are very famous for," Bobbi said sheepishly.

"I'm never going to get to see Steve again," Polly wailed to Bobbi from the bed.

"Now, now, calm down and take it easy. You know your mom. It will blow over quickly, and she'll be sorry for everything she said. She was worried about us and reacted. Do you feel well enough to wash up, or do you want me to go first?"

"You go first. I do feel a bit better." Polly's color had returned.

CHAPTER 22

Apology

*B*obbi watched Luke walk up the path to the cabin door looking apprehensive. He must be on the lookout for Aunt Jane.

Bobbi couldn't help but giggle at his expression as he held the door to the cabin for her.

"What?" Luke gave her a puzzled look.

"You look like you expect to get hit by a cannon," Bobbi whispered.

"Do you blame me?"

"No." Bobbi blushed, thinking about what had happened the night before, as they walked toward the car. She noticed Adam sitting in the front passenger seat.

Aunt Jane and Polly were sleeping in. "We are on vacation!" her aunt had declared when Bobbi had brought up the subject of church earlier in the week.

Just as Bobbi had expected, Aunt Jane's temper left as quickly as it came. She was joking and acting like the incident had never happened as they arrived at her friend's house for dinner, on time. Bobbi had noticed that after dinner Aunt Jane had used their hostess's phone. On the way home, Aunt Jane explained.

"Luke and his family will be picking you up for church at eight thirty tomorrow. I called from Barb's and apologized to him," Aunt Jane informed Bobbi.

"Thank you, Aunt Jane." Bobbi wasn't too sure what she was thanking her for, as she felt Aunt Jane owed *everyone* an apology.

"They will be taking you out for Sunday dinner afterward at a café near the church. I expect you back before five in the evening. Hopefully that will be enough time for you to spend with your friend."

Bobbi appreciated the opportunity to go to church. Besides, it was Luke's last free day while she visited the island. Aunt Jane had a big party planned for all her friends at the resort on Monday night, and both of the girls were required to attend.

"My, that is a beautiful dress, my dear." Rosa smiled as Bobbi settled in next to her in the backseat of the car. Luke walked around to the driver's side. "I'm so glad your aunt changed her mind and let you come to church with us."

"Thanks. I appreciate you picking me up and taking me, especially as it's out of your way." Bobbi smiled back at her.

She wore an outfit her mother had made—a white, embroidered A-line sundress that hit two inches above her knees with a matching short-sleeved jacket.

The church looked like something out of a picture book. The small, white, wooden building with strange detailing intrigued Bobbi. She stood by the car for a moment looking at it, puzzled by the unique architecture.

Luke noticed her questioning look. "It's a Norwegian design. Built by my grandfather Arvik Johansen himself," he said. "The day he finished it was most likely the last day he set foot in a church."

"That's too bad. It is beautiful." Bobbi and Luke walked into church together with Adam and Rosa behind them.

Luke introduced her to several of his friends and Pastor Bob. The old hymns they sang were wonderful. She enjoyed singing with the congregation, which sounded like a professional choir. There were some fantastic voices in the small group of about a hundred people. Bobbi loved listening to Luke's bass voice.

"That was a nice sermon," Bobbi commented later. She and Luke walked toward the café along the deserted main street of Eastsound, several paces behind Rosa and Adam.

Luke stopped at a storefront and pointed to the window. Several placemats and small rugs were attractively displayed. "Originals by Rosa Johansen," a simple sign read below the items.

"Oh how special!" Bobbi exclaimed. "She does such wonderful work!"

Luke smiled but didn't move. He stretched one arm up, leaned on the side of the building, and looked down at her. Adam and Rosa had disappeared into the café.

"Now about that sermon. What did you really think? Be honest."

"Well, it was good, but something seemed to be missing. I don't know." Bobbi looked puzzled. "I can't put my finger on it."

"That's how I feel. I knew you would understand. I always feel like I have really been fed after one of Pastor Ralph's sermons. What Pastor Bob has to say is always correct, but never quite enough. I introduced them to each other when Pastor Ralph vacationed here. I had hoped Pastor Ralph could help Pastor Bob out. But so far there's been no evidence of that happening. I just didn't want to say anything in front of Mom and Adam. That is the main reason I want to return to Olympia this fall, Pastor Ralph's teaching. It's what I need right now." Luke finally turned and they continued walking toward the café.

"I understand. I won't say anything." Bobbi smiled up at him. He seemed calm and sure of himself. She felt safe around him. Plus he was *so* good-looking and had a great physique. She kept trying not to think of *that* too often.

Bobbi had spent the summer in a Bible study led by Pastor Ralph's wife. Renee had originally planned to teach about being a godly woman. Since most of those attending were teenage girls, it became a class on dating and proper relationships with young men. Renee had emphasized the soul relationship as the most important and how young people needed to keep the physical relationship to a very minimum—handholding, a kiss now and then—and that God designed physical intimacy for marriage. Several of the girls called Renee a prude behind her back, but Bobbi knew that Renee was right. Many of the girls at school were sleeping with their boyfriends. Bobbi did not want to give in to that pressure and had thanked Renee for the summer Bible study.

"What a charming café," Bobbi commented as she sat down at the table.

"And you're sitting with some of my favorite customers." The owner brought menus; he knew the Johansens well.

They ordered, and Luke said grace when the meal came. Bobbi sat back, relaxed, and enjoyed watching the boys tease their mother. Rosa could give it back and tease them just as much. No one would guess she had been so ill just a year before.

"Let's all go back to the house for dessert. We have a few hours before Bobbi has to be back to the resort," Rosa suggested.

"And I would love to see your studio, if you don't mind." Bobbi said.

"I'd be delighted." Rosa smiled.

Once back at the homestead Rosa dished up rhubarb cobbler and took Bobbi to the back of the house. "My ex-husband added this portion on for me. This way I could work and keep an eye on the boys at the same time."

"Wow!" Bobbi gazed around the large room. There were two large-sized looms and one smaller one sitting in the middle of the room, with open shelving around the sides of the room housing all kinds of yarn and weaving equipment. In the far corner a desk and drafting board sat just below the window, with a view of the driveway.

"That's where I draw up my ideas and lay out yarn combinations. Weaving has never been a big breadwinner, but I do OK in the summer months around here. Before I got sick, I went to several county fairs on the mainland in the fall and sold a lot of my things."

Rosa and Bobbi were talking about her drawings and the various projects in production when Luke joined them. He stood there patiently for a while, watching them talk, and then he came over and grabbed Bobbi's hand and started to pull her away.

"OK, Mom, you've had her long enough." He smiled. "You can go visit her the next few days during the daytime; I can't."

Luke continued to hold her hand, gently guiding her outside and down to the dock.

"Sorry to end things with my mom. I guess I should have asked which of us you would rather spend the time with. Just got a bit impatient. We only have another hour before I have to take you back. Can you get into *Matilda* with that dress on?"

"Yes, I can." Bobbi sat on the edge of the boat and swung her legs around into the boat in a very ladylike fashion. "We must stay on calm waters; my aunt won't be understanding if I'm late a second time."

"We'll stay in Deer Harbor. I thought of taking you back to Rosario by boat, but with our track record lately, it's safer on land."

Bobbi laughed

They floated off Fawn Island most of the time, watching boats come in and out of the marina. Bobbi got Luke on the subject of his grandpa Johansen. It had not been the topic that Luke had wanted to talk about. Before he knew it, the time had flown by, and he was driving Bobbi back to Rosario Resort.

"Let's take a few more minutes for lunch," Captain Tom said.

Monday, August 11, was another ninety-degree day with no rain in sight. The smoke from all the forest fires hung over the Cascade Mountains and Mount Baker in a large gray layer. *The Claw* floated perfectly still in the quiet waters off the east side of Decatur Island, on the edge of Rosa Strait.

Taking a lunchtime together was a new concept in the first place. Usually he and Captain Tom just kept working all day long, eating their lunches when they were hungry between all the tasks that needed to be done.

Captain Tom hemmed and hawed for a few minutes, then finally started in. "I want to apologize. I've been kind of grouchy this past month. It is just all these problems with

Susan and now with us having to think about moving to a warmer climate. I don't want to leave Orcas. This is home! I want to die here."

Luke remained silent, afraid the crusty old man might cry.

"You go make something of yourself, son. You have the smarts. Don't get into crabbing. Look where it has got me. Barely breaking even, and it's tough work. I just have one question: How do you stay in such a good mood with all the problems you have faced these past few years? It's like you have a special strength or something."

Stunned, Luke quickly asked the Lord to give him the right words. He explained to Tom that his strength came from the Lord. He even got into the gospel. This time Tom listened as he spoke, unlike three years ago when Luke had given him the same information. Then Captain Tom had yelled and stormed down below deck, telling Luke to never bring up that subject with him again.

The two sat in silence for a while. Luke asked Captain Tom if he wanted to believe in Jesus Christ, but the captain didn't respond right away.

"Well, that is a lot to think about, son." The captain finally spoke, then stood up. "Thanks for the info. We'd better get back to work. Oh, by the way, I keep forgetting...I hope you don't mind taking tomorrow off. I've got to take Susan in to the doc's again."

"No, that would be fine!" excitement and disappointment hit Luke simultaneously—excitement about the day off, but disappointment because Captain Tom had not given him an answer about salvation.

A day off while Bobbi was still on the island! Another answered prayer. Maybe he would have a chance to talk to her about their relationship. He wanted her to know how he felt. He had tried on Sunday afternoon. Tuesday off! A whole day with Bobbi! Hopefully, she didn't have other plans. He and his family had received a last-minute invitation to Bobbi's aunt's party that night, so he could find out then if she was busy tomorrow. Bobbi would be leaving on Wednesday morning, which meant he wouldn't see her until school started in three weeks.

CHAPTER 23

Good-bye to Bobbi

*R*osa looked a bit nervous as she walked up the path to Rosario Resort with her arm through Luke's. Adam had declined the invitation, not wanting to miss baseball practice.

"You look especially beautiful tonight, Mom," Luke whispered as he opened the lobby door for her. She did. She had put on a touch of makeup and spent extra time with her unruly curly hair. She had pulled it up in the back and let some of the curls near her temples soften her face. She wore a new dress she had gotten for her trip to Hawaii. It was the perfect shade of blue, setting off her dark olive skin.

Luke knew this could be a difficult evening for the both of them. The circle of friends that Aunt Jane had been visiting all week were not the crowd that the Johansens socialized with. They were the crowd that the Johansen family had always worked for—the rich country-club set that came in from the mainland for the summer and weekends. Though, as a Miers, Rosa had been in better standing in the

162

community, she had lost some of that prestige when she married a Johansen.

"Hey, I thought you worked today." Luke shook Steve's hand.

"I came back on the ferry tonight, just so I can see Polly one more time. Then tomorrow, it's the early ferry for me," Steve explained. Steve was accepted in this crowd, as his father was the only pharmacist on the island and friendly with everyone, regardless of social standing.

Aunt Jane had reserved half of the main restaurant and the outside patio for the party. The decorations were fantastic, lots of large exotic flower arrangements, orchid corsages for all the ladies, and even an ice sculpture surrounded by more flowers.

"She must have had all this flown in from the mainland," Rosa whispered to Luke.

Aunt Jane kept Polly and Bobbi close to her side, introducing them to everyone. Luke noticed that most of Aunt Jane's friends had college-age sons or nephews in tow. It was like one of those East Coast coming-of-age parties. Luke barely got to say hi to Bobbi and tell her that she looked lovely before the dinner was served.

Afterward, he did get a few minutes with her out on the patio. "I have the day off tomorrow. Will you spend the day with me?"

"Yes, that's wonderful. But Aunt Jane has declared Tuesday to be "stay at the resort day." She says we have been wandering around all over this island and have not even enjoyed the amenities of the resort. Would you be too awfully bored if you came here and we swam in the pool or played tennis?"

"Well, the pool would be fine, but I don't know how to play tennis. How about if I bring *Matilda* by and give all of you a ride around East Sound?" Luke did not want to make a fool of himself in front of the whole resort.

Steve walked up next to Bobbi at the same time as Dr. Robertson and his son came up next to Luke. Unfortunately, they heard his last statement. Dr. Robertson was close to retirement and owned a summer home that was larger than the winter homes on the island. It turned out that his winter place neighbored Aunt Jane's. His wife and Aunt Jane were close friends.

"Now, Bobbi, I have just the young man for you to meet. This is my son, Harold. He is a freshman at Harvard. He happens to have the day off tomorrow from his summer internship in Seattle. I thought you might enjoy having him give you a guided tour of the island." Dr. Robertson slid in front of Luke with his back to Luke as if Luke did not exist. Harold, a skinny, bookish young man, looked like he was totally lost and kept looking down at the floor, not saying a word.

Bobbi looked a bit confused for a moment. Then she said, "Excuse me," politely danced past Dr. Robertson, and grabbed Luke's arm, forcing Dr. Robertson to turn around. "I'm afraid that won't be possible, Dr. Robertson. I already have plans tomorrow with Luke." She smiled up at Luke.

Dr. Robertson looked shocked at having been outmaneuvered. Luke struggled to keep from laughing.

"Well, Steve, it is good to see you." Dr. Robertson turned to Steve without acknowledging Luke. "It is nice to hear you have a job off the island this summer and plan to make something of yourself. So glad you're not in the dead-end job of crabbing like some young men. I hope your tennis game is in good shape. Sounds like Bobbi will need a partner."

Dr. Robertson grabbed his son by the arm and turned on his heel and left before Steve could reply.

"Poor Harold," Bobbi said.

"Should I go after the guy and make him apologize to you?" Steve asked Luke.

"No, it's not worth it. Besides, you don't want to get in a fight with Bobbi's future father-in-law." Luke glanced at Bobbi, a twinkle in his eye.

"Luke Johansen!" Bobbi exclaimed and gave him a playful punch on the arm.

The warm summer sun beat down on Bobbi as she floated on the inner tube tied off *Matilda*. Water drops glistened off her tanned skin. Luke floated nearby in another inner tube. Every once in a while he splashed some water in her direction, but never with enough force to make the spray reach her. They were both exhausted after a long, vigorous swim. The green forest surrounding East Sound framed the shimmering blue water.

She didn't want to leave tomorrow morning. This day was going by too fast. She wanted to relax and float on the water forever.

Luke had arrived in *Matilda* at ten in the morning. They had gone swimming in the pool with Polly while Aunt Jane sat reading in a lawn chair nearby. After a poolside lunch under one of the big plantation umbrellas, Luke gave the ladies a cruise around East Sound on *Matilda*. An hour later Luke dropped Aunt Jane and Polly off at the dock, then took the boat twenty yards offshore and anchored. Luke and Bobbi dove into the still water and swam laps to a buoy and back for twenty minutes.

Bobbi kept stealing glances at Luke. What a mystery. Every male of the species that she knew would have been angry with Dr. Robertson last night. Men's egos are a fragile thing, her mother had always told her. Luke didn't seem like the kind of guy to be a doormat. He seemed confident, but not stuck on himself. She liked it but didn't understand why he was so different. So far she had not seen any sign of a temper. She admired his self-control.

"Hey, it's getting close to time that we get back for dinner." Luke paddled his inner tube over to the swim platform. "Want me to pull you in?"

"No!" Bobbi wailed. "I don't want to go home!"

She started to paddle in. Luke helped pull her in the rest of the way when he realized she was teasing. They sat on the swim platform facing each other.

"I really don't want to go home tomorrow. It has been so much fun here," Bobbi said.

"I know. I don't want you to go. I'm going to miss you." Luke gave her a very serious look and then he took the plunge. "There is something we need to talk about and have settled before school begins. It's about us. It isn't easy to talk about all of this, but I think we both need to know where we stand and set some goals."

"Goals? Oops!" Bobbi realized she had responded out loud. What did goals have to do with this? "OK, go ahead."

Luke hesitated. Maybe she wasn't on the same wavelength as he was. Maybe she just liked him as a friend and did not feel this bond and attraction that he felt. But he had to know, and keeping silent would not give him the answer.

"I believe the Lord brought me to Olympia for three main reasons. To get better Bible teaching, to get better schooling, and to meet you. I'm not sure, Bobbi West, but I think we could have a special relationship. One that, if properly developed, might become a lifetime one. I'm very attracted to you. But this needs to be a relationship that is put together God's way, not man's. We need to take time to build the friendship part of our relationship first. That means we would be a bit of an oddity at school. We might both take some flack about it. I want to build this slowly and minimize the physical side of it as long as we can. I want what my grandpa and grandma Miers had."

Bobbi had been half-smiling, looking at him and not saying a word. She put one foot in the water and kept swirling it around and around. "That is a lot to think about, Luke Johansen. I'm not sure I know what to say." She paused for a few moments, looking at the scenery around her and then straight at him. Blushing, she said, "I feel the attraction, too. It's almost like an unseen bond between us. I have tried not to think about it."

Luke relaxed. "You feel it too?"

"Yes...I do know that I agree with you, and I want this relationship on God's terms."

"That's good! So it's a deal, then?" Luke smiled and put out his right hand for a handshake.

Bobbi laughed and shook her head back so her damp hair fell behind her shoulders and then shook hands with him. "Only you would start a relationship with a handshake, Mr. Johansen. But I like it. Hopefully it means that we know what we're doing. Now, you have to tell me more about these grandparents of yours."

They sat on the swim platform a bit longer, and Luke told her all about his grandparents and their special marriage. Bobbi sat spellbound and he described the special childhood memories he had of them.

After dinner, Luke and Bobbi walked down to the Rosario dock. "I need to get going. Looks like a stiff wind has picked up."

"Yeah, plus it's best if you reach dock before dark," Bobbi agreed.

"I'll call at least once a week." That would put a strain on the phone bill, but Mom would understand. "And I'll write."

"I'll write too." She helped him cast off.

Luke kept looking back at her. She still stood on the dock as he rounded Diamond Point. Three weeks seemed like a very long time.

CHAPTER 24

Fog

A thick heavy fog enveloped *The Claw*, making a cold, dripping wet working environment. So cold that Luke had actually put a sweatshirt on for the first time all summer. He shivered as he baited a crab pot. So the hot weather had ended, and they were back to normal Pacific Northwest weather.

Luke set the pot and watched it disappear in the fog. He hoped they would be able to find it again. He knew they were on the southwest side of Blakely Island. Exactly where was a guess. *The Claw*'s radar system didn't work. It had stopped working in June along with some engine trouble. With the good weather, Captain Tom hadn't bothered to invest the money in fixing it. Luke reassured himself with the fact that Captain Tom knew these waters like the back of his hand.

There had only been two other days of fog so far that summer. It had been the light friendly kind that made the sun look like the moon and burned off by midmorning, leaving wisps of clouds around the islands, like beautiful lacy shawls. He couldn't remember a fog this thick. He could barely see the bow of the boat. Usually he didn't mind the fog. This was different. The heavy air pressed in on his body, and its thickness gave him an eerie feeling.

"It's about zero visibility," Captain Tom mumbled as he headed to the cabin.

"Yeah. My mom didn't think we should go out today. The radio said that they cancelled the Port Townsend to Keystone ferry run this morning." *Mom might have been right*, thought Luke.

Luke baited more pots, trying to ignore the fog, and thought about a happier subject—Bobbi. It had been a week since she had left. He had called her twice and written to her every other day. He missed her. He wished he could just see her and be with her for a few minutes each day. She had written almost every day since she left. Her notes with little sketches were great.

Silence interrupted Luke's thoughts, dead silence! *The Claw's* noisy engine had stopped! Captain Tom and the engine had been in a constant conflict all summer. It hadn't wanted to start several mornings and had run rough several times, but never this. Stopping in the fog with no control of the boat wasn't a good thing, especially this close to Thatcher Pass!

Thatcher Pass, a narrow body of water created by Blakely, Decatur, and Frost islands, was a pivotal point on the Anacortes ferry run. Would the ferry's radar be able to pick them up before they rounded the wide south point of Blakely Island? Even if the radar spotted them, the ferry captains were used to any boats in their course scurrying out of the way.

Helplessness flooded over Luke. *We could run aground. Willow Island—we could hit Willow Island!* He wished he knew where they were in relationship to Blakely Island; then he would know how much trouble they were in.

Luke looked at his watch. The 10:00 A.M. ferry would be coming through in just fifteen minutes! Captain Tom went below to work on the engine. Luke went to the cabin and started sounding the horn every two minutes. In between toots, he found some old flare guns, matches, a bullhorn, and two life vests. *Lord, please help me think straight!* he prayed.

"Here, you need to put this on!" Luke had donned a vest and brought another one down to Captain Tom. "You do realize we're close to the ferry run, and it's coming through in about twelve minutes, don't you?"

"You really know how to pressure a guy. I always said this old girl's hull was stronger than the ferry's. Maybe we'll get to find out." Captain Tom stopped working on the engine for a minute, stood up, and looked Luke square in the eye. "I have one order for you. Promise you will obey?"

"What?"

"Promise?" The old captain yelled.

"OK."

"You're to abandon ship if you see we're going to crash. Now get back up on deck and sound the horn!" Captain Tom turned and started in again trying to get the engine going.

On the way back up the ladder, Luke asked the Lord for wisdom and asked for the fog to lift enough to see where they were. Up on deck, the fog seemed even thicker, if that was possible. He looked over the port side and noticed that they were moving at a good speed. A current had caught them. He estimated they were going about three knots. He went to the cabin and sounded the horn again. Then he looked at the compass. They were traveling southwest, right toward Thatcher Pass. *Must be an outgoing tide,* he thought.

A knot formed in his stomach. He didn't like being on a moving boat and not able to control it or know where they were going. He sounded the horn and remembered the story of David and Goliath. *The ferry's my Goliath and the Lord's bigger than the ferry. I need to trust the Lord and relax. David claimed that the battle was the Lord's, and this situation is the Lord's, too.* Luke thought of Isaiah 41:10: "Fear thou not, for I am with thee: be not dismayed for I am thy God; I will strengthen thee; yea, I will help thee; yea I will uphold thee with the right hand of my righteousness." A wonderful calm came over his soul and he relaxed.

He sounded the horn a third time and stepped outside the cabin. Then he heard it, the drumming of the ferry engine. It didn't seem too far away. A chill went down his spine. He grabbed one of the flare guns, lit it, and shot it into the air. It exploded in the dense fog, giving off a few seconds of muted pink light. Luke hoped that the ferry could see it. They must be in the middle of Thatcher Pass, and the ferry had just rounded the point. *Please, Lord, make them see us!* The ferry's engine sounded closer and closer. He went back and sounded the horn again.

"We are dead in the water!" Luke yelled over the bull-horn several times. He didn't think that the ferry attendants would be able to hear him above the ferry engines, but he had to keep trying everything he could think of. He didn't like Captain Tom's wry joke about who would do better in a crash. The ferry was at least four times the size of *The Claw*. They wouldn't have a chance.

Luke grabbed two more flare guns and shot them off. Then, a miracle! The fog opened up for about two hundred feet off the bow of the boat, and for a split second he could see the ferry. There it was, about one hundred fifty feet ahead, coming straight at them. He started to run back to the cabin to grab another flare before the fog closed in again, but he slipped on the wet deck and fell. He crawled the few feet to the hatch.

"Captain Tom! Get on deck! Now! It's going to hit us!" Luke yelled down the stairway.

Luke stood up on the starboard side. *Should I jump?* Then he heard the ferry engine slow, go into reverse, and then idle. They had seen *The Claw*! In those few seconds of visibility they had seen them! He knew they still might hit. A large ship like that couldn't stop its momentum that fast. At least it wouldn't be at full force.

Captain Tom came up on deck in time to hear the captain of the ferry on a bullhorn. "Will the fishing vessel please respond?"

Luke handed Captain Tom the bullhorn, but it didn't seem necessary as Luke could feel the ferry coming closer.

"I'm Captain Tom of *The Claw*, and we're dead in the water."

The fog lifted for a few feet again, and they could see the ferry just off the port side less than twenty feet away. They weren't going to collide. Luke's legs turned to jelly. He wanted to kneel down on the deck and praise the Lord, but he had to get the stern and bowlines ready. There was a lot of yelling from the ferry attendants once they saw *The Claw*. They threw out their own lines to Luke, which he quickly tied over cleats on the bow and stern of *The Claw*. The ferry crew walked the old boat back to the stern of the ferry. Slowly, they started forward, heading for the Lopez Island dock.

Land never looked so good, thought Luke, as they got close to the island. It was hard to make out the dock and the shore of Lopez through the fog.

"We have an extra passenger," one of the ferry attendants yelled to the dock attendant. "We will need your help. Got an old fishing vessel tied off our port side near the stern. Found it dead in the water, floating just to the east of Frost Island."

So that is where we were, thought Luke. Nice to know.

The passengers for Lopez unloaded, and the ferry attendants moved *The Claw* to a smaller emergency dock.

"I want you to grab your things and catch this ferry," Captain Tom instructed him. "They're still loading. Here's money to pay for your ride. Please call Susan when you can and let her know that I'll be on the six o'clock run. I'm afraid this might be the end of our crabbing. This engine's a goner. I'll call."

Luke wanted to stay and help, but Captain Tom wouldn't hear of it.

"Nope, no need to pay for a ticket. You're riding for free," the ferry attendant insisted. "We're glad that you're alive. The captain would like to talk to you. Follow Jim here to the wheelhouse."

"How did you know that we were in your path?" Luke asked the captain, once he was in the wheelhouse and introductions had been made.

"Well, we'd just rounded the south point of Blakely and saw this funny pink glow in the fog ahead. I thought it must be a flare, so I quickly looked down at my radar and saw a boat in the middle of the channel. As you can see, the fog is not quite as thick at times up here on the bridge. That is what made it possible to see your flares. Glad you set those off. Must have been a scary feeling, floating there helplessly in that fog."

"It was, sir, but I also knew that the Lord would take care of us," Luke responded.

"Well, chalk it up to what you want. Just glad that it turned out OK. Seems as if that old boat has seen its end." The ferry captain brushed off Luke's reference to the Lord's protection and changed the subject.

Luke knew the captain was right. *The Claw* had died. It was sad to see it end that way. She was still a sturdy old boat. But Luke knew that Captain Tom couldn't afford to put a new engine in her.

CHAPTER 25

"Roughing It"

*T*wo weeks of summer left, and no job. Luke mulled over his situation as he sat on a bench outside the marina store at Deer Harbor. Captain Tom and Susan had invited him for dinner the night before. They had settled up accounts and said their good-byes. *The Claw* had been sold to a boatyard in Everett. Luke had called every possible place he could think of on the island, trying to find two weeks' worth of work. *Lord, You know I need a job. Help me to be patient as You work out the details. Amen.*

Luke had been saving all his money that summer to buy a car. He was so close to having enough. His mother didn't like him spending the money, but he needed "wheels" if he was going to live in Olympia. Mom would need the '57 Chevy. He wanted to be able to come home to Orcas once a month. Plus he knew that he couldn't rely on his dad to take him to madrigal practices, church, or school events.

"I finally got a hold of Dad last night. And I let him know that I will be moving back to Olympia. He seemed distracted and in a hurry. He won't be driving me anywhere." Luke had presented his argument at dinner the night before.

His mom gave him a disappointed look. "But you need that money for college!" she insisted.

"The past four summers I have put everything away for college, Mom. I've got enough for one or two years. Besides, you can't afford to buy another car, and you and Adam will need the one you have. Let me do this. It is my way of helping out. Uncle Hank has a friend in the car business, and they are going to help me find the right vehicle."

Rosa had given in just because she had no other solution to offer.

"Luke Johansen?" a deep voice interrupted Luke's thoughts. A tall man in his late forties stood in front of him.

"Yes, that's me." Luke stood up and held out his hand.

"I am Ted Harrison. I hear that you are mighty handy on a boat. I have need of another deckhand. My boat is out there at the end of the south dock." Mr. Harrison shook Luke's hand and turned slightly to point to the end of the marina.

Luke turned and looked out at the far end of the south dock. A large, white seventy-two-foot yacht floated off the end of the south dock. It looked brand new. "Wow! That's some boat!" Luke had never seen a pleasure boat that big.

"We like her. Would you like to come on board while I explain what the job entails?"

"Sure."

"John, in there at the store, gave you a very good recommendation. He told me how you lost your job and said you might need some work for the next few weeks."

Luke glanced in at the marina owner through the store window and saw the "thumbs up" signal John gave him as they walked past the window and out to the boat. *Care Free* was the name on the stern.

"My wife, our two sons, and I have been in the islands a week. We were at Roche Harbor, Stuart Island, and Friday Harbor. We kept having trouble with one of our deckhands. He stole wine out of the stock down below and worked drunk most of the time. I fired him this morning."

"Sorry to hear about it."

"We are planning to stay for another ten days. We want to go up to Sucia Island, then down to Rosario Resort and to Spenser Spit, but we will need another hand to do that. You would be required to help take her back to Seattle, get her through the Ballard Locks, and into her slip at Lake Union. You'll receive a fair wage and be flown back home when the job is all done." Mr. Harrison finished up the job description as they arrived at the boat.

"Welcome aboard! I'm Captain Jim and this is our deckhand Bob."

"Thanks, I'm Luke." Luke stepped onto the large swim platform and shook Captain Jim's hand. "This is some boat!" Luke wanted to whistle but knew it would not be polite.

Luke wondered why the sons couldn't help out, when Mrs. Harrison, a medium-height redhead in her early thirties, appeared holding the hand of a three-year-old boy and balancing a baby on her hip. Luke smiled at the thought of one of them helping with the lines.

"Ted, could you please come inside and help me with something?" Mrs. Harrison asked.

"I'll show Luke the sleeping quarters, sir," the captain offered. He pressed a button, and the wall of the swim platform opened into a large walk-in engine room.

Captain Jim opened a door off the engine room, and inside was a small cabin with two berths. "You'll share this with Bob."

"Looks like he has the bottom bunk, so I guess the top one would be mine."

"It may seem small, but for crew quarters they are ample. These are the best people to work for. You should take the job. He pays generously and is not overly demanding. The food is very good. Mr. Harrison expects us to keep the outside spotless. The butler sees to the inside and the Harrisons' personal needs, and does the cooking."

"How soon do you need an answer, Mr. Harrison?" Luke asked when they were all back up on the main deck. "I need to check on a few things at home first."

"The sooner the better, but by tomorrow morning at the latest. I hope you will join our little cruise. John indicated you know the San Juans fairly well and are a responsible young man."

"Thank you, sir. I should be able to give you an answer by eight o'clock tonight. Will that be all right?"

"Great, see you then."

"I have a job, Mom." Luke walked into Rosa's studio. She sat at her fifty-four-inch Macomber loom, beating the beam hard. She stopped.

"Where? How?" she asked.

"By God's grace, and on the biggest yacht you have ever seen! It has two tenders, one the size of *Matilda*—the other's a twelve-foot pram—and they have bikes stored in the engine room. It even has a motorcycle on board for when they are at dock!"

"How do you know these people?"

"John recommended me for the job. He's known Mr. Harrison for a long time." Luke had stopped by the store on his way back to the house and asked John about his future employer. "John says they are from a very old Seattle family. I want to take the job, Mom. It looks like it would be a lot of fun."

"One more time! One more time!" Little Samuel floated in a small child's inner tube in the shallow warmer water on the east side of Sucia Island at Echo Bay. Luke spun him around again. It was Luke's afternoon off, but he had taken a liking to the little fellow and offered to take him to the beach to build sandcastles and play in the water. During the morning, the tide had been low and the sun had beat down on the sand. The afternoon high tide came in over the sand, making nice warm swimming conditions for the young boy.

Luke looked out at the yacht. He could see Bob polishing the railings, a job that Luke had started that morning. They had been there two days. Luke had showed the captain the best mooring area in Echo Bay. The boat was too big for the smaller coves on the island.

Luke brought Sammy up to the beach. Then went to his beach towel and glanced at the last part of the letter he'd written to Bobbi:

> Captain Jim was right about the job—easy work and incredible food. Mr. Harrison expects us to keep the outside polished and looking good, but we get plenty of time off each day. I can use the twelve-foot tender if the family doesn't need it. Yesterday, in the morning I took it around into Fossil Bay and had a good swim.
>
> Looking forward to school starting and seeing you again,
>
> Luke

Luke didn't like how he signed the letter, but he didn't know how else to sign it.

"Love" didn't work; they weren't at that point yet, and "sincerely" sounded too formal. He packed up his things. "It's four-thirty, Sammy. Time to go back to the big boat and get ready for dinner." Luke picked up little Samuel and put him into the twelve-foot pram and headed back to the yacht.

They pulled up anchor early the next morning and headed out for Clark Island. They stopped there for a four-hour break. The Harrisons took the larger tender around the island and then went ashore with a picnic basket. The crew stayed on board. They docked at Rosario just before dinner. Luke called his mom and mailed his letter to Bobbi. The Harrisons went to dinner at the restaurant and left the boys with the butler.

"My, oh my!" Adam let out a low whistle as he and Rosa walked down the ramp to meet Luke. "That's a ship!"

"Not quite." Luke smiled. "I have permission to show you the main lounge, galley, dining room, pilot house, and my quarters. We aren't allowed down in the family's state-rooms or up on the fly bridge." He took his mother's hand and helped her on board.

"Just look at this dining room set! It's rosewood, I believe." Rosa carefully ran her hand over the back of a dining chair, then looked around the room. "The colors are fabulous. They must have hired a designer."

"Do you eat here?" asked Adam.

"No, we eat on the back deck or at a table in the engine room."

The *Care Free* spent four days at Rosario. Luke wrote two more letters to Bobbi. Rosa brought him his mail and some blackberry cobbler. Saturday night he went home for a few hours and called Bobbi.

Hearing her voice made his heart beat faster.

"I will be in Seattle Wednesday night or Thursday morning. I'm going to stay with Uncle Hank and Aunt Sophie for a few days and look for a car." Luke let her know his plans.

"Really? Will you be there on Friday?" Bobbi asked.

"Most likely, why?"

"Because I'm driving up with Mom to Frederick's to go shopping. We're going to the Friday fashion show and lunch. Would you like to come?"

"Fashion show?"

Yes, Mom and I go at least twice a year. The models walk between the tables, and you can ask them to stop and turn so you can see every detail of the outfit. Mom went to college in fashion design and had her own business for many years before I was born. I let her know which outfits

I like best, and then after lunch we go down to the fifth floor and pick out the right fabric for each outfit. Maybe you could meet us for lunch on Friday?" Bobbi asked again. "The restaurant is on the eighth floor of the Fredrick and Nelson's store."

"I'll be there." *A fashion show?* Luke thought. Well, anything for another chance to see Bobbi.

The Harrisons were delighted to hear about Luke's church, and on Sunday morning they gave Luke a ride to the service. Mr. Harrison had secured the use of one of the resort vehicles.

Early Monday morning a chartered floatplane from Seattle brought in fresh produce and food for the yacht. Fully stocked they shoved off for Spenser Spit on the northeast side of Lopez Island. They anchored on the south side of the spit.

Luke looked up from his Bible and out at the yacht. What a job and what a dream world. He had the afternoon off and had taken the smaller tender into the beach. The larger tender sat in its perch at the back of the fly bridge. Luke looked down at his Bible again and started reading. Suddenly he heard little Samuel yelling.

"Help! I want...Help!"

Luke looked up and saw Samuel in his inner tube floating about two hundred feet from the yacht. A current had caught him, moving him quickly toward Frost Island. The narrow passage between the spit and the island was a passage frequently used by boats and no place for a child to be floating. Luke plopped his Bible down and took off running down the beach. As he ran Luke noticed Sammy starting to thrash around in his inner tube.

"It's OK, Sammy! I'm coming!" Luke yelled, hoping to calm the youngster, who needed to stay still to be safe in the inner tube.

Luke dove into the water and swam out to the little boy. They were still a hundred yards from the narrow passage by Frost Island.

"It's OK, Sammy. You calm down. I've got you! Now I'm going to take you in to shore." Luke reassured the little boy. Luke checked Sammy's position in the inner tube, grabbed the line on the side of the inner tube, and started swimming a modified side stroke so he could keep an eye on the youngster.

Luke got him into shore and sat Sammy in the tender. "Stay put now. I'll be right back." He picked up his Bible and his towel and loaded everything into the boat. By this time the whole crew and the Harrisons were on the back deck watching his every move.

"He's fine," Luke yelled out to them as he pushed the tender off from the shore.

"You were supposed to be watching him!" Luke could hear Mrs. Harrison say to Mr. Harrison as he brought the small boat up to the swim platform of the *Care Free*. "How did he ever get way out there from the fly bridge?"

"I fell asleep. Last I saw he was playing with his puzzle on the table." Mr. Harrison looked shaken. He picked up Samuel out of the tender, took him out of the inner tube, and gave him a big hug. "How did you get way out there?" he asked his son.

"I wanted...go swimming," Samuel answered, shivering from the cold water as he spoke.

"Well, I am very glad you put on your inner tube. That was the good thing. But you are *never* to go swimming without an adult around. Do you understand?" Mr. Harrison scolded the little boy and then handed him to his mother. Mrs. Harrison wrapped Sammy in a towel, hugged him, and they disappeared inside.

Mr. Harrison turned and helped Luke tie up the tender and thanked Luke profusely.

"I don't know what I would have done if I had lost him....You have certainly earned your keep. Thank you so much."

Wednesday afternoon, as they got closer to Seattle, Captain Jim signaled Bob and Luke to come to the pilothouse.

"Are you two ready for the Ballard Locks?"

"Yes, sir. We put the fifty-foot lines on the bow and the stern just like you asked us to." Luke tried to contain his excitement; going through the locks was something he had always wanted to do. Uncle Hank had taken him to watch the boats go through the locks several times.

"And we'll have plenty of fenders out," Bob added. "I showed Luke what height."

"Because we are a big boat, we will be on the 'wall' of the big locks, and several smaller boats will raft off of us. Luke you have the bowline. You are to keep the boat in control as it rises." The captain warned, "There will be a current caused by the water being pumped into the locks that will fight against the bow and make the bow of the boat pull away from the concrete wall of the locks. Don't let the boat hit the wall or pull too far away from it. You'd better go and get the fenders set."

"Keep a constant pull with the line against the cleat. Take up the slack as the boat goes up and you won't lose control," warned Bob as they entered the large concrete locks at Seattle.

Bob's advice proved valuable. Luke pulled steadily, keeping the boat in control as it rose. He could see how even an experienced deckhand could lose control for a second and end up causing the boat to do a one-eighty degree turn in the locks. He had heard stories about boats doing that. With all the other boats packed into the locks, if he lost control of the bow it could be a disaster.

They were quite the show for the tourists and visitors. Mrs. Harrison and her sons had disappeared down into their staterooms, while Mr. Harrison stayed on the fly bridge. As the boat came up to the lake level, Luke could hear people making comments. "Look at that boat! Have you ever seen something that big?"

"I wonder if those boys are the owner's sons?"

"No, they must be the deckhands. See the shirts they're wearing with the name *Care Free* above the pocket?" The whispers kept coming.

They docked the boat at the southwest side of Lake Union, near the bottom of Queen Anne Hill, but their job wasn't yet over. It would take the evening and the next morning to wash and clean the boat. He took a short break and called Uncle Hank and Aunt Sophie and told them he would be done at noon the next day. The Harrisons and their butler had packed up and headed to their Seattle residence on Lake Washington.

It was noon on Thursday when Mr. Harrison returned to the slip. He had paid the captain and the other deckhand, and they had taken off. "You did a great job," Mr. Harrison said to Luke.

"You have a decision to make. I have your money here in this envelope. I heard that you were saving up for a car. My wife and I were discussing last night about what we could do for you to thank you for saving our son. You see that 1947 Willys Jeep paneled wagon out there in the parking lot? It's yours if you want it. It is mine, but I never drive it. I just had our butler drive it over."

Luke looked over to the parking lot, and there in the front row, with the butler standing next to it, was the Jeep. *That's cherry!* he thought, silently admiring the blond wood paneling. It sat higher than others he had seen; it must have special tires.

"A Jeep! Wow! But Mr. Harrison, I can't accept that! It is worth way more than the amount I worked."

"Yes, you can, son; you gave us the best gift of all—our son back safely. If you had been a few minutes slower or not such a strong swimmer, he could have been hurt or drowned. We could not have gotten to him in time. We will always be grateful to you.

"If you would rather have the money, I understand. There is $1,500 here in the envelope, about the same value as the Jeep."

"May I please have a few minutes to think about it?" Luke didn't want to rush such a major decision. He walked out to the parking lot, said hello to the butler, and looked the Jeep over. What a cool thing it would be to own. It could handle any terrain—snowy mountain roads or sandy ocean beaches. He wouldn't have to worry about the roads or weather traveling back and forth to Olympia. Plus it only had twenty-two hundred miles on it.

"Hey, Luke! Are you all done? What's with the Jeep?" He turned to see Uncle Hank walking toward him.

"Well, I think it's going to be mine." Luke grinned from ear to ear.

"What?" Uncle Hank said in surprise. Luke explained the situation to his uncle.

"Come out to the yacht. I'd like you to meet Mr. Harrison.

"*The* Ted Harrison?" Uncle Hank asked.

"Yes, that's his name."

Uncle Hank looked impressed. "Do you know who he is?"

"No, I have no idea what he does," Luke responded.

"He owns several businesses in town, and his family is very well-to-do. I'll tell you more about him later." They walked out to the yacht.

Luke made the proper introductions. Then he told Mr. Harrison he would accept the Jeep and thanked him profusely.

"Here is the title in this envelope. You will have to go with my butler and get the title transferred. It has been a pleasure getting to know you. My business card is in the envelope too. If you ever need anything, young man, give me a call. Even if it is years from now, don't hesitate to call." Mr. Harrison walked back down the dock with them to the parking lot.

CHAPTER 26

Seattle

*T*here he is, Mom. I knew he'd come. He's most likely late because he couldn't find a parking spot. I forgot to tell him to park in the parking garage." Bobbi had just spotted Luke waiting in the foyer of the restaurant. She waved big and caught his eye.

He is so *handsome,* Bobbi thought as he walked to the table.

"Sorry I'm late, but I didn't give myself enough time for parking." Luke confirmed Bobbi's assumption. "Seattle traffic is heavier than I'm used to."

"Did you get a car? Oops, the fashion show is starting. And here's our waiter again. You need to order." Bobbi did not give him a chance to answer.

"Oh! Bobbi, take a look at that outfit! What do you think?" Mrs. West asked.

"For you or me?" Bobbi asked. It wasn't something she liked.

"For me, silly. Now Luke, you order anything you want. This is my treat." Mrs. West barely looked up. She quickly sketched the outfit modeled by the skinniest woman Luke had ever seen. *Is she alive?* Luke wondered.

Luke leaned over and whispered to Bobbi, "Why are all the women so skinny? And why does she keep twirling that card with number one on it?"

"Luke, all models are thin. The card corresponds with our program." Bobbi whispered back, while holding her program for Luke to see. Then she raised her voice. "Now, there is the pantsuit I want, Mom. It's just perfect."

Mrs. West looked at her program and underlined number two. "The program says it's Vogue pattern #1086."

"But you can't wear that to school. You know the dress code," Luke interjected as the waiter served him his lunch.

"It will be fine for evening church or other times when I'm not at school." Bobbi was not going to give up on that outfit. "Besides, there are some girls working on getting the code changed so we can wear pants to school."

Luke quickly realized he needed to keep his comments to himself. Mrs. West kept sketching, taking a bite of her salad once in a while. She and Bobbi shared a running commentary about each outfit. He now knew why Brad and Mr. West didn't come on these outings. He would make sure he missed the next one. He really couldn't see much difference between the dresses they were critiquing, and he didn't know there were so many starving women in the world. He felt like he needed to give them his lunch. Why would anyone think they were the best way to show off clothes? *Well, the best part is watching Bobbi enjoying herself*, he thought.

Finally, after an hour it was all over, and it was time to go to the fifth floor and find the right fabric.

"What about this soft plaid flannel for your pantsuit?" Luke pulled out a bolt of blue plaid fabric. Bobbi gave him a horrified look. He gave up and retreated to the corner with a few abandoned husbands. He watched Bobbi hold fabric up to her face in the mirror, make a face or smile, and then hunt for another bolt of fabric.

"It's best if you leave them alone," one of the husbands informed him. "They get through it faster."

"Thanks for the information. As you can tell, I'm new at this."

"They only bring us along because they can't carry it all," another husband chimed in.

Luke laughed. He was glad that Bobbi had been too busy to ask any more questions about the car. He wanted to show it to her and see her expression. Finally, the two women finished their shopping.

"I have something that I want to show you. It's just down the block. Then I'll get all of this to your car." Luke's arms were full of packages just like the man had said.

"There it is. See, the second one after the lamppost." Luke stopped to watch Bobbi's expression.

Bobbi stopped and made a face. "A Jeep? Why did you buy something so ugly?"

Luke flinched. "But it's a cool vehicle. They don't make these anymore. They're hard to find. The neat thing is that it can go anywhere. It doesn't even need a road. We can go to the mountains or the ocean and not worry about the weather or getting stuck." *Why doesn't she like it? Uncle Hank thinks it's the best thing since ice cream.* He gave her the condensed version of how he got the Jeep. She seemed to warm up to it some.

"It's just not what I expected." Bobbi back-peddled. She could see that she had hurt his feelings. He was a proud parent showing off his child. "I like it if it's what you wanted."

"Well, we need to get going. I am sorry to break this up, but we do want to be back in Olympia by dinner." Mrs. West had been standing back, watching this little scenario. "Luke, you don't have to carry the packages to our car. We can carry them." She started to take one of the bags out of his hand.

"No. I'll walk you to your car. It won't be any bother at all. I thought it would be nice not to have to be concerned about the weather conditions this winter when I drive up to Orcas and back." Luke continued to think of all the points he could to make Bobbi like the Jeep. It wasn't possible to take it back now.

"How am I going to get in and out of that thing in a dress?" Bobbi hurried along Fifth Avenue, trying to keep up with her mom and Luke's longer strides.

That had been Aunt Sophie's point when she saw the Jeep. "No young lady will be riding with you," she had commented.

"Well, Uncle Hank says he's seen them with a small running board added on to the side. Or I can just be the gentleman and lift you into the seat." Luke smiled, trying to make light of the situation.

"Or she can just wear the pantsuit all the time," Mrs. West joked and paid the parking attendant. He brought the car around.

"OK, I will see you in three days. I'll call when I get to my dad's." Luke opened the car door for Bobbi and shut it slowly. Even three days seemed like a long time.

Luke left Seattle with the windows down despite the cool, cloudy weather. He owned a Jeep! He couldn't get used to the idea. At least his mother should be happy that he didn't spend any of his college money. Not bad pay for ten days of work. *This is a gift from the Lord, a perfect*

example of God's grace I don't deserve. "Thank You, Lord!"
he shouted.

Adam came out of the garage where he had parked his
bike. He stopped suddenly when he saw Luke parking the
Jeep. "Wow! Do you have any college money left? Mom's
not going to be happy with you."

"No it's not like that—"

"Luke Johansen! That's not a car!" Rosa stood in the
kitchen doorway, looking at him like he had lost his mind,
her hand on her hip.

"OK, you two, you have to wait until you hear the whole
story." Luke put his arms up in defense. "Mom, I didn't take
a penny out of the bank. It's all intact, even the money from
this summer. This is my pay for working on the boat."

"You're kidding!" Adam ran his hand down the sides
and looked over the dashboard. "What a paycheck!"

Rosa looked relieved. "Well, I have clam chowder on
the stove and fresh cornbread. Why don't you tell us about
it over dinner? We're eating in the kitchen. It's too cool to
eat outside."

Over dinner Luke filled them in on the rest of the boat
trip and the reward he had gotten at the end.

BOOK 3
Senior Year

1947 Willys Wagon Jeep

CHAPTER 27

Back to School

Senior year! This is my senior year of high school!" Bobbi laid out five outfits on her bed and held them one at a time up to her face in the mirror, trying to decide which one she should wear. Rain had been forecast for tomorrow, according to Mrs. Larson. Bobbi had overheard her conversation when she picked up the phone to return Luke's call. He had called while she was out riding Missy. There were rumors that they were going to get private telephone lines out their way soon. Bobbi hoped they were true.

She liked the blue and white outfit the best.

"Luke's on the phone again." Brad poked his head around her bedroom door. "What's this, a clothing store? Better hurry up before Mrs. Larson gets on the line again. I think that lady lives on the phone."

Bobbi hurried to the kitchen and picked up the phone. "Are you all ready for tomorrow?"

"Yeah, I think so. I found my oldest pair of jeans with the most holes and a T-shirt I wore crabbing most of the summer." Luke had learned the hard way last year. The guys at Oly always wore the oldest and worst clothes they could find. The girls wore the nicest, newest thing they had for the first day of school. "Things aren't too good here with Dad. Not sure what to do."

"What's going on?"

"Deanne has moved in and is living with him. He told me that it's a final decision, and he doesn't want to hear any self-righteous sermonizing or he will cut off Mom's child support."

"But he can't do that. He's required by the courts to pay that," Bobbi answered.

"Yeah, but he won't change. I'd like to move out, but I won't be eighteen until March. Got any ideas?"

"How about just telling your mother what's going on?"

"I don't know. She doesn't even know about Deanne. I never told her because I didn't want to hurt her more." Luke didn't like keeping secrets from his mother, but he still thought it was the best decision.

"The only other idea is praying about it."

"You're right. Meet in the music building before school? The weatherman is predicting rain."

"See you in the music building."

The rain never materialized. Instead, a semi-cloudy day welcomed the students back to Oly High.

"Hey, you look nice." Luke met up with Bobbi.

"And you look cool." She smiled. "It feels different being a senior. There's something very final about it."

"Yeah, and it seems like the mood has changed around here. Did you notice all the guys with long hair?" They started walking toward the gym for the school assembly.

"Yes, and some of the girls look like models for the new hippie movement. See that group of girls over by the cafeteria building? They all have long flowery dresses. And look at the rough-looking sandals! I do like the flowers in their hair." Bobbi hadn't seen anything quite like that at the Frederick's fashion show.

During the assembly Principal Bain reminded everyone of the dress code and looked at the senior class the whole time he recited it. He made no bones about the fact that they were not his favorite class.

"Antiwar stickers are everywhere—on people's cars, notebooks, and lockers." Luke commented as he ate lunch with Bobbi on an outside bench.

"A new political awareness has evolved, and the main topic is Vietnam in every class."

"Well, one thing stayed the same, mixed chorus. Ready for madrigal practice tomorrow morning?"

Bobbi groaned. "It's so early in the morning. Oh, did you hear the announcement? We have a new ski coach. He called a meeting after school today, so I can't go out in your boat."

"There will be other times." Luke looked at his watch. "The bell's about to ring. I'll walk you to art class." Luke gathered up his books. "And then the next time I'll see you is in independent study English."

"Yes. Have you thought about your thesis topic?"

"Not yet. See you later." Luke left when they arrived at the art room door.

The last period of the day Bobbi and Luke sat by each other in the library conference room. The teacher explained the schedule on the board. "We meet as a class three times a semester: today, in two weeks to present your outline and thesis topic, and during finals week to turn in your written thesis and present it orally. The rest of the time you are free to study on your own in the library or off campus. A panel of three faculty members will decide your final grade based on your written and oral presentations."

"Hi. I'm Mr. Hendricks. Please put your name and phone number on the sheet I'm sending around. Up here on the blackboard is the conditioning schedule."

Bobbi looked at the board: stretching, one-mile run, stairs, weights, and dry-land courses. *He's taking coaching way more seriously than the last one,* she thought.

"We start in a week. Please wear appropriate workout clothes," Mr. Hendricks said.

As she headed out to the student parking lot she heard Scott yell, "Hey, Bobbi, can I have a ride tomorrow morning to madrigals?" Scott Thompson lived over by Big Fish Trap. He ran to catch up with her. Scott had been friends with Bobbi since third grade. He made it into madrigals this year.

"Sure, I'll pick you up at—"

"No, my dad goes to work early and he can drop me at your house," Scott interrupted. "Will six thirty be OK?"

"That's when I'm planning to leave. We have to pick up Patty Banks," Bobbi replied. She took a note off the windshield of her VW bug and opened it.

Bobbi,

I'm going out to the marina to eat dinner with Charlie. I'll call you later tonight.

Luke

Bobbi left ski team practice not sure if she could walk another step. They had been at it for a week. "Warm up" exercises, run a mile, then run the stadium stairs, weights, and then run the courses that Mr. Hendrix had set up. Mr. Hendrix had a system of tall metal drums set up to represent the bamboo poles used for ski races. He set up a slalom and giant slalom course, and once everyone mastered them, he would change it a bit and they would start in again. He wanted the team to be good at reading courses. Bobbi liked the weights, the courses, and the running, but the stairs of the football stadium scared her because they were so steep. Her balance and depth perception weren't very good. She feared she might fall and get hurt.

Today, unfortunately, most of the team had cheated on the mile run, and Mr. Hendrix caught them. He penalized all of them with one hour of running the bleachers.

By the time Bobbi met Scott at her car, she didn't feel like talking.

"Say, I saw you talking to that new guy from mixed chorus after school. What's his name, Jim?" Scott asked as he settled into the passenger seat.

"Yes, it's Jim." Bobbi had been nice to Jim, trying to make him feel at home. Apparently, Jim had gotten the wrong idea, because that afternoon before ski practice he had asked her out. She was still upset about it.

"Sorry, but I couldn't help but overhear him ask you out when I walked by. Don't get me wrong. Jim is a nice guy and all, but you better not go out with him. He doesn't seem like a good match for you."

Bobbi drove out of the school parking lot. "Who put you in charge of my social calendar?" she retorted. *This is too much. He gives me advice, acts like my big brother and now he tells me who I should date? Well he can just stew about it.* She had politely turned Jim down. She hated hurting people. If only Jim hadn't misread her intentions.

"Well, I don't want you to mess things up with Luke just because this Jim guy asked you out." Scott persisted. "Luke's a great guy."

Bobbi didn't answer. She gave him a dirty look and picked up the pace a bit. They flew through Priest Point Park in no time. She didn't notice the sunshine and cloudless sky; hunger gnawed at her stomach, every inch of her body ached, and Scott had stepped over his bounds.

Scott noticed the scowl on her face, got the message, and pulled out a book to read. As they passed Gull Harbor Mercantile, he glanced at the speedometer. This had to be the worst mood he'd ever seen her in. "Hey, want to let up on the pedal some, Lead Foot?" He hoped she would slow down.

She gave him another angry look, turned back to look at the road, and put the gas pedal to the floor in defiance. They quickly shot up to over seventy miles an hour and rounded the wide, gentle curve about a block after the store. There sat the sheriff on the far side of the curve, his radar gun poised, ready to catch the oncoming traffic. He immediately put on his siren and signaled to Bobbi to pull over. She pulled in front of the sheriff's parked car and put her head down on the steering wheel. *Could this day get any worse?* Now her temper had done her in.

"Well, we are making a habit of this speeding thing, aren't we, Miss West?" the sheriff asked as he walked up to her car. "Do you have any idea how fast you were going?"

Bobbi raised her head slightly. "Too fast, sir," she mumbled.

"Sir, it was my fault," Scott started in.

"Were you the one driving, Mr. Thompson?"

"No, sir."

"Well, then I suggest that you keep quiet and let Miss West and I finish our business." The sheriff took his time writing out the ticket. "Here you go, young lady. Twenty-two miles over the speed limit is inexcusable. You will be required to appear in traffic court."

Bobbi dropped Scott at his house, barely saying good-bye. She was in big trouble.

"I think someone had a very exciting afternoon." Brad passed the potatoes and grinned at Bobbi.

Bobbi looked up from her liver and onions. She had been deep in thought about how she could get that gross meat down her throat. One glance at Brad and she knew he knew about her speeding ticket. She had hoped to bring the subject up after dinner when her father and mother had eaten and were relaxed. Now, she had two problems—how to eat the liver and what to say to Brad. Her parents had a hard and fast rule that they had to eat what was set before them.

"Ski team practice today, right?" Mr. West asked.

"Yes, and it was brutal. I arrived late and had just started running my mile when the coach caught the rest of the team cheating on theirs. We had to run the bleachers the rest of the practice. I'm not sure I'm still alive." *OK, one problem averted for a few minutes. Now this liver. Where's Lassie?* Bobbi's eyes darted to the side of her chair.

"I know that this is not your favorite meal, but it is very good for you. It's full of iron, and we have to have it every so often. Now, don't try feeding it to Lassie." Mrs. West smiled and ordered Lassie to the kitchen.

Bobbi had been successful many times in slipping food that she couldn't handle to the fat beagle. But tonight would not be one of those times. Why did she have such an aversion to certain foods, like steak or roasts or this liver? Just the thought of those things almost made her gag—and then to have to eat it! It didn't help that her father referred to the meat they had two years ago as "Glenn Burgers." She had mourned the loss of her favorite steer. She hadn't known he was scheduled to be butchered, and she came home that afternoon and saw him half-gutted, hanging up next to the barn.

"No, ski team wasn't what I was referring to." Brad continued to smirk and took a huge bite of his liver and onions, chewing it slowly and savoring it like it was the best thing in the world, grinning and taunting her the whole time.

Jealousy swept over Bobbi for just a second. How could he eat everything under the sun and not gain a pound? He liked every single type of food. She wondered why she had the squeamish stomach *and* the tendency to gain weight. And he always did everything right. He hardly ever got into trouble. She often felt like she had three parents rather than two.

"OK! I got a speeding ticket on the way home from school." Bobbi burst into tears and started to get up from the table.

"Now, you just sit down here for a minute, young lady, and tell us about it." Mr. West spoke very quietly, but firmly.

"Dad, you aren't going to go soft on her, are you?" Brad always felt his father favored his sister.

"I want to hear what happened from her."

Bobbi wiped her eyes with her napkin and filled her parents in on the story.

"Next, I would like to know how you found out about this, young man," Mr. West said to Brad.

"Well, when the activities bus stopped at the store, Bobbi went speeding by. By the time the bus got to the curve, we all saw the sheriff giving Bobbi a ticket."

"I guess you had a front row seat. Well, young lady, you have had quite a day. If you would like to be excused from the table, you may. We will talk about it later."

"But, Dad, she hasn't even touched her liver and onions," Brad complained.

"Brad, enough!" Mr. West insisted and Brad kept quiet.

"Would Luke Johansen and Debby Robertson please report to the principal's office right after the announcements are finished?"

Bobbi sat doodling in homeroom that Thursday morning. *What is that all about?* she wondered. *Debby is one of the smartest people in school. And Luke hasn't done anything wrong other than forgetting to call me last night.*

After the dinner discussion, Bobbi had gone to her room for a good cry. Then she pulled out her Bible, confessed her sins of anger and self-pity, and got right with the Lord. *Sometimes life is just unfair. I should have kept my eyes on the Lord while I ran the bleachers, and then the rest of this mess wouldn't have happened.*

After mixed chorus Bobbi finally got a chance to talk to Luke.

"So what did the principal want? Did he catch you T.P.-ing his office?" she teased. A group of senior guys had done that the week before, and Bobbi knew Luke wasn't one of them.

"No. You better sit down." Luke guided her to a chair in the multi-level band room. She sat down, and he stood on the step below her. Then he leaned closer to her, resting one foot on upper riser. "Remember that test we had to take on a Saturday last spring?"

Bobbi nodded. "The SAT, right?"

"Right. I guess if you do well enough on it, you can get college scholarships." Luke went on. "Well, I qualified for a full ride to most any college in the whole country. So did Debby."

"Oh, my!"

"It's called a National Merit Scholarship. My mother's going to be happy. She won't have to worry about how we're going to pay for college. I can't wait to call her tonight." Luke grinned from ear to ear.

"That is fantastic! What's your score?" Bobbi asked.

"Fourteen fifty. By the way, you must be feeling better than you were last night. Sorry you were sick," Luke said.

"Who told you I wasn't feeling well?"

"Brad. When I called last night, he said you weren't feeling well and weren't taking any calls," Luke explained.

"That dirty rat." Bobbi felt her anger rise. How dare he decide who she could talk to. "I never told him that. I had kind of a bad afternoon and evening. I waited for your call."

"Oh. What happened?"

Bobbi filled him in on the afternoon's events, starting with Jim asking her out, ski team, and the ticket.

"I will most likely lose my license again. I'm so sore it really hurts to walk. We have another practice after school today. And who knows what punishment my dad is thinking up?" Bobbi moaned. "Sorry, but you did ask what was wrong." She and Luke laughed, and he walked her to econ.

CHAPTER 28

Relocating

While Bobbi sat in homeroom listening to the announcements Friday morning, she heard, "Will Luke Johansen report to the principal's office?"

My, this is getting to be a habit. What could it be this time? Bobbi thought.

Luke wasn't in mixed chorus and not anywhere to be found the rest of the day. What had happened? She couldn't help but worry a bit.

Luke left his homeroom and headed right for the office. There in the lobby of the administration building stood his mother!

"Mom? Is everything OK?" Had something happened to Adam?

"No. They said we could use this counseling room." His mother pointed to a small room off the lobby. They walked in and Luke sat down at the table. She slowly closed the door and stood up against it with her arms folded across her torso. Rosa glared at him for a full minute, making it clear that for some reason she was very angry with him.

"Why didn't you tell me that Deanne had moved in with your father?" she exploded.

Luke hadn't seen his mother this angry for a long time.

"I will not have my son living under those conditions." She walked over and pounded the table with her fist, making Luke jump. She continued through clenched teeth. "I would have expected you to fill me in on the problem. You usually have a level head on your shoulders."

"How do you know about Deanne?" Luke asked in surprise.

"I called yesterday at lunchtime. Deanne answered the phone. We had a little chat!" Rosa started shaking her finger at him and her voice rose. "Why didn't you let me know what was going on?"

"I didn't want to tell you about her because I didn't want to hurt you any more than you have been hurt. I tried to figure out a solution, but Dad threatened to take away your child support money if I did anything."

Luke's apologetic tone stopped Rosa. Her face softened as soon as he mentioned not hurting her. She walked over to the table, sat down, and covered her face with her hands. Silence reigned for a few minutes.

"Are you OK, Mom?" Luke took one of her hands away from her face and held it.

Rosa looked at him, defeat covering her face. "I suppose it is my fault for not telling you the entire reason for our divorce. I've known about Deanne from the start. She is the reason for the divorce. Your father promised me she would not be around when he took care of you and Adam."

So that's why! That jerk! Luke's jaw tightened and he clenched his fist. *It's a good thing Dad isn't here.... Took care of us? He ignored us!*

They sat in silence.

"I didn't want you and Adam hating your father. He needs your love, though he may not know it." Rosa tried a weak smile.

Finally Luke let go of her hand and gave her a shortened version of what had happened the past school year. "What do you suggest that I do, Mom? I want to stay here in Olympia. But since I'm not eighteen yet, I can't live on my own."

"There isn't anyone else you can live with? Is there someone at church? What about that old guy at the marina? Would he have any extra room?" Rosa perked up, and her color started to come back.

"Charlie? I don't know if he would even want me there. I know there's an upstairs, but I'm not sure what condition it's in. Charlie never goes up there because he can't."

"Well, I am not leaving Olympia until we get this settled. I have permission for you to miss classes today. Let's take a ride out to the marina." Rosa snapped into action.

Rosa quickly walked through the door as Luke held it open. "So this is the famous Boston Harbor Marina. You must be Charlie. I'm Rosa Johansen, Luke's mother." She didn't give Luke a chance to make introductions. She and Charlie shook hands.

"What brings you out this direction, Mrs. Johansen?" Charlie didn't look good. He had lost weight and looked a bit uncertain and shaky.

"Well, Luke has a problem. Do you want to explain it to him, Luke?"

"Sure. It looks like I'm in need of a place to live, and we were wondering if you might like to have a boarder." Luke hesitated. "I'm willing to pay you."

"Wow. Well, there's no more room on this floor...but there is the upstairs. It was my original residence, but once I ended up in this thing," he patted the wheelchair arms, "they moved everything I needed down here. You two can go up and take a look if you want. It will need some major cleaning."

Luke and Rosa went up the back stairs. At the top landing were two doors—one that led out to the street and one that led into a small entry, then into a large room with a terrific view. A sofa plus a small dining room table and chairs were still up there. They took a look at the empty bedroom, bath, and kitchen minus the stove and refrigerator. It *did* need of a lot of cleaning.

"It looks like the dust bunnies have become large rabbits. Well, you will need a bed, but the sofa is all right, and you can study on this dining room table. What do you think?" Rosa looked happier than she had all morning.

"I think it'll work," Luke replied. "The Wests might have an extra bed in their basement. I thought I saw one when I visited last winter. Maybe they would let me borrow it for the school year."

"Let's go down and talk to Charlie some more. I would like to get you moved out of your dad's place today."

Charlie had warmed up to the idea. "On one condition. You're not paying rent. You were the one who brought this marina back to life. I'll always owe you for that. Besides, I will enjoy having the company."

Luke used Charlie's phone and called Mrs. West. "Of course you can borrow the bed. But wait until Brad gets home from school. The headboard is heavy and he can help you."

"That should do it, Charlie. Ring it all up." Rosa placed another bottle of cleaning solution on the counter. "Oh, can we use your vacuum?"

"It's all yours. It's in the closet."

Rosa and Luke headed back upstairs and got to work. By early afternoon they had the place looking pretty good.

After school Brad helped Luke move the bed and set it up. Once Brad left they looked around the place.

"Now we need to go and get your things at your dad's place." Rosa looked apprehensive.

"Mom, let's pray." Luke sat down on the sofa and Rosa joined him.

"Father, please help us say and do the right things. Help me treat my dad with respect. Keep Mom from being hurt. In Jesus' name, amen."

"Amen." Rosa echoed.

"No one's home." Luke stood at the door of his dad's house. "Come on in and help me pack." Rosa left the side of the car and joined him.

As Rosa folded the last shirt and placed it in Luke's suitcase, she cocked her head. "That's a car that just pulled in." Her face drained.

Luke went downstairs and checked. "It's Dad. Come on down."

As Luke and Rosa loaded Luke's things in the car Mr. Johansen walked up to them, a frown on his face.

"What's going on?"

"You broke our agreement." Rosa turned and confronted him.

"What?"

"Deanne has been living with you. I talked to her yesterday. Didn't she tell you?"

"No."

"I still have full custody of this one until he is eighteen," Rosa reminded her ex-husband. "He only lived with you because I said he could. Now, I say he cannot, and he will be staying with Charlie!"

"OK, Rosa, OK." His dad fidgeted.

Why isn't Dad protesting the move? Luke wondered. Maybe he feels guilty about what he did to Mom and about the lifestyle he's living.

Luke shook hands with his father. "See you later. I'll call."

The two stopped at J. C. Penney downtown and got Luke some bed linens and bath towels. Then they picked up some food at Safeway. Everything was all set.

When they got back to the marina, Rosa made her famous spaghetti, a big salad, and garlic bread for Charlie and Luke.

"Now, how often are you going to come down and cook for us, Mrs. Johansen?" Charlie teased. "I could get used to this."

Rosa laughed. "I still have one more at home to raise. Dinner's ready. Come to the table."

Charlie cleared his throat. "Luke, would you mind saying grace?"

Luke tried to contain his surprise as he gave the blessing.

During the meal Luke noticed that when his mother talked about the Lord, Charlie seemed interested. Maybe Charlie's heart was softening. Wouldn't that be wonderful if he would believe?

Luke lay in bed, wide awake. He could hear his mother lightly snoring as she slept on the living room sofa. It had been quite a day! He acknowledged he had made a bad decision in not telling her about the situation with his dad. He was glad it was out in the open.

Saturday morning they woke to the foghorn going full bore.

"It's going to take some getting used to, having that foghorn so close," Luke mentioned at breakfast. Charlie had beat them to the kitchen and had scrambled eggs with cheese and onions, bacon, and toast waiting for them when they came downstairs.

"Can I borrow your kitchen for a while this morning?" Rosa asked Charlie. "Thought I might make several batches of cookies for you two before I leave." Luke and Charlie broke into smiles at the idea.

Luke went out to the docks to check on everything, and at nine o'clock one of the neighbor boys showed up for work. The fog began to burn off. It was going to be a beautiful September day.

Luke looked up at his new home above the store. *OK, Lord, why have You brought me here?* he prayed. *I know You always have a reason. I'd just like to know what it is.*

CHAPTER 29

Charlie

*R*osa left right after lunch, and Luke headed over to Bobbi's. He found her working with the horses in the "little pasture." He helped her groom Missy after she finished her ride. Then they worked with Lady, who had been recently halter-broke.

"She's quite the filly. Every time I see her she's sprouted a few more inches," Luke commented as Bobbi worked on her turns. "She has a lot of spirit and attitude."

"Yes, but she is still afraid of the rain," laughed Bobbi.

"The rain?"

"When she first came home the vet ordered her to be kept inside during the rain, to prevent her from catching cold. He said she was so weak she could get sick easily. Now, every time it rains she heads for the barn. Right, baby?" Bobbi petted the filly, then let her loose to play.

Luke and Bobbi went to the beach and rowed around Zangle Cove in the Wests' eight-foot pram and talked about the week's events. So much had happened.

"I'm so glad you're living close by. Now that you have a scholarship, what schools are you thinking of?" Bobbi asked.

"The school counselor says that I should apply to several schools. He suggests at least three out-of-state schools. But I don't want to be that far away. I'm going to apply to University of Washington. It has a great science department." Luke did not want to leave the Northwest because of his mother. If she had a relapse he wanted to be close by. "What about you?"

"Well, Mrs. Miller says the best vocal instruction would be at Pacific Lutheran University in Tacoma, unless I went someplace out of state like New York. I guess there's an excellent vocal school in Italy. Mrs. Miller gave information about it to my mother. I would really like to go to a Bible college, but my parents aren't too keen on the idea."

Luke's eyebrows rose. "Why don't they want you going to a Bible college?" He thought for sure that they would support that idea.

"Something about needing to graduate in something I can make money at. You know, in case I never get married or my husband dies. Dad wants me to have a university education." Bobbi made a face.

"What about being an interior designer? You're always buying house magazines, you took that drafting class, and you sketch all the time." Luke was sure Bobbi would be over with something to spruce up his meager living quarters.

"No, that's not what I want to do. Dad took me over to Washington State University in Pullman, and I toured their design department. I liked it, but I want to do something with my music."

Luke rowed the pram to shore and they headed up the trail. Mr. West was working in a flowerbed near the trailhead. He placed a new rhodie into a hole he'd just dug.

"Are you staying for dinner, Luke?" he asked.

"Not tonight. Thank you, though. I think I need to get back and make sure Charlie eats a good meal."

"That sounds like a good idea. Bobbi says he has been looking a bit poorly ever since he took that fall a month ago. So, I guess we will see you at church tomorrow. If you want a ride, we can swing by and get you." Mr. West tapped the loose soil around the rhodie down with his foot.

"What fall?"

"He fell getting from his bed to the wheelchair one morning, and one of the dockhands found him on the floor. He had been there for several hours. Bobbi kept going over and helping out until school started. I thought you'd told him about it." Mr. West looked at Bobbi.

"No, Dad. Remember? Charlie made me promise not to tell anyone except you and Mom. He's so darn independent."

Luke headed back to the marina with his thoughts on Charlie's condition. He'd better check a few more things out. He wondered if Charlie had enough insulin.

"OK, dinner is served." Luke walked back into the store with a salmon on a plate. He had taken advantage of the nice weather and barbequed out on the deck. He brought out the leftover salad from the night before.

Again, Charlie asked him to say grace.

"I suppose you will be going to church tomorrow." Charlie brought up the subject as they started eating.

"Yes, the Wests offered me a ride. I should be back by one, so don't wait for me at lunch time."

"Well, I was wondering if maybe I could go with you?" Charlie took his time asking the question. "But if that puts a damper on your plans, I don't need to tag along."

"No, I mean, yes. I mean, I want to take you to church, and it's not a problem at all." Luke couldn't seem to get the words out right. "I don't know about getting you into the Jeep. That could be a problem."

"We can take my car. You can drive it. We might need to get gas before we head home. I haven't driven it for a while."

"How long is a while, Charlie?"

"Over a month."

"Over a month? So what have you been doing with the bank deposits, and what about your insulin?" Luke knew that food wasn't a problem, as Charlie got his food and other supplies for himself when the vendors delivered to the store.

Charlie turned red and looked down at his plate for the longest time. "Well, I have the last month's deposits in my closet in my room. They are in bags, separated by week, each with a deposit slip. But I need to get the money in the bank so I can write checks. It's been too hard to even think of driving into town."

Luke got up and went to the refrigerator. There were two vials of insulin on the refrigerator door shelf, one almost empty. "So, when were you planning to tell me that you needed help?"

"Not sure. I just hate being a bother."

Luke walked over and leaned on the table with both hands and stared Charlie in the eyes. "You're not a bother." He sat down, and they finished their meal in silence.

Stubborn old man, Luke thought. *His pride just keeps getting in the way.*

Luke did the dishes and then called Bobbi to decline the ride to church.

"I'm so glad he wants to go!" she exclaimed.

After dinner, Charlie brought out the deposits and the store books. He and Luke came up with a plan for weekly deposits that Luke would take care of. Charlie explained his bookkeeping for the store, his budget, inventory, and accounts. When they were all done, it seemed like a big weight had been taken off his shoulders. He acted happier than he had in a long time. He even challenged Luke to a game of Chinese checkers and beat Luke four times.

"Four out of five does it, Charlie. It's time to hit the hay. I'll see you in the morning for breakfast." Luke headed up to bed.

Luke lay in bed praying. *Well, Lord, I think I know Your answer. You have me here to take care of Charlie. Just please give me the wisdom and the strength to do it right.*

Luke almost jumped straight out of bed at the first foghorn blast. *You sure don't need an alarm clock around here*, he thought. *That's worse than a rooster.* He looked at the clock; it was only five thirty. He didn't feel the least bit tired, so he decided it would be good to get an early Bible study in before church. At six thirty he heard the downstairs shower going, so he knew Charlie had gotten up. It was his chance to cook breakfast. Luke decided on hash browns with sausage, onions, and mushrooms mixed in. Soon the aroma filled the store.

"Wow, does that smell good!" Charlie opened his bedroom door and rolled out.

Luke smiled. "It's all ready. Do you want to say grace this morning?"

"No, I'm not on talking terms with the Maker yet." Charlie bowed his head, waiting for Luke to pray.

"Do you have a Bible, Charlie?" Luke asked after he prayed.

"Yes, I dug it out of my bottom desk drawer about three weeks ago. I remembered someone telling me to start reading in John. I have been doing that, and I am partway through Genesis, too."

"That's great!" Luke responded. "You might want to take a small notebook to write down verses and what the pastor says."

After breakfast, Luke did the dishes, and they both finished getting ready. As he wheeled Charlie up the ramp and got him into the car, Luke thought about how Charlie had done this all by himself for a long time.

The Wests pulled into the church parking lot just after Luke and Charlie did. Brad came over to help with Charlie.

"Hi there, Charlie! We're glad you could come to church this morning. How about if I give you a push into the church and we can let those two lovebirds walk in together?" Brad grabbed the back handles and pushed Charlie inside.

"I think our prayers are being answered." Bobbi whispered as she put her arm through Luke's, and they headed into church after her parents.

Charlie went with Mr. and Mrs. West to the adult Sunday school class. Then they all sat together during church. Brad saved back row seats and took out a chair so Charlie could park his wheelchair next to them. Pastor Ralph gave the gospel clearly several times.

After church, Luke took Charlie out to Bob's Big Burgers. They were halfway through their cheeseburgers when Charlie finally started talking.

"I'm glad I went. A very interesting morning. Your pastor answered a few of my questions. It's a bit different than the church I went to."

"When was that?" Luke asked.

"When I was a boy. My parents made me go every Sunday. We never took a Bible to church or read one at home. Just had to show up at church to meet everyone and look good in the community. When I left home to join the Coast Guard, I never went to church again. Just never saw the need." Charlie leaned back in his chair with a far-off look in his eyes. He was obviously thinking about the old days. "Then when I had my accident I was angry with God for letting me lose my leg. But after that fall I had in August, I began to realize that I couldn't fight God anymore. Now, I'm having a hard time with the fact Jesus would do all that, that He would die for me. Then all He asks in return is that I believe?"

My, he's at a crucial point, Luke thought.

"It's that simple, Charlie," Luke explained. "That is the ultimate love. He died for our sins even though He never sinned. He loved us so much He died for us. You just have to believe."

They finished their meal and went to get gas in the car before heading back out to the harbor. Luke had been curious how Charlie had lost his leg. But now wasn't the time to bring that up. The issue at hand was Charlie's need for Christ.

"Looks like you're all ready for Monday classes. So, did you have a nice time with Bobbi yesterday?" Charlie asked as he wheeled over to the table with oatmeal for Luke.

"Yeah, we got a lot of homework done yesterday afternoon. Youth group went well last night. How about you? Did you get that nap you were wanting?" Luke asked.

"Yes, I did, and then I had a real long Bible study. Luke, I'm now ready to meet my Maker. I'm in His family. I believed last night, right here at this table. I couldn't eat dinner without praying, and I knew that I couldn't really pray about anything to the Lord until I got salvation taken care of. So, if you don't mind, I would like to say grace."

"That's wonderful news, Charlie! I'm happy for you! Welcome to God's family." Luke bowed his head and it sounded like music, Charlie saying grace.

CHAPTER 30

Traffic Court

My, it's cold for October 11. Luke shivered. He sat in the fuel dock shack all bundled up in a coat, hat, and gloves, reading *Hamlet,* preparing for his English thesis on the common characteristics of Shakespeare's protagonists.

Normally, he didn't work the fuel dock anymore. Charlie now had four neighbor boys working different shifts. But the Saturday boy had called in sick, so Luke offered to take his place. Luke had rebuilt the fuel shack that fall. Even though it didn't have big gaps between the wallboards anymore, it wasn't heated, and it got fairly cold when you were sitting still for long periods of time.

Bobbi had gone skiing at White Pass with a group from the ski team. The lifts weren't open yet, but there was enough snow at the top to ski a medium-distance run. They were going to get one ride on the chair to the top and then they would be skiing and hiking back up for the rest of the day.

Luke missed her. He put *Hamlet* down and started thinking back over the last few weeks. They were getting to know each other better. Since they had two classes together at school, and church together, he got to see her every day. He had been invited to eat dinner with her family each week. She would come over for a meal with Charlie and him once in awhile. She would also come by with freshly baked cookies or cake. Just as he had expected, Bobbi and Brad had come over to see his new digs. Then she had returned a few days later with several throw rugs, some pillows for the sofa, a night stand, coffee table, and floor lamp for next to the sofa.

There were lots of adjustments in madrigals. Twelve of the members were new. Many of the new members were very serious about their music and had taken private voice lessons for years. Some of the girls weren't too happy with Bobbi as the nodder. They wanted to be in charge and lead the group by nodding and using slight hand motions. Mrs. Miller had paired Luke and Bobbi so they walked on stage together. It gave Luke a chance to give her a last-minute Bible verse or word of encouragement as they walked in for a performance. There had been a lot of speculation that this could be the most talented madrigal group that Oly had ever had. Each member was a competent soloist. However, Luke didn't think that they were as good as last year's group because they weren't working together as a team. He just kept hoping things would get better.

The "just being friends" routine with Bobbi was working so far. Luke often asked the Lord for the strength to keep it that way. There were times, though, he wanted to take her in his arms and start kissing her.

He had taken some flack from the guys in gym class about his relationship with Bobbi. They asked questions of a sexual nature, and he let them know that his relationship with Bobbi was none of their business. Another time he explained that he wanted to do things God's way and wait until he was married to have sex. Boy, they hooted and hollered about *that!* It was interesting, though, that the guys who gave him the most razzing were the ones who hadn't even been on a date. Big talkers. He really did not care what they thought; he only wanted to please the Lord.

So he walked around school being polite to everyone, but pretty much keeping to himself. He missed Joe. However, he and Scott were talking and spending more time together.

Bobbi, on the other hand, went around happy and friendly to everyone. She didn't give in to peer pressure, she accepted people as they were.

The past three weeks with Charlie had been great. At dinner they would talk about the Lord, the sermons that Pastor Ralph had given, Charlie's adventures in the Coast Guard, where Luke might go to college, and the day's events. They were becoming family. Luke helped more with the ordering, plus keeping the store and marina books. Charlie had lost interest in running the marina. Almost all the mooring slips were rented out, and people were coming in for fuel consistently. The best part was taking Charlie to church and watching him grow spiritually. Luke enjoyed Pastor Ralph's teaching even more this year. He wanted to get started on Greek lessons again, but it seemed impossible to find the time.

Now he needed to get back to *Hamlet*. He had set aside tomorrow's study time after church with Bobbi for pre-calculus.

After Sunday dinner Luke and Bobbi sat down at the Wests' dining room table to study. Bobbi had lot to tell him about the ski trip. "The way the weather is going, the ski resorts might be opening soon. It looks like the winter of '69–70 is going to be a great ski season."

Luke smiled at her. He liked it when her brown eyes danced with excitement. He opened his pre-calculus book.

"You know that Charlie's birthday will be coming up soon." Bobbi started sketching a sofa. "I think it's the twenty-fourth, a Friday. Maybe we should plan something."

"How old is he going to be?"

Bobbi kept sketching. "Don't know. He never gives out much information about himself. I didn't even know that he had been in the Coast Guard until you told me." She looked up at him, her eyes wide. "How about if we ask the Boston Harbor School if we can have the auditorium and invite the whole neighborhood? Have one big surprise party!

"How are the studies going?" Mrs. West walked through the dining room.

"Mom, what do you think about having a big surprise party at the school for Charlie?"

Mrs. West liked the idea, and the ball was in motion. Within a few hours, several women from the community were helping her plan the event.

Luke was assigned to keep Charlie in the dark about it, then take him to the school the night of the party. At least he had a bit of time to think up a way to do that.

Luke helped Charlie out of the car. He had gotten him to the school by telling him that there was going to be a community meeting about the new private telephone lines, which would be available at the beginning of November. That meeting was actually going to happen, but not for another week. Luke feared Charlie might get suspicious because he had insisted that Charlie wear one of his best shirts.

Luke rolled Charlie into an auditorium full of people. As soon as they saw Charlie everyone started singing "Happy Birthday" to the elderly man.

"What's this?" Charlie looked up at Luke.

"It's your birthday party." Luke rolled Charlie over to the place of honor set up for him.

"Looks like you have candles to blow out and cards to open. Wow, what big cards!" The schoolchildren had made six oversized cards, almost twenty-four inches tall. The cards had been passed around the community for people to sign. People started to form a line to wish him well.

Luke realized that the four elderly men talking to Mr. West had Coast Guard veterans' caps on. Luke walked over to join them.

"I am sure that he is older than I am, and I'm seventy-nine," one of the former Coast Guard men said to the group.

"Well, I know that he is not over eighty-two. He joined in— Now, there's someone who could tell you how old Charlie is." They all turned and watched another elderly man in a Coast Guard jacket walk through the door. "He went to high school with Charlie, and they signed up together."

"How did all these men know about the party?" Luke asked Mr. West.

"My wife is the best detective in the world. She thought it would be special for all of them to come, so she contacted the Coast Guard Veterans' Association." Mr. West turned to the older gentleman. "Did I overhear you say that Charlie is eighty-two?"

"Yes, I have known him for seventy years," the old man replied.

"Well, gentlemen, let's go over and see if he remembers all of you." Luke led the group over to where Charlie sat.

Charlie just stared. Then he smiled, and a few tears started to slip down his face. It wasn't long before the old comrades were laughing and telling stories about the old days.

"Kathy, have you seen Bobbi?" Luke asked one of Bobbi's girlfriends. Kathy lived in the harbor, on a hill to the east of the marina.

"I think she is sitting over in the corner by the door. She seems kind of bummed out. We didn't have much time to get the decorations up and the food out. We were working at a pretty fast pace," Kathy answered.

"Hey, there you are. I have been looking for you. You pulled it off! Charlie was very surprised. Your father and I know how old Charlie is!" Luke had found Bobbi over at the far end of the auditorium. She sat watching everyone else.

She looked up and forced a smile at Luke as he sat down. "OK. So spill it. How old is he?"

"Eighty-two and that is official, from a man who went to high school with him. So, I don't think you had enough candles on the cake. Why the sad face tonight? Oh, that's right. How did it go in court?" For a moment Luke had forgotten that Bobbi had gotten out of school early to appear in traffic court. Her dad had picked her up, and they had gone together.

"Let's just say not good. I won't be driving for a long time. Do you mind if we take a walk outside?"

"No."

Boston Harbor School consisted of two buildings—an old, wooden, white building with the auditorium at the back, and a newer, one-story brick building. They walked around the brick building in silence and ended up at the swings. Luke waited patiently. He knew she would talk when she was ready.

Bobbi sank down in a swing. "The judge took away my license for three months. He seemed nice and understanding. I agreed that I had been speeding. He told me that I would lose my license for two months, and then my dad got into the act." Bobbi looked at the ground for a minute and then continued. Her voice started to crack, and tears rimmed her eyes. "I'm not even sure how it happened, but all of a sudden they were yelling at each other. I do remember my dad telling the judge that it was a perfectly nice day and the curve was well banked and I had every right to be going that speed. Before I knew it, I had lost my license for three months, and the judge put me on probation until I am twenty-two! Dad almost got in trouble."

"So, your dad argued with the judge?" Luke tried to picture the scene. He wanted to laugh but knew Bobbi wasn't in the mood. She didn't answer. She just kept gently rocking and looking at the ground. Luke walked over to her, grabbed her hands, pulled her to her feet, and gave her a big hug.

"You know that the Lord will work all this out. You need to leave it with Him," Luke whispered to her. Bobbi kept shaking, and he realized she was crying. Then she stopped. He helped her dry her tears with his handkerchief. "Besides, I have wheels, and I'll make sure you get wherever you have to go."

Bobbi nodded and smiled, and they walked back in to the party.

CHAPTER 31

Thanksgiving

Swish, Swish. The big carving knife made a noise as Aunt Jane waved it in the air. They were all sitting at Aunt Jane's and Uncle Ray's dining table, and she kept waving the knife as she told about their last family vacation instead of carving the turkey. Bobbi looked at her watch. At this rate, they were never going to make the ferry. It was two o'clock already, and they needed to be in Anacortes by six. She and Brad were going to do a "walk-on" at Anacortes, and Adam and Luke would meet them at the Orcas Island ferry dock.

Thanksgiving was one of two holidays that the Wests spent with the Jameses, Aunt Jane's family. The other one was Easter. At Christmas, the Jameses always left for Mexico or Hawaii, and the Wests were left on their own. Both of Mr. West's parents had gone to be with the Lord years ago, and his other sister lived in Australia.

Three days at Orcas and staying at Luke's house! Bobbi tingled with excitement as she thought about it. Brad winked at her across the table. She knew he was thinking the same thing. He couldn't wait to see Adam again. They hadn't seen each other since Brad's trip to Orcas that summer.

"Mom, I think the turkey might be getting cold," Polly said very quietly and respectfully. She interrupted her mother's saga when Aunt Jane stopped to catch her breath. Aunt Jane started carving again. Polly smiled at Bobbi.

Polly seemed different this visit. Usually she would take Bobbi into her room and show off all her new clothes from the best stores in Seattle. When they were younger, she would show off her latest toys and dolls, desperately trying to impress Bobbi. This time Bobbi and Polly had sat and talked before dinner. She had mentioned her youth group and church several times and asked Bobbi about her church. Bobbi had assumed Polly was referring to the same church that Aunt Jane and Uncle Ray attended.

"Well, young lady, you wanted to say grace." Uncle Ray looked at Polly.

Polly gave a refreshing prayer. Not the usual mumbled, meaningless "nothing" often heard at that table.

"Polly is quite independent now that she has her driver's license and is going to her own church," Uncle Ray explained as they passed the food. "She has become a regular fanatic just like all of you, and she goes two or three times a week."

"Really? What church are you going to?" Mrs. West asked.

"It's a small, independent Bible church about a mile away. I visited their youth group about a month ago. They really teach the Bible. The second time I went there I finally understood that I needed to believe in Jesus Christ to be saved, and I am now a Christian." Polly smiled as she explained to the West family about her conversion.

"Well, you were always a Christian, Polly."

"No, Father, I was not. You have to believe in Christ to be a Christian." Polly answered her father quietly but with firmness in her voice. It was obvious that they had been through this discussion before.

"Well, to each his own. Going to church twice a year is good enough for me." Uncle Ray smiled, completely missing the point.

After dinner Bobbi and Polly offered to do the clean up. Bobbi wanted time to talk. Now she knew why Polly had seemed so different. Maybe they would become close friends.

Luke brought in more firewood. He shivered as he set the wood down. The temperature had dropped again. He paused to smell the turkey roasting and listen to the sounds of Uncle Hank beating Adam at checkers, and Aunt Sophie playing the piano. *This is what a Thanksgiving should be: a house full of love and good smells, a family together to praise and thank the Lord for another year of His mercy and goodness.*

Luke had tried to talk Charlie into coming up for the four-day holiday, but he had declined. He already had an invitation to dine with the Clark family that lived at the lighthouse. He'd been going there for years.

"How's the bird doing, Mom?" Luke could smell the stuffing. It had never smelled so good.

"Just fine. About another hour and I will have you start carving it." Rosa went over to start the potatoes on the stove.

"Just seven more hours and counting." Luke looked at his watch and smiled.

Rosa laughed and winked at Luke. She understood his reference to meeting Bobbi at the ferry dock.

"I think I am going to be glad I have that Jeep. It feels as if it could snow tonight." Luke went over to check on the pies.

"They are still there. Pumpkin, cherry, and apple. Remember, you can't eat them all. The rest of us get a piece, too. Now you move on away from there." Rosa grabbed a dish towel and shooed him away from the pies as Luke picked up a large spoon pretending to scoop into one of them.

Luke had been right. As he drove Adam to the ferry dock it started snowing, big thick flakes coming down very slowly. By the time Bobbi and Brad walked off the ferry, an inch lay on the ground. Brad walked slowly loaded down with three bags. Bobbi had a large suitcase on wheels. When she sat it upright on the dock, it stood almost as tall as she was.

"What a winter wonderland!" Bobbi smiled and did a little dance in the snow on the dock.

"Watch out or you're going to fall!" Both Brad and Luke yelled at the same time.

Luke and Adam helped Brad load the bags into the Jeep.

"Did you two know that you're only staying for three days?" Adam winced as he lifted Bobbi's big suitcase. "You have enough for a month."

"Don't look at me," Brad said defensively. "The smallest bag is mine. The rest all belong to her—and they're heavy too. You better start lifting weights, Luke, if you're going to hang out with her for long. Dad always asks her if she has her bricks packed every time she goes somewhere."

"OK, enough teasing. A girl has to make sure she has everything she might need." Bobbi smiled up at Luke.

Luke did have to wonder what on earth she had packed in all those bags. Poor Brad, he had been the pack mule on the ferry.

By the time they got back to the house, another inch of snow had fallen, and it kept coming down hard. Luke carried Bobbi's luggage up to his room. He was bunking out in the guesthouse with Brad and Adam. Aunt Sophie and Uncle Hank had Adam's room.

They all gathered in the living room for pie and ice cream. Luke looked around the room. Adam and Brad were playing checkers, Uncle Hank was stoking up the fire, and Bobbi was sitting with his mother and his aunt, enjoying a talk about the latest fashions. They were looking at the new 1969 December issue of *Vogue* magazine Aunt Sophie had brought. Bobbi filled the women in on the "wearing pants" saga at school. The principal had finally given in and allowed the girls to wear nice pants. But there were strict guidelines—no jeans or denim material and no front zippers. Uncle Hank put a record on the record player, some light jazz music. Now it was the perfect Thanksgiving.

The snow stopped late Thanksgiving night, leaving about three inches on the ground. The next morning, Bobbi and the boys had a snowball fight. All three ganged up on her. After about a half-hour of observing the slaughter, Rosa, Aunt Sophie, and Uncle Hank came out and declared themselves on Bobbi's side. Rosa and Sophie were not much help. Gradually everyone lost interest in the snowball fight, and they built a snowman together. In the afternoon, Bobbi and Sophie spent time with Rosa in her studio going over her projects and looking at all her yarns. That evening, Uncle Hank took all of them out to dinner in Eastsound. The snow had melted.

Uncle Hank and Aunt Sophie left Saturday morning after breakfast. Bobbi was sad to see them go. She liked them both. They were such warm, thoughtful people. *A lot like Luke,* she thought.

After Uncle Hank and Aunt Sophie left, Luke, Bobbi, and their brothers packed a picnic basket and headed out to Mount Constitution, a mountain just north of Rosario Resort. The one place Bobbi had not visited when she was on the island last summer.

As promised by all three of the Johansens, the view from Mount Constitution was fantastic. Because it was a clear day they could see other islands, the mainland, and even up to Vancouver, in Canada. Mount Constitution was the centerpiece of the large 5,252-acre Moran State Park, named after the man who built Rosario Resort and had owned most of the parkland at one time. They spent the day hiking on trails, exploring the park, and doing some off-roading in the Jeep.

Saturday night they played gin rummy. Luke and Bobbi battled it out in the championship round. Luke had won, but not by much.

At bedtime Rosa knocked on the bedroom door, poked her head in, and asked, "Bobbi, are you OK? Is there anything you need?"

Bobbi walked over to a Disneyland picture of Adam, Luke, and Grandpa Miers with Mickey Mouse.

"How old is Luke in this picture?"

"Oh, about seven. Their one trip to Disneyland." Rosa walked over, picked it up, and stared at it, her eyes misty.

"Tell me about it?" Bobbi asked.

They sat down on the bed together, each curled up with pillows and blankets like two girls at a slumber party.

"My father wanted to send all of us to Disneyland, but my husband and I were so poor at the time that we could not afford the time off from work. The trip evolved into just my father taking the boys down to Los Angeles for a week, as my mom didn't want to go.

"The three of them had so much fun together. My dad got a room at the Howard Johnson Motel and they spent three days playing at Disneyland and several days at the beach. I think he treasured every moment spoiling his only grandchildren. For years after, he would often talk about that trip ..." Rosa kept staring at the picture she held in her hand. "He really enjoyed that trip. I'm glad they went."

"Do you miss your parents a lot?" Bobbi asked.

"Yes, at times. But the pain has eased with the passing years. Knowing that they are with the Lord has helped. I'm not sure how people deal with such a loss when they don't know the Lord or their loved one didn't," Rosa answered.

Bobbi glanced around the room. There were at least six Bibles and many more Bible commentaries on the bookshelves. "How did Luke get so many Bibles?"

"Oh, some are my father's; others were gifts." Rosa laughed. "When he was four he asked for a Bible for Christmas. I can still hear him saying, 'Not a picture book. A big boy Bible.' He couldn't even read. He's always had this desire for God's Word. He's a bit different you know."

When Rosa left, Bobbi glanced around the room again. The pictures on the walls were of boats—*Matilda, The Claw,* and others she could not put a name to. She felt like she had invaded Luke's private space, no, she felt closer to him than ever before.

Luke glanced at Bobbi. She slept soundly in the backseat of the Jeep, curled up amongst the bags. Brad sat up front with him, reading a book. It was Sunday afternoon and they were heading south on I-5 on their way back to Olympia. Brad had suggested that Bobbi ride in the back, as she always fell asleep during long car rides.

"She won't be any company to you at all," he'd insisted.

Luke smiled as he thought about how pretty she looked with her hair blowing in the wind during the ferry ride. She had insisted on standing on the forward deck, despite the cold wind. Luke had pointed out to her the place where *The Claw* had the close call with the ferry. Once on the mainland she fell asleep before they reached the freeway, just as Brad had said she would.

It has been a great holiday, Luke thought. *Three and half days with Bobbi.* He reminisced about how she looked when he beat her at gin rummy. How her hand felt when he held it helping her over a log at Moran State Park. And how her hair shimmered in the sun when she threw a snowball at him. Before breakfast his mother had told him about her chat with Bobbi the night before. He was glad they were getting along.

The trip to Mount Constitution had been fun. He had not been there in a while. He had let Brad and Adam drive the Jeep while they did some off-roading. Brad had handled the Jeep the best.

Luke kept looking at her in the mirror as he drove. She looked so peaceful while she slept.

CHAPTER 32

Christmas on Orcas

Quiet! We're on in three minutes. Where's Scott?" Bobbi started to panic. This was the last madrigal performance for the Christmas season. Everyone kept talking and playing around. The last three performances had been disasters. No one had followed her, and they sounded awful.

This one had to be good; they were singing for Mr. Miller's Rotary Club's Christmas dinner. Mrs. Miller was in the audience, and they could not embarrass her in front of her husband. At this rate they would.

Luke went over to a group of the guys and talked to them. The group broke up and came over to stand with the girls. Things started to quiet down.

"We will start with 'Greensleeves,' then 'Behold the Star,' and last, 'Mary Had a Baby.' Please keep an eye on me. If we work together we can sound great. Let's make Mrs. Miller proud." Was she wasting her breath?

The entrance onto the stage went well. The girls sat down together. They were all watching her. Bobbi gave the note with the pitch pipe. Then she nodded the rhythm, and they all started in. What a relief! They sounded halfway decent tonight, and they were following her lead.

"Hey, we sounded pretty good tonight!" Luke whispered to Bobbi as they walked behind the curtain. "Hear that? They're still clapping. Should we go back on for an encore?"

"I don't think we should push our luck. Oh…the clapping stopped."

"You all sounded great! Thank you so much!" Mrs. Miller came backstage smiling. "Now, for those of you who are leaving early on vacations, have a good time. Merry Christmas to all of you!"

"I'm so glad that went so well. What an answer to prayer," Bobbi said as Luke opened the Jeep door for her, took her hand, and helped her up inside. Even with the running board he had installed, it was a bit of a struggle for her in the madrigal gown and heels.

"December has sure flown by. It was just yesterday that we were enjoying Thanksgiving break," Bobbi continued when Luke got in on the driver's side.

Luke nodded.

"Hey, why are you so quiet?" Bobbi realized Luke wasn't smiling or responding to her chatter. He just sat there looking at her, and he had not even put the key in the ignition.

"It just hit me that tomorrow you'll be gone for two weeks. That's a long time." Luke took her hand in his. "I wish you could spend Christmas on Orcas with me. I'm going to miss you so much!"

"Hey, they do have telephones in Iowa. I gave you all the phone numbers. I'll write you." Bobbi did not know what to do to make him feel better. He looked so sad. She knew she would miss him too.

She tried cheering him up on the way home, but nothing seemed to work. Once at Bobbi's house, Luke walked her to the front door.

"Is it still OK if I come in for awhile?" he asked.

"Yes, but we can't talk for too long. I still have to pack. Dad is keeping me to two suitcases, so I really have to plan what I'm taking." Bobbi glanced at her watch. "It's ten o'clock, so we better be quiet. Most likely everyone is in bed. We are getting up at three tomorrow morning so we can catch our six o'clock flight out of Sea-Tac."

Bobbi opened the door very quietly, and they tiptoed up the stairs to the living room.

"Why don't we sit down for a minute? I have a small Christmas present for you," Luke whispered.

Bobbi looked at him as she sat down. His hands were empty. Where was the present? He reached into his jacket pocket. This had to be small! Luke pulled out a small, very flat, light-blue box with a bright red bow. It said Tiffany's on the top.

Bobbi gasped.

"Merry Christmas, Bobbi. I hope you like it." Luke smiled.

She hesitated. *Not a ring! I'm not ready for a ring. I don't want to get that serious.* She wished the butterflies in her stomach would go away. "Tiffany's is in New York! How did you? Or is it…?"

"Just open it and see." Luke kept smiling. Bobbi's eyes danced with excitement. He couldn't wait for her to open it.

She took off the bow and lifted the lid. Inside was a simple silver-colored, banded bracelet. "Oh my! So beautiful!" Her words were barely audible.

"Try it on. I hope it fits. It's white gold. I know you don't ever wear gold." Luke reached into the box and slid the bracelet over her hand. "If you don't like it you can exchange it. It is from a jewelry store in Seattle. They carry Tiffany jewelry."

"No, I love it! It is beautiful! Thank you! Thank you!" Bobbi was completely blown away. She reached over and gave Luke a big hug.

She looked down at her bracelet again and then looked back up at him like there was something wrong. "What I got for you isn't nearly as nice. Just a minute. It's here under the tree."

She went over and picked up a large package. "I didn't know what to get you." Bobbi handed him the package wrapped in bright Christmas paper.

Luke tore off the wrapping paper to find book with a front-cover picture of Spenser Spit. *Crabbing in the San Juan Islands* was the title. Luke beamed. He started to thumb through the pages.

"It has a lot of pictures of your favorite haunts, and there is even a picture of *The Claw* on page thirty-two. I just thought it might be a nice memory as you move on to college." Bobbi turned red.

"I like it." Luke continued to smile. "Wow! Look, here's a picture of Blakely Island, and there it is, *The Claw*, at dock at Orcas. This is great, Bobbi! Where did you ever find it?"

"At a bookstore at the new South Center Mall. I had been shopping all Saturday with my mom and had nothing for you. I had just asked the Lord for help and walked in there and saw it on display. It seemed perfect."

They talked a bit longer and then Bobbi walked Luke to the door. He picked up her hand and kissed it. He cleared his throat. "I'm really going to miss you. You have a great Christmas, OK?" Luke didn't wait for an answer but headed out the door.

Bobbi walked to her room with a happy glow on her face. The two large suitcases on her bed quickly brought her back to reality. *How can I get everything I need in those things?*

She couldn't wait to spend Christmas in Iowa with all her mom's family. She loved being with the large family. Her mother had three sisters, and there were ten cousins all together—five boys and five girls. Two of the girls were her age, one she was especially close to, Lilly. At two in the morning, Bobbi had finished packing and looked at the clock. They had to get up in an hour. There was no sense in putting on pajamas or trying to go to sleep. She laid out what she wanted to wear on her bed and headed into the shower. Hopefully, she would be able to get some sleep on the plane.

Luke looked over at Charlie. He slept peacefully in the passenger seat of the Jeep. It was Tuesday, December 23, and they were heading to Orcas. Luke thought about how Bobbi had been so pleased with the Christmas present he gave her. His mother had suggested jewelry. Aunt Sophie had suggested something from Tiffany's. He had not even heard of the place before. The saleslady had suggested a bracelet. When he saw the simple band he knew that was Bobbi. He loved the way her face had lit up when he gave it to her. He would remember that moment until he died.

Charlie kept snoring. He had been sleeping from Seattle on. Luke had stopped in downtown Seattle to drop off a present for Mr. and Mrs. Harrison. Rosa had woven custom placemats for their yacht. Luke was surprised at

Thanksgiving when she showed them to him. She had remembered the dining room, the colors, and how many the table sat. Each one had a small ribbon label that said "Designed by Rosa Johansen." He hoped the Harrisons would understand how special the placemats were. Mr. Harrison had his office in the "Black Box," the first real skyscraper in Seattle. Everyone joked that it was the box the Space Needle came in. Luke found street parking and pumped the meter full of change. He left Charlie reading a book in the Jeep and went up to the forty-eighth floor office suite. *What an incredible view.* Luke looked south and saw to the Tacoma Narrows Bridge towers. He turned north and gazed at Whidbey Island off in the distance.

"Mr. Harrison will see you now," the receptionist finally informed him. Luke had been sitting and waiting for twenty minutes. She showed Luke into the large corner office.

Mr. Harrison got up from a beautiful, huge wooden desk and walked around it to shake Luke's hand. "It's nice to see you again, Luke."

"It's nice to see you too, sir. You have a fabulous view from your office! I came to give you and your wife this Christmas present and thank you again for the work this summer." Luke handed Mr. Harrison the present. "It's for your yacht."

"Thank you, Luke. That is very kind of you." Mr. Harrison seemed impressed. He turned and carefully laid the present on his desk. "How is the Jeep doing?"

"It's doing great, sir. I love it, and it was useful in the snow we had at Thanksgiving on the island. My girlfriend is on our high school ski team, so I've driven it to White Pass once. It is the perfect vehicle for me right now. I will never be able to thank you enough."

"That's good to hear. It would just be sitting in my garage. I am glad it's of use to you."

"Well, I won't take any more of your time, sir." Luke started to move toward the office door.

Mr. Harrison stepped toward him. "Luke, just one thing. If you ever need anything, please call me. Advice, money, a reference, anything. You are a remarkable young man, and I would love to help in any way."

"Thank you, sir. I will remember that." Luke left the office. When he got back to the Jeep, Charlie had fallen asleep.

Luke had convinced Charlie to join his family for the Christmas holiday. It was a struggle getting him into the Jeep, but Charlie's car wouldn't have made it to Orcas. Rosa had fixed up the den on the main floor for Charlie to sleep in so he could have easy access to his bedroom. They would stay until Sunday. Then they would head back to Olympia for a doctor's appointment for Charlie. Luke had been trying for over a month to get Charlie to agree to see the doctor. Finally, he just made the appointment and told Charlie they were going. Charlie didn't look well. Luke had to remind him about everything. Luke had taken over the books completely. When he would try to show the numbers to Charlie so he could see how the week had gone, Charlie would just nod and say, "I'm sure you are doing a good job. Can we go over it next week?" The past week Charlie had forgotten to place the order with the main vendor for the store. Taking over the ordering would be next.

"This is a wonderful dinner, ma'am." Charlie turned to Rosa. "I really appreciate you including me in your holidays this year." He passed the turkey on to Adam.

Luke looked around the table. Uncle Hank had carved the turkey this time. Aunt Sophie sat next to him. Then Pastor Bob and his whole family, a big group for Christmas Eve dinner. The table looked beautiful, and Rosa had the old familiar Christmas decorations up, plus several new additions. She had made fudge, peanut brittle, and all the traditional Christmas cookies. *But one person is missing—Bobbi.*

"So how did Miss West like her Christmas present?" Aunt Sophie asked Luke. They had finally stopped passing the food and started eating.

"She really liked it. I won't forget the look on her face. Thank you for suggesting that store, Aunt Sophie."

"Well, all I have to say is, it's a good thing that he will not have to pay for his college. That was a lot to spend on one Christmas present!" Rosa said. She had not approved of the amount that Luke had spent on Bobbi.

"Well, if it secures a place in the heart of that young lady for Luke, it is worth every penny." Charlie came to Luke's defense.

"What is this about your not paying for college?" Pastor Bob asked.

"I have a scholarship." Luke took his time explaining the scholarship to Pastor Bob.

Christmas morning they all opened presents and Luke called Bobbi.

"Keep it short," Rosa warned as Luke placed the call.

"Panther Creek Farm." Bobbi's aunt answered the phone. Luke could hear lots of talking and occasional yells in the background as her aunt went to find Bobbi.

"Merry Christmas!"

The sound of Bobbi's voice made Luke's heart speed up. Man, he missed her. "Merry Christmas to you, too. It sounds noisy there!"

"Oh, it is. It's been so much fun. I've hardly slept at all. Carol and Lilly and I stayed up all night the first night talking. Yesterday my uncle took us on a hayride in the snow. How are you and Charlie doing?"

"OK, we just opened presents. I miss you."

"I miss you, too,"

The rest of the week Luke relaxed. They played board and card games, Charlie slept a lot, and Luke gave him a tour of the island. Rosa hosted several small holiday parties.

After church on Sunday Luke and Charlie headed back to Olympia.

CHAPTER 33

Endings

"It's not looking good. His kidneys and his eyesight are starting to go all at the same time. It is typical of diabetes to act like this," Dr. Lange explained to Luke after he had examined Charlie. Charlie was still in the patient room getting dressed.

"How much longer do you think he will be able to see?"

"I am not sure. But you might not have to worry about that too much. His heart is also showing some signs of weakness. Are you the only person he has to watch out for him? Are you a grandson?" Dr. Lange asked.

"No, I'm just a friend and boarder. Charlie has two nephews who live back east. They never call or write to him. They don't seem to care. He's helping me out by giving me a place to live, and I'm helping him out more and more every day. Are you trying to tell me he's dying?" Luke wanted straight answers. He needed to know what to expect and to be able to plan for Charlie.

"Yes, he is a lot closer to death than he was at his last examination. I am not sure how much longer he will have. A month? A year? It is hard to say. Which will go first—his heart, his kidneys, or his eyes? I don't know. The best for him would be if he had a diabetic heart attack and went suddenly. You need to make sure he has all his affairs in order." Dr. Lange patted Luke on the shoulder as he stood up. "Oh, his blood sugar may start spiking or dropping drastically. Do you have sugar items around?"

"Yes, we always have plenty of cookies. He's good about only eating one if his blood sugar is dropping. Otherwise he likes to serve them to his guests. Have you told Charlie about all of this?" Luke didn't want to be the one to break the news to Charlie.

"Yes, I have. But you feel free to call me with any questions or problems." Dr. Lange shook Luke's hand and headed down the hall.

Luke walked to the patient room to check on Charlie. He struggled putting on his shoe and then had trouble tying it. Luke bent down and helped him finish the job.

As they left the doctor's parking lot Charlie starting talking. "Well, I guess it won't be too much longer before I get to meet my Maker, Luke. I'm just very thankful that I will be going to heaven. I've been reading every passage I can find about heaven lately."

"It will be wonderful, Charlie." Tears started to well up in Luke's eyes. "How about eating out tonight, an early dinner at the Falls Terrace? They always have good specials on Mondays."

"That would be nice. It's my treat, though. I owe you after that wonderful Christmas on Orcas."

Over dinner Luke brought up the sensitive subject of Charlie's affairs. "I think we should hire someone to come and help with the store during the day. What do you think, Charlie?"

"Yes, it would be a good idea. I have been having trouble lately with making change for the customers. It's hard to see the difference between the nickels and the quarters, and my fingers don't have much feeling in them anymore. I can't feel the difference. The Little Store closed last month, and we are getting a lot more of the kids coming in for candy after school. They mostly have change, and I'm not sure how many have cheated me or I have cheated them." Charlie looked down at his hands in dismay.

"What about Mrs. Clark? Didn't she work at the Little Store? Maybe she wants a job. I will call her tonight." Luke hoped that would be the answer to the problem. She only lived a block away at the lighthouse, and they could trust her. She cared about Charlie.

"The real issue, Charlie, is do you have a will? Have you made sure everything is in order for your nephews?" Luke pressed the subject.

Charlie gave a loud snort of disgust, which made several people at tables nearby turn and look. "My nephews!" He pounded the table with his fist and his face turned red. "You, you know how much they care?" He struggled for composure. Then he whispered in a tight-lipped tone, "I've given them my time and money all their lives. I took them in for a while when neither of their parents wanted them, and look what I've gotten in return. I even wrote them this summer, telling them I might not have much longer on this earth and that I would like them to visit and we could talk about the future of the marina. Then, I tried calling them and left messages with their wives. No answer or return call. They couldn't care less about me." He hung his head and a tear started down his cheek.

Luke fell silent. He knew not to push the subject any more at that point. They finished their meal in silence and headed back to the marina.

Mrs. Clark walked into the store midafternoon. "Hi, Charlie. Luke, thank you so much for calling. Working so close to home is a Godsend."

"And we need the help, so it works out perfectly," Luke replied. "Too bad about the Little Store closing."

"I'm surprised it didn't close before. Mr. Jackson never made much. What hours would you like me to work?"

"How does nine to three sound?" Luke asked. "One of the dock hands has worked here for more than a year. He's a hard worker and seems honest enough. If he worked the store for the after-school hours, then you could leave work when your sons come home from school."

"Wonderful. Now show me the ropes."

Luke walked Mrs. Clark through the slip rentals and the gas system and showed her where everything was. After she left he went over the books.

Later he took a break and gave Bobbi a call. The West family had traveled to northern Iowa to visit Mr. West's aunt Hazel in the small town of Humbolt. They would be leaving the next day to spend New Year's with friends, the Swensons, in Madison, Wisconsin, a university town. Luke filled her in on everything that had happened with Charlie and the store. It helped to hear her voice.

Saturday afternoon Luke decided to call Bobbi at the Swenson house. A pleasant-sounding lady answered the call. "Mrs. Swenson speaking."

"This is Luke Johansen, calling for Bobbi West. Is she available?" Luke asked.

"I am sorry, Luke, she is out on a date at this time. Should I tell her that you called?" she asked.

"No...no, that's OK." Luke hung up, confused. A date? A *date*? How could she be on a date? Well, better to find out all the details before getting upset. He kept working, stocking the shelves of the store.

About an hour later the phone rang. He ran to get it, hoping to hear Bobbi's voice. Instead he heard Joe's!

"Luke, this is Joe. How are you doing?" he asked.

"Just fine. And yourself?" Luke didn't know what to say.

"OK. Just home for Christmas vacation and thought I should check in with you before I leave for Iowa. I called your place on Orcas, and your mother told me you were living at the marina. What a surprise."

"Yeah, I enjoy it here, and Charlie is real good to me. I get to be out on the water on a regular basis. Charlie has a small boat he lets me use."

"Do you ever see Bobbi?" Joe asked.

Luke paused. How was he going to explain this one? "Well, we have mixed chorus, and madrigals together. And we spend a lot of time together —"

Joe interrupted Luke before he could finish. "So, she's doing OK. That's good. I was worried about her when we broke up. Do me a favor, big guy, and keep an eye on her. Or better yet, maybe you should date her. You two seemed to get along. Hey, I gotta go. My parents are taking us out for dinner, and everyone's waiting. Take care."

"OK, good to hear from you. Good-bye." Luke hung up the phone, shaking his head, and just as he turned to go back to stocking the shelves, the phone rang again.

"Luke? This is Bobbi. Did you call me earlier?"

"Yes, I did. Mrs. Swenson said that you were out on a date?"

"She did? That is her view of it! I went to a basketball game between Wisconsin and Duke with Greg, their son, who's my age. Greg and I were both forced to go. The original plan was me and Martin, their older son, and Brad going. So I agreed because it sounded like fun. But then she changed it all around, and when it came time to leave, it ended up being Greg and me. He didn't like it either. He had to break a date with his girlfriend. I overheard him on the phone trying to make her understand. We had a miserable afternoon. I don't think he said more than two words to me."

Luke started to laugh. "Well, as long as there isn't an arranged marriage that you're unaware of, what's the harm?" He could just see Bobbi sitting there, trying to suppress her anger. "Poor Greg. I would have gladly changed places with him."

"I wish, but it's over and we fly out tomorrow. Greg has disappeared to his girlfriend's house to do penance. I don't think I'll see him again this visit." Bobbi started to laugh, too. "I can't wait to see you Monday morning. You're still picking me up for school, right?"

"Wouldn't miss it for the world." Luke wished he could meet her at the plane Sunday night, but Charlie had developed a cold, and Luke didn't think he should leave him alone.

"Bobbi, Bobbi, wake up, honey."

Bobbi rolled over at her mother's touch on her shoulder. "Mom?" Mrs. West sat on the edge of Bobbi's bed. She had been crying. It was six-fifteen on Monday morning, the first day back to school after Christmas break.

Bobbi sat up. "What's wrong, Mom?"

"I was listening to KGY. They have some bad news. Patsy...Patsy was found this morning in the hospital parking lot in her car. She'd been stabbed twenty-six times. She's still alive, but she's going through blood real fast. They're asking for donations of blood." Mrs. West hugged Bobbi.

Bobbi went numb. She wasn't close with Patsy, but they had a class and ski team together. She had moved to Olympia from California this year. She immediately made friends because of her sunny disposition.

"Is she going to live?" Bobbi asked.

"The radio station is not saying. They are asking for anyone who might know anything to call the police and for people to give blood. You better get ready for school. Luke will be here in a half hour."

Bobbi usually warmed up her voice and sang in the shower every morning, but this morning she didn't. She stood there for a long time, letting the water run over her and trying to understand about Patsy. What could have happened to her?

"I want to give blood," Bobbi said as she walked into the kitchen.

"You can't, honey. You have to be eighteen," Mr. West replied. "But we can all do something more important, and that is pray."

Brad walked into the kitchen. They formed a circle holding hands, and the whole family prayed.

Luke arrived a few minutes before seven o'clock. She hadn't seen him for over two weeks. This was supposed to be a happy time, but it wasn't.

Bobbi opened the front door and asked Luke, "Have you heard the news about Patsy?" As Bobbi said the words she knew he'd already heard the bad news. The look on his face said it all.

"Yes, on the radio on the way over." Luke walked into the entry and gave Bobbi a big hug. Bobbi started to cry. They stood there for a minute or so.

"We'd better get going. School is going to be a bit different today." Luke broke the hug and stepped back. "Go get your books."

"Good morning, Luke. Did you have a nice vacation?" Mr. West walked into the entryway carrying his black metal lunch pail and briefcase, which he laid down on the entryway bench. Then he turned to get his coat out of the closet.

"Yes, it was nice. Did Bobbi tell you about Charlie?" Luke asked.

"Yes, she did. Charlie is fortunate to have you living with him. If you need more help with him, let us know. We want to help out." Mr. West headed out the door to his International Travelall.

The gray, drizzly day matched the somber mood at school. Groups of people stood around crying or talking in hushed tones. There were quite a few students missing in Bobbi's homeroom. Some of them knew Patsy quite well. Rumors were flying around that it was a drug deal gone bad;

after all, Patsy was from California. Bobbi didn't want to believe that, as Patsy didn't seem like the type to do drugs. Between classes people listened to portable radios in groups, hoping for good news. The whole school was in a state of shock. How could this happen to anyone this young?

As Bobbi arrived at her homeroom, she could hear Principal Bain clearing his throat over the loudspeaker. "This is a sad day for our student body. As most of you know Patsy Baker is in the hospital fighting for her life. The hospital is in need of blood donations. Any student over eighteen who wishes to give blood may come to the administration office. We will release five students each hour to go to the hospital. Ski team practice is canceled for today."

"Mary! Where are you going?" Bobbi bumped into Mary. She was going the wrong way on the sidewalk. "Mixed chorus is this way, remember?"

Mary had been crying. "I'm going up to the office to sign up for blood donation."

"Oh, that's right, you turned eighteen today. I'm so sorry this happened on your birthday." Bobbi gave Mary a hug, and Mary started to cry again. "I'll walk you to the office and then let Mrs. Miller know you'll be gone." They walked quietly up to the office with their arms around each other. Mary knew Patsy better than she did. Mary knew everyone.

Throughout the day and into the evening, there were regular updates on Patsy's condition on KGY. She kept going through blood very fast, and she had not woken up at all. It did not look good.

"I wish I knew if she is a believer." Bobbi said as she sat with her family at the dinner table.

"She seems like such a nice girl. Who on earth would have done this to her?" Mrs. West shook her head sadly.

"They say she drove herself to the hospital. The crime didn't happen in the hospital parking lot. She had to have been in a lot of pain as she drove. She had opened the car door, and she tried to get out of the car," Brad said.

"That's horrible." Bobbi tried to picture Patsy struggling to drive the car and get to the hospital. "Every one at school was in shock. I don't think anyone thought something like this could ever happen to one of us. Most of the kids have never thought about death. Lots of girls are scared."

"Hopefully, they will catch who ever did it, and soon. By the way, I postponed my trip to Oregon on Wednesday, Kay. I didn't think you would like it if I was out of town this week with this going on." Mr. West was being considerate of his wife. He knew she did not like it when he was away.

"Bobbi, Bobbi, time to get up." Mrs. West sat on the side of Bobbi's bed again.

Bobbi sat up. "How's Patsy, Mom?"

The look on her face gave Bobbi the answer. "She passed away early this morning. I am so sorry, honey." She took Bobbi in her arms and they cried together.

"This has been a strange two weeks. Finding out that Charlie doesn't have much more time, and now Patsy dying." Luke glanced at Bobbi sitting next to him in the Jeep. They were on their way up the Crystal Mountain Highway to the ski resort. Oly had a race against the Charles and Annie Wright Academies.

"Yes, it has. Not sure we are going to do too well today. Several kids on the team were very close to Patsy, and with only three practices this week we're not in the best shape." Bobbi put on her wool ski socks.

"You should dedicate the race to Patsy."

"Good idea. I'll mention it to Coach," Bobbi said.

"It has provided an opportunity to talk to people about the Lord. For once, people are thinking about eternity and not just about today. Several of the guys in my physics class asked me questions about heaven. I got a chance to share the gospel with two different guys."

"You're right people are thinking about what happens after they die. I didn't tell you what happened in art class yesterday. Candy and I were talking about the Lord as we were painting. Most everyone in the class was over at the potters' wheels and working with clay. This guy, Doug, who sits at the table behind us, overheard us. He started asking questions about how one gets to heaven. So we gave him the gospel. But he couldn't accept it. He kept talking about his mother and how good she is and how she does everything for others. He said God should let her into heaven because she's so good. We tried to explain that we all sin, even his mother. But he didn't understand that our goodness is never as good as God's. We had quite a discussion. Other people started to join in."

"Sounds like Doug needs our prayers." Luke pulled into a parking space at the Crystal Mountain Lodge. They sat for a moment watching the snow fall. "It looks like we're the first ones here. We even beat the ski bus. You go get 'em, tiger. Remember that I will be filming you and everyone else with Coach's movie camera, so smile as you ski."

Bobbi laughed and got out of the Jeep.

CHAPTER 34

Everything in Its Place

"No, Bobbi, for the hundredth time, I don't know why Charlie wanted to talk to us this afternoon. Come on." Luke opened the door to the marina store for her, and she marched through. She had been grouchy all day. Everything had been going wrong with ski team and madrigals.

Bobbi bumped into a middle-aged man in a suit, carrying a briefcase. Bobbi turned red. "Oh! I'm sorry. I didn't see you."

"Well, here they are." Charlie rolled over. He looked bright and chipper dressed in his best slacks and a nice shirt. "These are the two I wanted you to meet. This young lady is Bobbi, and this tall fellow is Luke. This is Mr. Ellis, an attorney."

"It's nice to meet you, Mr. Ellis." Luke and Mr. Ellis shook hands.

"Hello, nice to meet you." Bobbi nodded and smiled. "I'm so sorry about bumping into you."

"Well, I wanted you two to meet him. When I pass away, he's the fellow you are to call. He has all the instructions as to what is to be done. He left each one of you a business card here on the table."

"Yes, I put my home phone number on the back in case you needed to reach me on the weekend or evenings. Charlie and I had a good meeting. We got a lot of loose ends tied up."

"I'm glad to hear that." Luke was relieved.

"I hear that you two are a big help to Charlie. Not many young people would do such a thing for an adult," Mr. Ellis continued.

"Well, Charlie has been very good to both of us." Bobbi walked over and stood behind Charlie's chair. She put her hand on his shoulder.

"It was nice to meet both of you. Charlie, I'll have those papers ready for you to sign next week." Mr. Ellis said his good-byes, turned, and walked out the door.

"OK, you two. How about some milk and cookies? I have some chocolate chip cookies here that a very special young lady made for me. Come sit down. You both have been so busy lately I don't even know what is happening in your lives." Charlie rolled over to the refrigerator. Bobbi followed and got the glasses out for the milk and poured it, while Charlie put the plate of cookies on the table.

"It's not been good, Charlie. Everything seems to be out of control." Bobbi sat down at the table.

"Really?" Luke said sarcastically. "You know that you have nothing scheduled between midnight and six A.M. every day? I think we need to find you something to do during those hours."

"OK! You're right!" Bobbi snapped back at Luke. "I'm overbooked. But I gave my word and promised to do it all. So now I just have to get through it. It will be better after the ski season is over."

"What's this, a fight?" Charlie looked at Luke, then Bobbi, and back at Luke again. "I think you two need to knock it off and talk to each other nicer. You are developing habits for your relationship, so make them good ones. I'm disappointed in both of you." He rolled back over to the refrigerator to get more milk for Luke. When he turned around, both of them were staring at the table and glancing at the other when the other one wasn't looking.

"How about a handshake and make up? OK? On three now?" Charlie was determined to see his two favorite people getting along.

Bobbi started to giggle and Luke started to laugh. They shook hands and both said they were sorry.

"That's better. Now let's discuss this problem like grownups." Charlie rolled back over to the table. "What's the worst of your troubles?"

"Madrigals…and ski team. They are conflicting." Bobbi made a face. "We never perform on the weekends. But Mrs. Miller scheduled a Saturday performance for this weekend and the next weekend, a Friday night performance. That's the weekend of the big three-day race at White Pass, and we've been excused from school that Friday so we can go up there for the first races that afternoon." She folded her arms on the table and laid her head on them in defeat.

"Mrs. Miller is upset that Bobbi's going to miss those two performances. She has asked Susan to take Bobbi's place, and during practice this morning Susan took over. She's been a part of the opposition Bobbi has had all year. She thinks she can do a much better job than Bobbi and has been grumbling about that. Now she's acting like the prize peacock. It's more than we can stomach." Luke continued with the story. "On the way out here, we were discussing if Bobbi should skip the ski races."

"Then, there is the artwork for the spring concert program that I have to design and have to the printer by the beginning of next week, the music honor society meeting this week, the social club meeting to plan the May dance, homework—and my poor horses haven't been ridden or worked with in a week. I just need a few more hours in the day, Charlie. Can you take care of that for me?" Bobbi asked.

"I told her that she made her decision to ski, now stick with it no matter what the consequences. Madrigals have been a mess all year. Maybe if Susan falls on her face, everyone will start to respect Bobbi when she returns," Luke explained to Charlie.

Bobbi jerked her head up. "But what if it's the wrong decision? It's not too late to change it." Bobbi couldn't make up her mind.

"Stop it. Luke's right. Just let the cards lie. You made a choice, now stick with it. You've had a lot better year on ski team with that new coach. Go and enjoy the races and bring back some medals. This guy has a good head on his shoulders." Charlie pointed at Luke. "You need to listen to his advice."

"OK. You're right. It has been a better year on ski team. Did I tell you about the last practice?" Bobbi started to laugh.

"No, what happened?" Charlie smiled. It was good to hear her laugh.

"Some of the younger guys are very good skiers, and poor Mr. Hendrix is just a snowplower. It's his first year skiing. He usually barely makes it to the course. He reads books and watches ski films so he can coach us. The information is good; he just can't do it himself. Anyway, last week the guys purposely set up a practice course on an advanced run, so Mr. Hendrix couldn't get there. But the prank backfired.

He shows up midmorning looking like a snowball because he had fallen so many times." Bobbi laughed again. "Mr. Hendrix laughed about his inability to ski and made jokes about it. Then he got to work, putting us through some tough new drills and telling us what we were doing wrong. He *does* do his homework. I think the whole team respected him for making it to the course."

"You kids should respect him for even taking the job. As I heard it, none of the other faculty would take the team. At least he got all of you goof-offs in shape this year, and for once you're winning races." Charlie cleared the table. "There is something else you need to do, young lady." Charlie rolled back to the table, took her hand, and looked her in the eye. "Advice you always give me. Pray about it. Take it to the Lord. Ask Him for the time to get it all done. Remember, leave it with Him."

Luke smiled big. He loved it, Charlie giving Bobbi spiritual advice. It was great to see how much he had grown in the past months.

"You got it, Bobbi! Keep it going! You got it!" Brad yelled as loudly as he could.

Luke held his breath as he watched Bobbi take the final gates of the slalom course on that Saturday. She had done well enough in Friday's races to advance to the finals. She looked good. Cutting all the gates so close they were vibrating as she sped by. He hoped she wouldn't miss the last gates like she had the weekend before. He hadn't been there because of the madrigal performance, but he had heard all about it. She had the fastest time on the hill but had misread the last two gates and had missed them, disqualifying herself.

Bobbi finished the course and stopped with a hard turn in the circle at the bottom, spraying snow all over the place. The sprayed snow sparkled in the sunshine. She looked at the judges' table. Every second seemed like minutes. Then they announced her time. She had the fastest time! She was ahead! There were three more skiers. "Now all we have to do is wait," Bobbi said under her breath. She wasn't the best skier. The best she had ever gotten, up until now, was ninth place. But last weekend things seemed to come together, and she had really picked up some speed. She spotted Brad and Luke in the crowd and skied over near them, then bent down and unlatched her bindings. Luke stepped up and took her skis from her. Silently they stood there as the next racer from a school in Seattle came into the circle. They announced the time—four seconds slower than Bobbi's time. The second skier seemed to have a great run. Then just before the next to last gate she caught an edge and went shooting off the course.

"Oh, that poor girl!" Bobbi could identify with her. She had done that once last year. The skier stood up after falling. "At least she's not hurt." Bobbi looked up at Luke.

Luke nodded and looked back up the hill.

The final skier started down. She fell midway down the course. She stood up and completed the race. But she had lost valuable time. Bobbi knew that she had it, but stood very quietly. She wanted to hear it from the judges before she celebrated. Brad came up and stood behind her with his hands on her shoulders, as if holding down a jumping bean. Luke couldn't help but chuckle. Finally, they made the announcement. Bobbi started jumping up and down, hugging Brad, teammates, and even Mr. Hendrix. Luke stood there holding her skis and watching her with a big smile on his face. Brad took her skis from him. Luke walked over next to her; she had run out of people to hug. She turned and looked at him and then gave him a big hug. He picked her up and carried her over to the small stage and placed her on the platform to receive her trophy.

As he watched her stand there, listening to the judge talk, he couldn't help but think that she had made the right decision to ski the races instead of performing with madrigals. She had beaten the hill! Only he knew the mental battle it had taken for her to do that. She had to stay in fellowship and leave it with the Lord to win, and she had. She had not only won the ski race, she had won a spiritual battle! *I'm happy for you, Bobbi,* he thought and clapped as she accepted the trophy.

"Oh, Mom, it was horrible. I didn't know what to do! Before we performed, Mrs. Miller reminded everyone I was nodder, but Susan nodded and the group got confused." Bobbi picked up a dust rag and started in dusting the coffee table. Since they had not had much time to talk lately, Mrs. West had suggested they should pick up and dust the house together.

"What did Mrs. Miller do?" Mrs. West asked.

"Nothing. She couldn't do anything. There were at least two hundred people in the audience, and she had to stand at the back of the room. I decided to keep on going. Then Susan finally realized what she was doing and stopped. The rest of the group decided to follow me, and we got it together enough to finish the song. The second song went OK."

"That's too bad. Did Susan say anything afterward?" her mother asked.

Bobbi picked up a large vase so that her mother could dust an end table. "That was the best part. She came up and apologized to me; she said she didn't mean to nod. She told me the job was harder than she had anticipated." Bobbi had heard about the performances she had missed from Luke and some of the others in the madrigal group. A few had privately told Bobbi that they were glad to have her back, but there were some holdouts.

"Susan told me the first performance she led she froze, had trouble with the pitch pipe, almost forgot to nod, and messed up the rhythm. She wants to be friends and says she will support me from now on."

"That's great."

"When we got back to school I talked to Mrs. Miller and told her I would stop being nodder if that was best for the group. But she said that knowing music and theory, no matter how well, doesn't make one a leader. She wants me to do the job."

"Just don't get a big head about it, hon. Remember, God gave you the ability to lead, and He gave you that voice too."

"I know. But I really wouldn't care if someone else took the job." Bobbi finished the last table in the living room.

"Now, let's go back and tackle your room. It has gotten out of hand lately. Remember your grandmother always said, 'A place for ...

"'... everything and everything in its place,'" Bobbi chimed in with her mother and they finished the saying together, laughing as they walked down the hall to her bedroom. There were a lot of things that needed putting in place in her life but she was glad she had the Lord to take care of them.

CHAPTER 35

Birthday Party

"OK, on three and we lift this young man up the stairs." Brad had one side of Charlie's wheelchair and Luke had the other. They were lifting Charlie up the patio stairs and into the Wests' home. They had wheeled him around to the bay side of the house so they could take him up the shortest flight of stairs.

"I'm just glad it is a warm, beautiful day. If it was raining I would have gotten soaked by now." Charlie laughed. "Now, let's get inside so we can join the party."

It was Saturday, March 14, Bobbi's birthday. Her parents had agreed to an afternoon party with just a few of her friends. She had invited Amy, who was on spring break from her university, two other girls from church, and her Boston Harbor girlfriends. Not all of the Boston Harbor girls were able to come.

Luke and Brad got Charlie through the sliding glass door and rolled him a few feet to a place on the south end of the living room.

Luke bent over to talk to Charlie and check on him. "Is this OK?" Luke had recognized Amy, Mary, Kathy, and Jill as he had swung the wheelchair around.

"It's just fine. Now, you find out where Mrs. West wants these." Charlie handed him the birthday presents that they had brought for Bobbi. Charlie had been holding them on his lap.

Luke straightened up and turned around to ask. All of a sudden there were a lot more people in the room. Luke took a step back. They were all smiling. They began to sing, "Happy Birthday" to him. There was his mother, Aunt Sophie, Uncle Hank, Adam, Steve, Scott, two guys from church, and even Pastor Ralph! Luke stood there looking dazed as they sang, and then he went over and gave his mother a hug. Over Rosa's shoulder he saw Bobbi grinning big, and he knew who the culprit was. This was not just a party for her as she had led him to believe, but also a party for him.

"Happy Birthday, Luke!" Steve came over and gave Luke a slap on the back. "So, how does it feel to be eighteen?"

"I don't know yet. Officially, I'll find out in two more days!" Luke wanted to keep the record straight. "Boy, there are a lot of people here!" He noticed Mrs. Miller and two other guys from madrigals. "Hey, I want to talk to you for awhile, but right now I better go and find that little sneak who planned this."

Luke found Bobbi in the kitchen with a tray of punch glasses. He took them from her and put them down on the counter. He put his hands on her shoulders and said, "I know you're the culprit!"

Bobbi laughed. "Well, you have to admit that you were surprised...."

"Yes, that I was. When did you have time to plan this?"

"We started about a month ago," Bobbi replied. "I'm not in this alone. I think it would be good if you try to figure out who my partner in crime is." Bobbi took Luke's hand and led him into the dining room. "There's something you have to see."

The room had been rearranged. The large dining table had been reduced in size and moved to the end of the room to give more space for people to stand. There on the dining table was a huge double layer sheet cake, with a map drawn on the top. There was a miniature lighthouse at one end, which Luke immediately recognized as Dofflemyer Lighthouse, and at the other end of the cake, a small blue boat. Luke walked closer to get a better look. It was a map of Puget Sound and the San Juan Islands. Orcas was spelled out and Boston Harbor at the other end. In the center it said, "Happy Birthday Luke and Bobbi."

"Who made this? Is that *The Claw*?"

"Your mother and I." Bobbi pointed to Rosa as she walked over. "And yes, that is our version of *The Claw*."

Rosa smiled. "How do you like the cake?"

"It's great, but when? How did you two get this together?"

"Oh, I drove down yesterday morning, and Mrs. West let me use her kitchen. When Bobbi came home from school she helped, and we decorated it together."

"So you're the other person that helped her plan the party." Luke thought he had the right person.

"No, I volunteered to help with the cake and that was it."

"How did Steve and Adam get here?"

"They did a walk-on, the Seattle *Princess Marguerite* run. Uncle Hank met them at the Seattle ferry dock this morning. Oh, by the way, I hope you don't mind, but Steve will be spending the night with you. I'm staying here and so is Adam."

"That will be great." Luke and Steve hadn't had much time together at Christmas. They had written a few letters and called each other now and then, but Luke missed time with his good friend. It would be fun to show him the marina and around Boston Harbor.

Luke looked around the room. Who could be the other party planner? His eyes rested on Charlie sitting in his chair all relaxed and happy. He was watching all the people and seemed very pleased with himself. Luke noticed that the piano bench at the north end of the living room had a pile of presents stacked on the floor at each end of the bench. One side had a sign that said "Luke" and the other "Bobbi." He walked over and looked at his pile. The biggest box said from Charlie and Bobbi. Luke smiled and walked across the room. He knew Charlie had had to do some planning to get that present there without his knowing about it.

"I guess I better take away your telephone privileges," Luke said and sat next to Charlie.

Charlie raised an eyebrow. "Why would you do that?"

"To keep you out of trouble and make sure you don't plan any more surprise parties," Luke replied.

Charlie smiled. "So, you figured it out. I wasn't so sure we were going to pull this off, especially last night when you wanted to go over to Bobbi's. I didn't want you to see your mother or mess up the cake baking."

"So, all that about having to go over the books was just a ruse?"

"You bet. I know you are doing a good job managing the store and marina. I just couldn't think of anything else."

Luke made the rounds and talked to everyone. Then they sang "Happy Birthday" again and Luke and Bobbi blew out the candles on their cake. Mrs. West and Rosa took lots of pictures. People stood or sat around the living and dining rooms while Bobbi and Luke opened their presents.

By four o'clock most of the people had left, and just Uncle Hank, Aunt Sophie, Rosa, Adam, Steve, Charlie, and the Wests remained.

"There is one more thing on the agenda, Luke," Rosa said as she started to pick up stray plates and cups. "Uncle Hank is taking all of us out to the Falls Terrace for an early dinner before he and Sophie head back up to Seattle."

"Wow, that's very nice of him." Luke started helping with the cleanup.

"So, did you enjoy your party?" Bobbi had her hand resting on Luke's elbow, as they walked along the Falls Terrace path to the lower falls after dinner. Steve, Brad, and Adam had run on ahead, the parents were lagging behind, and Charlie had stayed back in the park by the restaurant.

"Yes, I did. You and Charlie really pulled it off. I really appreciate having my family here for my birthday. That was the best part. Uncle Hank outdid himself, taking us all out to dinner."

"He is so thoughtful. He would have made a wonderful father. Too bad they never had children." Bobbi knew it would be impolite to ask why. Uncle Hank and Aunt Sophie had left for Seattle right after dinner. Uncle Hank had wanted to get home before it got dark.

They rounded the corner and headed for the bridge that went over the lower falls. They could see Brad, Steve, and Adam standing on the bridge and pointing to something below. There was so much water coming down the Deschutes

River from the spring run-off that the falls were deafening. Bobbi and Luke stopped at the bridge to look down at the falls breaking and plummeting to the narrow pool of water thirty feet below.

There below them on the rocks were three boys in swim trunks, taking turns diving into the falls. Luke had heard stories of guys diving off those rocks. Guys at school would brag about diving there. The river narrowed at this point and the falls were not very wide; large jagged rocks lined the sides making it dangerous. The falls plummeted into a small pool surrounded by sheer rock sides, and the water spilled out the north side of the pool to a lake. Rumor had it there was a cave behind the falls that one could swim into and come up for air. Even though it had been a warm March day, the temperature was cooling down fast, and an evening chill had set in. The ice-cold mountain water sprayed into the air, creating a mist as it tumbled over the rocks.

Luke took Bobbi's hand and they headed down the stairs to the observation deck, partway down the falls. Brad, Adam, and Steve were already down there watching the divers. Bobbi knew what Luke was going to do. He was going to tell the young boys to stop diving and that it was too dangerous. They had just arrived at the platform and were looking up at one of the young boys when they heard him yell, "It's my turn" over the roaring water. As he started to dive, his foot slipped on the wet rock. He fell out of control, hitting his head on one of the big rocks partway down. He continued to fall into the churning water below.

Bobbi didn't even have to look at Luke. She could feel him next to her pulling off his shoes, socks, and shirt. He climbed over the railing, turned, and yelled, "Go get help!"

Bobbi wanted to yell no, but she knew that it would not do any good. Luke would not stand by and let anyone die.

Instead she closed her eyes and started praying. She didn't want to see him dive.

Luke stood there for a second and then dove into the churning water below. Brad had taken off, running up the stairs and along the half-mile trail back to the restaurant to get help. Bobbi opened her eyes and looked at her watch.

Adam put his hand on her shoulder. "He made a perfect dive. Now you stay here and keep an eye on the falls and signal if you see him surface. You will be able to see him better from here. I'm going to join Steve down below."

Bobbi watched Adam disappear over the railing to the left. The bank on that side wasn't as steep. A narrow trail led down to the side of the small lake, fed by the falls. She looked back at the pool below the falls. Still no sign of Luke. Her parents and Rosa joined her. Her dad looked around and found a section of rope under one of the benches and headed out after Steve and Adam.

Bobbi looked at her watch again. It had been two minutes. Maybe they were behind the falls.

"How long has it been?" Rosa asked.

"Over two minutes. But there's a cave behind the falls, so he might be in there," Bobbi informed her.

"Well, he is a strong swimmer. If anyone can swim in that, he can." Rosa seemed amazingly calm.

The time dragged on. Steve had yelled up to Bobbi several times, asking if she had seen anything. The spray from the falls hitting the pool created a mist that made it hard for them to see down at that level. Each time, she shook her head no. Adam, Steve, and her dad had positioned themselves as close to the pool as they could get. But the pool's steep, rocky sides would not let them get any closer.

Brad should be arriving at the restaurant about now. She checked her watch again. It had been five minutes. Then she saw Luke's head bob up next to the falls. He waved his hand in the air and started for the bank. There was no sign of the boy. Mr. West had tied the rope onto a tree in the bank, and he threw it out to Luke when he got closer, pulling him onto the riverbank. About that time Bobbi heard sirens. Help was on the way. Luke kept talking to her dad. Steve and Adam were standing around Luke.

She heard sobbing; the other two young divers were standing on the platform by them, dripping wet in their swim trunks, clutching their clothes. One was crying, and they were both shaking with fear.

Steve came scrambling up the bank. "Luke got the boy into the cave. He's not doing too well, and Luke couldn't make it back through the falls with him. He says it will take two guys to get him back through the falls. I'm going out to the road to meet the medics."

Bobbi saw Luke head back into the water and swim toward the falls. He was going to go back into the cave, most likely to stay with the boy till the medics arrived. Her heart seemed to leap up in her throat as she watched him disappear under the falls again.

Please, Lord, keep Luke safe, help him make good decisions. Please keep the boy alive, Bobbi prayed.

"I am going up to be with Charlie. He should not be alone this long," Mrs. West said and headed up the stairs to the trail.

Bobbi turned to see the medic and fire trucks out on the road. A metal gate and a fence between the park and the road kept the rescuers from getting in.

"There's Brad with a parks guy!" Rosa yelled over the roaring water. Bobbi saw her brother and a man working on the lock on the gate so that the medics could get through. They were all standing on the other side of the fence with medical bags and stretchers. One of them dropped some gear over the fence and started to climb it. Brad and the park attendant continued to struggle with the lock. The medic climbing over the fence hit the ground and started to run toward Steve, who signaled him. They headed down the path. Another medic started to climb. Two others threw a stretcher over the fence. Bobbi noticed that the first medic wore a small backpack with a first-aid kit and supplies. He quickly got to the shore, took off his boots, ran into the water, and swam to the falls. He disappeared under them. Now they just had to wait.

Bobbi realized that she and Rosa had their arms around each other and were holding tight.

Finally, they got the gate unlocked, and other medics and firemen joined the group at the bank of the lake. Another rescuer swam into the cave.

It seemed like forever, but finally two medics and the boy came up out of the churning water next to the falls. Then Luke came to the surface. They got the boy to the lakeshore and onto the stretcher. Other medics took off with the stretcher up the bank to the medic unit.

Bobbi looked back down at Luke. They were wrapping him in a blanket and talking to him. He kept shaking his head no. Her dad came up the bank and gathered up Luke's shoes and shirt. "Luke is fine, just very cold," he yelled to Rosa and Bobbi. "I don't know about the young boy. He is unconscious. They want to take Luke into the hospital to check him over, but he's refusing to go."

Rosa went over and leaned over the railing, yelling to Mr. West as he headed down the bank. "You tell him to go to the hospital and that's an order!"

Mr. West smiled and nodded.

They heard the first medic unit start its sirens and head off with the boy. The other medics escorted Luke to the other vehicle. Bobbi turned; there were two policemen on the platform talking to the two young boys. One of the policemen came over to her and Rosa.

"Can we ask you a few questions?" he asked.

Bobbi and Rosa agreed. Once he found out that they had seen the whole thing, he suggested that they walk up the path away from the noise of the falls. They found a bench, and Rosa and Bobbi sat down. Between the two of them, they filled the officer in on the details. He thanked them and headed back to his partner and the two young boys. Rosa and Bobbi headed up the trail. Mr. West, Adam, Steve, and Brad were right behind them.

Luke lay in his bed, listening to Steve snoring. It was midnight and he couldn't sleep. He just kept playing the events at the falls over and over in his mind. It bothered him that he had come up on the wrong side of the falls and had to leave the young boy in the cave. If only he hadn't lost his sense of direction. But the force of the water hitting the pool made the current so strong, he could hardly see under the water. As soon as he had hit the water he tried to look around for the boy. He had aimed his dive to land close to the same spot where the boy had gone in. He had also asked the Lord to guide him in the split second that he had stood on the edge of the cliff.

God had answered his prayer. He found the boy almost right away, but he was unconscious, and blood oozed from his head. Luke knew that he needed air, but the force of the falls hitting the water kept taking them deeper into the pool, and then the current would bring them partway up again. Luke had struggled, trying to gain control and finally had figured a way out. He thought he was going out into the lake, but instead he swam into the cave. At least there was air and a shelf of flat rock to lift the boy on to. Luke had pumped his chest and got him breathing again, but there was nothing he could do to stop his head from bleeding. He made sure that the boy would not fall into the water before he headed back through the falls to get help.

It took forever at the hospital to get checked out. The police were there with lots of questions. The doctor suspected Luke had broken a rib, so x-rays were taken. It was only bruised. Once released, Luke went up to the waiting room where everyone waited for news of the boy.

Finally, about ten thirty the doctor came out and talked to the boy's parents. By the look on their faces everyone else could tell it was good news. He was going to be all right. His parents came over and thanked Luke. He wished that they hadn't. He still felt like he'd botched the job.

Sunday morning came too soon. Luke sat up. "Ouch!" he yelled and grabbed his side.

Steve jerked awake. "What?"

"Sorry, it's my rib. Man, is it sore!"

When Luke and Steve got downstairs, Charlie had milk and cereal on the table.

"I know that this is not the best food for a hero, but it is the best I can do." Charlie rolled back to the refrigerator to get juice.

Charlie pointed to the paper on the table. "You made the front page."

Luke glanced at the paper. "Teenager Saves Tumwater Falls Diver," it read.

At church, Luke realized how difficult it is to sing with a bruised rib. He was still not sure where he had gotten that, maybe when he was being tossed up and down in the pool. He remembered bumping something hard, like a rock, as he struggled to get out of the current. Thankfully, he didn't have a solo or a duet in the spring concert on Friday.

CHAPTER 36

After School

"*H*ey!" Luke exclaimed. "Stop that, or I *will* throw you overboard!" He wiped the drops of water that Bobbi had splashed on his face off onto his shirtsleeve.

"Oh! You wouldn't do that to little old me!" She wrinkled up her nose and smiled at him, dipping her hand in the water and threatening to sling more at him.

"Seriously now, I need to stay at this a bit longer." Luke looked back down at his notebook, and Bobbi took her hand out of the water.

They were anchored out in Zangle Cove. Usually they would go to Squaxin Island to study, but Luke didn't want to take the time. He was behind on his English thesis paper. Bobbi had hers almost completely written. *How did she find the time?* he wondered. *She's a faster reader and writer than I am, but still!* But then, she wasn't spending her evenings going over paperwork, writing orders for Mrs. Clark to place, and keeping books for the store and marina. Plus, Charlie needed more of his help each day as he physically declined.

Ever since ski team had finished up the first week of March, Luke and Bobbi had fallen into a routine of coming home from school and checking on Charlie and the store. They would grab their homework and head out in Bobbi's twelve-foot runabout. The exceptions were Tuesdays and Thursdays, as Luke had started to take Greek lessons from Pastor Ralph again. Bobbi spent those afternoons with her horses.

"OK. It's five thirty and we're going to have to head back in soon. Can you take a break and talk?" Bobbi put her books and notebook into her tote bag.

"What about?" Luke looked up.

"Everything, nothing! You just have seemed very distant the past three weeks. What's going on?"

"Nothing." Luke had not realized he was acting any different.

"You're not mad at me about anything?" Bobbi continued.

"No." Luke looked down at the water. "I just have a lot on my mind. With Charlie, and the store…I guess I'm still dealing with that day at the falls."

"The falls? You were the hero!"

"No. Don't say that."

"Well, I didn't see anyone else jumping in to help. If you hadn't acted so fast he would have drowned."

"It was all the Lord. I didn't want to make that dive. It bothers me that I came up on the wrong side of the falls and lost valuable time and it could've cost him his life." Luke felt relieved talking about his mistake.

Bobbi fell silent for a moment. "But God took care of that. He kept the boy alive. Besides, maybe you wouldn't have been able to get through the falls to the north; the force on the outside might have kept you from getting through. I think you need to let this go. You sound like it all depended on you and that you have some self-pity going on. God forgives and forgets our sins and the mistakes we make, and you need to leave it behind now."

Luke gave her a curious look. This was the first time she'd told him he was wrong about something. He smiled. She was right. He had been feeling sorry for himself and feeling guilty that he hadn't done it perfectly the way he wanted to. He liked the fact she straightened him out when he headed the wrong way. "You're right. Sorry if I've been ignoring you."

Luke closed his notebook, started the outboard engine, hauled up the anchor, and they headed back to the harbor.

Luke enjoyed the view as he warmed up a casserole that Mrs. West had sent over. The evenings were getting longer. The word must have gotten out about Charlie's condition. Almost every other day one of the neighbor ladies would pop in with a casserole or main dish. Luke appreciated not having to cook, and Charlie could no longer do it. He got up in the morning, and after they ate breakfast he would sit in his chair by the window. Mrs. Clark said he would sit there all day, dozing off for hours at a time. She had started making him a sandwich or soup for lunch because she had noticed he didn't fix himself anything. Getting him to church the last two Sunday mornings had been a major struggle. Luke heard the downstairs shower turn on every morning, so he knew that Charlie was still taking showers. Their dinners had gotten a lot quieter this past week; Charlie did not seem to have the energy to keep up a conversation.

Luke had been concerned about leaving him over spring break. Luke had gone up to Orcas to be with his mom and Adam for four days. Mrs. Clark and the Wests had convinced him to go. All of them took turns making Charlie's meals and keeping tabs on him.

They had just finished up dinner and Luke cleared the last of the dishes when he heard a knock on the door. Luke turned and saw Dr. Lange and Dr. Peterson through the window.

Luke opened the door. "Come in. How can we help you?"

"We need to talk to you and Charlie," Dr. Lange stated.

"Have a seat." Luke motioned to the table.

Charlie looked up and nodded to the men.

Both men sat down at the kitchen table. Luke found some of Bobbi's cookies, put them on a plate, and poured the men some coffee.

"We are here to talk to you, Charlie, about your getting some help." Dr. Peterson started in. "Every time I come over here, you're sleeping. You aren't doing too well."

"We know that Luke is taking good care of you when he's here, but he needs to go to school. We think the time has come that it might be best for you to hire a nurse to care for you during the day." Dr. Lange picked up Charlie's wrist and checked his pulse.

Charlie stared at them and did not respond. He smiled and then finally nodded.

Dr. Lange got up and opened up his medical bag and took Charlie's temperature and blood pressure. He made a face and then checked Charlie's heartbeat. He signaled to Luke, and they walked over by the cash register.

Dr. Lange spoke in a hushed toned so Charlie couldn't hear. "His temp is up and his heart rate is low. He most likely has a low-grade infection somewhere. I think we are getting closer to the end. Probably he will not last over a month. I have a list of four nurses I know who would do a good job taking care of him."

"OK." Luke fought back tears. Charlie had become family. "I really do appreciate what you and Dr. Peterson are doing. Will you tell Dr. Peterson that if I don't get the chance to?"

"Sure. Now here's the list. Call tonight!" Dr. Lange pulled a folded piece of paper out of his shirt pocket.

The two doctors chatted with Charlie a bit longer and then said their good-byes. Luke started calling.

It would be nice to get some help, Luke thought as he and Charlie watched the sun go down over the Olympics. As the sky turned pink Luke pulled out Charlie's Bible. They had gotten in the habit of reading together every night. Luke knew that was the only time Charlie got to be in God's Word, as he could not read for himself anymore. Charlie seemed to appreciate it.

Charlie fell asleep as Luke finished the evening's psalm. Though they were studying in 1 John, Luke always ended with a psalm of comfort for Charlie. Luke had picked the Twenty-third Psalm that night, as it seemed apropos.

Two of the ladies were able to come out the next afternoon for interviews. It was very obvious they should hire the tall Norwegian woman named Sigrid who could easily lift Charlie, if needed. Not that Charlie was that big anymore. He had lost so much weight that winter Luke feared he might disappear. The other nurse was about Bobbi's size.

After the interviews, Luke took a walk out on the dock. He sat down at the end of the pier. He asked the Lord for the strength to get through the coming month. It was going to be a busy one with music competition, prom, the May concert, graduation ceremonies, and parties. It was already getting crazy at school. Kids were cutting classes left and right. Senior pranks were being played. Someone had filled the administrative offices with old rubber tires. They had also put tires over the flagpole, making it impossible for the janitor to fly the flag. Principal Bain had gone ballistic over that one. Luke wished he wouldn't get so angry and react so much. It seemed to egg on the troublemakers in the class and make matters worse. It had become an undeclared war between the senior class pranksters and Principal Bain. The troublemakers needed to be punished, but the principal's inability to control his temper did not help the situation.

Conversations had turned from politics to parties. It seemed like every day you would hear kids talking about how drunk or stoned they got at the last party.

With most of his free time spent working or taking care of Charlie this past year, he hadn't taken Bobbi out on very many real dates. They had gone out for a movie one Friday night in the fall. He had taken her out to the Falls Terrace for Valentine's dinner. This past Sunday he bought roses after church, went to her house in the afternoon, and asked her to prom. Maybe now with the nurse coming he could take Bobbi out more often. Sigrid had offered to work a few evenings.

Luke walked back up the ramp to the store. Once in the store, he nodded and said good night to the young clerk closing up. Charlie came wheeling out of his room with a small metal box in his hand. He rolled over to the table.

"What do you have there, Charlie?" Luke asked as he closed the door behind the clerk.

Charlie just smiled bright-eyed and opened the box. He fumbled through some papers and came up with a passbook. "For the nurse," he said and handed Luke the passbook.

Luke opened up the passbook. It was a savings account from a local bank. The amount—over one hundred thousand dollars! Luke's jaw dropped. Then he regained his composure and sat down at the table. "Well, we won't be needing all of this for the nurse, Charlie."

Charlie shook his head. Then he reached for a pen and took the passbook back from Luke. He fumbled through the passbook and found the withdrawal slips. Then he carefully signed six of them. "So you can take out…what's needed."

Luke nodded. He hated watching Charlie struggle, but at the same time Luke felt complimented that Charlie trusted him like this. "I will only take what is needed, Charlie." Luke patted his hand and put the passbook back in the black box.

"I don't think we are going to have to dip into that account for a while, Charlie," Luke said as he got up to start the dinner. "You are making a good living off the marina now. And you still have your Disabled Veterans and Social Security checks. You should be just fine. You put that box back. I'll let you know if we need it."

Charlie looked surprised and happy. He turned his chair around and headed back into his room, signaling for Luke to follow. He wheeled over to the closet and put his hand on a built-in set of drawers. He opened the second drawer down and put the black box under a false bottom. Then he took a key out of his pocket and locked the drawer. "Now you know."

"Now I know." Luke patted Charlie's shoulder and pushed him back into the main room.

CHAPTER 37

The Music Competition

*B*obbi honked the horn one more time, and Patty Banks ran out of her house—an old, small, one-story cabin— her long red hair flying. Bobbi had her told they could not be late. They still had to pick up Susan. They were trying to get to school early to practice for the music competition. The Southwest Washington Music Competition was this weekend in Kelso. Mrs. Miller had decided just a week ago that the three senior madrigal girls should sing as a trio. She thought the number that they were planning to do for graduation would be good. That meant extra practices to get the piece ready in time.

Bobbi headed in on Boston Harbor Road, through Priest Point Park, went through downtown and up the west side to pick up Susan. She lived in a beautiful three-story house overlooking Capitol Lake. The Mercedes she had gotten for her sixteenth birthday was in the garage for an oil change, so she had called and asked Bobbi for a ride the night before.

Bobbi dreaded having Susan and Patty in the car together again. Once, earlier in the year, they had both ridden with her. Bobbi feared her little red VW bug would explode from the heat of their discussion. Both were very smart girls and both politically active. The problem was that Patty was a devout Marxist and Susan a devout John Bircher. Bobbi concentrated on keeping the car on the road and tried to find things to say that would cool off the heated debate. In Bobbi's view, both were off the deep end, and they both needed Jesus Christ.

Today was different. Patty had started warming up her voice and doing scales, and when Susan got in the car, she joined in. By the time they arrived at school they had gone through the piece twice.

"I'll call you around noon. I really do appreciate your working extra this week." Luke handed Sigrid a check. "This should cover today with some extra included."

Luke heard Mrs. West honk the horn again. He started out the door and up the ramp to the road. Then he realized he had forgotten his madrigal suit and ran back to the store and grabbed it off the back of the door.

"Sorry I'm late. I just had to give Sigrid final instructions." Luke slid into the back seat of Mrs. West's red VW Squareback. Bobbi snored in the passenger seat. It was six in the morning, the last Saturday in April. They needed to be in Kelso by eight thirty. It was going to be a big day. Madrigals were performing, he had a duet with Bobbi, and she was singing with Susan and Patty. He appreciated Mrs.

West's offer to drive. He could sit back and try to relax a bit on the way down.

Mrs. West started to back up the car, took one look at Bobbi, and stopped. "OK, you two, out and switch places, please!"

Bobbi jerked awake. "Ugh?" Then she nodded off again.

"I am not going to whisper to Luke all the way down with you sleeping here in the front seat. Switch places. Now." Mrs. West grabbed Bobbi's shoulder and gently shook her awake.

As they switched places, Bobbi mumbled "Hi" to Luke and plopped into the backseat. She lay down, closed her eyes, and fell asleep again.

"She doesn't stay awake on long trips, does she?" Luke asked Mrs. West as they headed out of the harbor on Boston Harbor Road.

"No, not unless she's driving. But it is better to have her sleeping than the alternative."

"What's the alternative?"

"Carsickness. She either sleeps or gets sick on long trips," Mrs. West explained. "She will give out a little yell, and my husband knows he has to head for the side of the road."

"Oh no!" Luke glanced back at Bobbi sleeping so peacefully.

"Oh yes!" Mrs. West smiled. "However, on boats it is a different story. *She* is fine, and *we* all get seasick on rough seas. Once we were all so sick out on the straits, and she wanted to eat lunch. We thought she was crazy."

As they drove, the landscape flowed from forest to pasturelands with rolling hills and rivers adding interest. Luke and Mrs. West kept up a conversation most of the way to Kelso with only a few moments of silence. They had a lot to talk about—Bobbi, Charlie, church, school, his future, and his mother.

Bobbi washed her face and then put on her eye makeup in the locker room at the community college in Kelso. She was glad that they had come early. They had just enough time to freshen up, change, warm up, and then they were on at 9:10. The trio would perform at 10:00 and madrigals at 11:30. They would have the rest of the afternoon to relax, watch other performers, and wait to find out if they made any of the twenty slots for the evening performance.

When she came out of the locker room, Luke was standing there waiting for her in his suit. He looked taller.

"Hey, handsome!" Bobbi came up and slid her arm through his. "I have been wondering lately, have you been growing?"

"Growing?" Luke smiled down at her.

"Yes, you seem even taller lately. I have to tilt my head back more, and I know the top of my head use to be equal with your shoulder. Now I'm below it," Bobbi said as they headed down the hall.

"Maybe so. Come to think of it, you've seemed shorter lately. I'll have to measure when I get back to Orcas. We have a measuring wall in the kitchen. Now, let's warm up. There's a room here."

After their warm-up, Bobbi and Luke prayed together. They were both relaxed. The audience was small because of the early hour. The judge nodded for them to start. Bobbi and Luke had so much fun with the piece that when it was all over and the audience started clapping, Bobbi snapped back to reality. She had forgotten about the audience. The judge gave them a nine, the highest mark given. The audience clapped again when the rating was given, and Bobbi and Luke bowed and left the stage.

Mrs. West met them. Now they had to find Patty and Susan.

"Here is an open practice room. How about if you camp here and relax a bit, and your mother and I will split up and scout out Patty and Susan." Luke opened the practice-room door for her.

"Sounds like a plan." Bobbi sat down at the piano and began to play the piece she would be performing next. She wasn't concerned about the trio. They were sounding good together. They had put aside their political and social differences and had been working hard at blending and singing as one. Madrigals...madrigals she had some concerns. The old competition problem had reared its ugly head again the past month, and they were not sounding good. *It's interesting,* she thought. *This time Patty and Susan aren't the problem. They're trying to help. It's the juniors.*

Patty and Mrs. West walked into the room, and a few minutes later Luke, Susan, and her mother joined them. The girls had changed and were ready to warm up. After a few times through the piece, both mothers commented on how nice the girls sounded. Then it was time to go to the performance room they were assigned to. Bobbi liked the way they sounded together during the performance. Susan grabbed Patty and Bobbi's hands when they were all through, and they waited for the judge to make his comments and give them their score. He just kept writing and writing. Finally he raised his head and looked at them.

"You three are very pleasant to listen to. On the second score you could have made the forte a bit louder. Good job." He looked down at his paper again and wrote some more.

"What is our score?" Susan whispered under her breath.

"I give your trio a nine. And don't forget to check the evening performance board at the end of the day," the judge said.

All three clapped their hands and jumped a tiny jump in delight. "A nine! A nine!" Susan exclaimed in delight. The audience continued to clap.

"OK, girls, we need to get off the stage before we look like idiots. Come on," Bobbi whispered, and they walked off the stage.

The next hour turned into a nightmare. No one knew where they were supposed to be. Mrs. Miller was busy with the Good Day Singers. The Good Days were another ensemble group, all girls, who sang and did dance routines. They did songs from the 1930s and '40s. Mary sang mezzo-soprano in that group. They were very good that year. The Good Days were scheduled to perform at 11:15, so Mrs. Miller was with them. Bobbi could understand that, as the Good Days actually had a chance of winning everything.

Bobbi, Luke, Patty, and Susan had walked the halls for twenty minutes trying to find the rest of the madrigal group. They found the room that they would be performing in and the door for entering the stage. But all the practice rooms nearby were full.

"How about if you two stay here?" Luke nodded to Patty and Bobbi. "Susan, Mrs. West, and I will split up and try to find the rest of the group. If you see a practice room open up, grab it."

"Oh, there's one!" Bobbi saw a door opening, and a madrigal group filed out. She ran and grabbed the door.

A teacher from another school stood on the other side of the door opening. "Sorry, but we were in line next." She gave Bobbi a look that said "buzz off" and ordered her group into the room.

After several more attempts Patty finally found a room. By then, several of the madrigals had joined them. They had to be on in twenty minutes. Bobbi started to play scales and warm up the group.

"Ted is singing a solo right now in the other wing of the school." Scott came into the room. "I left instructions for him on how to find us. He should be here just before we go on."

Bobbi felt herself starting to panic. This was going to be the most embarrassing performance ever. Then she stopped herself, and as she played the scales on the piano, she asked the Lord for help.

Luke came into the room with five other members; then Susan came with three more. They were just missing Ted. Mrs. West left to help him find his way back to the room.

Luke walked over to her and whispered in her ear, "I can do all things through Christ who strengthens me. The battle is the Lord's. Take a stand and you will be fine."

She smiled. "We will have two more minutes of warm-ups," she announced and turned back to the piano.

After warm-ups she stood up. "I have something to say in the remaining minutes." Just then Ted walked through the door. "What I have to say is more important than practicing the song. We all know it forward and backward." Bobbi continued, "At the beginning of the year people expected us to be the most talented madrigal group that Oly has ever had. You all know that's saying a lot. The problem this year has been that we haven't acted like the most talented group.

Our performances have been awful. We are not singing like a group but a bunch of soloists thrown together. I know that I'm not the most talented among you. Most likely, I'm the least. But any group has to have a leader, and for some crazy reason I'm it. Like it or not I *am* in charge. So, today you have a choice. You can go out there and work together, listen to each other, and follow me. Or you can continue to sing like we have been. I know that we can sound really good. It's your choice."

Mrs. West stuck her head in the door. "They are announcing you. You're on!"

Everyone lined up and they headed out couple by couple, with Bobbi and Luke last.

"Very good," Luke whispered to her and smiled as they walked to the stage door.

"Thanks for the encouragement," Bobbi whispered back.

As they filed onto the stage, Bobbi glanced at the packed audience. The stage was the lowest part of the room. The seats were on a steep angle looking down on them. On the left side of the room, near the top, sat the judge, a thin, middle-aged, dark-haired man. He sat behind a desk and watched them intently through his glasses.

Once in her chair, Bobbi had a clear view of the judge.

She brought out her pitch pipe and gave the note. She nodded the rhythm, and they began perfectly on the same note. Then the tenors broke off from the basses and the sopranos from the altos, each section sounding like one voice. Bobbi hid her amazement. It felt right, and they were all following her perfectly. She signaled for pianissimo, and they followed, quiet and in control. Then they built up to the forte and they shone. She didn't want the piece to end. They were sounding so good. She glanced at the judge several times, and he kept staring at them and not writing anything down. Was that good or bad?

The piece ended, and they sat very still, looking at the judge. He sat there for a moment and stared back. You could have heard a pin drop. No one clapped. The judge rose from his chair and walked out to the aisle. He walked down half of the stairs, sat down on a stair, and took off his glasses. All eyes were on him.

"That was the most enjoyable thing I have ever heard. I want you to do me a favor and sing it again just like you did, but make the fortes a bit more forte and the pianissimos a bit more pianissimo. I am going to sit here with my eyes closed and listen." He smiled and closed his eyes.

Bobbi looked at the rest of the group. They were all smiling. They had done it! Bobbi gave the note, nodded the rhythm, and they started in again. What fun. Everyone paid very close attention, and they were finally a team. As they finished the song, tears started coming down Bobbi's cheeks. She couldn't help it. How beautiful!

The judge stood up and went back to his desk. The audience started to clap. Then they stood and the clapping got louder. Then there were shouts of "Bravo!" It was totally magical.

The judge sat and watched; then he started to write. The audience quieted down. The judge looked up and announced that they had a nine and he had written a recommendation for the evening performance.

As soon as they were off the stage and in the hall, they all started celebrating. The girls were hugging and crying and the boys slapped each other on the back. The Good Days and Mrs. Miller joined them.

Mary rushed up to Bobbi and gave her a hug. "We made it from our performance in time to watch you guys. Mrs. Miller is walking on cloud nine."

Susan came up and gave Bobbi a hug. "Thank you. You did it! I'm so sorry for all the trouble I have caused all year. You're the best leader."

"The sun is shining. It's warm. This has to be the best day ever!" Bobbi exclaimed as she lay on the picnic blanket. Mrs. West, Luke, and Bobbi had just finished the picnic lunch Mrs. West had brought. They had changed clothes and found a park near the school. "I don't think it could get any better."

"I think you're right. It has been pretty good," Luke agreed. "I'm going to call home and see how Charlie's doing." Luke pointed to the pay phone and stood up.

Everything was fine at the marina. Luke talked to Charlie and told him all about the performances. Then he talked to Sigrid, and she said that Charlie had smiled very big when Luke told him the good news.

Bobbi walked over as he finished up. "I'm going to call my dad."

"Hi, Dad. Boy, do we have a lot of good news for you!" Bobbi started in.

"And I may have some good news for you!" Mr. West answered. "You go first."

Bobbi told him all about the performances. "We most likely will be staying for the evening performance, so Mom says it might be midnight before we get home."

"That's fine. You enjoy and sing your best. Now, I have three letters that came in the mail for you. One from Seattle Pacific University, one from Washington State University, and one from Pacific Lutheran University. Do you want me to open them?" Mr. West asked.

"Yes! Oh Mom, Dad is opening letters from colleges. They came in the mail today," she shouted over to her mother sitting on the picnic blanket.

"Well, young lady, you have been accepted to PLU, and they have offered you a music scholarship! They will pay your tuition. Congratulations!"

"I'm in! I'm in!" Bobbi did a little dance. That was where she wanted to go. "Luke, Mom, I'm in PLU with a scholarship, too!"

"There's more. You got almost the same offer from SPU and WSU. Looks like you will have some choices to make, young lady! Very good! I am proud of you."

"Thanks, Dad. Mom wants to talk to you. I love you." Bobbi handed the phone to her mom.

She stood there, stunned. This was the most unbelievable day!

"Bobbi West is speechless?" Luke came up and gave her a hug. "Now, there is front-page news!"

She laughed and gave him a quick kiss on the cheek.

Back at the community college they ran into Mrs. Miller. She was pleased that the whole school had done well. She joined them, and they spent the rest of the afternoon listening to other groups perform.

At three thirty, they announced the evening performance participants in the cafeteria and then posted it.

First up, West and Johansen/Olympia High School; fourth, Ted Olsen/Olympia High School; twelfth, the Olympia High School Girls' Trio; fourteenth, the Olympia High School Good Day Singers; and last of the evening, Olympia High School madrigals. Five out of twenty for one high school!

Mrs. Miller gave all of them instructions on when to be back and where to meet. The performance would be in the school gym. They all took a break for dinner. Mrs. West drove Luke and Bobbi to a restaurant across town.

"Now, young lady, I want you to be quiet for a while and calm yourself down. You have been talking nonstop and you need to rest your voice." Mrs. West leaned across the table and looked at Bobbi very sternly as she talked. She looked at Luke sitting next to Bobbi. "You will help me with this, right?"

Luke smiled and nodded. Bobbi was always intense about everything. It had been such an emotional day for all of them, but Bobbi ran the chance of burning out first.

Luke paid the bill and they drove back to the community college in complete silence.

Once in the practice room, Bobbi and Luke warmed up. Bobbi's voice felt rough on the scales. Then they started the duet and she went up for the high note at full force. The most awful noise came out of her throat. She had cracked!

Bobbi looked at Luke in horror! "My voice! It's gone!" she croaked.

"No, no," Mrs. West exclaimed. "It will be fine. It is just all the excitement of the day. Here is a cough drop, and I will go and get you some water. I have done this before myself. Just rest it for a minute." Mrs. West headed out to the hall to get water; she could see people filling up the gymnasium seats.

Luke took both her hands in his and asked the Lord to make Bobbi's voice strong again.

Bobbi drank the water her mother brought back and finished up the cough drop.

They tried some gentle scales, then tried the song again. She backed off the high note and just hit it lightly. She made it through.

"That's good. Maybe not your best, but very nice." Mrs. Miller walked into the room. She had heard from Mrs. West about Bobbi's voice. "Just let your voice float up to that note. Don't force it. Not tonight."

Bobbi nodded and looked at her watch. "It's time," she whispered, and they walked to the stage door.

All the performances went well that night. Luke had whispered more Bible verses in her ear before they went on stage each time. He was such a comfort and strength. What was she going to do without him next year?

CHAPTER 38

Last Dance

"Now you stand still, or I will poke you with a pin," Mrs. West mumbled through a mouthful of pins.

Bobbi tried to stand still, but it was so hard. "It's really beautiful, Mom. You have outdone yourself." Bobbi looked at the midnight-blue velvet evening gown. She hoped that Luke would like it. "Hi, Dad. We're almost finished, and then we will start dinner. What do you think? Do you think Luke will like it?"

"Well, if he doesn't, I think he needs to have his head examined. That really looks good on you. You have done a good job as usual, Kay." Mr. West had just come up from the beach and walked in the sliding glass door. He walked over and gave his wife a kiss. Brad came through the door.

"Wow. How much did you two spend on that?" Brad asked. "You know, someday when you get married, your husband's not going to spoil you like this."

"Brad, you know that your mother saves a lot of money by making Bobbi's clothes. A dress like that from a store would cost three times what your mother spent on it."

"OK! That is it, the final fitting. You are not to lose any more weight in the next three days. I'll not take it in again." Mrs. West straightened up and looked at Bobbi in the mirror. "You do look perfect!" She gave Bobbi a kiss on the cheek.

"Thanks, Mom. There is only one opinion I care about, and we won't find that out until Saturday night." Saturday night seemed like a long way off.

"Sigrid, you can leave at eleven since he will be in bed, but please make sure that he is asleep. I won't be home till one at the earliest." Luke walked over to the window and kneeled down next to Charlie's chair.

"Now, we should be coming by in about twenty minutes. We won't be able to stay long, OK?" Luke looked the old man directly in the eye, hoping that he understood. Dr. Lange had told Luke that even though Charlie didn't talk much anymore, Luke should keep talking to Charlie and treating him just like normal.

Luke went over and got Bobbi's corsage out of the refrigerator. It was a wrist corsage, a large white orchid. Mrs. West had suggested the wrist corsage and given him a sample of the dress material. The florist had suggested the white orchid, the most expensive corsage they made. Luke decided it was worth it. He took one last look in the mirror at his midnight-blue tuxedo. It had seemed to match the swatch of the dress material just fine. He hoped so. It would be different; most of the guys were renting the popular white or light blue jackets.

As he drove the Jeep over to Bobbi's, Luke couldn't help but reflect on last year's May dance, when Bobbi had been Joe's date. This year he could say whatever he wanted. He could tell her how beautiful she looked.

They were double dating with Scott and Susan, who were going as friends. He and Scott had disagreed on who would drive. Scott refused to take Susan anywhere in the Jeep.

"Susan drives a Mercedes!" was Scott's winning argument. "I'm not taking her anywhere in that Jeep of yours."

Luke had given in, and Scott had made arrangements to borrow his dad's Buick Riviera. Then there was the issue of Charlie. Charlie wanted to see Bobbi and Luke all dressed up. They got it figured out. Luke would pick up Bobbi in the Jeep and take her to the marina. Then Scott would pick them up at the marina, and they would get Susan in town. The guys had planned a big surprise for the girls. They were taking them out to dinner at the best restaurant in Tacoma, Jonah and the Whale, right on the waterfront.

Luke had also talked to Scott and they had agreed that they were not on any great deadline. If they came in a bit or a lot late to the dance, it would be all right. It would be an evening of fun with no pressure. Luke did not want a repeat of last year's fiasco.

Luke rang the Wests' doorbell.

"Well, young man, you look good enough to take out my daughter," Mr. West said as he opened the door. "I swear you seem to be growing, Luke. How tall are you supposed to be?"

"Six foot, sir," Luke replied as they walked up the stairs.

"No, you have to be taller than that. Come over here, take off your shoes, let me get a chair, and we will settle this. Bobbi has mentioned that you are growing, and I think she's right." Mr. West took him to the kitchen doorframe and had him stand against it. He felt a bit awkward.

"Don't worry. Last I heard from the fashion end of the house, there was some kind of big disaster, and I doubt Bobbi will be emerging for a while. So we have time to find out how tall you really are."

Luke stood up tall, and Mr. West made a mark with a pencil and wrote a big L next to the mark. Then he pulled out a small silver tape measure from his pocket.

"Wow, six two! You have been growing, son! Now you are officially a foot taller than Bobbi." Mr. West pointed to Bobbi's last mark, a foot below Luke's.

"What are you two doing?" Brad came into the room.

"Finding out how tall Luke is. He has been growing on us. He's now six foot two," Mr. West exclaimed.

"Really? You can't grow any more. There is a limit, you know." Brad smiled at Luke. "I heard 'ready to come out' noises from Bobbi's room, so thought I should get out here to see the show." Brad picked up a camera from the kitchen nook counter and walked into the living room.

Mrs. West walked into the living room. "She is all ready, are you?" she asked Luke.

Luke nodded and kept his eye on the entrance to the hall. Bobbi walked through the door opening. He could not think of a thing to say. Finally the word "Gorgeous" came out of his mouth. The midnight-blue color of the dress made her olive-colored skin glow. Her hair pulled up on the sides fell in curls down her back.

Luke voice was full of admiration. "Wow! You really look beautiful!"

Bobbi smiled even bigger and walked over to him. Brad had been clicking away on the camera. Mrs. West went to get Luke's boutonniere out of the refrigerator.

"I have your corsage here." Luke handed her the white box and let her open it. The look on Bobbi's face was worth the extra money.

"It's a wrist corsage. Let's see, which wrist do you want it on? He looked down at her right wrist and she had on his bracelet. On her left was a delicate silver watch with a chain for a band.

"Oh! Let's put it above the watch. It was my grandmother's. You know this bracelet hasn't left my wrist since you gave it to me."

Mrs. West handed Bobbi the boutonniere, and Bobbi struggled to put it on Luke's lapel. Finally, Mr. West came to her rescue. Bobbi grabbed her shawl and purse, and they were on their way.

Charlie had his camera on his lap when they arrived at the marina.

He got the biggest smile on his face when Bobbi came into the room. "Look at my girl!" he exclaimed. "You are one lucky guy. I hope you know that," Charlie told Luke.

"I know, Charlie, I know," Luke agreed. They posed for a few pictures.

It surprised Luke how alert and talkative Charlie was.

Sigrid came into the room. She had been changing Charlie's sheets and getting his bed ready. Charlie went to bed earlier each night. "Well, look at you two! I must be looking at the prom king and queen!"

"Hardly," Luke replied. "We weren't nominated for court." There were eight couples in the May court—eight senior boys and six senior girls, then a junior princess and a sophomore princess. "We aren't in the popular crowd."

"Well, you look like you should be, right, Charlie?"

Charlie agreed. He just kept taking pictures and smiling from ear to ear. It meant a lot to Luke to see Charlie this happy.

At that moment, Scott knocked on the door. Bobbi opened it for him, and he stepped into the store.

"You two look terrific. Hi, Charlie. Sorry to break this up, but your chariot awaits." Scott opened the door and bowed.

The three said their good-byes and headed up the ramp with Scott in the lead. He opened the back door of the Buick and they slid inside.

"Hey, why are we getting on the freeway? Where are you taking us?" Susan asked as Scott approached the on-ramp of I-5 heading north.

Scott smiled. "You will just have to wait and see."

Susan looked radiant in a strapless, light blue sequined gown. Bobbi remembered seeing that one at Frederick's in Seattle. She knew it cost a small fortune.

The girls were delighted when they found out where they were going for dinner. The guys insisted that they order anything they wanted off the menu. Bobbi ordered lobster and Susan a New York steak. Luke had the Dungeness crab, and Scott got the same as Bobbi.

"Crab! You and your crab. You might even recognize it when it comes to the table. Maybe it's one you caught last summer." Bobbi teased Luke after they ordered.

"I hope not. Besides, the menu said fresh not frozen. For *that* price it better not be frozen."

"Are you going to be crabbing this summer, Luke?" Susan asked.

"No, most likely not. I'm not sure what I'm going to do this summer. A lot depends on Charlie. I can't desert him at this point. We're just trying to get through each day."

"I'm so glad we went there tonight. You should have seen him, Susan. He was so awake and alert, almost like the old Charlie. You could see it meant the world to him that we were together, and he loved seeing us all dressed up," Bobbi commented.

Luke laughed, "I think he took a whole roll of pictures. But you better not count on those photos Bobbi, with his eyesight who knows what he took. At least he was having fun."

"Oh, here come the salads," Scott said.

Scott said grace before they started their salads. Bobbi could tell that Susan was a bit uncomfortable with saying grace in public. Bobbi silently asked the Lord to make it possible for one of them to give the gospel to Susan that night.

"What a fairy tale evening! Thank you so much for making it perfect!" Bobbi leaned against the front door.

"No. Thank you. You were the prettiest girl there. It was a pleasure to be your escort, Miss West. I loved dancing with you," Luke replied. He bent over and kissed her on the forehead and then picked up her left hand and kissed it.

"I would invite you in for a few minutes, but I doubt that Scott wants to wait much longer." Bobbi gave Luke a kiss on the cheek and headed inside. Maybe it was good that Luke had not come inside. In the past they would just sit and talk, but tonight had been so romantic that she really wanted him to kiss her. She knew it was best if they waited.

It's been a perfect night, Bobbi thought, as she got ready for bed. She thanked the Lord again. They had gotten to the school gym in time to see the crowning of the May court. Then it was on to the dance at the Tyee. Susan and Scott had been a lot of fun to be with. On the way out to the harbor, Scott informed them that he and Susan had taken a walk in the Tyee garden and he had a chance to give Susan the gospel. Yeah!

CHAPTER 39

Senior Sleep Out

"*H*i there. You're up." Luke walked across the room and sat down on the side of Charlie's bed.

It was Thursday morning, the seventh of May. Charlie was sitting up in bed! Lately, he would sleep until nine or ten when Sigrid would wake him up. Luke missed having breakfast with him every day.

"Yeah! The foghorn woke me up this morning. There is something going on today, isn't there?"

"Tonight. It's tonight, Charlie. It's Senior Sleep Out, but I don't have to go," Luke replied.

"Yes, you have to. That's one of the oldest traditions at Oly. Sigrid takes good care of me. I'll be fine." Charlie smiled. "Besides, she's a much better cook than you."

"I'll be home after school for a while. Just to change and pick up a few things. You will see an extra boy working on the docks this afternoon and evening. I know a lot of the seniors are going to Squaxin for Senior Sleep Out. I'm hoping they will stop here and get fuel, so I scheduled extra help."

"Is that where you and Bobbi are going?" Charlie asked.

"No. That's going to be one big drunk. No, remember I told you we'd be with some of the seniors from the music department? We are going up to Seattle for dinner, and then eventually we will end up at Mrs. Miller's house. She lets everyone come and sleep on her rec room floor. She has a big house on American Lake, in South Tacoma. It's a place for those of us who don't want to drink or do drugs."

"That's nice." Charlie rubbed his eyes and looked like he might doze off.

"I will leave the Millers' number with Sigrid. Now, you go back to sleep. I gotta get to school."

Luke stopped laughing. "Bobbi, get in! The light's green!" he yelled at the top of his lungs. Cars behind them continued to honk their horns. Bobbi jumped onto the running board of the Jeep and collapsed into the backseat, laughing loudly. Luke took off, then looked in the rearview mirror. She grabbed her sides and trying not to laugh.

"It hurts!" she gasped.

Luke smiled at her predicament. Then he frowned. *Someone could get hurt.* They were in downtown Seattle. He slowed down and stopped at the next intersection. Scott pulled up next to him in his dad's Riviera, and one of the guys from band pulled up behind Scott. Bobbi had suggested playing Chinese fire drill about four intersections back. Since then, the girls had been racing around the cars at each intersection and jumping into a different car each time.

"We are going to get arrested for something. I just know it," Luke mumbled. "Public drunkenness, impeding traffic, something." Now the guys had joined the action.

"Oh Luke, loosen up. You know none have us have been drinking." Tanya from orchestra punched him on the shoulder and headed back out the door at the next intersection. The light turned green, and there was no one in the Jeep but him. Where did they go? He didn't want to leave anyone behind, but the car behind him kept honking. He looked to his right. People were jammed in Scott's car so tight you couldn't see who was who. He laughed. He did enjoy seeing Bobbi and everyone having so much fun. But the way everyone was acting, anyone watching would think that they were drunk or high. Bobbi could get so silly sometimes.

At the next intersection Bobbi and two guys from band climbed back into the Jeep. "OK, we're through. Scott's as worried as you are. The game's over. He wants to head south to Tacoma and go to Mr. Sims's house."

Mr. Sims? I thought we were spending the night at Mrs. Miller's." Luke looked dubious. Mr. Sims was the orchestra teacher.

"We are. But Bill brought a whole case of toilet paper and he wants to TP Mr. Sims's house first. It's just a mile from the Millers'," Bobbi explained.

It was midnight before they arrived at the Millers' house. Bill brought out the toilet paper and they TP-ed the trees in the Millers' front yard. Then they noticed a sign on the front door:

Music department seniors, please take the path to the right of the house to the back yard and go in through the sliding glass doors. Breakfast is at 5:30 in the morning. We leave for school at 6:30. All toilet paper will be picked up before anyone is fed.

Love and hugs, Mrs. Miller.

"She has been through this before," Bobbi whispered to Luke. "I wonder if she wants us to pick up the paper at Mr. Sims's house, too?"

Everyone grabbed their bags and sleeping bags and headed down the path, trying to be quiet. When Bobbi and Luke got to the door, Tanya stood guard. "Guys to the left and girls on the right. There are two bathrooms down here. The boys' is straight ahead and the girls' is on the right down the hall. Sorry, you two; no smooching tonight."

"That's fine with us," Luke and Bobbi said at the same time.

"I have an alarm clock and I'm setting it for five o'clock." Scott announced. They decided that the boys would get up at that time and clean up the toilet paper, and the girls could help Mrs. Miller with breakfast clean-up and the dishes.

Bobbi woke up to Mr. Miller playing "reveille" on his trumpet. She rolled over. All the boys were up and had packed up their sleeping bags. She could hear a shower going. Three of the other girls were still in their sleeping bags.

"Look at this spread! Thanks so much, Mrs. Miller." Scott had his eye on the donuts. There was fresh fruit, bacon, croissants, donuts, and scrambled eggs, enough for twenty-five people or more; too bad that there were only fourteen of them.

"Well, we were not sure how many seniors we would wake up to this morning." Mrs. Miller patted Scott on the shoulder. "I had hoped more would have chosen to come here." She knew what went on at the other parties.

"It looks like the guys did a great job cleaning up the yard, so you're all allowed to dig in after we say grace." Mr. Miller gave the prayer and they all lined up.

It was different driving to school from Tacoma and all of them walking into the gym together. Another part of Senior Sleep Out was an all-school assembly first thing in the morning. The seniors were expected to straggle in late in the clothes they had worn all night. The big deal of the day: the girls were allowed to wear jeans!

Principal Bain got up and gave some announcements. The yell squad led the class cheer competition. Usually the seniors won, but this time they were all so tired and so many were missing, the juniors easily took the trophy.

Just as Principal Bain got up to announce the speaker, a large group of seniors came in late. Most of them looked drunk.

Principal Bain lost it. He started in, his voice laden with sarcasm. "Welcome to school today. Glad the senior class could make it." Then his voice increased to a yell. He stomped his feet and waved his hands in the air. Pointing at the senior class, he said, "No, truthfully, I am really looking forward to when this senior class graduates! You are the worst class to ever graduate from Olympia High School. And the first class to have Senior Sleep Out all year long. I will be so glad when you are gone!" He turned and walked off the stage and out of the gymnasium. The whole school got very quiet. The vice principal stood up and went to the microphone and introduced the speaker.

Luke felt sorry for Principal Bain. Yes, many in their class had been disrespectful, rebellious, and often got into trouble during the year. But he didn't like the way the principal handled the situation. Getting mad at everyone didn't help to enforce his authority; it made all the students who were behaving dislike him for including them with the troublemakers.

It made him think about what Pastor Ralph had been teaching about this spring: God's authority. He had taken them through Christ's life and showed how He was obedient to God the Father and respected His authority. Then Pastor Ralph spent a lot of time explaining God's plan for man and the authorities that God had placed on earth. He gave a lot of verses showing how people should show respect for authority. Luke did get tired of the rebellion in the class, but not everyone was like that. There seemed to be a larger group that did obey the rules and respected the teachers and staff.

Luke looked at Bobbi. He could tell she felt the same way.

At lunch Bobbi used the phone in the music department office and called her mother.

"You should have seen all the boats scampering across the bay this morning from Squaxin Island, full of kids. A regular mad rush to get to school by boat," Mrs. West told Bobbi. "How was Mrs. Miller doing with all of you?"

"Just fine. We did the breakfast clean-up so she didn't have to. We had a good time. I'm just exhausted." Bobbi yawned. She had not gotten to sleep until two. "I didn't have time for a shower this morning, so guess what I'm doing this afternoon?"

CHAPTER 40

God's Time

*T*he foghorn let out one more blast. Luke lay there. He had been listening to it for a while. He rolled over. It was only five thirty on Sunday morning. He would let Charlie sleep a while and then decide if he should try to take Charlie to church. Last Sunday had been such a battle getting him there, and Charlie had slept through most of the service. Luke wasn't sure what to do. He knew Charlie wanted to go.

He got up and took a shower. Then he went down and got out the cereal bowls and cereal for breakfast. He needed to wake up Charlie, dress him, and feed him.

The minute Luke walked into Charlie's bedroom he knew that taking Charlie to church was not going to be an issue. Charlie was with the Lord. Luke could tell just by looking at him.

"Charlie, Charlie," Luke said, just in case. Then he picked up Charlie's wrist and felt for a pulse. There was none.

Luke stood there, stunned. Then loneliness and fear swept over him at the same time. Why did he feel this way? He had known this would happen. He sat down on the side of the bed and started to cry. Charlie was family. An uncle, grandpa, or father, Luke was never sure, but he was *family*.

"Well, Charlie, no more pain and no more sorrow," Luke said quietly. Charlie looked so peaceful.

Luke wiped his eyes and took a deep breath. Now what was it that Charlie had told him to do when he died? Oh yes. Call that lawyer, Mr. Ellis. Luke walked out to the main room and found the card the lawyer had left, in the little drawer next to the cash register. It was seven when he placed the call.

Then Luke called the Wests. Mr. West answered the phone. "I will be right over," he said when he heard the news.

Luke was relieved. "Would you please tell Bobbi for me?"

"I will."

Bobbi arrived with her father about ten minutes later, her face red and blotchy, tears still streaming down her face.

Luke gave Bobbi a hug and held her for a while. "We know that he's happy now. He's not in any pain." Mr. West went into Charlie's bedroom for a minute.

"I know. I'm going to miss him so much," she sobbed.

In a short time, Mr. Ellis, the police, and the medical examiner arrived, one right after the other.

"Now, you take it easy. I'll take care of everything." Mr. Ellis said. He peeked into Charlie's bedroom at the medical examiner and the police. "I need to talk to them, but here's a letter that Charlie wrote explaining where he wanted to be buried. He already paid for the stone, casket, and burial. Charlie took care of every last detail."

Luke scanned over the letter. Mr. Ellis came back into the room and shuffled through his briefcase.

"There are several letters that Charlie wrote to you two. These are the first two that he wanted you to read. The other two will be given to you at the reading of the will," Mr. Ellis explained as he handed Bobbi and Luke each a letter.

Luke signaled to Bobbi and they went outside on the deck and sat down on a bench. They each opened their letter and read in silence. Then Luke handed Bobbi his letter and took hers and they read each other's.

Charlie had written each of them that he loved them and how special they were to him. To Luke, he had also written, "I have thanked the Lord every day for bringing you into my life and here to live with me. You are the son that I never had. Don't be sad for me, be happy. I am enjoying being with the Lord."

And to Bobbi he wrote, "You are my little ray of sunshine. Always stay your happy self. Just remember I am with the Lord and don't be too sad."

He asked them to contact Pastor Ralph and set the memorial service for a time that was convenient for both of them. Charlie had left an outline of songs and what he wanted Pastor Ralph to say, with Mr. Ellis. He had also asked Mr. Ellis to contact his nephews. Bobbi and Luke were to be present for the reading of the will.

The undertaker arrived and Charlie's body was taken away. The policemen and medical examiner left. Mr. West and Mr. Ellis were still inside. Luke just sat on the bench with his arm around Bobbi. He couldn't move. "I'm no help at all," he whispered to Bobbi. Finally, he found the strength to stand. He walked over to the store and poked his head in the door.

"I'm sorry that I've not been much help," Luke said to the two men.

"It's OK. We haven't needed any help. You are in shock. That's normal," Mr. Ellis said.

"Maybe there is one thing you can help us with, though. We are trying to find a special box that has all of Charlie's valuables in it. The letter to Mr. Ellis says that he is to take it and open it at the reading of the will." Mr. West stood in the bedroom doorway looking puzzled. "I've looked everywhere I can think of. It is supposed to be a black box."

"I do know where that is. He showed me that a month ago when we hired Sigrid." Luke walked past Mr. West into the bedroom. Luke looked at the bed. The bedding had been stripped off of it, and it looked bare and lonely in the room. It hit Luke hard. *No more Charlie,* he thought. Luke started to feel a bit woozy, and then things started to turn dark.

"Over here, son," he heard Mr. West say. "Sit down here for a minute."

Luke felt a chair under him and he collapsed. He caught his breath, and things started to focus again. He started to cry and then stopped. "This is ridiculous," he said and tried to stand up. He collapsed in the chair again.

"Just sit still for a minute. We have time. There is no hurry." Mr. West put his hand on Luke's shoulder.

Bobbi came into the room. Tears ran down her face. She just kept looking around as if she was looking at everything for the first time. No, she was looking for someone—Charlie.

"The box is in the closet. There's a chest of drawers. The second drawer down has a false bottom. The box is in there." Luke pointed to the closet and then leaned back in the chair again. He still felt weak. But then he sat up, alert. "But you're going to need a key that Charlie always kept in his pocket. I hope that didn't go to the undertaker's!"

"Is it this key?" Mr. West opened a little box on the nightstand, and inside was the key.

"Yes." Luke leaned back in the chair again.

The men found the box, and Mr. Ellis said that he would be leaving. "Luke, remember that since your name is on the business checking account, you have access to funds to cover expenses for the store. Charlie told me that you always kept enough in there to cover two months' expenses."

"Yes, we have plenty. It will be fine. Besides, this place actually makes money," Luke answered.

"I will call you later today, and we can start to make plans once you have had a chance to think and rest a bit," Mr. Ellis said as he walked out the door.

Mr. West stood by the window, looking at the view. He turned to Luke. "Luke, I want you to pack a bag and come to our house for the day and spend the night too. I think you need to get away from here for a while. You two need to decide later this afternoon when you want the memorial service. We can call Pastor Ralph this afternoon.

Later that afternoon, Luke woke up to a knock on the Wests' guest bedroom door. "Yes, come in."

"It's Mr. Ellis on the phone for you and Bobbi." Brad stuck his head in the door. "Bobbi is going to get on the phone in my parents' room, and you can use the one in the kitchen.

"Thanks."

"Well, I talked to the nephews. They were just as awful as Charlie had said they would be. They have no interest in coming to the memorial service. They don't want to pay extra for plane tickets, so they want to have the reading of the will in two weeks or later so they can get a discount on their plane tickets," Mr. Ellis said. "You can set the memorial service for any time you want."

"We've talked to Pastor Ralph, and he says the church is available this next Saturday the twenty-third. The weekends after that, the church is booked with weddings. So we decided to have it the twenty-third," Bobbi explained.

"Well, then the twenty-third it is. What time?" Mr. Ellis asked.

"One o'clock," Bobbi answered.

"Luke, you and I need to go over all the business accounts. The bank accounts will require death certificates so that they can be transferred to the right party. Would you have time after school tomorrow?"

"Yes, that would be fine, sir. I can come to your office, or would it be better at the store?"

Mr. Ellis agreed that the store would be the best place. They also set a date for the reading of the will. June fourth. Two days after graduation. Luke went back down to the guest bedroom and collapsed on the bed again. He should be finishing up his English thesis paper and practicing for his presentation that was due at the end of the week. Bobbi had presented hers on Friday, so she was all done. There were finals in two weeks, to study for, but Luke didn't care. He just needed to be alone.

CHAPTER 41

Memorial

*B*obbi stopped brushing her hair and looked at herself in the mirror. She looked tired and she was. This past week had been a blur. There had been so much paperwork for Luke to go through.

She had organized the memorial service. Her mother and the ladies of the church were pros at this kind of thing, and they had helped her out. She would not have made it through without them. Bobbi looked at her watch; the service would start in an hour. She just hoped everyone had done their jobs and that everything would go well.

Thursday night had been the last music concert of the year. Rosa, Aunt Sophie, and Uncle Hank had come down for the concert. Uncle Hank and Aunt Sophie came just for the evening, but Rosa stayed for the weekend and Charlie's memorial service. Rosa was concerned about Luke and all he had to do, as was everyone else. The concert had gone well. Since neither she nor Luke had any special solos or special parts, they just blended in with the chorus and enjoyed the evening.

Bobbi had helped Luke at the marina. He taught her how to write up the orders and how the books were kept. After school each day she would come right out to the marina and help Mrs. Clark for a while and take care of the orders and books. That freed Luke up to deal with the scheduling, the paperwork concerning Charlie's death, and his homework.

Yesterday Luke had presented his English thesis. Though his oral presentation was a bit rough, the content of his thesis proved he had been working hard all semester, and Bobbi hoped he would get the A he deserved.

Bobbi ran the brush through her hair one more time, checked her outfit in the mirror, and headed out to the living room. She missed Charlie. It didn't seem possible that he was gone.

"Is everyone about ready?" Mr. West looked up from his paper. Bobbi nodded, and Brad walked into the room. He raised his voice so his wife could hear him in the bedroom. "OK, Kay, we need to get going."

"Hey, you have done a great job. The flowers look great." Luke put his hand on Bobbi's shoulder.

"Well, the only flowers we bought were the ones in the middle. The rest are all given by friends of his. I think the big arrangement on the right is from his Coast Guard mates." Bobbi straightened Luke's tie as she talked.

"That says a lot about how many lives Charlie touched. Just look at all those flowers. The steps are covered," Luke said in amazement.

Bobbi and Luke were standing at the back of the church in the small overflow room, waiting for the signal from Pastor Ralph to walk down the aisle. Since Charlie's nephews weren't coming, Pastor Ralph asked Luke and Bobbi to stand in as Charlie's family. They were to sit in the front row reserved for the family, and the Wests and the Clarks were to sit in the row behind them.

"Have you seen all the people? I don't think we are going to get them all in. I'm sure some will have to stand at the back. There are so many people from the harbor!" said Mr. West.

"I just hope we have enough food for everyone. The ladies have it all ready, but it may not be enough." Bobbi looked worried. She had expected quite a few people, but not this many.

"Well, some of these people will be hearing the gospel for the first time, I'm sure. What an open door God has given Pastor Ralph," Luke commented. "It's one o'clock. There are still people standing out in the hall. We won't be starting on time."

Luke was right. Pastor waited another eight minutes before signaling the families to walk down the aisle.

Pastor Ralph opened with prayer, thanking the Lord for taking Charlie home. He talked about how Charlie, even as a new believer, had grown quickly and was an eager student of God's Word. He explained that all the hymns they were going to be singing that day had been chosen by Charlie himself. Then he asked one of Charlie's old Coast Guard mates to come and give the eulogy.

"There are so many stories I could tell about Charlie. An outline of his life is on the back of your memorial program. I will go right to the reason we all loved Charlie so much. He had a big heart. He always thought about other people.

He would do anything for anyone, even strangers. There is one story that explains exactly who he was.

"We were working out of Port Angeles up on the straits. Charlie and I had been working the same shift for years. We were on a small rescue craft with two crew members. A bad storm came up quickly one day. Visibility was bad, the waves were high, and we got a call on the radio that there was a pleasure craft in trouble out in the straits. We found the vessel fairly quickly, but then the problems got worse.

"To make a long story short, due to the rapidly deteriorating conditions with the waves and wind, we ended up in a bad position with the pleasure boat hitting up against our boat as it began to sink. The family on board the boat started to panic. Charlie became the hero and got all four people off the boat and onto ours before the boat went under, but at a huge cost to himself. In order to get the last person off the boat, he positioned himself between the two boats, hanging on to a lifeline. Just before the craft sank, it crashed against our boat, hard, one more time. Charlie's leg was in the way. His leg was so badly crushed that the doctors had to amputate it. Charlie would have done anything to help someone else in need, even give up his own life.

"That accident changed Charlie's life. He was medically retired from the Coast Guard, and he moved to the small marina he had purchased several years before in Boston Harbor.

"After Charlie's birthday party this last fall, I started going to visit him about twice a month, in the mornings, while Luke was in school. I could tell that there was a big change in Charlie for the better. So I asked him about why he seemed so different. He explained about his coming to know the Lord. Then he took me through some verses in John. About three months ago he gave me the gospel again.

I am glad to say that I responded, and on that day I believed that Christ died for my sins. Even as he was dying, Charlie never stopped being interested in saving lives." The man went back to his seat.

Bobbi felt the tears coming. She had promised herself she wouldn't cry. Luke handed her a tissue from the box on the seat next to him. She glanced at Luke, and he had a tear going down his cheek. Well, now they both finally knew how Charlie lost his leg. It was not too big of a surprise that he had lost it helping someone else.

CHAPTER 42

The Ride

*L*ady nudged Bobbi in the back. "Shoo! You go eat and leave us alone!" Bobbi scolded the one-year-old and pushed her away. Bobbi turned back to Missy and cinched up the saddle.

She had left the memorial service as soon as she had dared. The line of people shaking their hands and giving their condolences seemed to never end. It was wonderful to see how many people cared, but it was almost more than Bobbi could handle. Mary had offered her a ride back home, and Bobbi had jumped at the chance. She asked Luke if he minded and he said he didn't. Bobbi wanted a long ride in the woods, and she needed a long talk with the Lord. Oops, she better not break the long-standing rule her dad had set. "If you're going out in the woods, always take the saddlebag." The saddlebag had a first aid kit and other survival things a person might need in case of an accident. She had left a message on the kitchen nook counter telling her family she'd be riding in the woods. She slung the saddlebag over the back of her mare, behind the saddle.

She would clip it onto the saddle in a minute. But first she came up to Missy's side and gave her a quick jab in the ribs with her knee. The mare sighed, letting out the air she had been holding, and Bobbi cinched the saddle up tighter. It was a game they played. Missy would hold her breath so the saddle would be looser, and Bobbi would always find a way to surprise her and make her let the air out. A loose girth could be a dangerous thing.

It seemed like there was one more thing she wanted to do, but she could not think of it. She walked the mare through the pasture gate and closed it. She didn't want Lady following them. Bobbi mounted her horse and rode through the barnyard. As she started down the lane to the lower pastures, Bobbi started to pray. She asked the Lord to help her through this. She found a lot of peace knowing that Charlie was with the Lord. She thought of all the verses she could about heaven. Charlie was enjoying streets of gold. He had no more sorrow or pain.

At the far end of the stump pasture, Bobbi stopped at the iron gate into the woods and opened it. She walked the small mare through the gate and closed it so the cows wouldn't get into the woods and get lost.

As she slung back into the saddle, she thought about Luke. He had been such a tower of strength through all of this. He had been quoting Scripture to her and talking about what Charlie must be doing in heaven. She hoped he didn't mind her leaving him to deal with everything, but she just had to get away.

The trail was overgrown. They hadn't been riding this trail very much lately. She kept dodging branches that were at head height. She and Brad needed to brush this trail out some more. Just a little way further and she would be to the "forty," and the trails there were a bit wider.

She ducked again, missing a large branch. Just as she sat up, Missy startled and Bobbi gasped. A dark shadowy figure stepped out from behind a tree and grabbed the bridle. Bobbi screamed. The man turned and sneered at her. He was dirty and unkempt. He held on to the bridle and kept trying to pull the reins out of Bobbi's hands. Bobbi fought back. Missy reared up and came down hard, trying to shake the man loose. It seemed like she was trying to trample him when she came down, but the man was too quick and moved his body out of the way.

For several minutes the fight continued, with Missy rearing up and coming down hard. Bobbi wished she had a whip; then she could beat him off. She tried kicking him, but her legs were not long enough to reach him. Out of the corner of her eye Bobbi saw several other men coming out of the woods. There had been stories circulating in the harbor about a band of hobos living in the wooded areas.

Missy reared up on her hind legs again, pawing the air, and Bobbi held on tight to the saddle horn. Missy came down hard, jolting Bobbi so hard that she lost her grip on the reins. The man grabbed the reins and backed up a few feet away. He pulled so hard on the reins that the bit began to tear at Missy's mouth. "Stop it! Stop!" Bobbi screamed.

The mare reared up again. The man kept on pulling on the reins. It was a tug-of-war between man and horse. Things were happening so fast that Bobbi couldn't even think. The frantic mare reared up on her back legs and stood tall, pawing the air for balance; Bobbi held on tightly to the saddle horn.

It was as if time stood still. The bridle slipped off Missy's head, and Missy and Bobbi propelled backward, crashing to the ground. Everything shattered, and the world went black for a second. Then she felt her mare's spine and the full weight of her body against her left side, pressing hard.

Half of Missy covered Bobbi. For a moment Bobbi felt the warm, soft body smothering her, but then she felt Missy roll off of her to the left. Everything went black again. A few seconds later Bobbi woke to trampling hoofs, and she realized that Missy was running around her in a tight circle, warding off the hobos. Bobbi heard a man yell, "That horse is going to kill us. It's crazy! Let's get out of here!" Blackness engulfed her, and all thoughts and sounds stopped.

Luke washed his face and looked at himself in the mirror. "I hope Bobbi is OK," he said to himself. She was probably sitting on the beach somewhere, mulling things over. The interment of the body had taken place at nine in the morning, then the memorial service at one. He was exhausted, even though it was only three thirty. He needed to finish changing his clothes and get back out to the Jeep. Brad was waiting. They had the Jeep full of flowers. They had dropped some at the Clarks', and then they stopped at the marina and unloaded a few arrangements for the store. The rest of the flowers were going to the Wests. The largest ones they had left at the church.

"Oh, it looks like Bobbi went for a ride." Brad pointed at the note on the Wests' kitchen counter.

"Really? I thought she would be on the beach. Oh good, your parents just pulled in. It would be nice to know where your mother wants all these flowers." Luke set the largest arrangement on the coffee table in the living room. "Once we get these flowers in, I may take a walk up to the barn and check to see if she's back yet."

"I'll go with you; just give me a chance to change." Brad headed back to his bedroom, and Luke carried in the last of the flowers.

"It looks like she took a long ride; the saddlebag's gone," Brad noted as he and Luke walked into the small horse barn.

Luke looked out the broken window to the main barnyard. "She probably went down the lane. How about we walk down to the lower pastures and see if we can see her. I'm concerned. All the emotion was too much for her today."

"Yeah, it was about all she could do to make it through that long line of people," Brad agreed, and they headed down the lane.

As they neared the end of the lane, they could hear the mare frantically neighing. Brad and Luke looked at each other and started to run. The loud, high-pitched, frenzied neighing signaled something was wrong. Once they rounded the corner and headed into the stump pasture they could see Missy on the far side of the iron gate, which entered into the woods. She was pacing and pawing the ground—with no rider on her back.

Brad and Luke sprinted across the pasture toward the gate. As they got closer, Brad yelled, "She's missing her bridle, and there's blood dripping from her mouth."

The horse calmed down for a moment. But her pacing changed into running down the trail a short distance, looking back as they climbed over the gate, then coming back for them as if to say, "Let's go." Once over the gate, both boys followed her at a dead run. Finally, she slowed down and put her head down on a small heap in the trail. It was Bobbi. Missy gently nudged her as both of the boys arrived.

Brad cried out, "Bobbi! Oh my! Bobbi! Is she dead? Bobbi!"

Luke knelt down, picked up her wrist, and felt for a pulse. Thankfully, there *was* one! For a split second he wanted to cry and yell like Brad was doing, but he knew that wouldn't help Bobbi. He needed to stay calm. She was still alive, and they needed to get help.

He stood up and grabbed Brad and shook him. "She's alive. Stop it! I need your help."

Brad calmed down. "What do you want me to do?"

"One of us needs to go get help. I think you should go. Ride Missy. She should head straight for the barn even without a bridle. Call for medical help and drive the Jeep down here as close as you can get it." Luke pulled the keys out of his pocket and handed them to Brad.

Brad nodded. "I'll go." He looked at Missy while he put the keys in his jeans pocket. She came up alongside Brad. She knew what her job was. Brad put his foot in the stirrup and hopped into the saddle. As soon as his seat hit the saddle she took off down the trail at a fast trot that quickly turned into a gallop. Brad grabbed on to the saddle horn for dear life.

Luke took another good look at Bobbi and noticed blood on the back of her head from a small cut. She had scrapes and some other small cuts. Otherwise, she looked fine. No visible broken bones. He hoped it was only a concussion, but there could be internal bleeding. He didn't want to move her. He needed to think. He asked the Lord for help, his heart aching as he looked at Bobbi.

What on earth happened here? This wasn't simply a horse getting spooked and throwing its rider. More had gone on. Luke stood up and looked around. The saddlebag lay on some ferns a few feet away. He looked inside. He found a first-aid kit and some water. He took out his handkerchief and poured water on it. He washed Bobbi's face and talked to her, hoping that she would wake up. But there was no response. "Please, Lord, let her live," he prayed.

He stood up and took another look around the area. About twenty feet away he came across Missy's bridle. It had blood on the bit. Luke went back over to Bobbi and noticed a deep indentation in the dirt and tree needles next to Bobbi's left side. He took a closer look. The horse must have fallen backward! He looked around the area where the bridle had been, and he saw boot prints. Then he walked a bit farther and saw more shoe and boot prints. They were not all from the same pair of shoes. The marks were large, the size of men's shoes and boots!

Then it hit Luke. Those rumors of hobos living in the woods were true. He had to get Bobbi out of there now! From the footprints it looked like there were a whole gang of them. He had nothing to defend her with. What if they came back? He decided that he'd better try to take her to safety. He slung the saddlebag over his shoulder and the bridle around his neck. Then he carefully picked Bobbi up in his arms and headed down the trail to the iron gate at a fast walk. He kept praying and asking the Lord for His protection.

Brad gripped the saddle horn tightly as he and Missy galloped down the trail, he leaned forward, his face close to her neck. It was weird riding a horse at this speed and having no control over her. *She's amazing,* he thought. She wasted no time getting to the iron gate. She pawed the ground impatiently as Brad opened the gate for her. She went through and waited for him on the other side, neighing for him to get back on.

Once he sat back down in the saddle, she took off again at a full gallop, skillfully dodging the old decaying stumps scattered across the stump pasture. She kept the pace all the way up the steep lane and into the barnyard. She tore across the barnyard and impatiently nudged the lock on the main gate. Brad told her to stay, and he jumped over the gate and ran down to the house.

"Mom! Dad!" Brad yelled as he ran down the drive. His dad was in the vegetable garden to the right of the driveway, and his mother was weeding a flowerbed near the front door. "Bobbi is hurt! Mom, call for help and have them meet us in the barnyard. Dad, come quick! Jump in the Jeep!"

Brad was glad he had driven the Jeep before. He started it up, his father jumped in with a concerned look on his face, and they headed up the drive.

Luke laid Bobbi down very gently by the iron gate in a patch of grass. He got the gate open and turned to pick her up again. Bobbi moaned and moved her legs. She tried to talk. Her eyes were closed.

"It's OK, Bobbi. We are going to get help. It's Luke. I'm here." He put his arms under her and picked her up again.

"Missy…Missy, it's not her fault," Bobbi mumbled again. "Don't let them shoot her." Then she was quiet.

"I know it's not her fault. She's a good horse," Luke replied, though he didn't think that she'd heard him. He turned as he carried her through the open gate and looked back down the trail. In the shadows, he thought he saw a group of men walking toward him. He hurried through the gate, laying Bobbi down on the grass on the other side. Just then, he heard the Jeep coming down the lane.

Luke quickly closed the gate and looked back again. Yes, there were figures walking down the trail toward him! They were still some distance away. He picked up Bobbi and started toward the lane. Brad rounded the corner in the Jeep speeding across the pasture.

"Let's get out of here fast!" Luke tried to yell over the noise of the engine as Brad pulled up next to him. But Brad and Mr. West couldn't hear him.

Brad stopped the Jeep, and Mr. West jumped out to help Luke lift Bobbi into the backseat. Luke knelt down on the floor next to her.

"We need to get out of here!" Luke said as Mr. West got in. Brad took off, making a wide turn, barely missing a stump, and heading back across the pasture.

"There's a gang of men heading down the trail. I'm pretty sure they tried to attack Bobbi, and Missy fought them off. Look, here's her bridle. Look at the blood! There were lots of footprints the size of my shoes or bigger back there. It looked like Missy fell backward with Bobbi still on her, and that's how Bobbi got hurt."

As they sped across the stump pasture, Luke held on to Bobbi, making sure she didn't fall off the seat from the bumpy ride. Just before they rounded the corner to go up the lane, he and Mr. West looked back. A group of five men stood at the gate. One held a rifle, and another one had a large chain.

Bobbi woke up. A bright light blinded her. Where was she? She saw her mother's face and then everything went black again.

"Doctor Peterson, I just saw her open her eyes." Bobbi heard her mother's voice. Then she started to worry. Something was wrong. Had she made madrigals?

"Mom...Mom, did I get into madrigals?" Bobbi mumbled.

"It's OK, honey, you made it in." Mrs. West looked at Dr. Peterson with a confused look on her face.

"No, I didn't!" Bobbi thrashed. "Please...please call Dave....Tell him I'm OK."

"OK, honey," Mrs. West agreed.

Bobbi closed her eyes again and blacked out.

Mrs. West signaled to Dr. Peterson, and they went out into the hall of the hospital. "She is talking about things that happened two years ago. Dave was her boyfriend when she was a sophomore in high school."

"That is normal. Just give her more time and rest, and she should snap back soon. Her x-rays are looking good. Nothing is broken and there is no hemorrhaging on the brain. It's most likely just a concussion." Dr. Peterson went on. "Now, you were answering her just fine. Go back in and keep her company. The fact she is waking up from time to time is a good sign. I'm going to find Dr. Hokoto. I want a second opinion on these x-rays."

Mrs. West went back into Bobbi's hospital room and sank down in a chair next to Bobbi's bed. She looked at her daughter sleeping peacefully. *Please, Lord, help Bobbi to heal and be well again. And help Joe and Brad,* she prayed. Where were those two and Luke, anyway?

The medics had taken over twenty minutes to get to the barnyard from town. She was perturbed that it had taken so long. She had gone up to the barnyard to wait for them. She could have driven it in a lot less time. In fact, often she did. Fortunately she had never got caught speeding.

Thankfully, Dr. Peterson had been monitoring his ham radio and heard the urgent call for the medics. He headed over with his black bag right away. He had just arrived when Brad drove the Jeep into the barnyard. She was grateful he had come and cared for Bobbi until the medics finally arrived.

Joe had insisted that she ride in the ambulance with Bobbi. He said he and the boys had something else to take care of and had headed down to the house. Now that she had time to think about it, she wondered what was going on.

A nurse came in and offered her a glass of juice and checked Bobbi's vitals.

Luke felt like he needed to be two places at once. He wanted to be with Bobbi at the hospital, and he also wanted to help catch the guys who had done this to her. But he had been given orders by Mr. West to wait for the sheriff. Mr. West went down to the house and called the sheriff and then the vet for Missy, while Brad and Luke put the mare in the horse pasture, put a halter on her, and tied her to the fence. They took the saddle off her, quickly groomed her down, and put a warming blanket on her.

Brad mentioned that he wished he could feed Missy something as a reward, but with her mouth all cut up, he knew it was best not to.

The sheriff and his deputies arrived in a large truck, pulling a horse trailer. Luke and Mr. West took them down to the stump pasture. Brad stayed with Missy. Two of the deputies rode the horses, and the rest of them walked into the woods.

Luke showed the men where Bobbi had been lying, the deep indentation where Missy must have fallen, the footprints, where he found the bridle, and the location of the saddlebag. They agreed with Luke's conclusion that there had been a scuffle.

After Mr. West went over a rough sketch of how the trails were laid out in the woods, with the sheriffs' men, he and Luke headed back up to the barn. The sheriff and his deputies started their search for the vagrants. The vet had just finished up when they got back to the barnyard. The vet went over the mare's treatment with Mr. West and Brad. Then the three headed to the hospital in the Wests' VW hatchback.

CHAPTER 43

Finals

*B*obbi rolled over in bed and turned off the alarm. "What day is it?" she moaned. Her head still hurt, and every-thing looked fuzzy. She had spent all Sunday in bed. She was glad she didn't have to spend the night in the hospital. Once she had woken up and stayed awake, they were fairly quick to discharge her on Saturday night. Sometimes when she looked at people, she could only see half of them. It kind of scared her every time it happened. This…this must be Monday.

Her room door opened slowly and Brad peeked in. "Hi, sleepy." He smiled and walked into the room."

Bobbi sat up in bed. "Hi. How's Missy? Ouch!" Her head started spinning faster than before.

"She's OK. Doing better than you. Her mouth has started to heal. The treatments the vet gave us seem to be working. Did Mom tell you?"

"What?" Bobbi lay back down. Her head didn't hurt as much in that position.

"The sheriff and his men found the group of vagrants and arrested them for trespassing, and stealing. They had a camp in the woods, just a quarter of a mile from where you ran into them. The mystery of the disappearing chickens from the Lilly ranch has been solved. There were chicken bones all over the camp. The sheriff recovered all of Mrs. Wright's pots and pans, Mr. Greenberg's radio, plus the Brentons' missing blankets and pillows, and lots of other stuff."

"Hi." Mrs. West walked into the room with a breakfast tray for Bobbi. "Finish getting ready for school, Brad. You need to catch the bus." She set the tray down and turned to Bobbi. I have some juice and your pain meds. Let's start with that. You have the econ final this afternoon and Luke's going to drive you to school."

"Econ?" Bobbi sat up again. "OK. I'm glad it's not this morning."

"It's nice of Luke to take you, even though he does not have any finals today. He says he will study in the library while you take your test."

Bobbi felt guilty, not helping him with the marina and store. Luke had insisted that he could handle it. All the paperwork and decisions resulting from Charlie's death had been taken care of, and they just had to wait for the reading of the will.

"I wonder what the nephews will do with the place," Luke mused as he drove Bobbi home.

"I know. I've been thinking about that too. Most likely they'll sell it, get all their money, and run," Bobbi answered.

"Yeah, I'm not looking forward to meeting them. I've been praying I won't hit one of them." Luke looked at Bobbi and smiled. "Unless you want to take them on?"

Bobbi laughed. "Oh! That hurts! No more jokes for several days." Her hand went up to her forehead. She had almost passed out during the econ final, and twice she had looked at Mr. Easton and she could only see half of him. At least tomorrow was her art final, and she didn't have to study for that. Right now the idea of bed sounded very good to her.

Luke lifted Bobbi out of the Jeep when they arrived at the Wests'. She looked a bit woozy, so he didn't put her down but carried her to the front door. Mrs. West opened the front door, obviously concerned.

"No, it's OK, Mom. I made it through. I just need to sleep." Luke carried her up the stairs to the living room. "Luke, I can stand. Please put me down." She turned and sat down in a chair.

"You're sure you're OK?"

"Yes. I need to sit here for a minute, and then I'll go back to bed for the rest of the day. Thanks for taking me to school." Bobbi leaned back in the chair.

"Well, I should go. I'll call later."

Bobbi headed back to her room. She watched Luke get into his Jeep. What a handsome guy! But that wasn't the best part. She really cherished the relationship they had. She thought about how unhappy she had been with Joe just a year ago. Luke cared about her. He was more spiritually mature than she was, and she really appreciated his leadership in that area.

Luke turned off Zangle Road and headed down Main Street to the marina. He had the books and the management details to take care of. He had given Mrs. Clark more responsibility, and a raise. What a blessing. Without her help, Luke knew he wouldn't have made it through the past few months.

"Your father called," Mrs. Clark told Luke as he walked into the store.

Luke looked at her with surprise. *What does he want?* Luke thought. He had only heard from the man once all year, during the Christmas holidays. Luke had left several messages with Deanne for his father when he first moved out to the marina, but there was never any response. Luke had given up trying to contact him. Luke went over to the phone and called, expecting Deanne, but his father answered!

"Hi, Dad. It's Luke."

"Hi. I hear that there is going to be a graduation this next week, and I wondered how I could get an invitation," his father said.

"Well, I don't think you need one. It is just in Oly High's football stadium. There's one request, though. Please don't bring Deanne. Mom will be there and I don't want Deanne there." Luke knew it would be hard enough for his mother to see his father again. He wanted his mother to have a great evening, and seeing Deanne would not be good.

"Not a problem, Luke. By the way, congratulations!"

Luke walked out on the dock to check everything over. He needed to remember to check over the fuel sales records tonight. It had been a while since the fuel barge had been in, and they might be running low. He was going to miss all of this. He actually enjoyed overseeing the marina and store. Bobbi had planted some flowers in big tubs on the deck a few weeks before. Mrs. Clark had started selling fresh-brewed coffee at the store, and people were hanging out on the deck more. He liked watching the business grow.

Luke sat down on the bench out on the end of the main dock. He looked north to the mountains and islands. Yes, he was going to miss this. The nephews would sell the place. He had been so busy with school and Charlie's death that he hadn't even thought about what he would do this summer. To go back to Orcas or not was the question.

Luke bowed his head. *Dear Father, Please give me wisdom to know where I'm supposed to live and work this summer. If You want me on Orcas, You will have to give me the strength. I'm not sure I can survive without seeing Bobbi every day.*

Luke wondered why he and Bobbi had to be present at the reading of the will, but then he remembered the letters that Mr. Ellis had referred to. It would be interesting to see what Charlie had written.

CHAPTER 44

Graduation

"Now which side is the tassel supposed to be on?" Bobbi switched the little gold tassel on her graduation cap back and forth.

"This side." Luke reached over and put it on the left side. "Now leave it there until they tell us to move it to the other side to show that we have graduated."

"Oh my! Isn't this sad?" Susan walked up to them and started to cry. "We will never be a class again! We will never see these people again."

"Well, considering that we don't know all of them ..." Luke started in and then stopped. He had been watching Patty Banks, the valedictorian. "What is she doing?"

"I don't know. Giving people something." Bobbi stood on her tiptoes trying to see, but she was too short to get a good look. They were all standing out in the entry courtyard between the gym, the lunchroom, and the little theater, creating a sea of royal blue gowns.

"She is passing out black armbands, and people are putting them over their gowns on their left arm. Something's going on here," Luke said.

"Oh, you know Patty. There's always some issue to protest about." Susan sighed. "I just wish she would get over here. It won't be long before we have to walk out to the stadium."

Patty, Susan, Bobbi, and Luke were to march in first on the left-hand side of the podium and stage and sit in the front row, in that order. The chairs and stage were set up on the edge of the football field facing the bleachers, half the chairs on one side of the stage and half on the other side. Bobbi and Luke were scheduled to sing first, after that the principal would say a few words, then the trio would sing, Patty would give her speech, next the guest speaker, and finally the graduates would march across the stage one by one and get their diplomas.

"I can't wait to walk across that stage and get my diploma!" Bobbi exclaimed.

"OK. It's time to walk out to the stadium," Mr. Hendrix spoke into a megaphone. "Everyone in their places, just like we practiced this afternoon."

The students scrambled for their places, still no sign of Patty, so Susan started leading the line on the left side out to the stadium, hoping Patty would show up. Just before they got into the stadium, she came running up from behind them.

"Where were you and what's with the armbands?" Susan asked.

"There's no time to explain, and I knew you guys wouldn't want one." Patty gave a slight laugh as she finished the sentence and took her place as first in line. She ran her fingers through her red hair and put her cap on just as they rounded the corner and walked into the stadium.

Bobbi got a bit scared looking at all the people. The stadium was packed. How would she ever find her parents in that crowd? As they stood there waiting for the rest of the class to file in, she started at the left side and systematically scanned the entire crowd, group by group. Finally, just as they were sitting down, she found them. They were almost right in front of her about three quarters of the way up the bleachers. Rosa, Uncle Hank, Aunt Sophie, and Adam were there too. The only one missing was Charlie. She wished he could have seen them graduate.

"I found them!" Bobbi whispered to Luke. "They are straight ahead."

"Yes, I see them. But we're up. Let's stand together on three. One, two, three," Luke interrupted Bobbi.

Bobbi put her hand through his elbow, and they walked up the stairs to the stage. Bobbi's nervousness kept her from singing her best. How sad that this might be their last time performing together.

Principal Bain said a few words and introduced the trio. That song went really well. Bobbi had relaxed a bit, and the other two gave it their all.

Patty stayed on stage. Principal Bain introduced her as the valedictorian. Susan and Bobbi returned to their seats, and Patty started in.

"Good evening, my fellow graduates, parents, teachers, and school staff." Patty waved her arm first to the left and the right, pointing at the class. "This is the generation that will change the world!" The students cheered. "Gone will be hunger, war, and materialism. This generation will make sure that everyone shares and gives to everyone so there will no longer be hunger or poverty. We are going to live on the earth like one big happy family; no one will own anything, and we will all live together and work for the common good." As she expanded on this theme, the students wearing the black armbands cheered at various points, and the audience of parents grew restless. Many of the men were World War II veterans and had risked their lives for their country and freedom. They didn't like what they were hearing.

Patty kept on. Some members of the audience were beginning to yell remarks at her. One man yelled, "Move to Russia." Bobbi couldn't make out what the others were saying. Patty raised her voice and continued over the noise. "We need to change now! Especially Olympia. It's a white racist ghetto."

At that remark, the whole place exploded. All the students around Susan, Luke, and Bobbi wore black armbands. They stood up and started chanting and yelling and raising their arms in protest. It seemed as if the whole class stood up in support of Patty's viewpoint. People in the audience yelled back. Men on the stadium bleachers raised their fists in the air and yelled at the top of their lungs at Patty. Patty tried to finish her speech, but the noise was deafening. She gave up and stepped back. Principal Bain came to the mike, but no one could hear him. Patty started crying.

Susan yelled to Bobbi and Luke, "I'm not standing up!"

"Neither am I," Luke and Bobbi said in unison. The three grabbed each other's hands and held on tight. The tension in the air intensified. It was frightening.

Bobbi looked up at her parents. They looked surprised and her dad looked angry. But he wasn't yelling. He looked at her and concern covered his face, concern for their safety. They had become a sitting target in the front row with chaos on every side. But what could they do—run for it?

"Duck your heads!" Luke yelled and the girls put their heads down just in time as something came sailing by in the air. Then something else flew by.

Some of the parents were throwing things at the students. Mr. Hendrix came running up onto the stage with his megaphone and started yelling into it. "Everyone sit down! Everyone sit down!" he kept yelling.

The adults started to quiet down and then the students. Susan and Bobbi raised their heads and let go of each other's hands. Then a hush came over the mass of people. They could not believe what had just happened.

Principal Bain stood up. "The graduation is over. Everyone go home. The diplomas will be mailed to the graduates."

Bobbi and Luke looked at each other. She couldn't stop shaking.

"That wasn't even a graduation!" Bobbi said disappointment showing on her face. "We didn't get to walk across the stage."

Luke was disappointed, too. The students filed out of the stadium row by row. They ran into Luke's father and talked to him for a few minutes. He had a present for Luke. Then they walked over by the parking lot and met up with the Wests and Luke's family. They all hugged. Everyone kept shaking their heads in disbelief at what had just happened. Thankfully no one had gotten hurt. It was surprising how quickly the students and parents had turned into an unruly mob. Both Bobbi and Luke were glad to hear that most of the students on the other side of the stage hadn't stood up in protest. In fact, about half of the class had remained seated. It wasn't as bad as it had seemed.

Many of the students were trying to find friends. There was a big party planned at Ocean Shores over on the Pacific coast. Luke had heard of a few other parties. Luke and Bobbi and their families were heading out to the marina for a party on the deck. Luke had invited the whole music department and their families. But most of the kids had opted for the all-night parties at the ocean.

In spite of that, a nice-sized crowd showed up at the marina party, enough to finish off the graduation cake Rosa had made. The Clark family had come. The parents stayed for an hour and then left the twenty-four students to party. Luke had set the rules, no drinking or drugs. The girls would sleep upstairs and the boys in Charlie's room. They had enough food and games to last the night.

CHAPTER 45

Charlie's Wishes

*B*obbi rolled over and bumped into Tanya. They had slept on Luke's bed with their clothes on. She sat up and looked around. Were they the only ones in the room? The rest of the girls must have decided to stay up all night. No, there were three more over in the corner in sleeping bags. She heard the foghorn going. So that's why she woke up. She looked at her watch. It was eight o'clock already.

She went into the bathroom and freshened up a bit and then headed downstairs. She had been the first one to call it quits just after midnight. She was still having some headaches from her concussion and knew she couldn't stay up the whole night.

When she walked into the store, she saw Luke on the phone. He didn't look happy. She looked around the room. Some of the kids were sitting at the table still playing gin rummy. They barely had their eyes open. Several others had crashed on the sofa. The rest of the guys must be asleep in Charlie's room. A light fog had started to burn off, promising a beautiful day. Bobbi walked over to the refrigerator and pulled out some eggs. Food ought to help the situation.

Luke hung up the phone and leaned up against the wall. He just stared into space. Bobbi walked over.

"What's wrong?" she asked.

"That was one of Charlie's nephews. They will be arriving this afternoon about four. They demanded that I pick them up at the airport. They also demanded that I move out of the marina today. They are planning to take over tonight. They want the books and everything tonight." Luke looked confused.

"Luke, they can't do that to you. The reading of the will is tomorrow morning. They have to wait until it's theirs," Bobbi said calmly. "Call Mr. Ellis. He will tell you what to do."

Luke looked at her with a determined look on his face. "You're right. Now where's that card?" He walked over to the cashier counter and fumbled through the drawer.

Bobbi went back over to the kitchen table and found out how many wanted breakfast, then started making bacon, toast, and scrambled eggs. She watched Luke out of the corner of her eye.

"Say, Scott, did Luke get any sleep last night?" she asked as Scott came over to help her serve the plates.

"Yeah, he headed into Charlie's room a short time after you went to bed. You two are great partiers," he added sarcastically.

Luke hung up the phone again and walked over to Bobbi. He grabbed her hand and took her out to the deck.

"Thanks for the advice. That was the right thing to do. Mr. Ellis is going to meet the nephews at the airport. He says that they can't kick me out. They have to give me thirty day's notice, and I can demand it in writing. He will take them to a motel." Luke sighed like a big weight had been lifted off his shoulders. He gave Bobbi a big hug. "You are a gem. We need to be praying about tomorrow. It's going to have to be the Lord in control tomorrow when we meet those two jerks. I want to deck them already, and I haven't even met them."

"I know it's hard. It's because we know how they treated Charlie," Bobbi agreed. "What are you going to do this summer?"

"I don't know. I have been praying and asking the Lord to show me where He wants me. It all seems to hinge on tomorrow. It seems like the nephews would want to keep me on for the summer, running the marina and making it look good while they put it up for sale. I can't imagine them keeping it."

Mrs. Clark came down the stairs from the road. It was nine o'clock and time for the store to open. Luke and Bobbi greeted her and went inside to clean up after the party. Tanya and the other girls came downstairs. Bobbi fixed more eggs, bacon, and toast. As she stood at the stove looking out at the wonderful view—with the fog lifting and the sun coming through in patches—she couldn't help but wonder, *What is going to happen to this place?* She hoped that whoever ended up with it would fix it up even more. It would be nice to take down the wall and expand the store into Charlie's room. It would also be great to turn the north section into a café.

The graduates began to leave in groups of threes and fours and head back into town. Scott helped Luke and Bobbi do the dishes. Then they gave Scott a ride home before heading to Bobbi's house. His mother and Adam were scheduled to leave after lunch for Orcas, and Luke wanted to spend some time with them.

Luke enjoyed the sunshine as he walked back up the ramp from the docks, Bible in hand. This was it, the morning of the reading of the will. He had gotten up early and walked the docks one last time. He hated saying good-bye to this place. He loved this old marina. It was home. Luke had studied out on the bench at the end of the main dock. It was amazing, the peace the Lord had given him about today.

He left a note for Mrs. Clark, checked his tie in the mirror, and headed up to the Jeep to pick up Bobbi.

Bobbi waited by her front door in a yellow and white sundress and matching short jacket, with white high heels.

Mr. Ellis greeted them in the lobby of his office. "Charlie's nephews are in my office right now. We will start right away. Thank you for being on time."

"Joe and Bob Swain, this is Bobbi West and Luke Johansen. And this is my secretary, Mrs. Reed." Mr. Ellis made the introductions as they walked into the room. "Please, everyone, sit down and we'll begin." Mr. Ellis sat down behind his big wooden desk, and they all sat facing him. It was exactly nine o'clock.

"First of all, Charlie had a sealed envelope for each of you. Inside is a letter he wanted you to have. These are to be read in private." Mr. Ellis passed them out to each of them.

Bobbi caressed her letter. Her last bit of Charlie lay here in her hand.

Mr. Ellis brought out Charlie's black box and placed it on his desk. He used the key and opened it up and picked up a letter in Charlie's handwriting off the top.

"This letter explains what to do with the contents of this box. This old gold compass Charlie specified for Luke." Mr. Ellis handed it to Luke.

Luke turned it over and read the engraving: *May you always find your way through life.*

"This penknife is for Bob Swain; it belonged to your great-grandfather. And this pocket watch is for Joe Swain; it was your other great-grandfather's." Mr. Ellis passed the treasures to both the men.

"And for Bobbi there's an antique diamond and sapphire ring. It belonged to Charlie's mother." Mr. Ellis smiled at Bobbi as he handed it to her.

"Now, Mr. Ellis, you can't be giving things like that to her!" Joe Swain exclaimed. "It has to stay in the family!"

Mr. Ellis looked at Joe and calmly explained, "Things are going to be done according to Charlie's wishes. He wrote it all down on this sheet of paper, and Charlie specified that Bobbi is to get the ring."

"Now, the reading of the will." Mr. Ellis read a few opening remarks. "To each of my nephews, you were not even courteous enough to answer my letters or calls or even inquire as to how I was doing for the past six years. To each of you, I leave twenty-five thousand dollars. You will receive that amount only for my brother's—your father's—sake."

Luke was taken aback. He knew that Charlie had much more than that in cash alone. He had seen the bankbook. What was going to happen to the rest of the money?

"To Bobbi West and Luke Johansen I leave fifty thousand dollars, the marina, the store, and both businesses' current holdings, including the boat."

Bobbi and Luke both gasped. Luke could not even begin to understand what had just been said.

"This is an outrage!" Bob Swain stood up and shook his finger in Mr. Ellis's face. "We will contest this will! The old man was out of his mind. We deserve to get everything. They aren't even his family." He pointed at Luke and Bobbi. Blood vessels were standing out on his face as he struggled to control his anger.

"Actually, there is more. Please sit down." Mr. Ellis looked Bob straight in the eye and continued. "To my nephews: I am sure you are upset and wondering how I can give all this to Bobbi and Luke. They have been my family these past years. This will was signed in the presence of four witnesses that can attest to my sound mind at the time." Mr. Ellis stopped and looked at the two nephews. "As you can see, you have no grounds on which to contest this will."

He continued reading the will. "The remaining twenty thousand or so will be given to Westside Baptist Church for missions."

Luke rejoiced that Charlie had given some of the money to the Lord. He would have to talk to Bobbi; maybe they should give some more. Luke looked at her; there were tears in her eyes. She was speechless.

On the way back to the marina, Bobbi kept looking at the ring on her right hand. She would smile, then a tear would slip down her face, and then she would smile again as she fiddled with the ring. As they pulled into the harbor and turned onto Main Street, they got a good look at the marina. It was as if they were seeing it for the first time. All this was theirs? They looked at each other and smiled.

"We have to keep it…and fix it up," Bobbi said, barely above a whisper.

"Yes, partner, I agree. Let's take Charlie's boat out and float for a while and read his letters. We need to talk. Mrs.

Clark will want to know." Luke walked around the Jeep, lifted Bobbi out, and stood her on the ground.

"Well, what's the verdict?" Mrs. Clark walked out of the store and met them on the deck. "Do I still have a job?"

"Well." Luke had a twinkle in his eye and Bobbi could tell that he was going to drag this out. "Let's see. We'll have to talk to the new owners. Right, Bobbi?"

"Now, Luke, be nice and just tell her," Bobbi said.

"OK, one half of the partnership says that you do. What does the other half say, Bobbi?"

"Yes, you have a job. We are the new owners! Can you believe that?" Bobbi started to do her little jumping routine.

"Oh my!" Mrs. Clark looked like she might faint. "Oh my! How wonderful. I'm so glad those horrid nephews are not the owners. I had made up my mind I was quitting on the spot if they were in charge." She gave Luke and Bobbi each a hug and then walked back into the store to answer the phone. "What a relief!"

Bobbi called her mother and then her father at work. She ditched her jacket, heels, and nylons in Charlie's bathroom. Then she got to work making sandwiches for her and Luke to take out on the boat. She also took a package of Kleenex off the shelf of the store and told Mrs. Clark to charge it to her. Wow, she was the owner. She owned all this. She was still trying to grasp all the ramifications.

"Are you sure you are going to be OK in that dress?" Luke asked as he came into the store from upstairs. He had changed into a T-shirt and shorts.

"Oh, I'll be fine as long as you don't throw me overboard," she teased.

They floated off the southeast side of Squaxin Island. There wasn't a ripple on the water; the boat barely moved. They each got out their letters and started to read.

"'The compass was given to me by my grandfather who was a sea captain. He gave it to me when I first went into the Coast Guard,'" Luke read out loud to Bobbi. "That's special."

He kept on reading to himself. "You are free to do with the marina as you wish. Keep it or sell it." Luke looked at the date, February 2, before Charlie needed nursing care. "You were a great son to me." Luke's eyes got misty. He looked at Bobbi, and tears were flowing down her face. "Keep your eyes on the Lord and take care of Bobbi." As Luke finished reading the letter he looked across the water at the marina. They needed to have some long talks.

Bobbi read Charlie's letter slowly, savoring every word. "The ring was my mother's, given to her by her parents when she turned eighteen at her 'coming of age' party. She had always treasured it. My mother was a happy woman full of life, and you often reminded me of her." Again, he made it clear that they could do with the marina as they wished. They could even sell it. "Bobbi, you have been the daughter I never had. Thank you for filling that gap in my life. Thank you for all the sunshine and cookies that you gave me. Take good care of Luke," he wrote. Bobbi looked up through her tears. Luke gazed at the marina across the water. They did have a lot to talk about.

"Do you agree with me about keeping it?" Bobbi asked after a few more minutes of silence.

"Yes, I do. I think it will be OK. We need to get everything set up on a good system. We have the summer to get it running like clockwork before we leave for college. We will need to ask Mrs. Clark to take on more responsibility and give her another raise."

"I would like to take out the wall between Charlie's room and the store to expand and add a café to the north side of the room," Bobbi confided in him.

Luke looked surprised, then smiled. "That's a good idea. First of all, we need to go over the books. It would be best if we could leave most of the fifty thousand alone and just let it earn interest. If something goes, like the fuel tank, we could be facing a huge expense." He put his hand in the water and thought for a minute. "Remember Mr. Harrison that I worked for last August on his boat?"

Bobbi nodded.

"Well, he told me if I ever need anything to just call. He's a very successful businessman. It might not be a bad idea to take him up on that offer and ask him if he could come and visit us one afternoon when he has time. He would be able to give us sound business advice." Luke's face lit up as he talked about the idea.

"That sounds good. You're right; we need to look at where things stand financially before we take on any big remodeling projects. I agree about not touching the fifty. Wait till your mother hears about this. Won't she be surprised?"

"Yeah," Luke agreed. "I'll give her a call when we get back in."

"Well, Mr. Johansen, I guess the Lord has answered the question as to where you'll be spending your summer." Bobbi smiled up at him. She turned to the old picnic basket and got out the sandwiches.

"Yes, He has. I will be working and planning with you!" Luke leaned down and kissed her on the forehead. "We have a lot of work ahead of us. Are you up for it?"

Bobbi nodded and handed him a sandwich.

The sun started to set over the mountains, ending a momentous day. It looked like the sunset was going to try to match the day's events and be spectacular. Luke looked around the deck. Everyone had left. The Clarks, the Wests, and Scott had come over in the evening after the store had closed. Mrs. Clark had invited several other people from the harbor. They barbequed salmon, and everyone brought food. It had been one big dinner party on the deck to celebrate Bobbi and Luke being the new owners.

Now where was Bobbi? He checked the store but couldn't find her anywhere. He walked back out on the deck and looked out at the docks. Out on his favorite bench at the end of the main dock sat Bobbi looking out at the bay. He locked the store door and headed down the ramp.

A seal surfaced as Luke stepped onto the dock. It swam alongside Luke as he walked. He stopped partway out on the dock and stared at Bobbi. He loved her. He knew she was the one. He knew they could have the same kind of relationship that his grandparents once had. He hoped she wanted that too.

Luke walked up to the bench and sat down beside Bobbi. "Hello, partner," he said softly as he put his arm around her. She leaned against his chest.

"Hello to you too," she replied. Then she looked up at him and smiled. "This partnership has grown some since we shook hands up there at Rosario. Remember?"

Luke looked down at her face. "Yes, I remember." He put both arms around her and gave her a full, long kiss on the lips.

Maps

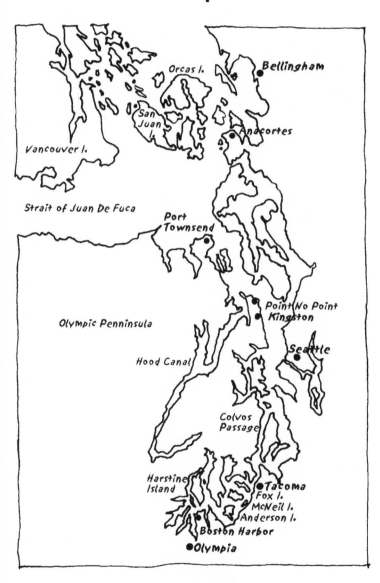

Puget Sound

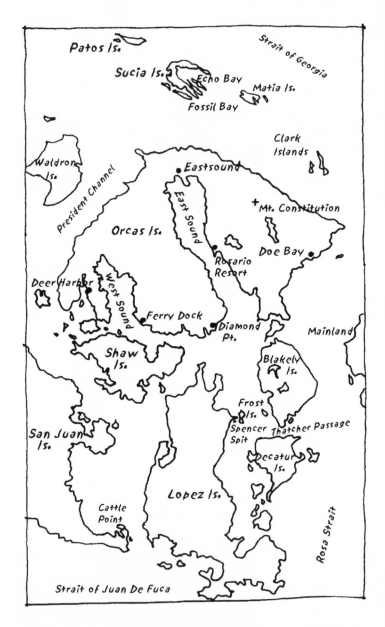

Patos Is.

Sucia Is.

Echo Bay

Strait of Georgia

Matia Is.

Fossil Bay

Clark Islands

Waldron Is.

President Channel

Eastsound

Mt. Constitution

Orcas Is.

East Sound

Rosario Resort

Doe Bay

Deer Harbor

West Sound

Ferry Dock

Diamond Pt.

Mainland

Shaw Is.

Blakely Is.

Frost Is.

Spencer Spit

Thatcher Passage

San Juan Is.

Decatur Is.

Lopez Is.

Rosa Strait

Cattle Point

Strait of Juan De Fuca

San Juan Islands

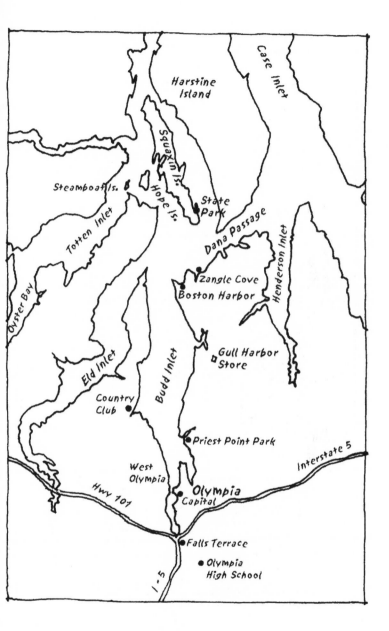

South Sound

"For God so loved the world, that He gave His only begotten son, that whoever believes in Him should not perish, but have everlasting life."

—John 3:16

"But God demonstrates His own love toward us, in that while we were yet sinners, Christ died for us."

—Romans 5:8

"For by grace you have been saved through faith; and that not of yourselves, it is the gift of God; not as a result of works, that no one should boast."

—Ephesians 2:8 & 9

"If we confess our sins, He is faithful and righteous to forgive us our sins and cleanse us from all unrighteousness."

—I John 1:9